# *The*

# STATION

OASIS OF THE OUTBACK DUOLOGY

## Volume Two

# MEL A ROWE

# Also by Mel A ROWE

# COPYRIGHT

**\*The following is written in Australian English\***

When a journey of over a thousand
words brought you here—
let the adventure begin...

Mel A Rowe

The STATION

EST. 1885

# One

S unset reds mingled with twilight mauves that chased the sun as it dropped behind an endless horizon. In the centre of this vast outback countryside was Danbunnan Station's homestead. Jake Cullen stood in the growing shadows, inhaling the aromas from the muster room's kitchen, as the men's laughter carried across Danbunnan's compound. He was tempted to go into the muster room and invite his lady to share a midnight picnic under the stars. Sienna would love that. She loved any type of romantic gesture.

But he couldn't because no one could know about them. And it was getting harder to find time alone with her.

Instead of spending what precious time they had left together, Jake had to keep up the façade for the family.

He headed up the front steps to the grand stone house that stood on the small hill watching over the expansive station.

At the back door, Jake slipped off his boots before stepping inside the kitchen, where the twins were reading aloud from their new books. They'd collected them from the area school today, on the weekly visit to town. Jake hated town days because that's when Jess brought home the mail. And mail meant bills.

'Uncle Jake.' Kate, with bracelets jangling, hugged him around the waist as if she hadn't seen him in decades.

'Hey, Kate.' He hugged her back. It was nice to come

home to this. Not that long ago it had been just Jake and an empty table, while his father sulked in the shadows of the lounge room.

Now the changes were evident. Young Aaron sat at the table set for dinner as his twin sister climbed onto her chair beside him. Gone were the boxes of jam jars and newspaper piles, revealing the faded wallpaper.

'You got a new kettle?' It was bright red and modern compared to the rest of the outdated kitchen.

Jess grinned from behind the counter, dishing up dinner. 'No more killing the curlew in the kitchen.'

Jake grinned. Sienna's habit of making an amusement out of simple daily items was catching. 'But red?' Jake asked, washing his hands in the sink.

'Red goes faster, Uncle Jake,' said Aaron, his napkin tucked under his chin. 'That's why Sienna's rally car's red.'

'I see.' Jake's laughter rolled with ease. Sure, he had the mother of all problems hanging over him, but he'd learned from Sienna to enjoy the little things. He enjoyed every second spent with her, too, and she'd enjoy this. One day she might eat with them.

No, he couldn't think like that, because they couldn't have an *us*.

'Gotta sec, son?' Bob beckoned to Jake from the lounge room, holding up a letter.

They hadn't talked much since the Simmons's rodeo the other week. Jake was still ticked-off by his father's behaviour.

'Don't be long you two. Dinner's ready,' said Jess.

'What's up, Dad?' From the open window, the breeze wove through the cluttered lounge room. The lights were on, with Bob standing well away from the beaten-up leather reclining chair he'd practically lived in for over a year.

'Got a letter,' said Bob.

*Not another bill.* Jake hated town days.

'We've been nominated.'

'For what?'

'The local cattle station competition.'

'Bullspit!' Jake snatched the letter to read the formal notice. 'Those mongrel motherf—'

'*Jake*!' Jess closed the door shutting out the young twins, seated at the table with wide eyes and stunned grins.

'Sorry, Jess.' Jake then turned to his dad. 'Simple: it's a no.' He spotted the address tag. 'Here, you say no, it's addressed to you, not me. End of discussion.' He opened the door and took his seat at the table. 'Man, I'm hungry. I hope there's plenty for seconds.'

Bob followed, waving the letter. 'Jake, we can't say no.'

'No.' He said it again. 'I will not get sucked into their bulldust.' Jake attacked the lasagne, his mouth watering at the hearty richness and meaty flavours. He knew Sienna and Elliott handmade the pasta sheets as part of Elliott's cooking course, and Sienna had used buffalo meat for the sauce. Sienna was reaching new heights with her meals, using all sorts of food found on this property. He'd never eaten so well. 'This is good for buff mince.'

'I know. Sienna says not to tell Elliott, or he'll get an even bigger head,' said Jess with a giggle.

Bob took a mouthful, raising his grey eyebrows. 'This is all right. Not as good as the mushroom meat one Sienna made with yoghurt. That's my favourite.' Bob wiped his mouth with the napkin, then sipped from his water glass. 'Jake, you can't say no.'

Jake shovelled in more food to not respond. But chew.

'What's going on?' Jess asked.

'We've been nominated for the Northern Cattle Stations Competition,' replied Bob.

'Oh, no.' Jess's cutlery clanged onto her plate and her hands dropped into her lap, her fingers fidgeting. 'I'm so sorry, Jake.'

'Not gonna happen. I'm not having those sons of ...' Again, Jake hesitated for the sake of his young niece and nephew. 'They're not coming here.'

Bob's frown deepened. 'They have to.'

'They're only coming here to stickybeak. And it's all

your fault, Dad.' Jake glared at Bob at the opposite end of the table with his sister and the twins stuck in the middle.

'My fault? How?'

'If you hadn't bragged to your mob of mates at the Simmons's rodeo, they wouldn't have nominated us.'

'What has gotten into you?'

'They're only doing this to see what we have, like buyers visiting an open house inspection prior to an auction. They're not interested in what we're doing, and you aren't either.'

'I am so. This is my place too, you know,' grumbled Bob.

'You haven't even stepped outside the compound and seen what I've done.' Jake pushed his plate back and wiped his mouth on the napkin. 'You know what? We should ask the men.'

Bob darkly scowled through knitted brows. 'This does not involve them.'

'This is their death warrant too. Forcing us to put on a show for those buzzards—*which we can't afford.*' Jake's words bounced off the walls forcing everyone back in their seats.

After a moment, Bob muttered, 'We can't say no.'

'I'm not having the crew work harder for this show-pony bulldust when we get nothing out of it.' Jake resumed eating, conversation over.

Bob sniffed sharply, with his nose in the air. 'We'll be offending them if we don't do it.'

'Don't care.'

Bob's chin jutted higher as he rolled his shoulders back. 'Well, I already told them yes.'

'*What the hell!*' Jake dropped his cutlery and glared at his father. 'You. Had. No. Right.'

Bob sniffed deeper, resting fists on either side of his plate, as if digging into his place at the head of the table. 'I had every right; my name was on the letter.'

'Yeah, but your name's not on any of the bills, is it?' Jake eyeballed his father, furious.

'What do you want to do, Jake?' Jess asked timidly.

Jake wanted to talk to Sienna. But she was serving

dinner for everyone on the station. Did he talk to Tom? His dad wouldn't want Jake talking to staff about family business, because it was against the rules. But they weren't just staff. If anything, Sienna had shown him they were a team. A good team. 'Dad, you're calling a meeting.'

'What for?'

'Twins, I've got a job for you.' Jake winked at the pair who sat up eagerly. 'I want you two to go and tell Tom that Grandpa wants a meeting to talk to everyone in half an hour in the muster room. Can you do that?'

'Yes.' Their little heads bobbed up and down like toy emus sitting on a dusty ute's dashboard.

Jake opened the screen door, turned on the outdoor lights as the twins' chairs scraped across the kitchen floor. 'Off you go.'

'But they haven't finished their dinner,' said Jess.

'They can eat when they return. Twins, only talk to Tom, then come straight back. I'll be watching.'

The young twins burst through the door, quickly slipping on their boots.

Their childish laughter echoed as they raced across the compound, the stars sparkling above them. They rushed up the muster room's wooden steps, barrelled through the double screen doors and straight to Tom, the trusty 2IC, seated at the table closest to the door.

Tom was bombarded with the news. Then his niece and nephew rushed out the door with Tom following.

Jake waved to Tom at the muster room's screen doors, who gave a nod, then turned to face those seated, his strong no-nonsense voice echoing. *'Meeting, muster room, thirty minutes. Be there.'*

Within seconds, the first out the door to spread the news was Elliott, the trainee muster cook, dashing for the cottages. Next was Josh, the jackaroo, who headed for the stockmen's quarters. While Jake held the door open for the twins as they came huffing and puffing up the stairs. And that's how the bush telegraph ran at Danbunnan Station.

'Good job, twins. Let's finish dinner and go to the meeting.'

'Us too?' Aaron dropped into his seat, while his sister brushed back her plaits.

'No, honey, that's for the staff,' said Jess.

'This involves everyone, Jess. You and the twins should come,' said Jake, returning to his seat.

*'Why are you doing this, Jake?'* Barked out Bob, red in the face.

Gone was the newly acquired *son* tag. His father's chiselled lines of the old boss shining through.

'You're the one who accepted the nomination, not me, so you can tell the staff.' That was what Bob used to do. He ordered. Barked. Never asked, only shouting his demands, and it was never open for discussion. That was the old boss, who Jake had feared as a child. But not anymore.

'This doesn't concern them.' Bob pursed his lips whitening with rage.

'Yes, it does.'

'How? They're just staff!'

He was sick to death of that term. Jake had heard Sienna say she was just staff, when she meant so much more to him. 'Who's going to do the extra work? Not me, I'm busy, and they are too.'

'But—'

'Look, Dad …' Jake took a deep breath to calm not only himself but also his father before they screamed the plaster off the walls. As a kid he hated his dad shouting the fear into him, so he wasn't going to do that in front of his nephew and niece.

Jake didn't want Bob to take over either, but he also didn't want him to return to his zombified status on the couch. He wanted to show Bob how much Danbunnan had changed for the better—or so he'd hoped. 'You can tell everyone you've accepted the competition's nomination.'

'Why? It doesn't concern them.'

'That's our skeleton crew down there, now the

contractors have gone. Those people in that muster room care what happens to Danbunnan and treat this place as if it was their home. So why not let everyone decide if they want to be involved. You do realise, Dad, the men running that competition are only here to see how they can buy us out. They've blocked all avenues for us to sell our beef in the co-op, except through your mate Simon Simmons. They know I can't afford to do this and, somehow, they must know this muster is it for us.'

'Is it that bad, Jake?' Jess asked.

He didn't want to worry his sister, or his niece and nephew either, but he wasn't going to lie to them. 'Not yet. I won't let it come to that.' Not when he'd been working with Sienna on his secret project. But it wasn't enough. 'Dad, can you see why I'm saying no?'

'I had no idea it was that bad.'

'Yeah, you did. You just didn't want to admit it.' Jake stood from the table. 'I'm going to have a quick shower. Dad, start thinking about what you want to say. If you want this, you'll have to sell it to the crew, not me, because I'm voting no.' Jake walked out with a sick knot in his stomach. He was sick of people forcing his hand, especially his father who still didn't listen to him. He'd already accepted it was going to cost him his happiness, which was only snippets of secreted time left with Sienna. But he'd sworn to his dying mother that he'd save the station and there was no way he was going to surrender Danbunnan, not today. Not ever, if he could help it.

# Two

Elliott rushed through the muster room's side door calling out, 'The cottage crews are coming, Uncle.'

'Good.' On the other side of the kitchen bench, Tom nodded from his seat.

'What do you want me to do?' Elliott asked Sienna who'd stepped inside the coldroom.

'Can you refill the urn? I'll dish up supper.' Sienna carried out a large plastic container that held her cake stash.

'Don't go to too much trouble, Sienna,' called out Tom.

'I don't do meetings without coffee and snacks in hand or I'll fall asleep.' It had to be something big, because meetings weren't often called, and this was Bob's first public speech in years.

But that was family business and Sienna tried not to get involved.

She began dishing up cake slices on serving plates, doing what she was paid to do: feed everyone as the relief cook until Rhonda, their full-time station cook, returned from her holiday.

Josh barrelled through the front doors. 'Tyson's coming, but Annie won't.'

'Why not?' Tom's frown deepened at the jackaroo.

'Said she's not hungry.' Josh shrugged, beelining straight for the serving bench.

'Did you tell her it's a meeting.'

'Yeah.' Josh nodded while watching Sienna plate up

biscuits and cakes. 'Oh yum, custard slice. Sienna, you've been holdin' out on me.' He pinched a slice and took a big bite.

'I thought you only liked bread-and-butter pudding?'

'It's custard. I like anything custard.'

'I'll remember that.' Because she liked spoiling the crew with her cooking, which was so much easier these days. A few weeks ago, they'd been cooking for over forty men. Now it was only the regular team and the Cullen family.

She set the platters out on the tables, placing one in front of Tom.

'Not for me.' Tom patted his stomach, as he pushed his empty dinner plate away.

'I'm selfishly thinking of me.' Sienna put her coffee mug near Tom, claiming her spot in the back corner. Its where she sat and faced the screen doors.

Across the red dust compound stood the house on the hill all shiny with lights. It was the first time she'd seen it lit up, making it seem almost inviting. Even with its solid front door that she'd never seen open.

'Have ya got any more coffee?' Tom asked.

'For you, never. But I've got a ute-load of that bushman's billy-tea though.' She grinned sideways at the tough cattleman, surprised at how country she was sounding. But slowly everyone was being converted to her coffee. 'Should I brew a big pot of coffee?'

Tom nodded, expressionless as always. One day she might see him smile.

'I will.' With her back to the room, Sienna said quietly, 'Tom, how is Annie? I never see her anymore.'

Tom gave her a sideways glance. 'What do you mean?'

'Annie hasn't stepped inside this kitchen for a sit-down meal in weeks, long before the rodeo. The only time she comes in is to grab a box of cereal for her room.'

Dropping his elbows onto the table, he rubbed his creased forehead. 'I've been watching her like you said. At lunchtime she nibbles her tucker like a zebra finch. She'll tear up her sandwiches but doesn't eat them... She's skinny. And if this keeps up, she's not gonna have the strength for the job, especially with the build-up coming.'

'I've got some cheesecake I was saving for tomorrow.'

'Reckon you'd dish it up with some blueberries?'

'I can.'

'Save me two plates while I go muster up the mob.' And with a nod, he was out the door.

Sienna collected his empty plate for the sink and then headed into the coldroom to grab the cheesecake and blueberries.

'Where's Uncle Tom going?' Elliott asked. 'Oh, baked cheesecake! I'm so there.'

'Uh-uh.' She slapped his hand away. 'Your uncle has gone to get Annie.'

'You're not sucking up to her again, are you?'

'Me, no.' Sienna wanted to test if Annie was suffering with an eating disorder by dishing up the jillaroo's favourite. 'Have you spoken to Annie since the rodeo?'

'Me, no. But ...' Elliott peered around to make sure no one was nearby, then leaned in closer while Sienna sliced up the cake. 'Annie was found in the gutter, legless at the rodeo.'

'It was actually in the car park. I was there and she had wobbly legs on her way to bed.' The lovely Lyn and her husband, station mechanic, Joe had helped her. 'Hey, I'm not ashamed to admit I've indulged in a few gutter parties with my BFF Mail-order Biatch. Which reminds me, Jess fetched the mail today, right? Has she brought it down yet?' Sienna loved mail days, it was like Christmas considering the packages she received from her fabulous friend, Ricky, who loved to shop for her.

'I guess she'll deliver it at the meeting. What do you think it's about?'

'No idea.' She plated the cheesecake while Elliott added the blueberries. 'Do you think Annie is embarrassed and hiding from everyone because she got a little messy at the rodeo? I know I wanted to hide in the coldroom after the

Zombie hunt.' Which had to be the worst hiding spot ever.

'You didn't do anything wrong that night, but ...' Elliott, her Kardashian-obsessed sidekick, inhaled deeply, enjoying the dramatic pause. 'Annie propositioned Josh. Josh said so.'

'Josh said what?'

'Josh said Annie was rotten drunk, propositioning both him and Tyson. Josh told her they were mates only, and thought she was gay.'

'Annie's not gay, she's a tomboy.'

'I know that, and you know that, but that crowd ...' He waved his arm at the stockmen watching the widescreen. 'But I do know Josh said Annie wasn't pretty.'

'Poor girl. Men suck when they say stuff like that—Hey, hold on, that's not like Josh?' Josh was cheeky, but never cruel.

'Josh tried to apologise heaps of times, but Annie's ignoring both of them, which of course doesn't bother Tyson.'

'Um, I do that, ignore people when they've ticked me off.' She'd done it to Jake in the past, although now she was enjoying a hot lustful affair with the man. Whether it was a quick kiss, a stroke of the fingertips, or an afternoon of pure indulgence, it was hot, heavy, and extremely addictive.

'Yeah, well, Annie's been acting stranger than normal lately. She won't talk to anyone, except ask me for her cereal, so she doesn't have to come in here.'

'Is that because of me, or what she did at the rodeo to Josh and Tyson?'

'I think ...' Elliott raised his finger as if stirring an invisible pot. '... all that and then some.' He gave a flourished air kiss, picked up the cheesecake plates and headed to the tables.

'Let's hope Tom can get Annie over here, because there's not going to be much cheesecake left.' Because Sienna was determined more than ever to see if the jillaroo would eat.

# Three

'Thanks for coming at such short notice,' said Bob, standing in front of everyone in the muster room. 'The reason this meeting's been called is that in six weeks it'll be Danbunnan Station's turn to be presented for the local Northern Stations competition.'

The room gave a collective groan. Boots shuffled on the floor. Heads were lowered and shaken in disbelief, as denim-clad behinds shifted in seats.

'So, ah ...' Bob wiped his palms on his jeans, as his frown faltered. 'So, there's little time to organise this. We've gotta fair bit of work to do ...'

Sienna was seated at the back table between Elliott and Tom, while Annie sat on Tom's far side, with plates of cheesecake and coffee set before them. 'What's going on?' Sienna whispered.

Jake sat at the front with his forearms resting on his denim thighs, staring at the floor with palms pressed together as if praying. All while the rest of the room moaned in pain at what Bob was saying.

Bob continued. 'Besides the judges coming to overlook our operations, we'll need to put on a show for them. So, has anyone got any ideas?'

Boots shuffled, cups of coffee were drunk, and cake forks scraped across plates. But no one spoke up.

'What do they do for the judges?' Sienna whispered to Elliott.

'It'd be like the rodeo thing we went to at the neighbour's station.'

'Can the station afford to waste time on that when you're finishing up the muster?' Not that Sienna had a clue what they did, only what the crew said, and only if she figured out the local lingo.

'No,' muttered Tom, keeping his eyes on Bob. 'But it's an offence to say no.'

'So, they have to throw a horse-jumping thingy in a fenced field with a band and a barbecue.'

Tom remained expressionless, rubbing his eyelids. 'No one's been here since Jake became boss.'

'Oh, no.' She now understood why Jake wasn't happy. 'They're coming to nitpick, aren't they?'

'I do when I visit the neighbours,' said Elliott.

'You don't do cows.'

'I know.' They both giggled at the irony of working on a cattle station.

Tom shook his head. 'Oi, Bob's speaking, unless you've got somethin' to add.'

'Me? Nope. I'm not getting involved.' Arms crossed, she sat back and watched the room. Poor Jake, he looked so uncomfortable up there. 'Tom?'

'Yeah …'

'What does Jake get if they do accept this challenge?'

'It'll promote his name among the peers. The nomination alone is considered an honour.'

'Hmm … So how many times has Danbunnan been nominated?'

'It's Danbunnan's first time. Bob used to be a judge, so he couldn't be nominated.'

'But Bob's not boss anymore … Has Danbunnan got a chance of winning?'

'I think the comp's a crock these days, judged by a mob of bullies. It's meant to be judged by the peers that run the co-op that controls the local beef market. Yet, it might get the boss the respect he deserves.'

'Does it have to be a rodeo?'

'No. Why?' Tom's grey eyes narrowed at Sienna. 'What are you cookin' now, girlie?'

'Nope. Nah-uh.' Crossing her arms tighter, she clamped her lips together to stop speaking.

'Boss needs help.'

'I don't know cattle.'

'You do know projects.'

'I'm only temporary, remember?' Her time here at Danbunnan was limited, unlike the rest of the people within this room, who would be affected the most.

Is that why Bob and Jake were asking for ideas?

Although Bob looked uncomfortable speaking to the room, who mostly weren't listening. Jake remained silent with head down as if he didn't want to be there, and Jess was furiously fidgeting with her fingers.

'Sienna has a question,' called out Tom.

She frowned at the head stockmen. 'Hey, what's the go, Tom?'

'Sienna?' Bob asked.

'Go on, girlie, get ya giggle on.' Tom gave her a nudge.

'Thanks, Tom. *Not*.' She had no choice but to face the front, clearing her throat. 'As someone who knows absolutely nothing about this competition or the industry, does it have to be a rodeo?'

'No. It's an event for the judges, which ends with a celebration where our neighbours are invited,' replied Bob.

'What are the judges looking for?'

'To see how the station is managed and its product.'

'So, can it be other products, besides beef?'

'Yes. But it must be produced on the station.'

'Does any other station show other produce, besides cows?'

'Cattle.' Bob glared at her with furrowed brow. 'Some stations show feeding pastures they provide for cattle that they sell. It's judged by cattlemen. Anyone else got any questions?'

'Excuse me, Bob, I have questions.' Her hand shot up in the air. 'Does it need to be for the judges' benefit only?'

'No, that's why there's a party at the end for guests.'

Sienna sat taller; she liked parties. 'Does that mean anyone can be invited, even if they're not directly involved with the cattle industry?'

'We don't want every man and his overfed dingo here, Sienna. Now let someone else speak who knows what they're talking about.'

*Rude much.*

'Anyone else got any ideas?' Bob asked.

*'I do.'* Sienna stood and spoke to Jake. Because Bob wasn't boss anymore. 'Couldn't this be used as an opportunity for you to meet and expand on your marketplace?'

'It's a lot more complicated than that, woman.' Bob's steely blue eyes peered below his knitted grey eyebrows.

'But this event can be anything you want it be, right?' She wasn't talking to Bob, but to Jake who'd raised his head forcing her to swallow down the desire that rose just from the intensity of his royal blue eyes. Her heart flipped because, stupidly, she was in love with the man who could promise her nothing. But she hoped he was getting the message.

Bob scowled, as he hitched up his jeans. 'Listen, woman, this is to do with stations and the cattle industry, and you've just admitted you know nothing about that.'

'I know, but—'

'You're just the relief cook.'

Which put her at the bottom of the station hierarchy, but she couldn't stop now. 'I know, but what I'm trying to suggest—'

Bob held up his palm. 'I suggest you leave the questions to the others who know this industry.'

'But—'

'Anyone else got something to say?'

*'Dad, let Sienna speak.'* They were the first words Jake had said all night. 'What are you suggesting, Sienna?'

'Why not show this place off and advertise the fact Danbunnan's under new management. You can show them your processes for creating your cattle.' A few men chuckled as Bob's frown deepened. So what if she was damning herself for not using the correct terminology for this industry but she needed to say this. 'Please, hear me out … Why can't you invite your marketplace here?'

'We're meant to only invite the neighbours, who are part of the co-op who sells the cattle,' said Bob.

'I understand that.' *Sheez!* What was Bob's problem. 'Jake, forget the rodeo and do something different.'

'They always do a rodeo,' said Bob.

'Why? Is it mandatory as per the rules of this competition?' She snapped back.

Bob faltered. 'No.'

'Jake, Danbunnan is one of the oldest stations still owned by the original pioneering family. There is so much incredible history here, which alone makes this place unique. So why should Danbunnan follow the herd? You're not cowboys that need to do a rodeo, you're *cattlemen*.'

The men murmured their approval. Jake kept on his poker face, but she knew he was listening. It was Bob who wasn't happy. Sienna knew she'd breached the boundaries of staff speaking up about station business, especially being female—which went against all of Bob's archaic ways—but wasn't that the point of this meeting?

'Why not invite these guests and judges to a dinner party and show off the food in the best possible way.'

'This is a cattle station, not a restaurant.' Crossing arms over his chest, Bob gave her the evil eye.

'Why serve up slabs of steak slapped on a barbecue when you can give them an entire experience? Especially when Danbunnan beef is *not* some nameless supermarket cut, shoved at the bottom of the shopping trolley as part of the weekly food shop.' Sienna inhaled deeply to calm her passion down, while also trying to work out a way they could all get excited over this golden opportunity. 'Don't you get it, guys?

Danbunnan beef *is* top shelf. Danbunnan beef is the steak the guy buys at a restaurant taking his lady out on their first date, or to celebrate his wedding anniversary. Danbunnan beef is the roast a mother seeks out for her special family occasion where the butcher gives his personal recommendation. Your produce is the plated dish that makes the centrepiece of the table.' She patted the table where she'd shared her first meal of Jake's farmed Barramundi. 'Danbunnan deserves better than a dusty rodeo in a paddock. Come on, people, we can do better. We don't need to buy votes by putting on a show when this place *is* the show. It's what you do every day. So why not let the product speak for itself?'

'I've got to think of what this is going to cost,' said Jake.

'We can get creative. Come on, this is the Northern Territory, the land of mate's rates. We have a worthy product we can use to barter with and make contra deals.'

'Like we do with Tom's chillies for our coffee,' said Elliott with hand in the air like it was a school.

'Exactly. The Territory is a small place, where someone always knows someone. We can borrow or barter for what we'll need. Let's use our creativity and think outside this station's boundaries. Okay, use me as an example …' Waving her hand in the air like Elliott. 'I'm new, and I have no idea what goes on at a muster.'

'We know that,' said Tyson.

Jake sat up, with his eyes narrowing at Sienna. 'Yet Sienna sees things differently, because she's never been here before.'

'Exactly! You guys have no idea how incredible this place is. And you live here. This is a secret world people never see. Why not give these guests an experience they'll never forget? Jake, if you tap on the right circles, it'll create a huge rippling effect across a very big pond.'

Joe, the station mechanic, scratched his head. 'You've lost me on the pond part, luv.'

'Why not show these people the fabulous, flavoursome

food this place produces. Have a dinner party in the garden beside the house. Take them out on your stock horses to get them up close to the cattle and your organic pastures. Be proud of what you've achieved, Jake, because you have every right to be.'

'I didn't think you knew what we're doing, Sienna,' called out Charlie, his bald head shining under the light as he stroked his long wavy red Viking's beard.

'I hear things, and I'm learning.' She shared a timid smile, considering all cows and horses scared her. 'But I do know how to throw a good party.'

'Does that include your jelly shots?' called out Josh. That had the room murmuring.

Sienna rolled her eyes. *Freaking jelly shots.* They'd resulted in her memory loss while on a zombie hunt, that ended up with Jake carrying her to bed. Where Jake was now grinning at her like he had some secret.

'*All right,*' called out Tom above the din, and the room went quiet. 'Boss.' Tom's slow nod communicated a secret language from the head stockman to the boss.

Everyone faced the boss, seated at the front of the room, and waited for his answer.

Jake kept on his poker face, his eyes shifting from Tom to Sienna. 'What else do you suggest, Sienna?'

'Um …' Now she was winging it. 'Why not do a classy dance in one of the worksheds as a fundraiser. You don't need someone to pat you on the back because you fed the neighbours and gave them a good show. You need buyers, here and up close, and with a personal invitation they will come. If Tom says it's an honour being nominated, then there's your excuse to get them here, because Danbunnan is already considered competition standard. So why not use this competition to advertise this station's long-term future, the way you want as boss.'

Again, Jake's blue eyes narrowed at her. 'Do you really think we could do it?'

'Definitely. And you know what? Let's make it a

fundraiser to the suicide prevention group. Everyone is aware of what happened with your brother, Duncan. So let's help raise awareness about depression to save another life, and create a new reputation for this place. Don't you think it's time that you turned this tragedy into a triumph?'

Jake rubbed the back of his neck.

Everyone waited for his response.

And they waited.

And waited.

'Well, Dad, it looks like you've got your show. Sienna, what do you suggest first?'

'How about each person tells us about their favourite place on Danbunnan Station and why they love it. They've worked this land, not me.' Jake would need teamwork for this to work, hopefully motivating them too.

'Good idea. Dad, the floor is yours to run this meeting. Sienna can help me manage this because we've all seen what she can do with projects. And where's that coffee?'

'I'll get it. Looks like the cook's gonna be busy,' said Elliott, making a dash to the kitchen.

'Nicely done,' muttered Tom beside her. 'Do you believe that bulldust you just spouted?'

'I do.' The once sad and silent room had now erupted with excited conversations, she could feel the energy building. 'Are you going to make any suggestions?'

'I'll see what everyone says. I don't wanna double up.'

'So, missy,' said Jake, taking Elliott's spot, close beside Sienna. 'What's your favourite place on this station?'

'The muster room. It's the heart of the station, where it all began.' Hoping she'd done the right thing for Jake's sake, or Danbunnan was done for good.

# Four

Jake leaned back in his chair inside the spacious office. The printer whirred away beside the fax machine that never got used anymore. The door opened and Bob strolled in, carrying a dog-eared manual.

*Slam*, went the screen door behind him.

'I keep meaning to fix that,' said Jake.

'Me, too.' Bob dropped into the spare chair beside the desk. 'It was a good meeting last night, eh, son?'

*Son, huh?* Jake swivelled in his seat to check on the printer. 'It looks like Sienna sold everyone on your comp, Dad. You should be thanking her for that.'

Bob raked nails over his grey crewcut. 'I reckon I owe Sienna an apology for how I treated her last night.'

'Yep, or she'll give you the silent treatment for a while and that's no fun.'

Bob crossed his arms over his chest, tucking his boots beneath his seat. 'Are you really doing this now?'

'I can see what Sienna wants to do. Can you?' Because his cunning little kitchen wench had many ideas for using this competition to his advantage. Proving again that Sienna's talent for seeing things was a gift.

Bob shrugged. 'Do you want to do this?'

'I know you were a judge of these things, but it never interested me. You and Duncan did that, not me.' Nope, Jake used to hang at the bar with Craig. All while his older brother, Duncan, was made to stand beside his dad and stare at stock.

Jake tried it once and that was enough.

'Look, I understand this promotes good relationships with the neighbours. What Sienna is suggesting is risky, but we've got everything to lose if we don't do *something*.'

With a frail sun-spotted hand, Bob rubbed the back of his neck. 'I don't want to get in your way. I've always used the co-op to sell my beef … and yeah, I mucked up with that poison.' Bob sucked back the air so deep his chest rose as his bottom lip quivered.

Jake stopped rocking in his seat and the printer became silent. It was hard for his dad to say this. It was even harder to watch.

'I only know one way of farming, from my father who taught me. Duncan tried to tell me other ways, like you did, but I never listened. And Duncan … He was different to you and your sister.' Bob frowned so hard at the floor, Jake expected the tiles to crack any second.

'Dad, I'm not Duncan.'

'No, Duncan had your mother's patience. You had passion and lots of ideas, which is why we clashed, so you moved on.'

'You kicked me out! I only came back because Mum called me in tears, telling me Danbunnan was in trouble.' And that was just the beginning of a never-ending trail of tragedy.

'After all I'd put you through, you still dropped everything and came back.' Bob's frown faltered, softened even. 'I'm ashamed of what I did to Danbunnan, to the family, and what I did to you, too. Which is why Danbunnan deserves you as her boss. You're the one who built this herd from scratch.'

'Dad, this is meant to be home.' Yet it felt like a heavy dog's chain strapped around his throat, keeping him a prisoner to this land.

'But you did this when there was nothing left. You got the cattle to this standard, not me. I had it easy. My herd numbers came from my father's hard work, holding my hand the whole way, which is what I tried to do with Duncan.'

'It's the past.' And it was stopping Danbunnan from moving forward.

'I'm sorry I never helped you when you needed it after your mum ...' Bob lowered his head to his chest, where he heaved in shaky air. 'But that's when you proved you are so much better than me.'

'Huh?' Did he hear that right?

'Last night, the way those men listened and looked up to you with respect and loyalty, I never got that. I'm sorry I accepted the nomination when I should've spoken to you first.'

'It might've turned out for the best with everyone's ideas.' Jake had been impressed, hearing about their favourite places on Danbunnan.

'I've got to hand it to Sienna, her ideas are ... different.'

'That's what we want. What do you think about the barn dance, when we don't own a barn? Sienna and Elliott are trying to come up with a name. I think I heard 'workshed rave' tossed around in their wordplay.' Jake chuckled. 'I like the idea of it being a fundraiser, by turning a tragedy into a triumph.' And the Cullen's had suffered with more than their fair share.

'Sienna's proving to be a clever woman.'

'You have no idea.' Jake was only beginning to discover her hidden depths. Even though they'd agreed to be friends with secret benefits, it was only limited to time Sienna was at Danbunnan. It had to remain a secret because he was engaged to another woman to save this station.

He'd sworn to his mother, on her death bed, he'd do anything, and he would—even if it meant pimping out his soul. The soul that died the day he'd been named as the new boss of Danbunnan Station.

A soul that had once been buried beneath the dusty workload, only to be awoken by the arrival of the relief cook, Sienna.

Bob placed a dog-eared manual on the desk. 'Here's my

copy of the competition's rules. It'll be outdated.'

'That's what this is, the latest version.' Jake grabbed the paper from the printer and bundled them together with a bulldog clip. 'Sienna wants them. I'm hoping you'll help me with the rules.' Jake cocked an eyebrow, as he thumbed over the many pages.

'I'd doubt anyone's read them in a while. I didn't. I got invited because it's what my father did. Mind you, it's not the same anymore. Back then it was just a friendly competition, sharing a feed at the neighbours, when they were all family-owned stations.' Bob's chiselled features shifted as he cracked a small smile. 'When I was a boy, my father made us travel five days, one way, just to show up for one of these things.'

'Really?'

Bob's smile softened as if at some happy memory. 'As kids we all camped together on the verandah, while the grownups partied. Back then, it was a time for the neighbours to come together, to share stories and techniques, and check out their cattle stock. I remember roosters were swapped regularly. The women swapped recipes, garden seeds, kid's clothes and toys. It wasn't the competition it is now. Sienna had a phrase for it …' Bob waved his hand in a circle. 'Commercialised corporate something-or-other.'

'Nice way to phrase a bunch of backstabbing bullies.'

'And I used to be the biggest bully of that mob.' Bob stared at his fingers where they fidgeted in his lap.

It was the same trait that Jess had. Jake had never noticed it before. 'How is this competition judged?'

'We check out the stock, produce, and their future management plans to check their suitability to stay within the co-op. Then we'll do a secret vote that gets locked away and counted at an end-of-year dinner.'

'So, it could be months before we find out who wins?' Would it be worth the wait? When the co-op was blocking him now from selling his cattle.

Bob gave a slow nod. 'I'm happy to help.'

'What would you want to do?' Jake didn't want Bob

taking over, or over-sharing with his mob of mates, who were nothing but a pack of vultures ready to pick Danbunnan to pieces.

'I want to finish the cattlemen's quarters. If the judges are staying there, I'd want it looking its best. It'll be easier now, most of the cosmetic stuff's been done around here.' Bob peered through the screen door to the garden. 'It's like she knew.'

'Who?' *Cosmetic* was one of Sienna's words, a term he didn't expect to hear from his father. In fact, this whole conversation was unexpected.

'That relief cook, the way she's been chipping away, cleanin' this place up.'

Through the open office window, they had the perfect view of the renovated muster room, the thriving kitchen garden, and the cleaned-up cook's quarters.

Even his office had been rejuvenated by Sienna's touch, transformed from a choking closet of junk and dust to a spacious room with a view.

Bob was right, Sienna had project managed all of these various areas, the homestead's clean-up was almost complete. 'You can come out and help beyond the compound.'

'There's plenty to do around the house. I'm not that fit anymore, and I'd only be a hindrance. This is your time, son. You're the boss, and I'm proud to stand behind you.' Bob patted Jake's shoulder.

'Thanks, Dad.' He'd never needed that pat on the shoulder from his dad before, but it felt good to hear.

'So, who are these guests Sienna's suggesting?'

'Not sure. I'll be catching up with Sienna shortly to discuss it.'

When he noted the date on the desk's calendar. The competition's dates were only a few days before Rhonda's return from her holiday, when Sienna was expected to leave the station. How much would his world change then?

# Five

Sienna sighed as she enjoyed her favourite morning view through the kitchen window—Jake in his dust-stained jeans crossing the compound with that long-legged confident stride of his.

'Morning.' Jake gave a nod as he opened the screen doors, the men mumbled their replies from their scattered seats in the dining room. 'Sienna.' Giving her a sly wink.

'Morning.' She slid his cup of coffee across the bench, trying to suppress a smile, along with the increased heart rate from just being near the guy.

'I've brought you a present.' Jake held out a ream of paper.

'For me? Is it flowers?'

'It's the rules for the station's competition.'

'Rules are boring,' she said, screwing up her nose. 'But it is paper, and paper comes from a tree and trees have flowers, so you almost brought me a flower, right?'

Jake chuckled, shaking his head. 'Okay, I'll play.' He grabbed the pencil tucked behind his ear. Flicked past the cover page and scribbled on the paper. 'There, now ... You can't say I didn't give you any.'

Sienna turned it around and smiled at the simple flower he'd drawn for her. 'Aww, it's a one-of-a-kind, precious piece of petal prowess.'

Jake winced at her. 'What's in your coffee this morning?'

'Elliott and I've been word-playing trying to come up with a name for the shed party. How's your morning?' She sipped her coffee to hide her smile, because Jake had only snuck out of her room when she went to work.

Jake cleared his throat, keeping his poker face, but the intense shine to his royal blues gave him away. 'Had a yak with Dad about these rules.'

'Did Bob give you any insider information?'

'The basics. I tried looking at this stuff but started going cross-eyed.'

'I don't blame you,' said Sienna, flicking through the pages. 'Any thoughts on what you want to do first?'

'Can you grab us some lunch, your laptop, that fancy camera, and tourist brain of yours and we'll go through everyone's suggestions?'

'I'm up for an adventure, and we'll be searching for the wow factor.'

'The wow what?'

'It's for the guests. I'll tell you when I see it, so you have to surprise me.' She slid over the list of places the crew suggested at last night's meeting.

Jake tilted his head to read it. 'Okay, I can do that. The cascades—you've been there with Jess.' With his pencil he struck it off the list.

'And the waterfall by the third turn-off after the front gate. That's my favourite so far.' And the things they did there.

Jake's darkening eyes narrowed at her, with a hint of a smile across his lips. 'I think we can outdo that one. I hope you've prepped Elliott to do dinner because you might be back late.'

'I can do that.' With a chance for a one on one with the boss all day—she was so there.

'Good. Which reminds me, that front sign needs fixing.'

'Who's gifted at signwriting?'

'Jess is. She's into her arts and crafts. So, what other ideas do you have?' He angled towards her lists of paper.

'Heaps. I'll power up my tablet soon because my phone's too small for all my notes. Hey, you should pinch one from the twins and I'll network it with mine.'

'Why, when you'll be playing secretary and can tell me instead.'

'Wow, from chook-poop shoveller to kitchen scrubber and now this, it has to be the fastest occupational growth I've ever done.'

Again, Jake chuckled, pausing to sip his coffee. He never did tell her if her coffee was any good.

'So, what's topping the list of lists?' Jake asked.

'To call your water guy.'

'My what?'

'The guy who does the water readings.'

'We don't have water meters out here, Sienna.'

No, they had bores that pumped water from some underground water basin to fill the large tanks outside of each dwelling, which then flowed through to the taps inside. It was a whole new way of being water wise. 'You know what I mean.'

'My mate, Barry, calls himself a water analyst.'

'Excellent. Can he do a testimonial for the website? Will he also be able to provide any official water certification? It'd be great if he could come to the dinner too?'

'How many cups of coffee have you had this morning?'

'Oh, I'm just starting, sugar.' Sienna smiled wide because she loved working on new projects. 'If I was a potential buyer, I'd want to know how pure the water is, and have physical evidence. If your water expert's present at the dinner he can answer any questions, mostly mine.' Especially after the toxic poisoning that ruined this station's reputation. The reputation she was trying to help Jake restore.

'Okay, I'll call Barry. Next question?'

'Do you know any vets willing to visit all the way out here?'

'Yes. Ryan. He's another boarding-school mate. I'll get him to check the cattle for transport certification.'

'Great. Does he do fish too?' Because they needed a vet's tick for the licensing paperwork.

'I'll talk to him.'

'Excellent. I'll contact the Department of Primary Industries and Fisheries to—' She stopped before she blurted out too much about Jake's secret barramundi farm. 'I'll fetch lunch and we can chat more on the road.'

'Good idea.' With coffee in hand, Jake sat next to Tom at the back of the room. 'Morning, Tom.'

'Boss.' Tom sipped his mug of billy tea.

'SNAKE! SNAKE!' The twins screamed as they ran from the orchard.

Jake led the stampede of boots and met his niece and nephew in the dusty centre of the compound. 'Where?'

'At the chook pen,' cried Kate, hugging her uncle's legs.

'It's wrapped around the wire hanging from the roof, Uncle.' Aaron twisted his arms as if performing a weird contortionist trick.

'Josh?' Jake looked back at the staff gathered on the muster room's verandah.

'I'm on it, Boss. I'll get my gear.' With a wide smile the jackaroo dashed to the stockmen's quarters.

'I'll show you,' said Aaron.

'Don't get in the way, Aaron,' said Jake.

'I won't.' Aaron ran as fast as his little legs carried him, holding onto his mini-cowboy hat, chasing after Josh.

'I'm not going,' said Kate, hiding behind her uncle.

'Do you want me to take you up to the house, Kate?'

Kate pouted up at him. 'Yes please, Uncle.'

'Okay, your mum's there.' Jake picked up his niece, giving Jess a wave where she stood at the house verandah. 'Sienna, I'll drive round to pick you up, and I'll email Barry and Ryan now to see when they can come visit?'

'No rush, focus on the snake situation first.' Sienna shuddered, rubbing her upper arms. '*Ick*, hate snakes. Which reminds me why I don't do country.'

'Must be warming up with the snakes on the move,' said Tom, adjusting his Akubra.

'They can move right on outta here for all I care,' said

Sienna.

Jake turned around with his niece in his arms. 'Tom?'

'Yes, Boss?'

'Get Elliott to do a low mow over the compound's firebreak and get rid of any weeds around the base of any buildings. That should lessen the likelihood of any snakes crossing if they've got nowhere to hide. Also, I want the front sign taken down and passed to Jess to paint. Get Charlie to fix the office screen door. And Dad wants to start painting the cattlemen's quarters, so prep the crew for a room shuffle. I believe Sienna gave Dad a work plan already.'

'Will do, Boss.' Tom gave his signature nod to Jake. He then turned to Sienna. 'Have you got me a work plan too, girlie?'

'I wouldn't dare, Tom.' She grinned at the head stockman who never smiled, but heard Jake chuckling as he carried his niece towards the house.

Tyson came up beside them, sipping from his coffee. 'Snake whisperer's onto it. Hope it's not another bloody Taipan for his room.'

Josh, with a long rod in hand and black bag in the other, jumped off the deck of the stockmen's quarters. With Aaron following, they raced up to the orchard where the henhouse lived beneath a massive mango tree.

'Josh doesn't keep snakes in his bedroom, does he?' Sienna winced at the thought.

'Oh yeah, he's got glass cages with heat lights.'

'Why?'

'For the injured snakes he nurses back to health, then he sets them free down the track,' said Tyson. 'It looks cool. But there's no way I'd sleep with that.'

'Sounds kind of cool.' Sienna watched Josh and Aaron disappear inside the corrugated dwelling that made up the chook-pen.

She'd never seen a henhouse until she'd come to Danbunnan, let alone experienced the true rich colour and flavour of free-range eggs. When she'd first arrived, they'd had to buy their eggs. Now after the clean-up and repair of the henhouse they enjoyed a healthy daily supply.

'I think I'll suggest staff interviews for the website. Such as Josh the jackarooing snake whisperer.' She pulled out her phone from her apron's pocket and tapped in her ideas. Even though there was no reception to make calls, it held her notes, carried her music, and the battery lasted longer now. 'I could interview Tyson about having the best ute on the property while he explains what a ute muster is.'

The cowboy of cuteness puffed out his chest like a proud rooster. 'My baby's the winner of the many I've entered.'

'How's Josh keeping those heat lights on in them snake cages when the generator goes off?' Tom asked.

'We've hooked up a solar panel and an old spare battery with a timer that leads out of Josh's window,' replied Tyson. 'Boss and I made the panels from broken ones, experimenting to see what we could salvage.'

'Have you got much stuff to move, because they want to paint the rooms?'

'Just my tools. I'll shift them back to my ute and get rid of the wiring. Guess my ladies will need to be lifted too.' Tyson grinned, hooking thumbs into the belt loops of his jeans.

'Ladies?' Sienna cocked her eyebrow at Tyson. 'Let me guess, *Playboy*?'

'Buckle bunnies wearing bikinis. Signed by the ladies themselves, from the rodeo finals in Mount Isa. They're a collector's item.'

'*He's got it. He's got it,*' shouted Aaron, skipping alongside Josh who was carrying a wriggling black bag to his room.

'Looks like Josh has got a new bunkmate.' Tyson drank the rest of his coffee and put his cup on the kitchen's front deck. 'Better go see what type this one is.'

'What's Josh going to feed it?' Sienna asked.

'You don't want to know.' Tyson tapped the brim of his Akubra and headed for the cattlemen's quarters.

'I'd better go warn the lad he'll be shifting them cages if Pina and Lyn are painting,' said Tom, 'because Pina's terrified of snakes.'

'She's not the only one.' Sienna shuddered, rubbing her upper arms.

'You've got Sally.' Tom pointed to the blue cattle dog lying under the bench seat. 'She's the best snake dog around.'

'Sally's not my dog.'

Sally raised her head, her dark blue and grey ears twitching. With a grumble and a groan, she stood to walk down the steps and sit beside Sienna's leg. The perfect height for a head scratch.

'Are you sure about that?' Tom glanced back at her while walking after Tyson.

'I don't know how to look after a dog.' Sienna looked down at Sally, creating dust clouds from her wagging tail.

Sally wasn't a pet, but a retired working dog.

'You're my friend, aren't you?' She patted the blue cattle dog who used to be her stalker. 'Come on, Sally, we've got a play date with the boss.' They had lots to do, but it was the type of work she enjoyed the most—planning for a party.

# Six

Jake pulled his ute to a stop along the arid wallaby track, with Sienna sitting beside him, her laptop open and camera at the ready. They'd been working through everyone's list of favourite places on the station, discussing the options for the pending competition.

'Why are we stopping here?' Sienna lowered her sunglasses, to peer at the dirt track hemmed in by thick clusters of pink flowering turkey bush.

'For that wow factor you're after. Can you give me your scarf, please?'

'Sure, but I don't think it's your colour, honey.' She unwrapped it from her fair hair and shoulders. It reminded him of a silver screen Hollywood actress from the movies he watched with his mother as a kid.

The soft delicate material slid between his fingers. 'Do you trust me?'

'Well, that depends—'

'Oi!'

'Of course, I do. Why? What are you up to?'

'I'm going to blindfold you until we get there. Are you up for that?'

'Oh yeah, how cool.'

'Do you ever say no?'

'To you? Um ...' She sat with her back to him, sliding her sunglasses onto her head. 'Should I?'

'Not today, I hope.' Jake wrapped the scarf across her eyes. 'No peeking.'

'I won't, I don't want to ruin the surprise.'

'I'm glad you're willing to play along.' She'd been playful ever since he'd told her to go for it with this competition. Surprisingly, he'd been enjoying the challenge of planning this event as much as he enjoyed working with her. 'How's that?'

'I can't see a thing.'

His nose rubbed against her slender neck.

She squirmed. 'Hey, that tickles.'

'Hmm … The things I could do to you while blindfolded, baby,' he murmured into her ear, watching the goosebumps spread across her skin.

'If this is your wow factor, I'm so there.'

'But we're not there, yet.' He helped her back into her seat, then put the ute into gear and began the steep climb.

'Whose favourite place is this?' Sienna called out over the roar of the powerful diesel engine.

'Mine.' The ute crested the top and he parked in the centre of the flat summit. 'Wait there, I'll come get you. Don't peek.'

'I won't.' With hands in her lap, she waited for him, blindfolded.

Jake dashed around to the passenger side, and gently lifted her out. 'Okay, it's just a few steps, I've got you.' He couldn't wait to see her reaction. 'Are you ready?'

'You sound nervous?'

The lady missed nothing. 'I'm removing the blindfold.'

Sienna blinked until her eyes adjusted to the sunshine, then they widened, as her jaw dropped.

'Sienna?' Had he done the right thing?

She clutched his arm.

'Is this what you're looking for?'

'This … this is amazing.'

'This is the North Ridge. It gives you a unique view of Danbunnan …' He led her closer to the edge, wrapped his arms around her waist, holding her back to his chest. Her silky hair floated against his cheek, as her delicate floral fragrance mingled with the fresh breeze. Spread beneath their boots was an endless vista of green treetops, black soil plains, broken up by a sparse scattering of red dirt roads, and wide rivers that glistened like ribbons under the sun. It was Danbunnan Station in all its glory, stretching further than the curve of the horizon in all directions.

'I've never shared this place with anyone.' On this plateau it felt like they were untouchable, giving him a rare moment of freedom from his world.

'Jake, you've just redefined the meaning of magnificence.' She spun around, hugged him, then peppered his face with kisses. But her eyes soon returned to the view. 'Thank you for sharing this.'

'Stay here, I'll get our lunch.'

'I'm not moving.'

Jake didn't know what was more spectacular, the scenic Danbunnan, or Sienna. But he was damned glad he'd shared this with her today.

He used Sienna's camera to take a snapshot of his favourite place with his favourite lady. They looked perfect together.

Through her eyes she'd made him start to see the beauty of this place again. Sienna was his lady, the one he could never have, because of the bigger lady that stood behind her, Danbunnan.

It was going to kill him to say goodbye to one to keep the other, when his family's legacy already dictated which one he had to choose and which one he had to let go of.

But not today. Today he could pretend he had both.

# Seven

Jake parked his ute inside the worksheds. At the benches was their station mechanic, Joe, busily filling a wheelbarrow with junk. He could see the stuff everywhere, now he'd been made to look at it, courtesy of Sienna's wise eyes.

'Hey, Boss.' Joe gave a wave.

'How'd you go with that water pump?'

'It's ready. Are you gonna give it to Charlie?'

Jake wanted Charlie's opinion about his secret barra farm pump works but couldn't. Not yet. Only Sienna knew about his side project because he could tell her anything. 'I'll take it.' He put the pump in the back of his ute. 'What else are you up to?'

'Cleaning up.' Joe adjusted his grease-stained trucker's cap.

'Has Sienna got you into it too?' Sienna's enthusiasm was spreading and the pride in his team was showing.

'Yep. Now she's set up that recycling area out the back with your dad, it'll make it easier to sort stuff.'

'The what?' Jake knew she'd organised an archiving system with Bob, but a recycling centre?

'We've sorted aluminium tins, steel, and copper wiring into piles. You know, it's all worth something for the bickie tin. You name it they'll recycle it, and someone'll buy it. Sienna showed me on her laptop over coffee this morning. All about recycling and bein' organic. We're almost a green station, huh.' Joe gave a snort-laugh, pointing out to the fields where large rolls of feed dotted the dry outback landscape.

'In a few months it'll be green.' And that's when the place became an inland sea, where everything slowed down in the wet season. Normally he looked forward to the break. But not now, because then Rhonda would've returned, and Sienna would be …

'I'm finding lots of treasure. You should've seen that girl's eyes light up goin' on about using this an' that for your shed dance. You've got lots of great ideas, Boss.'

'Ah huh.' With Sienna adding to that list daily.

Was the junk his dad had collected for half a century really worth something? He headed for the muster room to find out.

'Boss?' Tom called out from behind.

Jake stopped. 'How's the branding going?'

'Catching up from yesterday.'

'What happened yesterday?' Jake had the best day with Sienna, and he trusted Tom enough to not stand over the man.

'It's um, Annie …' Tom crossed his stocky arms over his barrel chest. 'She fainted at the yards and fell off the rail.'

'Is she okay?'

'Seems to be, she's not complaining about any head or body aches from her flat drop.'

'Was she dehydrated?'

'It's complicated.' Tom sighed with a slow head shake, rubbing the back of his suntanned neck. 'Sienna would be better at this stuff than me—'

'What's this got to do with Sienna?' Jake's fierce protectiveness over Sienna flared up like a match scratching to burn beneath his skin. 'Annie had better not be playing games again with Sienna.'

'I dunno what's going on with Annie. But back at the Simmons's rodeo, Sienna told me Annie wasn't eating right and lost lots of weight. I took no notice until Sienna told me.'

'Aren't girls always on diets?' Jake liked his women soft

and curvy, like Sienna.

'I didn't think much of it. But Sienna said to keep an eye on Annie, so I did.' Tom let out a long slow breath, and with an unusually remorseful tone to his voice, he said, 'Boss, Annie isn't eating. I caught her throwing up yesterday morning after I'd made her sit and eat a spoonful of eggs and a mouthful of toast.'

'If you're crook you can't eat, and we can't force someone to eat, Tom.'

'Right before Bob's meeting, Sienna said Annie hasn't stepped inside the kitchen since before the Simmons's rodeo and that she's only getting cereal for her room.'

'What else did Sienna say?' Why hadn't she mentioned any of this to him?

'Sienna had cheesecake she was saving so she dished it up coz it's Annie's favourite. Yet that kid took an hour to eat a tiny piece, when not that long ago she would've wolfed it down in a flash. But then I find out from Josh, she threw it all up after the meeting.'

'You don't think Annie's suffering a stomach bug? I'm not a doctor.' But he knew Tom rarely spoke about anything unless there was a reason. 'What do you think it is?'

'Buggered, if I know. I don't know women. But when I picked that girl up outta the dirt, yesterday, she weighed nothing. Not like she'd done a few months back when I'd helped her up after being pushed over by one of the cattle. The thing is, Boss, if Annie had fainted before she'd closed the latch on that gate the cattle would've trampled all over her.'

*Damn.* 'If it's a risk to her safety and if she's not eating, what do we do about it?' His job didn't come with a manual for dealing with staff eating disorders.

'Sienna and I both agree we need to get Annie to the doctor. I asked Annie yesterday about it and she said no. And, I hate to say this, but …' Again, Tom hesitated as he thumbed up the brim of his Akubra. 'It's our duty of care to help that kid.'

Tom, who was normally expressionless, looked worried.

'Look, get Jess to take Annie to the doctor in the morning. I won't risk our jillaroo's health and safety, especially when you're worried about her, when we all need to focus on the job.'

'Agreed.' Tom gave his nod.

Jake narrowed his eyes at Tom who'd agreed way too fast. 'How is Annie's work performance?'

'It's gone downhill. I told her not long ago to pick up her game, but she's just not focusing.'

'Give her a warning. The first and last. If she's not performing her job, we can't afford to keep her. Not when I've got dozens of other kids emailing me their resume weekly.' One of the benefits of having a website he hadn't expected.

'How long do you think I should give Annie for the warning?'

'The warning is on her work performance only. I'll let you be the judge on time. But tell Annie she *has* to see the doctor at Elsie Creek. I'll pay for it; I've still got an account there from Mum. If Annie's fainted on the job in a dangerous situation, I want a medical clearance before Annie returns to work. If Annie's got a health problem, the doctor will see it and give the kid the help she needs. They're the health professionals, not us. Do you want me there when you speak to Annie?'

'Nah, I wouldn't want to shame the kid if she's, um, Sienna called it, delicate.'

'Do you want Sienna to help you when you speak with Annie? Sienna can be tactful.' And secretive. Why hadn't Sienna mentioned this before?

'Believe me I would, but Sienna thinks it's because of her Annie's stopped eating.'

'What?' Jake adored Sienna's cooking, everyone did.

'Annie's on some food strike. Sienna and I tested her theory out where Annie will eat Elliott's food, not much, but she does. But she won't eat Sienna's food at all. Annie will stab at it with a fork or just pull it apart, that's it. The girl's jealous, you can see it.'

'Women.' Jake wiped his mouth, realising he sounded just like his father. 'Look, go and see my sister to make the doctor's appointment. Then you can give Annie her warning and tell her when to be ready to visit town. If Annie says no, we'll have to let her go.' Damn, he was depending on everyone's help.

'Will do. How are you going with your preparations?'

'I'm about to get an update.'

'You can see Sienna's loving it,' said Tom.

'Yeah, can't miss that.' Because her eyes glowed, her smile was wide, and her creativity was amazing to watch.

At the back of the kitchen, he noticed the wood stockpile was getting bigger. There was no reason for it when winter was passing, and the wood stove use was slowing down with less people to cook for.

Jake stopped by the woodpile where the large rotisserie had been pulled out from the pig truck. Inside Elliott was busily cleaning, obsessed with the thing. 'What are you doing?'

'Um ...' Elliott's skinny shoulders rose to his ears, his hands wringing the cloth.

For some unknown reason Elliott feared him, and at his lady's gentle request, Jake had promised to be more mindful around the kid. 'Relax, Elliott, I'm just asking.'

Jake rubbed at his forehead. When did this pandering to the staff's personalities start?

But Elliott was part of his lady's team, and he certainly didn't want to upset her. Not when they were playing so well together, and he liked playing with her every chance he got.

'I'm, ah,' Elliott mumbled, 'polishing the spit for Sienna, for the barn carnival.'

'Is that the new name, is it?'

'We're still word playing with it. We're going to see if we can re-organise the pig truck for the food tour.'

'We're using the pig truck?' Jake cocked an eyebrow at

the patchy pieces of scrap metal, welded together to make a four-wheel drive food van. It wasn't pretty, but it was practical for feeding the hordes when they did scrub work.

'Sienna's waiting to see how much paint will be left over from the cattlemen's quarters. She said we could give the pig truck a makeover for the next muster.'

Jake had to finish this muster first, and Sienna wouldn't be here for the next one because Rhonda would be back. *Damn.*

'Keep cleaning, Elliott.' Because the kid liked the pig truck and was starting to come into his own with his cooking. How long before Elliott left for some food tour of his own? 'Where is Sienna?'

'In the kitchen talking to some guy.'

'What guy?' Jake frowned as he walked around the kitchen's back corner that was closest to the cook's quarters. He knew this path well because it's how he snuck into Sienna's room nightly. The effort to see his lady didn't bother him, but it was getting harder to restrain himself whenever they were in the company of others.

Jake passed the flourishing veggie patch, vaulted up to the side verandah to find Sally sniffing at the bottom edge of the dry goods storeroom door. 'What's with you Sal? I can't let you in there.' He patted the old dog. She was Sienna's constant companion these days; and if the dog was here, Sienna was nearby. 'Sienna?' He gripped the door's handle, grinning at the thought of a grope in the storeroom.

'In here,' Sienna replied from inside the kitchen.

*Well, so much for that idea.* The storeroom self-closed with a loud click, which reminded him to check if the office door got fixed. The work was piling up with all these little jobs. He didn't do details, he did the big stuff—but it had to be done.

Inside the kitchen, Jake washed his hands at the small basin. An ingrained habit from way back when he used a footstool to reach the sink. 'What are you doing with the pig truck and recycling project? Do you want me to tell the men to stop collecting wood?'

'Want a coffee?'

'Sure.' He never said no to her coffee, like the woman. 'Tom told me about Annie.'

'Barry, do you want a refill?' Sienna nudged her nose towards the dining room.

'Thanks, Sienna. How are you, Jake?'

Jake spun around and there was Barry seated at the table. Wearing his cheesy smile, covered in freckles, with eyebrows that matched his auburn hair.

'G'day mate.' It was handshakes and man-hugs of long-time friends. 'Stay right there.' Jake dug around the pantry's top shelf. 'For you,' he said, putting a bottle of rum down in front of Barry.

'It's not my birthday.' Barry tilted the bottle to inspect the label.

'I know, but I've got a favour to ask.'

'What favour does the Black Prince need?'

'Black Prince?' Sienna gave a light laugh, serving up Jake's coffee and a plate of gourmet sandwiches.

'One of those names you get as a kid. Don't ask, it's a long-forgotten story.'

'Yeah, sure, I'll forget it.' Barry chuckled behind his cup and pushed his empty plate forward. 'Besides the top feed, mate, what's with the rum?'

'I need a water certificate.' Jake sat down, eagerly scooping up a sandwich. The aroma of roast beef and mustard relish had him salivating, with the fresh homemade bread soft in his hands.

'I've always said I'd do it for you, anytime. I've kept regular records ever since the poisoning.'

'How come?' Sienna asked.

'We had to. It's part of the national environmental protection standards. So, I'll get fresh samples today and send them through. You should have your test results and certificate by the end of the week. I'll email you a copy when I do the testimonial for the website too.'

Jake swallowed his food and looked at Sienna. How

much did she say?

'Elliott and I told Barry about Danbunnan's nomination for the competition. I'm sure it's all over the district,' she said with a shrug.

'Mate, I had to look twice when I walked inside. It's good to see,' Barry said, looking around the muster room's renovations.

'Yeah, it's all happening.' Even if Jake felt a bit out of the information loop.

'I'll be outside helping Elliott. You two have fun.'

He couldn't reach out and ask her to stay, even if he wanted to. 'I'll catch up after.'

'Thanks for lunch, Sienna. Great cuppa.' Barry then turned to Jake. 'She's a stunner, mate.'

Jake wanted to agree but couldn't, his relationship with Sienna had to remain a secret.

'So, are you up for a short drive? I want to show you something, and I'd appreciate your honest opinion.'

'Sure, what is it?'

'Can't tell anyone.' Yet another secret. When would it end?

'Is that what I'm getting the rum for?'

'We're gonna do some fishing.' Jake grabbed his coffee and sandwiches. 'Come on, grab your water-testing kit.'

They headed to Barry's large ute, complete with rooftop tent and aerials, covered in a thick layer of red dust.

Barry put his rum inside the cab and reached for a large bag. 'So, do I get an invite to this shindig you mob are chuckin'?'

'What did you hear?'

'Sienna and Elliott asked if I could suggest any names for this dance thing. Mate, I haven't got a clue.' Barry chuckled. 'But it sure made for interesting conversation while waiting for you.'

'Yeah, Sienna does that. You'll be copping one of those official invitations when they're done up.' Jake didn't have a clue on that stuff either, but he was grateful Sienna loved working on the details. He was relying on her heavily, now mustering up his best mates for this one occasion. 'By the way, you should know that your name is on top of the guest list.'

'Nice. And you are so keen on that relief cook.'

'I'm engaged to Angela.' And shoved the last of his sandwich into his gob to not speak about the subject.

'Yeah, Craig filled me in already. Sorry mate, anything I can do to help I will. But I only know water.'

'You always were a little wet behind the ears.'

'Says the Black Prince. Hey, can I bring Jenny out to the dance? She'd like it.'

Jake had never danced with Sienna—would he ever get that chance? 'Sure, we want you here for the dinner and food tour. But you don't dance, and you don't want Craig dancing Jenny away from you.'

'I'm aiming to beat Cowboy Craig's dust-dancing ways, because I've been having dancing lessons.'

'For what?'

'My wedding.'

'You're getting married?' Jake pushed up his hat's brim.

'Yeah, that's my big news. I would have told you sooner but you're never at the house to answer the friggin' phone.'

'You're worse, working on the road all the time.'

'I was on my way back home when I got your email and I wanted to tell you in person, because, mate, I'm engaged to Jenny.' Barry grinned wide with pride.

'Congratulations.' Jake shook Barry's hand with a pat on the back, delighted for his mate.

'You know it was the scariest thing I'd ever done in my life. We were down at the wharf having a candlelight dinner. I was so nervous I almost dropped the bloody ring over the side of the wharf.'

Jake's engagement had been entirely different. He'd been sitting in the Elsie Creek pub getting tanked, ticked-off from being knocked back by the stock buyer. With no one to buy his cattle, he couldn't see a way forward. Then in walked his brother's girl, Angela, with a crazy idea: as they were both angry at their fathers, they should team up. With 'team up' meaning they get engaged. Jake was just drunk enough to agree, and it took very little to convince everyone else, especially when they got a hotel room. Except Jake slept on the floor; Angela had the bed. How romantic. All staged for the benefit of the co-op, who wasted no time getting word to Angela's daddy that his one and only daughter was engaged.

'You didn't pay Jenny to say yes, did you?'

'Very funny. But it's costing us now with Jenny's wedding planning and dancing lessons.'

'Why dancing lessons?'

'Bridal dance. Jenny likes it, and it makes her happy. So, I've got my brother as best man and I want you, Craig and Ryan as my groomsmen. So, would you want to be my groomsman? I'd like you there, mate.'

'I'd be honoured. I'm happy for you, mate. Jenny's a nice lady.' He could see Barry was beaming with that cheesy grin. Jake even had a touch of green envy that his mate got to celebrate his engagement for the right reasons.

'Where are we going?' Barry asked.

'To bash a few golf balls around. Do you still play?'

'Every Sunday morning. Next time you're in Darwin we'll have a hit.'

'Who knows when that'll be, but it'll be good.' At least one job could get ticked off the growing list towards saving Danbunnan. But would all the sacrifices he was making, including his happiness, be worth it in the end?

# Eight

'That'll do. Don't you think, Elliott?' Sienna stepped out of the trailer with her bucket filled with rags and cleaning solutions, to inspect the metallic patchworked monstrosity known as the pig truck.

Elliott stood beside her, admiring it. 'It's so blah. It could do with a coat of paint, sure, but I think it deserves more.'

'You should design a logo for it, it's your beast. Jess can paint it.'

'I will.' Elliott's eyes shone brighter than the spotlights showcasing a department store's window display.

'Let's take this gear back inside, get some lunch and have a picnic under the banyan tree. You can research logos, and I'll do more of my other stuff.' She gathered her cleaning supplies, an all-too-common accessory these days, and headed for the kitchen.

'Excuse me, Sally.' She pushed past the dog who was sniffing under the door to the storeroom. 'What is she doing?'

'Probably doing some Jedi mind trick for her dog biscuits,' said Elliott with a shrug. 'Talking about bickies, I want to do a blog post about those shortbreads we made, and I'll see if my results are through from my last assignment.'

Sienna slid her bucket of cleaning goods under the bench in the kitchen. 'Wi-fi in the muster room would be handy.'

'But it's like checking the mail at the local post office when we visit the banyan tree.'

'If anyone in my past life knew that they'd laugh.' Wow, it'd been a while since she'd thought of her past life, even though the countdown was ticking faster. Yet the idea of leaving only made her shuffle to a sullen standstill.

'Sienna, there you are.'

Sienna spun around to the main screen doors. 'Hey, Jess, were your ears burning?'

'Why?'

*Oh, no!* In walked Angela, Jake's fiancée, with her father, Simon Simmons, and Bob. 'Elliott can explain.'

Simon removed his wide-brimmed hat, his eyes focusing on her chest, as his tongue flickered over his thin lips. 'Good to see you again, Sienna.'

'Afternoon, Simon. Angela.' *Holy roasted coffee beans!*

'Heya.' Angela waved with her ring-covered fingers. 'Wow, Jess, you've done an amazing job in here. I love the artwork. Where did you get it?'

'The twins did this.' Jess smiled widely at her children's collages hanging on the wall.

'I must say, the place looks … too good.' Simon's small eyes peered around then back to Sienna's breasts, again his tongue flickered across his lips.

'I've accepted the nomination for the station's competition with the co-op,' said Bob, with his nose in the air.

'I'm surprised you did.' Simon aimed for the open laptop sitting on the dining room table. 'Where is young Jake?'

Sienna moved fast to her equipment, closing the laptop, snatching up her camera, sliding them all into her bag. 'Excuse the mess, I've been helping Elliott with his food blog.' She quickly gathered her notepad and maps of the station, all to do with this competition, looking to Bob for help.

In an instant, Bob stepped forward blocking the neighbour. 'If you'd given us some notice, Simon, we would've had Sienna whip something up for us.'

'There's a cake and fruit platter if you want, sir.' With everything crammed into her laptop bag, she tucked it safely out of the way behind the kitchen counter. Giving Bob a nod, playing her part as the relief cook, all hot and sweaty from cleaning the pig truck. How glamorous—*not*.

'Sure, we'll have a cuppa in 'ere.' Simon dropped his Akubra onto Tom's hat chair.

Sienna frowned, because they were Tom's chairs, like the guy who owned the seat in the bar where everyone knew it.

'Help yourself to the urn, Simon.' At the large radio Bob picked up the handpiece and flicked a few dials. 'Jake, you there?'

Sienna hated this and ducked into her favourite hiding place, the coldroom. 'Elliott, can you serve these, please?' She removed the plastic wrap from the trays prepped for tonight's supper. 'I'll get our lunch, while you get our coffee, and we'll sneak out the back door.'

'Good idea.' Elliott took the platter, raising his chin, always proud to serve.

'Yeah, Dad?' Jake's voice carried over the radio's speakers.

'Simon and Angela are here for a visit. Can you come in?'

Silence.

Sienna grabbed their lunch, hating this jolt to her reality. She was only staff, a relief cook. So what the hell was she doing getting involved by helping the family sell beef and fish?

Yet no matter how much she tried not to get involved, she did it for Jake, because, yes, she loved him.

Sienna felt sick, because Jake was engaged to Angela, and she couldn't be in the same room as Angela. Not when the guilt slammed hard onto her shoulders and knotted her stomach. She felt guilty not only for Angela, but that she was also a part of the secret Jake kept hidden from his own family. So how many other secrets did Jake keep from her?

'I'll be half an hour, Dad.' The boss's voice was cold.

Sienna recognised it from Jake's many sides and tones, but did she truly know the man?

'Good, son. We're in the muster room admiring the twins' artwork.' Bob patted his puffed-out chest—the posturing of the old boss was back.

'I'll leave you to it, sir.' Scooping up her laptop bag, Sienna opened the side door for Elliott who hurried through with their coffees.

'Where are you going, Sienna?' Simon called out from the other side of the dividing bench.

'I'm on my break. I work split shifts. I'll be back before dinner.' She nodded to Bob, as she walked backwards to her freedom.

'Sienna starts at four to bake our bread ...' and on prattled Bob.

With coffee in one hand, and his laptop bag over his shoulders, Elliott said, 'We're so outta 'ere.'

'Come on, Sally, come for a drive, we'll go for a swim at the falls.' Sienna didn't want to hang around. She might be sleeping with the boss, but that didn't mean she was on call twenty-four-seven.

It sucked being in love, because no matter what she did for the man she adored there could never be an *us*.

So why was she putting herself through this?

For what?

All she saw in her future was a whole load of heartbreak destined to hit on the day her contract ended. And the countdown was on ...

# Nine

'Have they gone?' Sienna peeked into the kitchen.

Elliott peered around the empty room. 'The coast is clear.'

She put their esky onto the spotless counter. Unlike the dining table, covered in empty plates, cups, and saucers. 'More cleaning to do,' she mumbled, collecting the discarded crockery, and was back at her station in life at the bottom of Danbunnan's staffing structure.

'Where did everyone go?'

'Who cares?' It was nice to be away from the scrutiny of others. 'Okay, dinner is …'

Elliott flicked the dark fringe out of his chocolate-coloured eyes. 'Tonight's dinner of deliciousness is my stupendous handmade fettucine noodles and your sauce of magnificence. We are so organised.'

'That's what preparation is all about. We'll need to plate more fruit and cake for supper. Wow, they cleaned this up.' All that was left were cake crumbs on the tray she kept beside the steaming urn that never stopped.

'Ooh, lookie here.' Elliott pointed at the windows above the sinks.

It was Annie.

'Didn't Annie have the day off, sick?'

'I thought so too. Hey, is it me or does Annie look like a walking clothes hanger?'

'You can see that?' She was worried about the jillaroo, who'd lost that healthy glow, entering the muster room.

'Hi, Annie, are you feeling any better?' Elliott asked.

'Okay, um, better. I'm wondering if I could hassle you for some more cereal.'

'I'll get it, you two can talk.' Sienna headed for the storeroom.

'Thanks. So, how's it going, Elliott? I saw you cleaning the pig truck earlier. Does that mean we're going on another muster?'

Annie was rather chatty. Which seemed odd when Annie had been nothing but a sulky sourpuss for weeks—no, months!

Outside, Sienna pushed on the stiff handle to the storeroom.

Sally pounced from her favourite hiding spot under her bench seat and pushed her nose straight to the door.

'Hey Sal, you can't go in here, it's not for animals.' She squeezed past the dog, flicked on the light in the narrow room, lined with floor to ceiling wooden shelves.

The newly organised room was a sight to behold. A Tupperware consultant could use it as a showroom on the clever ways to use their containers. Which reminded her she needed to email Rhonda.

Sienna grabbed a box of cereal, ordered specially for Annie. At least the girl was eating that. She then grabbed a box of milk to go with it. 'Yep, just getting some cow from the cupboard on the cattle station.' She giggled at the irony and turned for the door. 'AUUUUGGHH.'

'Sienna, what's wrong?' shouted Elliott from the other side of the door.

'SNAKE. *There's a snake at the door.*' Sienna's back hit the shelves along the far wall.

It was huge! Thick and scaly. Its body coiling into a spring, with flickering tongue and beady black eyes. And fangs. FANGS.

Her panic hitting an all-time high, she threw the milk and cereal box at the snake before climbing the shelves like a ladder.

Annie pushed the door open, forcing the snake into the corner. 'I know what to do.'

'*No, Annie, don't.*' Sienna clambered onto the top shelf beside the rolls of toilet paper, watching the snake search for a way out amongst the spilled cornflakes, toilet paper, and tins of beans.

'I'll do it, Josh taught me.' Annie snatched at the snake.

Cornered, it reared up and attacked Annie, striking her bare forearm.

'Bugger, it bit me!'

The snake's glistening fangs struck out again as Annie went to grab it and again it bit at the jillaroos' forearm.

'OW.' Annie gripped onto her arm and stumbled, scattering tins of fruit from the shelf. She knocked over the flour bucket. The lid flipped off one way as the bucket spun the other, spewing white powder across the room.

The snake had to be six feet long, with its thick body wrapping into a coil of thick mooring rope. It reared high in the corner by the door, with its fangs exposed. It swayed in its stance, hissing, as it prepared to strike again, as the flour fell like snow in the room.

'SALLY. SALLY. *Elliott, get Sally.*' Tom told her Sally was the best snake dog, it was time for the dog to earn her biscuits.

'She's here.' Elliott pushed open the door and like lightning the blue cattle dog bolted inside and dove into the corner. Growling, with teeth snapping, Sally lunged at the snake and latched on to it, shaking it viciously in her mouth.

'*Get out, now.*' Elliott held out a broom like a blunt-ended spear.

Sienna leapt down and pushed Annie outside. Behind them the dog growled as jars and tins fell off shelves from the snake being flicked around like a stockwhip.

'Quick, the first-aid kit is in the kitchen.' Sienna dragged Annie inside.

'What do we do for a snake bite?' Elliott asked.

'Ah, wrap the wound, I remember that.' Sienna grabbed

the kit from the pantry shelf, while Sally continued to destroy the storeroom like a toddler chucking a tantrum over a toy. 'Is Sally going to be okay?'

'Sally's tough. She's the best snake dog there is,' said Elliott.

'She's been sniffing at that door all day. I should have realised it meant something.' At the bench Sienna opened the first-aid kit, grabbed the book, and flicked through the index. 'Okay, instructions say bandage the area, keep the patient calm and still, and to seek medical attention.'

'I don't feel so good.' Annie plonked down onto a stool, holding her bleeding arm.

'What kind of snake is it?' Elliott asked.

'How would I know? I don't know snakes.' With trembling fingers, Sienna unwrapped the roll of gauze.

'Elliott, get on the radio and ask Josh what to do. Come on, Annie, sit back down. You need to stay calm and keep your wound below your heart.' While her own heartbeat hammered faster than a power drill as Annie washed her face under the gushing taps.

'Josh? Come in, Josh? We need you, man.' Elliott spoke over the two-way's handpiece, adjusting the volume, while Sienna wrapped the bandage around Annie's arm.

Tom's voice came over the speakers. 'Josh is outta range, Elliott. What's wrong?'

'Annie's been bitten by a snake. Sienna's doing first aid now, and Sally's still killing it in the storeroom. What do we do, Uncle?'

'How is Annie?'

Sienna snatched the handpiece from Elliott who was pulling at his hair. 'Tom, she's weak, bleeding from the puncture wounds, and showing signs of going into shock.'

'Sienna, this is Tyson.' His voice clear over the speakers. 'Don't panic.'

'Yeah, right.' Sienna looked at Elliott, both of them with wide eyes on the edge of panic.

'In Josh's room he keeps an antivenene kit on the

dresser. Read the instructions on how much to administer. Then get Annie to the hospital.'

Without a word, Elliott dashed out the door faster than an Olympic sprinter.

'Where is the nearest hospital?' Because there were no shops or asphalted roads here. No power stations or streetlights, where everything either ran on generator, gas, or solar power.

'Sienna, it's Tom, drive towards Elsie Creek. There's a bush hospital there. I'll organise an ambulance to meet you on the road. It'll be quicker than getting the Flying Doctors to land at the airstrip.'

'We have an airstrip?'

'You've gotta take the snake with you for identification,' said Tyson.

'*What the hell?*' Sienna looked at Annie, all pale and sweaty. Her arm fully bandaged, leaning over the bench as if she was about to faint.

Tom said, 'You can do it, Sienna.'

'Greeeaaaat! Once Sally's finished with it, consider it done. Later.' She tossed the handpiece onto the shelf. 'We're going on a road trip, Annie, so I want no backseat driving, right? It's time to test my rally racing training. Stay there.' Sienna snatched up the longest pair of tongs she could find, as well as a garbage bag, and headed for the storeroom.

It was far too quiet behind door number one.

Sienna opened the door and Sally barrelled out huffing and puffing, leaving a trail of white powdery footprints behind her.

'Are you okay, girl?' She patted the panting dog where spots of white flour blended with her grey and dark blue coat. The dog seemed fine, wagging her tail as she drank thirstily from the water bucket.

Sienna timidly pushed open the heavy door. On the floor, the snake lay in pieces among plastic containers, various tins, toilet paper, and flour.

'The poor thing.' It would've been a horrible way to die.

With tongs, while trying to keep her stomach, Sienna picked up the scaly pieces, swallowing down her fear and revulsion. She had to do this for Annie, and there was no time to waste.

'*I've got it.*' Elliott ran up to the deck, waving the small rectangular kit.

'Good. You read the instructions and I'll do the deed.' Not that she wanted to but she did it, with steady hands while Annie sat on the stool sweating profusely. 'There... All done, Annie.'

'I don't feel so good.' Annie rushed to the sink and retched.

*Not good!*

'We've got to move. Elliott, you'll sit in the back with Annie. Good thing I refuelled this afternoon. Car needed a spin.' But not like this.

Annie's cheeks were shiny with tears. Clutching her bandaged arm she pushed through the screen door. 'It's one of Josh's snakes.'

'From Josh's cages?' Sienna asked, and with Elliott they escorted the patient to the cook's quarters.

'It was only meant to be a joke. I'm sure it's a python I pinched. But they're not meant to bite.'

'Nooooo.' Sienna's eyes widened with fear. 'This morning Tyson said Josh had a taipan in his room, not a python. *A taipan.*' And that was one snake Sienna knew was deadly.

Doors slammed and with a rumble of the engine, the toy-car reversed from the carport. Then with a pouring plume of dust from the spinning tyres, the red car flew out of the compound and raced for the outback town of Elsie Creek.

# Ten

Jake's ute skidded to a stop in the compound. Before the dust could settle, he was slamming the driver's door behind him. *'What the hell happened?'* His boots echoed like thunder on the muster room's deck as he made his way round the verandah.

'There was a snake in the storeroom,' said Tom, meeting him at the side door.

'How? Because that room is vermin proof.' Jake knew Sienna had spent ages making sure all holes, cracks, and crevices were patched because one of his ancestors had died from a bite to the throat from scaring a snake sleeping on the storeroom shelf. It was a tale of warning his mother had obsessed over, ensuring the house and verandah had no places for snakes to hide.

Jake pushed on the stiff handle and watched the door shut automatically. 'It's impossible.' He then re-opened it to examine the fight scene inside. It was a stark contrast when Sienna had this storeroom in such an immaculate condition, calling it her Tupperware showroom.

'We know.' Tom held up a black cotton sack.

'Why are you showing me one of Josh's snake bags?'

'We found it in the corner. It was planted, Boss.'

Jake strode into the muster room, spotting the other men, and his eyes landed on Tyson. 'Where's Josh?'

'He's doing a boundary bore run with Charlie and won't be back until tonight,' replied Tom.

'Boss, this isn't Josh,' said Tyson. 'One of his bags and a

snake disappeared this morning. We thought it might've escaped while we were reconnecting the new heat lights to the solar panels last night.'

Jake was well aware of the solar experiment because he'd supplied all the gear. 'Are you saying one of Josh's snakes got out?'

'We couldn't work out how, because we've put latches on the cages, so they'd never get out. We did it so Pina could clean his room. But one of them went missing.'

'Which species of snake is Josh missing?'

'I wish I knew, Boss. Sally destroyed whatever it was, and Sienna's got the rest of it. Until Josh comes in, we won't know.' Tyson removed his hat, holding it to his chest 'Boss, Josh wouldn't do this. Josh adores Sienna, and he'd never hurt any snake, not when he's all about saving them.'

'I know.' It didn't fit.

'Joe's manning the radio trying to catch Charlie and Josh now,' said Tom, 'and as soon as we find out the snake's type, we'll let the hospital know.'

'And Sienna?' Jake faced the cook's quarters, looking empty without her red car. It was another reminder of Sienna's not-too-distant departure.

He also knew she was scared of snakes. Her panicked voice over the radio had really worried him, and the way the storeroom looked told the story.

It reminded him of the time she'd been trapped with Chris.

Why was Danbunnan trying to scare off Sienna, who was instrumental in helping him try to save this station?

'Sienna is on the road, and the ambulance is on their way, watching for her red car,' said Tom.

'Has anyone tried to contact Sienna?' *Damn*, he was sleeping with the woman and didn't have her number! What kind of a bastard was he, treating her like a cheap one-night stand at the back of a B&S ball. He'd learned lots of other things about Sienna, but nothing as simple as her phone number. Being on the station he hadn't needed it until now.

'I know Sienna doesn't have a radio in that car,' said Tom. 'But that girl's always got her phone on her.'

'Does anyone have Sienna's phone number?' Jake asked. And they all shook their heads. 'Damn.'

# Eleven

'I'm so sorry,' whimpered Annie from the back seat of Sienna's toy-car.

'You'll be okay, Annie,' said Elliott seated beside the patient, directly behind the driver.

'Stay calm, Annie, you've had the antivenene, you'll be fine.' With a white-knuckle grip on the steering wheel, Sienna raced ahead of the dust plume that hid the spindly black-trunked gum trees and monstrous ant mounds that stood on either side of the dirt track.

'Those rally racing lessons are really working for you. Have you got springs on this thing?' asked Elliott.

'The lot.' Because the car was flying. 'Don't ask me what's in the toy-car, I don't know any technical-mechanical terms, but it works. Come on, Annie, enjoy this. We're off Danbunnan's dirt and heading to civilisation. Hey, we should stay in Elsie Creek for the night. Because if the sun's setting I'm not driving amongst the wandering wildlife.'

The so-called peak hour was massive from sunset to dawn; she'd never seen anything like it. Even safe inside Jake's big beast of a ute, she watched in awe as he'd been forced to dodge wallabies, possums, dingoes, and many other creatures that wandered onto the dirt road, even a crocodile doing a midnight river crossing. There's no way she could compete with that sort of traffic in her small red car.

Elliott brushed down his T-shirt. 'I'm not dressed for town.'

'It'll be a good excuse to go shopping, right?' Her laptop

bag held her purse, which she hadn't used in months.

'We can get junk food!'

'Bathe in unlimited hot water.' So glad Elliott was getting with the program to ease Annie.

'Sienna, we can finally get you a pair of jeans.'

'Don't you own any jeans?' Annie asked.

'I own jeans, I just forgot to pack them. Hey, what is in Elsie Creek, besides fuel?' Her mobile phone was docked in its cradle on her dashboard waiting for it to come into range. And for the first time she wished she had a two-way radio. But where would it fit?

'Elsie Creek is this cute country town. The pub has the best bushman's burgers that's to die for. They've got a small supermarket down the road for chocolate and crisps and oodles of junk food. Can we go? Pleeeeease? I need a burger with cheese, or I'll die.'

'You're learning how to cook fine foods and you want a burger?' Sienna peeked into her rear-view mirror spotting Elliott's cheesy grin.

'I'll have that with fries, thank you.'

'*I did it*,' wailed Annie as the tears streamed down her cheeks. 'They'll never let me back onto Danbunnan now.'

'Of course they will, you're part of the team,' said Sienna.

'Stop being nice to me when I've been nothing but a bitch to you.'

'Don't stress, you've been a bitch to everyone,' said Elliott matter-of-factly.

'Let's focus on getting you to the hospital, Annie.' Sienna hoped her voice was calm, but—*where the hell is this ambulance?*

'They'll kick me out because of what I've done. You shouldn't be nice to me. You should leave me on the side of the road to die.'

'Why?' Elliott asked.

'I planted the snake.'

Elliott's eyes widened as big as his gasping mouth. 'You

did *what*?'

'Old news. Where were you?' Sienna said.

'Panicking.' He shrugged his skinny shoulders.

'I didn't know it was a taipan, I thought it was a python and *now I'm dying*.' Annie wailed so loud, both Elliott and Sienna cringed.

'Annie, calm down.' Sienna eyed the back-seat passengers through her rear-view mirror. 'It was a prank gone wrong.'

'Tom gave me a warning.'

'Why?' Elliott's head was busy swivelling from the driver then to the wailing Annie.

'For not doing my job.' With her unbandaged arm Annie wiped at her tears. 'I fainted at work yesterday, so now the boss won't let me go back, not until I've got a medical clearance.'

'You'll get that at the hospital now,' said Sienna, passing back the box of tissues. What a brilliant idea on the medical clearance from Jake, who was smart and sexy, yet full of secrets he kept from his own family.

'Consider this a priority appointment, with an escort,' said Elliott.

'*But I did it*.' Annie clutched Elliott's shirt, slamming him against the rear door.

'You're not making sense, Annie. Are you hallucinating?'

'Is Annie reacting to the antivenene?' Sienna grabbed Annie's shoulder, pulling her off Elliott.

'*I did it all*.' Annie's cheeks were stained with tears and her bloodshot eyes were huge. 'I was the one who snuck the chooks onto your verandah every night. It was me who gave Chris the rum that night and swore to him you wanted to sleep with him and liked it rough. I even pulled the leads off the other ute to make the crew use the kitchen-ute, so you'd be forced to take the blue rust bucket. It was me who stole that ute's map, so you'd get lost and be left defenceless. And it was me who dumped the poisonous taipan in the storeroom to scare you because I wanted Josh to get sacked for it, so I'd keep my job and you'd run away. *I planned all of it. Me.'*

'*What the—*' The fury blinded her so thick and fast that Sienna slammed her foot on the brakes and the car skidded in the dirt. She jumped out before the red rain of dust had settled, filling the car through her open door.

'*Aww come on!*' Her body trembled with white hot rage. 'You've got to be kidding me.' She spun away from the car, gripping her hair. She needed to hit something, anything but the passenger bawling in the back seat of her car.

'Ooh, Sienna's gone all kung fu-ey on that ant mound.' Elliott waved at the dust swirling inside the car. 'What did you do that to Sienna for? She's always been nice to you.'

Annie bawled louder, suddenly leaning out of the car to retch. Wiping her mouth, she sank deeper into her seat hiding her face in her palms.

Sienna returned to her seat, re-adjusted her sunglasses, and took some deep breaths to control her anger. What the hell did she do to deserve this?

Tears poured down Annie's cheeks, her bottom lip trembling as she blubbered, 'I'm sorry.'

It took every ounce of self-control to not turn around and slap the wounded girl in the rear seat. 'Let's find this ambulance. No more talking. I need to concentrate on the drive.' Sienna slammed the car into gear and put the music on, loud, and her red car raced the large plume of dust to the tiny Northern Territory town called Elsie Creek.

# Twelve

Jake was in the office trying to concentrate on his paperwork when the phone rang. He snatched up the ancient handpiece. 'Yeah?'

'Jake, it's Sienna.'

'Babe, are you okay?'

'Fine. We're at the Elsie Creek Hospital.'

He sighed deep with relief to hear her voice. 'It was a python.'

'A what?'

'A children's python; they're harmless. Josh confirmed it from what was left in the storeroom, and we've told the hospital.'

Her deep exhale echoed over the line. 'The doctor had the park ranger confirm it. He also said that Annie may be a little ill from the antivenene, but she'll be fine in a few days, and he's running some tests to ensure her overall well-being.'

He flexed his hand into a fist as he said, 'We know the snake was planted. Annie stole it from Josh's room. Look, we believe Annie was setting you up, but there's no way to prove it.'

'Annie confessed.' Her tone was terse.

'She did what?' Jake scowled, gripping the phone tighter.

'Annie got all hysterical, I think she was having a reaction to the antivenene. Elliott called it her dying confession.'

'Annie's not dying, Sienna, it was a non-venomous snake. It was a set up.'

'I know. Annie told me she put the snake in the storeroom to scare me off and to try and get Josh sacked. She also planted the chickens on my verandah, and she fed Chris the rum while whispering into his ear that I wanted to meet up with him that night.'

His knuckles whitened on the phone's handle as his jaw locked.

'Annie also told us she took the map from that blue ute you all call the rust bucket. She said she'd pulled the plugs on the other ute that day hoping I'd get lost'

Jake winced. 'We guessed that one about Annie playing with the utes and taking that map.'

'How? I didn't have a clue.'

'Joe told us about his suspicions on the ute's repairs, and Tom suspected the chooks were deliberate. It all came out while we were talking in the muster room waiting for news. I've had Lyn and Pina go into Annie's room to get some of her gear to take to the hospital, and it's a mess.'

'What did you find?'

'Loads of Chris's brand of rum, all half-drunk. We've been wondering if Annie's an alcoholic.'

'What else did you find?'

'Boxes of cereal, sour milk cartons, and rotten fruit. You know, I hire cleaners, so the stockmen don't have to worry about it, because it's the best thing to come in from down the track to a decent feed, a shower, and to sleep in clean sheets. I also keep the cleaners because my mum reckoned single men are pigs, but Annie was worse. She needs help.'

'I'll tell the doctor, to ensure she gets treatment.'

'Annie is not welcome back here, Sienna.' If Annie was male, he would've dragged the kid by the throat and —

'I don't think Annie wants to face anyone after this.'

'I'm sorry this happened to you.'

'It's not your fault and thank goodness for Sally. Is she okay?'

'She's being well looked after. I've fed her myself.'

'And everyone else? What are they having for dinner?'

He was proud she was thinking of them. 'Pina, Lyn and Jess found the fettucine and are doing an early dinner.' Everyone was hanging around the muster room, while he waited for this call. 'Babe, I don't have your number.' He felt foolish asking at this stage of their relationship.

'Well, I don't give it out to just anyone you know,' she said with a giggle.

It was a relief she wasn't upset over his slackness in dating simplicities. But then again, they weren't dating because he couldn't promise her anything. How much of a selfish bastard was he?

'Not that it'd do you any good when my phone doesn't work out your way except to play music and hold my notes. But it's working now, and I'll be spending the rest of the night going through all of my messages.'

'Are you staying in town tonight?'

'If that's okay?'

'I was going to suggest it. I don't want you driving back at night in that toy-car. I'll book you a room at the pub and you can have dinner on me.'

'With unlimited hot water, please, so I can have the longest shower ever and not worry about draining the tank, having to run the bore, which might upset the boss about wasting generator fuel.'

Jake chuckled. 'Now you're sounding like one of us.'

'I'm only a tourist passing through.'

*Damn.* He hated that she was only temporary.

'This is the first time I've stopped and visited Elsie Creek. Hey, you should ask everyone if they want anything, while I'm in town. Elliott's trying to find me a pair of jeans, and then we're doing dinner.'

'I can do that, it'll give me an excuse to call you later.'

'You can.'

His heart expanded just hearing her smile. 'So, what did you email me?'

'I've finished your business plan and sales proposal. It's my best work ever. Hey, how did the water testing go?'

'Barry said it's crystal.'

'*Yes!*'

'Did you just do the air punch thing?' He grinned, just picturing it.

'I did.' Her laugh making him smile wider. 'What did Barry say about the barra?'

'I shocked him. Barry liked the ponds, and he knows a guy who owns a barra farm outside of Darwin.'

'You should get an intro.'

'I knew you'd say that. So next time I head into Darwin, Barry will organise a visit, and promised me a game of golf on a proper course.'

'Great idea. You should see if you can visit a bottling factory too, because Danbunnan's spring water is worth bottling.'

'One thing at a time, babe. I haven't gone public with this first project.'

Her sigh was deep, as if disappointed. 'Barry's a nice guy. He said you went to boarding school together?'

'There is four of us from the same area: me, Barry, Ryan and Craig, who you met at the rodeo.' Jake could always count on his mates and was calling in all his favours.

'I hope you've added them to the guest list for the barn-shed-fundraiser-shindig?'

'I'm writing it down now. Still no name for it?'

'No. Which is unusual for me.'

'You've got a lot to work on at the moment.' He hadn't overloaded her, had he? 'I'm sick of always losing my paper and pencil—what did you say about a tablet?'

'We can network them, so we can see what's going on between us and not double up.'

'I got one for Christmas, it's in my room somewhere.' Where would Sienna be for Christmas?

'So, Elliott's coming back and we're in desperate need of a coffee. Please have a look at the proposals I've emailed you.

I'd appreciate it if you sent me any comments or questions so I can think of some solutions on the drive back. I've also included a costs projection with ways to pay for this event too.'

Her creative thought processes and intelligence were amazing, her beauty and sensuality a brilliant bonus. 'Is that the recycling area, cashing in that junk to pay for the competition?'

'I'm hoping it will be. I won't be sure if it's worth anything until Joe finishes sorting it out. I only talked to Joe about it this morning when he stopped in for his coffee.'

'Does our station mechanic normally do that?'

'Oh, yeah. Now I'm talking out of school.'

'I don't like secrets,' said Jake.

There was a pause because their relationship was one big secret.

'Um, have I done the wrong thing, Jake?'

'No, I just hate not knowing what's going on.'

'You are the boss, and I'll tell you whatever you want to know. Networking the tablets will help, too.'

Work they could talk about, but not long-term futures or movies or dates, because everything was all about Danbunnan.

'Why didn't you mention Annie to me?'

'Part of me forgot. Also, I have the utmost respect for Tom and the relationship you two share. Should I have spoken to you?'

'You can talk to me about anything.' But did she? 'Were you concerned?'

'Yes. It's why I spoke to Tom, because I knew he would've been the only one to get through to her. Hey, kudos for saying she needed medical clearance to return to work.'

'Wish I had a staffing manual for stuff like this.'

'I can relate,' Sienna said with a laugh.

'You can? How?'

'That reminds me, did you call Annie's parents?'

'I will. Their number I do have.' Again, she'd avoided

answering any questions about herself.

'My number is at the bottom of the email I've sent you, and just because I'm not there doesn't mean you can have the night off from reading those documents either.'

'Thanks. Not.' He chuckled.

'You need it for the competition. But we can also use it for your buyers, and I'll use snippets for the website too.'

'Like your meals, from one dish you create many.'

'Exactly. It's all in the details.'

He hated bothering with details. 'Do you think I should move forward on the fish?'

'Yes. Although you seem hesitant, and I understand it's a big change for a cattleman. But now that Barry has seen the ponds, I think it's time you got another opinion.'

'I'm not ready to show my dad.' Aware he was procrastinating.

'I meant Tom.'

'Really?'

'Jake, you told me Tom is always thinking of what's best for Danbunnan. So I'm hoping he'll give you the boost you need to either move forward or pull the plug on this project. I think you'd respect Tom's opinion more than your dad's. Sorry, I shouldn't have said that.'

He could picture her bunching up her shoulders for saying that too. 'I appreciate your honesty, and Tom's.'

'Well, that's your business, not mine, but I wish you would at least talk to Tom about it, please. I've gotta go.'

He wanted to hug the woman. 'Can I call you later?'

'Sure. And I might even answer.'

Just hearing her smile made him grin.

'But call me only if you can though, Jake.'

'I will. They'll think I'm talking to Angela.' As soon as he said that he could've kicked himself.

'Yeah, like I said, Jake, that's your business, not mine. Later.' And she was gone.

Jake opened his email account and there it was: an email from Sienna Jacobs, complete with her email address and phone number. He may know her personality and some of her history, but he realised he knew very little of the woman away from the station.

Jake opened the attached documents and his eyes widened. 'No way.' His PC screen displayed graphs, photos, including the history, the cattle and barramundi farm, presented in a professional business document.

How did Sienna do that while sitting on her laptop on the roof of her car beneath the shade of a banyan tree in the middle of the outback? It looked like it came from a blue-chip company in Sydney and not a cattle station situated in the remote Northern Territory.

Just who was Sienna Jacobs in the real world?

# Thirteen

Beneath the muster room's windows sat an old bench seat, where Sally watched the main entrance to the homestead. She gave Jake a low thump from her tail.

'She'll be back in the morning, girl.' Jake gave the old dog a pat and then stepped inside.

'Any news?' Jess asked from behind the kitchen counter with Pina and Lyn dishing up dinner. Bob and the rest of the crew were spread out amongst the tables like customers in a café.

But there was no coffee, no music, and no smile from Sienna that was better than a sunrise. Is this what it'd be like when she left Danbunnan?

His heart dropped and he shoved his hands into his jeans pockets. He missed her.

'Any news, son?' Bob asked Jake.

'Annie's at the hospital. Sienna and Elliott are staying in Elsie Creek for the night and going shopping, so if anyone has any requests make a list and I'll give it to them later.'

Relief spread across everyone's faces. And his eyes fell on Tom, seated at the back of the room, always watching. 'Boss?'

'Got a minute? I'll shout you a beer.'

'Sure.' Tom swiped up his hat from its chair and followed Jake out the door. 'Where are we goin', Boss?'

'For a drive.'

They drove in silence until they'd gone through the padlocked gate and Jake had parked next to the pump shed on top of the small rise.

'What the hell is this?' Tom pushed up the brim of his Akubra.

'It's a fish farm, filled with billabong barramundi. There's about a thousand kilos per pond, but I'm only guesstimating as Sienna would say.'

'What the ...' Tom stood on the rise, scratching beneath his hat, while clutching his beer can. 'Billabong barra's muddy this time of year.'

'These are spring-fed ponds.'

'Is this where you've been sneaking off every night. To do this?' Tom's grey eyes narrowed at the man-made crest of dams.

'Yep. I've just had Barry test the water this morning. He gave it the all clear and took a decent feed home.' That seemed like aeons ago now.

Jake flicked on the water filtration system to start pumping through the many rolls of black plastic pipes that ran from the shed like octopus legs.

And like he did every night since he'd created the job of manning the pump, he carted his bucket of balls to his makeshift tee on a patch of scrappy carpet. Grabbed his golf club wedged into the corrugated roof, lined up his shot, and *whack*.

The golf ball arced into the air and flew across the pond.

It then hit the old net, haphazardly strung between two trees that stretched before the barbed wire fence that protected them from the river's many man-eating crocodiles. 'Are you sure you don't play golf, Tom?'

'Nope, never.'

'It's a good stress relief. I come out here to bash a few balls and have a beer, while manning the pump. Sienna's shots are scattered everywhere, but she's improving.' Jake chuckled at Tom's surprised expression, it was as rare as the man's smile.

'The relief cook knows about this?'

'Sienna's more than a relief cook, Tom.' Jake knew it.

'It's Sienna who urged me to tell you before I tell Dad about this project.'

'Why?'

'I don't know if this is a good thing for Danbunnan's future. This barra farm happened by accident, and last wet season it washed away. But this year I have a product. Sienna's been testing it by feeding you and the men this fish for weeks. Come on, I'll show you.' Jake reached into the feed bin and threw a handful of pellets into the nearest pond. In a matter of seconds, the water bubbled like it was a pot on the stove.

'How come the relief cook knows about this barra farm?'

'I needed someone to feed the fish while we were mustering out at the outstations.'

'That giggly girlie never let on. Not once.'

'Sienna's good at keeping secrets.' What else did she keep from him? When Jake wanted to know everything. 'Sienna has been working on a business plan and it's ready to go.'

'For this?'

'Yep. And it's brilliant, Tom. From the one document Sienna's created it has plenty of scope for any other project we might take on in the future.'

'Are you looking at doing this barra thing full time?'

'I want to diversify. I don't want to get caught out like Danbunnan did when Dad poisoned the cattle, or when the government froze the export markets, sending a lot of our neighbours broke.'

'The cattle industry is still recovering.'

'So is Danbunnan. And you know we're on the bones, which is why I've been looking at other alternatives. The main reason I showed this to Sienna is because I saw what she did with your chillies and Elliott's website. You should see the website Sienna's created for Danbunnan. It's classy, Tom. Even Dad likes it.'

'I always said that giggly girl has got an entrepreneurial mind.'

'Sienna does, and she thinks we can sell the water too.'

Tom rubbed the top of his head with his hat. 'Are you gonna do it?'

'Do you think I should?'

'You're the boss.'

'I'm asking your opinion, Tom.'

'You shouldn't be asking me—ask your dad.'

'Tom, you were there to help me when this place fell. You've always been there helping me.'

'What do *you* want to do?'

'I'm not sure.' Surprised at himself for openly admitting that to Tom. It's something he'd never admit to his father. But Tom had been a part of Jake's entire life at Danbunnan, still living in the same cottage he grew up in with his father, Mick.

Tom sipped his beer, while doing a slow turn. 'So, you're tellin' me that this came from that poison spill.'

'The following wet season, yes, because I'd blocked off the contaminated area so nothing disturbed it.' Jake never wanted to go back to that place again.

'Was this what Sienna meant by turning a tragedy into triumph at that meeting?'

'Yep.'

'And all that other stuff for the competition she went on about, it was to do with this fish farm?'

'Not just the fish, we want to use everything else we produce, as well as the beef and the fish. Our guest list is a mixed crowd and Sienna's ready to promote all our produce as competition standard. She says we're winners without even bothering to race.' He was a winner for having her in his life—if only he could keep her.

'Bugger me …' Tom swallowed his can dry.

Jake exchanged a cold beer with Tom's empty and looked at the aluminium can in his hand. 'Did you know Sienna's got Joe sorting out a recycling centre? Apparently, there's money in rubbish.'

'I heard Sienna callin' it someone's treasure.'

Jake grinned at his lady's wordplay. 'Sienna's sent me the links to these recycling yards who are willing to buy heaps of that junk Dad's collected for the past half century. She's estimated it'll pay for the judge's show and more, but I'm sure it'll buy us a good drink.' Jake tossed the empty can into the back of his ute.

'I've been wondering how you were gonna pay for the competition; it's sounding schmancy.'

'You're telling me! We've gone highbrow.' Jake rolled his eyes. 'I don't do fancy either, but if we're promoting Danbunnan as top-shelf beef …'

'You need to get schmancy. I get it. So …' Tom jerked his thumb at the ponds. 'You're doing this to keep Danbunnan going?'

'Always. Same as you, Tom. But I'm not sticking to just cattle. I want to include the barra too. Who knows, the way Sienna was talking we'll make you the chilli king with our own bottled water to cool them down.'

'And that face cream her and Elliott couldn't stop bloody eating,' said Tom, sharing a rare chuckle. 'Imagine that pair loose in Elsie Creek?'

'Nope. Don't want to.' Jake was tempted to jump into his ute and meet up with her for the night. But then again, he had the worst reputation in that town, which might hinder what Sienna was hoping to achieve.

'How much work is there on this fish thing, if you were to go ahead, Boss?'

'I check on it once a day to feed them and man these pumps. When it's time for harvesting I'll need help, same as mustering, just different.'

'That's why you've kept the crew you have?'

'Yep, they're all multi-talented people. And I've always got you, Tom. I hope?'

'I'm not going anywhere unless I'm sacked. It's a bloody shame Annie went astray.'

'How many staff have we seen pass through here, Tom?' Yet one in particular would hurt the most when she left, and

Jake was not looking forward to that day.

Tom shrugged. 'I've lost count.'

Jake plucked another golf ball from the bucket, placed it on the tee and lined up for his next shot. 'I can get you another apprentice. I've got a big list of kids willing to work. But only after we've sold the cattle and got past this competition.' *Whack*. The golf ball arced high above the sunset and landed with a plonk amongst the rest that lay on the red dirt.

'The jillaroo's not coming back?'

'Look, Annie confessed to Sienna what she'd done,' and Jake explained all to Tom. 'Some of what Annie did is against Josh, too. So, I'll have a chat with him later, because I don't want Josh to stop doing his snake rescuing. But at least Annie will get the help she needs.'

*Whack*. From the sweeping swing of Jake's club, the small white golf ball sailed over the ponds in its arc. Suddenly a barramundi broke free from the pond's silvery surface, leaping high in the air with mouth wide open, aiming for that white ball. Its large scales reflected rainbows from the low-lying sun as it flicked its thick tail, spraying water like glitter into the air. 'That's beautiful.'

'I'd never imagined that this was what you were doing every night you nicked off.'

Jake balanced another ball on the tee wedged into the dry red dirt as he adjusted his dusty boots on the worn carpet strip to resume his swinging stance. 'Why? What did you think I was doing every night?'

'Visiting Angela.'

'Huh?' Damn! *Whack*. And he slammed the golf ball into the net. 'I've been here, feeding the fish and manning the pumps.'

'So, only you and Sienna know about this fish farm?'

'And my mate, Barry, who won't tell anyone until I'm ready. And now you.' Jake leaned against the golf club and faced the man he truly respected. 'So, Tom, any thoughts?'

Tom's grey eyes surveyed his surroundings with his

stern face expressionless. He was tough and determined as always, and as steady as the sun rose and set as Danbunnan's head stockman.

'The day I called you Boss, I knew this place was in good hands,' Tom said. 'You've always had your heart in this place, no matter how hard your dad tried to squash that in you. Danbunnan's in your blood, and don't you dare believe any different. You've done well here, Boss. Any man who likes their fish would brag they've got their own supply of barra out the back.'

Jake was speechless.

'So, can ya explain this pumping system you've rigged up, and we'll work on gettin' the crew involved. The only problem we might have is …'

'What problem?' With a mountain of other problems to deal with he didn't need any more.

'It'll be keeping Tyson and Josh's fishing rods inside their flamin' ute.' Tom shared a grin as Jake chuckled with him. 'Do you ever catch any?'

'I keep the rod and net up here.' Jake grabbed the fishing rod he had tucked in the grooves of the corrugated roof. 'You should've seen Sienna land her first fish. I think they heard her screams of joy all the way to Elsie Creek.' It had been one of the best afternoons he'd shared, seeing Sienna's smile and enthusiasm. He was proud he'd taught her, even taking a photo of that memorable moment.

Tom inspected the fishing rod as the keen sports fisherman he was. 'I like that giggly girlie, she's done a lot for Elliott. Shame there's no job for her when Rhonda comes back. I'd hate to see Sienna work for the Simon Simmons, it'd tick off China. She's a good station cook who's been mates with Rhonda for years.'

Jake didn't want Sienna to leave either, but what could he do? 'As Sienna would say, business is business.'

'And you've got good business here, I'll take my hat off to you, Boss.' Tom flicked the lure into the pond and *whack*, the fish took the bait. *'I'm on.'* Tom grinned as the rod flexed and the reel whirred at the pull as he fought with the large fish splashing in the water.

'Bring it in, Tom.' As Tom reeled in his catch, Jake looked over the ponds, and truly believed it was a good thing. But how was the old cattle king, who hated change, going to react?

# Fourteen

From the muster room's verandah, where she hid beneath the bench seat, Sally flicked her ears as she lifted her head. Her grey tail thumped as she shuffled to her feet, her excited barking alerting everyone to the incoming car.

'*They're here. They're here*,' yelled the twins, skipping down the stone steps out front of the house.

Tom peered through the office screen door, while Bob craned around in his seat. Jake grinned from behind his desk at the small red car leading the towering dust plume.

'I'd better find out what mischief that pair got up to last night.' Tom put on his hat and was out the door.

For once, the office door didn't slam shut.

'Did you fix the screen door or did Charlie?' Jake asked Bob.

'Charlie. I supervised. That's a funny car that girl drives.'

'It's been tricked up.' The rumble of the engine was the music of his siren calling. 'Sienna was learning to race in off-road rallies.'

'Strange hobby for a girl. Did she race?'

'Navigated in a few as co-driver.' *Why did she stop?* 'So, do you have any thoughts on the barra farm, now you've seen the photos and the proposals?' Because Bob still wouldn't leave the compound.

'They're good. Where did that extra history about Danbunnan's ancestors come from?'

'Wasn't that your input?'

'I spoke to Sienna about some things. I guess she's just jazzed it up for advertising. Ya can't trust everything you read these days with all that fake news they waffle on about.'

'I'll check with Sienna, because I don't want any false info on these documents.' Not when they were trying to rebuild from a crappy past.

'It's real flash, that document. I had to look twice to realise it was Danbunnan in Sienna's photos.'

'I took those photos, Dad. Sienna edited them.'

'Did you?'

'I used Sienna's camera that day we went to everyone's favourite places.' The day Sienna had made him see Danbunnan's beauty, now presented in a document about to be shown to the world.

'I can't comment anymore on your stuff, son. I've always relied on the co-op to buy my beef and didn't need to hunt a buyer.'

'Buyers. I've got fish to sell too.'

'I only know cattle and it's your hobby, son.'

*Hobby, huh?*

It was like déjà vu tapping on his shoulder all over again. Just like the many times he'd tried to speak to his dad about the grey water system, wind, and solar projects too. Back then Bob ignored him.

His father still ignored him, standing at the door, watching the staff gather in the compound.

His dad spoke to him the same way the men who ran the co-op did. They'd made it clear that they thought what Jake was doing at Danbunnan was a joke. Jake was just the new kid in nappies still skidding along in his training wheels and they were all waiting for him to crash.

Like hell that was going to happen.

Jake shut down the PC. Tom's feedback on the documents were blunt and brutal, but the man was on board, and his men were happy about the new jobs. Bob, however, had been non-committal, tiptoeing around the edges. Why didn't Bob get more excited?

Jake turned off the office light and closed the door for the night. 'Are you coming, Dad?'

Bob stood on the corner of the verandah with hands in pockets watching the scene below. 'What for?'

'To hear about Elliott's adventure. I'm sure he'll make it interesting in his retelling.' If the kid didn't run away from him in fright first.

'He's like his grandfather, Tom's father, Mick.'

'I don't remember much about Mick.'

'Tom's old man was good at spinnin' a yarn. He had a flair for it.' Bob's grin deepened the crevices across his skin. 'Whenever we were out mustering with Mick, he'd share his stories around the campfire, keeping us entertained for hours. We all knew it was bulldust, but it was entertaining bulldust. It's better than them reality shows on the telly these days. You know, they've got this show now where they marry complete strangers who first meet each other at the altar.'

'I don't watch TV, Dad.' Arching an eyebrow at his dad who was talking about weddings.

'They're doing arranged marriages but using science to matchmake couples. Your mother would have said it ruins the magic of marriage. Hey, when are you and Angela planning on having your wedding?'

'Look, my main focus is on the competition and the sales first.' He hated lying to his family about his engagement, but he had good reason.

# Fifteen

Sienna slowed her approach into the main compound, and there it was: Danbunnan's homestead. The large horseshoe compound, the stables, and its stockyards, with cattle fattening up on organic grasses in nearby paddocks.

At the row of worksheds was their station mechanic, Joe, waving from the front.

On the other side stood the house on the hill with its rich river rock and deep verandah, shielding the occupants against the harsh outback sun. A lush green belt wrapped around the grand house, an oasis in the outback with its tropical garden. It was a stark contrast against the surrounding lands of golden grasses, spindly olive-leafed native gums, and roads of red dust.

'Wow, look at the laundry shed.' Elliott pointed from the passenger seat, his shoes crunching on the Christmas paper, junk food wrappers, and water bottles littering the floor. The back of the car was so full of boxes they couldn't see out the rear windows.

When Sienna had first arrived to start her contract as the relief cook, she was the sole occupant in this car. Back then the passenger seat had been covered in maps, a half-eaten bag of lollies, with empty wrappers and bottles of water rolling around on the floor. So similar today, but now she took in the changes.

'The place is cleaning up nicely.' Elliott gave a nod of

approval, similar to his uncle.

'It's a huge change from when I first arrived. I thought it was a place full of red dust shipwrecks.'

'You know, when you first arrived, we thought you'd be Rhonda's age in a four-wheel drive, not this cute little car and not who you are.'

'Who am I?'

'Why you're my mentoring goddess, queen of the kitchen, my fabulous friend, and stylish sober driver.' Elliott smiled, flicking the fringe out of his eyes. 'You're also the best person to escort shopping.'

'You should try shopping with my BFF Mail-order Biatch. He's a scream to go shopping with.'

'You talk about Ricky all the time. Why don't you invite him for a visit?'

'Oh no, Ricky doesn't do dirt.' She laughed at the thought. 'But he'd love all these cowboys. Sorry, cattlemen.' Who knew the word cowboy was an insult to cattlemen?

'See, you're learning.'

'I am indeed.' She parked in front of the muster room in the same place where she'd parked when she'd first arrived months ago. This time there was no Rhonda barrelling out the door with her soft grey curls and flour-dusted apron. Back then everyone had peeked at her suspiciously from the shadows. Today they all waited on the kitchen's verandah, with wide smiles.

'It's nice to be home.' Elliott waved, bursting from his seat to greet everyone.

But Danbunnan wasn't Sienna's home.

She glanced up and there he was: Jake, in those dust-stained jeans, crossing the compound with his confident stride. Her palm slapped over her heart as it threatened to burst free from her rib cage. And then when he gave her his crooked grin, her smile broke wide and everything was right in the world again.

Which kinda sucked.

She'd tried so hard to build an immunity against her

feelings for Jake, but he was impossible to resist. Her soul was sold to a man she could never have. If she was smart, she should be creating some distance between them now, because it wouldn't be long before she left for good.

'Sienna.' Her door opened and Josh pulled her from her seat to gather her into a huge hug.

'What's that for?'

'To say I'm sorry for Annie scaring you with one of my snakes.'

'Hey, it's not your fault.' She might not know what it was like to have siblings, but she imagined that Josh would make the perfect little brother.

'And, yeah, I missed you too.' Josh blushed a bright sunburnt red.

'Aww, you're so cowboy cute.' She playfully tapped the brim of his hat.

'Don't call me a bloody cowboy,' Josh mumbled.

'Joke, honey.' She popped the hatch for everyone to unload. 'Okay, I've got all your booze in the back, boys.'

'You're not cookin' tea, are ya, luv?' Lyn asked, grabbing a beer carton.

'Nope, I gave myself the night off and bought pizzas.' Sienna handed a stack to Pina.

'They missed your cooking,' said Pina with her Spanish accent. Tossing her thick black plait over her shoulder, her eclectic mix of hair clips caught the sunlight. 'I don't know how they'll cope when you leave and Rhonda comes back.'

'You're still stuck with me for a few more weeks yet, and we've got the competition to get through first.' With a large shopping bag over her shoulder, Sienna entered the muster room, which she'd spent hours scrubbing, painting, and polishing. It was surreal observing the obvious changes. Would Rhonda be impressed?

Rhonda, the long-time station cook everyone adored, treated these people like family. So why did Rhonda take holidays in the middle of Danbunnan's first muster since the poisoning, when it meant so much to everyone? It was a question she hadn't considered before.

Jake came up beside her carrying a carton of beer on his shoulder. 'How was the drive?'

'Good.' She dug nails into her palms to stop herself from wrapping her arms around his neck and inhaling his manly outdoor aroma. She wanted to nestle into the safety of his arms and talk to him about everything, and to just hold him and say nothing.

But she couldn't. She had to distance herself *today*.

'I've been told that beer isn't nice hot, Boss.' She opened the coldroom.

He winked, before sharing that crooked grin with her as he stepped inside.

Again, she had to pat at her expanding heart to calm herself down. How did he do that with one look? Every. Single. Time.

Her head tilted as she watched his delicious denim derriere. Maybe she should wean herself off Jake tomorrow. Diets didn't begin until Mondays, and in the morning, not late afternoon, right? She could start …

*Ugh,* she was pathetic.

Her cheeks flushed, staring inside the coldroom at the near-perfect male. It was too hot. So she went in search of other heat sources and turned on the oven.

Great, her body temp was all over the freaking place. *Focus.* If she didn't go near the guy, she'd be fine. 'We'll reheat the pizzas now.'

'I'll do it,' said Jess, pulling Sienna back from the oven. 'I enjoy the luxury of not cooking when I return from my town trips.' Jess then reached up and gave Sienna a hug. 'I missed you.'

'I was only gone one night.' Sienna blinked back the beginning of tears.

'It wasn't the same. Who knows how we'll cope when you leave.'

'Jess, you and the twins are welcome to visit me, anytime.' That's if Sienna didn't end up as another blubbering mess, on another drive across the country.

'Excuse me, there's someone I've got to see ...' She headed to the side screen door to escape the sentiments and there was Sally wagging her tail, waiting.

'Hello, girl.' Outside, she hugged the dog.

Sally's whole body wagged with her tail, her furry face wearing a huge smile.

'I've got a present for you. I've never done this, Sally, so I hope you'll approve of your treat.' Sienna giggled at Sally sniffing inside the bag. Her cold, wet nose, and coarse fur was a welcome-back delight, so different from when she'd imagined Sally was a stalker that used to scare her.

'What's that?' Jake asked, standing behind her.

'Roo sticks. The guy in the stockfeed store said dogs love them.' And Sally snatched it from her fingers. 'I'll take that as a yes, shall I? I bought Sally all sorts of gifts and more food that looks like kabanas for her to try.' Because the cattle dog had saved her butt a few times now.

'Don't leave those around, the men might think they're for human consumption. Dad's the worst for salamis and kabanas.'

'I'll remember that.' Then her smile faded as she stared at the storeroom door.

'The women cleaned it up for you. I know it's not how you'd had it, but they tried. I didn't want you returning to that mess.'

He was perfect, which sucked when she was trying to distance herself. 'I made a mess climbing onto the shelves.' A chill ran up her spine at the flashback of being trapped inside a room with a snake.

'I'm sure Sally made most of the mess. Hey, are you okay?'

No. Not when she wanted to hold him. 'Yeah, you?' Hugging herself she checked her vegetable garden.

'Right now, I want to hold you so bad, but ...' He sighed, looking back at everyone gathered inside the kitchen.

'Yeah.' Those people were friends and she felt guilty

hiding this affair like it was some dirty secret.

Part of her was glad to be back, but part of her was sad knowing it wasn't permanent and she couldn't fall into the fantasy—no matter how much she dreamed.

This had to stop and soon. Because everyone she'd ever loved in her past had either died, deserted her, or destroyed her trust. Whatever the reason, they had all crushed her soul. She didn't think she'd have the strength to cope with another knockback.

'Are you sure you're okay?' Jake narrowed his eyes at her.

*No.* 'Yes.' She inhaled deeply, put on her game face, opened the door and stepped inside. 'I've brought presents for everyone.'

'It's not Christmas, is it?' called out little Aaron, looking up with hope.

'No. But when I saw these things I just couldn't resist. They're only small, so no complaints.' Sienna opened her large bag and started unloading the presents she'd bought, hoping to boost the team's morale after what Annie had done.

'You should've seen Sienna play shopping queen all over Elsie Creek. We went to every single store they had— which isn't much.' Elliott unpacked one of the many bags on the bench. 'I can't believe we packed so much into that little car.'

'You'd be amazed how much fits inside the toy-car.' It wouldn't be long, and it'd be packed again for her to leave.

'We missed you, Sienna.' Kate, with her hair in plaits, her bangles lining her wrists, she held out a cream frangipani flower.

'Aww, I missed you too.' Sienna hugged the little girl, then tucked the flower behind her ear. 'I love flowers.'

'Me too.'

'I don't,' said Aaron, hitching up little jeans. 'It's girlie.'

'I am a girl,' said Sienna. 'Twins first. Here's some new movies and don't worry Jess, they're kid approved. And for you, here are your favourite chocolates, and five pairs of gardening gloves, considering we ruined those first pairs together.'

'Oh, *so* mine.' Jess's smile was huge. 'Thank you.'

'Pina, a new mask, and some cute hair accessories. Tell me how that mask compares to the one I make.'

'I'm so there, thank you.' Pina gave a flick of her long thick plait.

'Lyn, here's a CD of the top one hundred trucker songs. I'm pretty sure you'll rock the cab.'

'Champion, luv.'

It was like she'd been on holiday and brought souvenirs, except they were everyday normal items found in any local supermarket aisle. But it was a novelty for residents in the outback, considering the nearest shop was hours away. 'Tom?'

'What?' Tom stood beside Bob at the back of the room.

'Catch.' Sienna threw a thin piece of cardboard.

Tom effortlessly caught it. 'I don't want nothin'. I don't need nothin'.'

'Too bad, you've got it now.'

Tom shook his head, wearing that same stern expression as he ripped open the paper. 'What the hell?' He held up the *Reserved* sign.

'That sign is for your hat chair, so no one else dares make the mistake of putting their hat on there.' She didn't like Simon Simmons claiming Tom's spot on his last visit. But she was delighted with Tom's firm nod of approval.

'And this is for the muster room. I saw it and loved it.' She pulled out a heavy, badly wrapped package. 'Tom, the honour is yours.'

Tom shook his head as he unwrapped the Christmas paper. He then held it up and cocked an eyebrow at the row of welded horseshoes. 'What is it? You know we've got plenty of horseshoes in the stables.'

'It's a hat rack sculpture. This guy had amazing pieces of art, all made from junk. You should've seen the small museum at the Elsie Creek train station. I'm going back for sure.' Sienna grinned at the men admiring the blokey bit of iron. 'It suits this room.' And those men. 'Tom, I want you to find the best spot for that hat rack, so no one uses your hat chair again.'

'Thanks, Sienna, that's very thoughtful,' said Tom as the rest of the men shared their own nods of approval.

'Here, Charlie, I got you the coolest comb for your beard.' Because the man shaved his head, yet fastidiously pampered his long red beard. It was in excellent condition. 'Oh, and these swimming goggles coz I could.' Sienna giggled at the quietest of the stockmen who played with water.

'Thanks, mate, I might have to hide the comb from my wife, though.' Charlie grinned, tucking the comb onto his red Viking's beard.

'Joe, my tools interpreter, this is for you.' She passed a paper bag and a jar of industrial hand cleaner to the station's mechanic.

Joe snort-laughed, pulling out a crown that had everyone laughing. 'Told you mob, Sienna called me king of the junk pile.' He placed the toy crown over his oil-stained well-worn truckers cap, his eyes as shiny as the fake jewels.

'Bob, this is for you.' Sienna passed the gift to Lyn, who passed it to Charlie, who passed it to Josh, who passed it to Tom, who handed the gift to Bob by the double doors.

'What's this?' Bob's grey brows lifted, inspecting the box a few times to find the opening.

'Sunglasses.' The first time they'd met Sienna had blinded him by opening the curtains when he looked like Dracula's older cousin. Now Bob had no excuse to hide indoors. 'They're magnetic and clip onto the top of your frames. I brought you three pairs to keep you out of trouble.'

'Cheeky woman.' Bob tried to suppress his smile as he clipped on a pair for the room. 'What ya think?' Again, grunts of approval came from the men.

'Looks good, Bob,' said Sienna and got a sly wink from

Jake. It was the wink that made her feel extra good. 'Josh, this is for you. I can't wait for this one.'

'What is it?' Josh tore at the tacky paper and his eyes widened as if it truly was Christmas morning. 'No way! Where'd you get this, Sienna?'

'What is it?' Aaron asked, as the others craned around Josh for a closer view.

'It's a proper snake identification kit with their differing types of antivenene. How did you get this?' Josh asked with an even wider smile.

'Sienna totally chatted up the doctor,' piped in Elliott.

'Oh, a doctor, luv. That's a good choice for a single girl like you,' said Lyn.

Sienna faltered as Jake narrowed his eyes at her as if she'd done the wrong thing. 'Behave, Elliott.'

Elliott sniggered, while his eyebrows bobbed up and down beneath his fringe. 'It was the same doctor that was in the ER when we first arrived, and Sienna drove back this morning to personally deliver his coffee. The local women called him the Hot Doc.'

'Delivering coffees to doctors, were we?' Jake's voice had an edge to it she hadn't heard before.

'I wouldn't say no,' said Jess, fanning herself with her gardening gloves. 'I saw the Hot Doc when I took Dad in for his check-up.'

'Oi.' Jake frowned at his sister.

'Oh, come on, Jake. I'm a mother, not a virgin—'

Jake cringed, holding his palm up to his baby sister. 'Stop, please.'

'The doctor called the park ranger to identify the snake, and I had to explain we had a snake whisperer because the ranger would've slapped us with animal cruelty.' Sienna said to Josh, 'the doctor's housemate is a senior park ranger who supplied the antivenene kit. All it cost me was a coffee. Her business card is inside. She'd love to speak with you about that kit, and we can organise a Skype meeting. But …' She then winced. 'The ranger said what you're doing is a good thing, she'd love a snake wrangler in the area, but to do that you'll need a permit. Which means doing some paperwork. Sorry.'

'You mean, like go legit?'

Jake had told her over the phone how upset Josh was for losing a snake he'd been helping to heal, preparing to release it back into the wild, only for it to be massacred by a dog. It broke the jackaroo's heart.

'You can use the office to talk to the ranger, Josh,' said Jake, standing beside Sienna. 'We don't want you to stop what you're doing, and I'm happy to co-sign for the permit as station manager.'

'Hell, yeah, I'm in. You guys are the best.' Again, Josh hugged Sienna. 'Thanks, Boss.'

'I swear that cop was chatting you up.' Elliott was so excited his eyes practically glowed.

*'What cop?'* Jake demanded, and the room fell silent.

*Big mouth!* She glared at her offsider. But they all deserved an explanation. 'The doctor contacted the police after we told him how Annie got bitten by a snake. Elliott and I filed a police report over everything Annie confessed to in the car. But I also made it clear I wasn't going to press charges as long as Annie accepted medical treatment.'

'Did she?' asked Tom, showing his genuine concern for the jillaroo. 'I know Annie didn't want to see the doctor in the first place.'

'The Elsie Creek doctors are transporting Annie to Darwin Hospital, and her family is flying in to meet her. This is no one's fault,' Sienna said, patting Josh's shoulder. And she needed to change the subject. 'So, on to the next present in this mid-year Santa sale, because the wrapping paper was on sale for twenty cents. You can blame Elliott for the wrapping, where I swear there's more paper on the floor of my car.' She pulled out a flat rectangular box. 'This is for the boss.' Who she was a complete sucker for.

'You didn't have to do this, but thank you.' His hand brushed against hers and the electric current squirrelled up her arm.

'I know.' This gimmick-gift giving was having the effect she'd hoped for. Aaron stood beside Josh and Tyson gawking over the snake kit. Joe beamed beneath his crown. Charlie adjusted his swimming goggles to fit over his Akubra, with his comb still stuck in his red beard. Tom and Bob were inspecting the workmanship of the hat rack. And the women shared hand cream and chocolates, while putting hair accessories into little Kate's braids.

Jake opened the wrapper and smiled a glorious smile that only made her sigh. 'You didn't.'

'I did.'

'What did you get, Jake?' Jess craned in for a closer look.

'An indoor golf putting station, a hole in one.' Jake laughed, holding up the box.

'All CEOs have them, you know, and you have plenty of room in the office to play.'

'Thank you. I'll truly be mixing up my swing.'

'Love that driving range you showed us this morning, Boss,' Josh said.

'You're sneaky, Sienna,' said Tyson. 'Not telling us we were eating the boss's barra and telling us it was farmed fish.'

'It is farmed. I never lied to you guys, I just didn't say it was Danbunnan barra. Do you want your gift or not, Tyson?'

'You brought me my beer, thanks, that's enough.'

'Well, I can't take it back not when I went to so much trouble for this.' She passed him the laminated roll.

'Me, why?' Tyson unrolled a poster displaying a group of women in bikinis. 'Oh hello, I have new ladies for the wall, and signed to me. What did you two get up to last night?'

'Were you in the bikini competition too?' Josh asked as they all stared at her.

'No.' Crossing arms over her chest, Sienna suddenly felt under the spotlight.

'Nooo. Ah huh.' Elliott shook the fringe from his eyes. 'Much more than that—'

'Hey! What happens on the road stays on the road,

Elliott.' But Elliott was a man who loved an audience.

'I've never had so much fun in Elsie Creek before,' said Elliott. 'But you should've seen Sienna driving that toy-car, I swear we've broken the land speed record for Danbunnan to Elsie Creek.'

'No, I didn't.' And she didn't like this kind of attention either. 'I've got stuff to unpack before I can catch up on my to-do list for this competition. I'll let Elliott fill you in. Later.' Escaping out the side door.

'Did you get me those samples from town for the competition?' Jake asked, following her out.

'In the back of the toy-car.'

'I'll come over and get them. You can drive.'

She peeked back at everyone busily listening to Elliott. How obvious was this? 'Okay, Boss, but no complaining about my driving.'

'We're only going to the cook's quarters.' Jake sat in the passenger seat with knees close to his chest. 'This is low and small.'

'You'd feel like you're dragging your arse on the ground, right?' She giggled, slipping the key into the ignition.

'Compared to my ute, yes. Seats are comfy, but the leg room sucks.' He dug around beneath the seat and found the latch to shift the seat way back as his boots crunched on the wrapping paper. 'You didn't have to get me the gift.'

'I saw it and couldn't resist.' Like she was having trouble resisting the man whose presence filled the car. She'd missed him. 'Now you can perfect your putting, and ...' She reached behind her seat and dumped a large heavy plastic bag in his lap. 'For you.'

'What's this?'

'Another bag of golf balls to replace the ones I've lost in the ponds.'

'Thank you. I might need to ship in more, now I've shown the crew my driving range.'

'Did they like it?'

'All the men were impressed and keen to be rostered for

pump duties. They're okay with the extra tasks for this competition too.'

She drove them across to her room. 'What did Bob think of the barra ponds?'

Jake sighed. 'Dad didn't want to leave the compound.'

'Oh? Wow, um …' Her lips narrowed to a thin line as she parked her car in the shadows of the lean-to that faced the open countryside.

'I had the same reaction.'

Out of the car, she retrieved more parcels from the boot.

'What else did you get?' Jake eyed off the bags in the back. 'For one impromptu night away, you brought back a lot.'

'Leave those grey bags for later, they're from the recycling plant for the cans. I've got their brochure on what materials they're after and spoke with the council guy who knew the manager. I also found a fabulous selection of hire chairs, tables, and linen, and negotiated a discounted rate, along with heaps of other brochures for regional businesses.' She walked into her room, admiring the shabby-chic style. It was only temporary accommodation, being Rhonda's room, yet with all the familiarities it almost felt like home.

As a perfectionist with her work, why was her private life such a mess?

Yet it was amazing how one night away opened her eyes to the bigger picture. Because, this room, this place, all of it was temporary.

Jake kicked the door shut, dropping her gear on the floor.

'Ah, hey?' Stepping back from his fast approach. 'What do you think you're doing?'

'What I wanted to do as soon as I saw you.' His palms cradled her face, and he kissed her. Tilting her back, his fingers gripping her hair, controlling the kiss that went so much deeper than the physical.

'We shouldn't.' She struggled feebly against the kiss of impossibility and irresponsibility. Cursing at the pleasurable waves she was helpless to fight against. His lips pressed against hers and her reluctance was consumed in flames because his kiss owned her.

It was like she was standing on a fault line, paralysed by the tremor in her legs. One of her hands fisted in his shirt. His chin was prickly against hers, as her fingernails scraped through his hair. He held her tighter, like the anchor at the centre of their storm, and their lips never parted.

'Can't stop.' He carried her to the bed and laid her on the soft covers. 'I don't want to stop.' His breath was hot beside her ear, creating deliciously heated sparks across her skin. His fingers roamed over her curves as his lips ghosted across her skin, then he looked at her like she was his entire world.

She peeled off his shirt to mark her territory across his defined muscles. His hardness pressed against her, as his nimble fingers made quick work of her buttons, making her skin come alive under his touch. Her lust awakened and all logic was put to sleep.

'Hello, ladies.' His hot mouth ravished her lace-covered breasts with kisses.

'Jake ...' Her back arched and her traitorous heart surrendered to this beautiful madness. 'They're just outside.'

'Not stopping.' His tongue teased her throat, playing with her pulse. His hand cupped between her legs, and her underwear disappeared. With committed fingers he teased her past the edge of heaven and opened a hell's fire dance of passion. 'Can't stop now.'

'Don't you dare!' She clutched his face and her lips meshed with his with a raw and intense crush of despair, and of love, and of devotion. He owned her. Now she wanted to own him.

Naked, she arched beneath him as he entered her. Ecstasy flowed with each stroke as her eager hips met his. Joined as one, their breathing synchronised, fingers burrowed into flesh, skin on skin, her eyes rolled as the tremor built in her belly. She clung to his body, bucking beneath him, unaware she'd given voice to their shared passion that imploded to the galaxies of colour behind closed eyelids.

His deep rumbled groan travelled from his chest through to hers, as his embrace tightened with his release. And it was the safest place in the world. It was as if she'd truly found her *home*.

And knew she was in trouble.

# Sixteen

Sienna's fingertips skimmed the muscles across his back and shoulders. 'You can't stay here much longer, people might talk.'

'I don't want to move.' Jake could lie here forever feeling her voice against his skin. 'But you're right.' He sat up, and quickly dressed. 'Is there much more stuff to get out of the car?'

'There's some plastic bags in the esky. I had to restock my fridge due to the regular raids from my midnight visitor.' Sienna buttoned up her dress as she headed for her bathroom.

'I'll get it, considering it's me doing the damage.' He chuckled, as he tucked in his shirt and stepped out into the daylight, soon returning with a stash of shopping bags. 'I can still hear Elliott yakking.'

'Oh, he'll embellish it.'

'What happened last night?' Jake placed the shopping bags next to her bar fridge. His stomach grumbled as he unpacked assorted cheeses, chocolates, and other fine delicacies for the late-night in-house picnics they shared.

One night he'd take her on a midnight picnic under the stars so she could name the constellations like she wanted to, if he could.

'I told you I spoke with the pub's manager about the drinks order for your shed dance. I was looking for the best deal. I've got you their business card for you to decide if you want to use them or not.' From her laptop bag, she removed a black leather compendium that she unzipped.

'That's flash.' Jake pointed to the open case that carried what he had on his desk, a notepad, tablet, and business cards stored in a neat folder. 'Whose business cards are those.'

'From the various businesses in Elsie Creek, and surrounding areas.' She pulled out the small bundle bound by a rubber band, while the rest remained neatly slotted in the folder she promptly put away. 'The pub's manager also knew some waiting staff we can hire for the shed dance. I also spoke with a few sales reps, who were passing through, who gave me some great tips on where to find things locally. You said you wanted to use local gear, right?'

'I did.' He flicked through the cards, recognising a few names. 'I didn't think Elsie Creek was that big of a town. How much did you party last night?'

'I only had three drinks while babysitting Elliott. I drank more with you over the phone in my room.' She passed him a collection of brochures and papers as he sat on the end of the bed. 'Hey, what did you think of the proposals I emailed you?'

'Tom's impressed. Dad's being non-committal, saying it's above him, but he wasn't too sure about the history you wrote. Look, I love all of it, but I want to be sure we've got the facts right for those judges.'

'I understand.'

'So where did you source your information from?'

'It's legitimate.' She sat on the bed with her lips twisted.

'Babe?' Grabbing her small soft hands in his, he made her look at him.

'You shouldn't be calling me that, Jake. You might slip up in front of others.'

'Stop changing the subject. You do that too well.'

'Do I?'

'Every time I ask what you do outside of this place, you avoid answering.'

'Do you have to know everything?'

'I want to know because I hate secrets.' He leaned forward, cradling his head in his hands. 'I feel like I'm drowning in secrets. Us. My engagement. And the one secret I've kept for so long—was the barra farm. I'm relieved it's out. Although, I'm disappointed with Dad's reaction.'

'What were you hoping for?'

'I wanted Dad to at least see what I've done.'

'Was Bob the type of father to attend your school functions and graduations?'

'Dad never left the property. It was Mum who flew with us to boarding school to make sure we'd settled in.'

'You were lucky to have that with your mum.'

'Hey.' He squeezed her hands, aware she didn't have a family, while his family felt like a burden. 'It wasn't all roses—yes it was, coz roses have prickles on them.'

'Are you talking flowers?' Giving him a coy grin but the smile shone in her eyes.

'No, never. And again you've hanged the subject.'

'What were we talking about?'

'Don't you flutter your eyelids at me.'

'They say it's a form of flirting.' Fluttering her eyelids as she melted against his torso.

'You can flirt all you like.' He slipped his arm around her shoulders, kissing her nose, glad she was back. 'First, tell me how you researched Danbunnan's history. Is it fact? Because Dad was talking about fake news, he reckons you made it up.'

Sienna frowned and her eyes darkened. 'I'm not a liar.'

'I'm not saying that, but you called the garden the *oasis of the outback* and told me how it was created from suitors carting exotic flowers for my great-great-aunt Madeline. How cattle were used as dowry, and my great-great-grandmother was a botanist.'

'And a herbalist.'

'See, how?' He cupped her cheek and gazed into her wise eyes where intelligence had never looked so sexy. 'Please, Sienna, I tell you everything and anything you want to know. Yet, I feel our conversations are one-sided and it's all about this place.'

'Everything I'm doing is for you to save Danbunnan, so all those people have a job. This is their home too.'

'What do you get out of it?'

She barely shrugged. 'We all know I leave when Rhonda returns. And I'm not sticking around while you're engaged, when I have no obvious reason to stay on.'

A stabbing ache churned inside his chest. He was trapped and couldn't promise her anything.

'I'll prove I'm not lying, but I've been sworn to secrecy too.' She shifted to the far corner of the room and removed a swathe of thick velvet material to reveal a row of leather-bound journals in a bookcase. 'Rhonda is going to kill me.'

'Hey, I know those.' He moved in for a closer look.

'You do?'

'Mum kept those books in the schoolroom, where Jess homeschools the twins. These were among Mum's black-and-white-movie collection and her Frank Sinatra albums. Do you have any of those movies and records?'

'No, just these. I've been minding them for Rhonda. I told her to put them away, but she insisted I read them. Aren't they amazing?' She flicked one open showing him the detailed sketches of plants like a vintage botanist's notebook. The artwork was impressive.

Jake crouched in front of the leather-bound journals. 'We weren't allowed to touch them. Mum had them on a special shelf inside this fancy cupboard. I haven't seen that cupboard in a while.'

'Was that the fake cupboard that hid the indigenous children when the government were separating them?'

'Who told you about the fake cupboard?'

'I read about it in these journals. They start with your great-great-grandmother,' said Sienna, sliding the journal back on the shelf. 'When I first arrived, Rhonda said these journals were stored in this room as part of the cook's tradition.'

'No, they're not. These were my mother's. Only a month back, Dad talked about how that cupboard used to live in the cellar. So, how did these books end up here?'

'I have no idea. But this ...' She pulled out another leather-bound volume. 'This is my resource for history, recipes—'

'The face creams?'

Sienna nodded. 'Herbal remedies and wood stove recipes. The beeswax polish I used for the tables in the muster room. The gardening tips, table settings and the proper etiquette for entertaining guests. I learned all of that from your ancestors.'

He flicked the thick creamy pages covered in a flowery cursive. 'It's hard to read this writing.'

'I agree. For the record, Rhonda swore me to secrecy. That's why I couldn't tell you.'

'Why?'

'Rhonda said it was a cook's privilege passed along by the women not born into the Cullen family. I wasn't even going to read them until you told me how your family and this place came to be. It was the first time we spoke, the first time you said my name. Back then I saw your pride in the way you spoke about Danbunnan's history and your sadness too.'

He stroked her soft fair locks, adoring her empathy and how she remembered the details.

'Aaand because I had no TV, no books, and with no wi-fi that first week I had nothing. I was totally unprepared, and I also did it to impress you.' She rolled her eyes at his grin, as he lifted her hand to kiss her fingertips. 'But once I'd started reading them, I could relate to their stories. Rhonda said I would.'

'In what way?'

'When I arrived, I didn't know about cattle or cattle stations, I still don't. But I was the same as your ancestors. The first pioneering women who came here didn't have a clue about what they were getting into. They came out here with no phone, no instruction manual, nor any form of farming experience. The men left them to run this place on their own. They had it tough, so I had to respect them for it.' Her fingertips caressed the spines of the journals as if they were made of fine crystal. 'They are also a lady's private thoughts, too.'

He arched his eyebrow at the bookcase. 'Diaries?'

'Sure. But a lot of it is to do with the weather and planting of food crops, and herbal remedies. They even mention the station competitions too and how excited they were to attend … Please don't get mad at Rhonda.'

'I won't. Are you still using them?'

'I'm three-quarters of the way through the story. I've been looking for recipes to use for your competition functions. I found a great consommé and the perfect gravy using my super stock. There's a wild-goose pâté, a native bee honey sauce, and there are some great recipes for beef jerky I can't wait to try. The notes to set up their smokehouse to cure salamis might be outdated. I hope the plans I sent you were okay?'

'I've added some scribbles to it. But why the salamis?' It seemed like a lot of effort.

'It was Henry Cullen's hobby. Taught to him by his grandfather and loved by Danbunnan's stockmen. That's what I'm up to now.' She opened a page she'd bookmarked.

'It's hard to read.'

'It took me a while to get the hang of it. It's like interpreting a foreign language, but it's such a romantic use of words.'

'You, being a word player, would've enjoyed that.'

'I do, and the penmanship is beautiful. Winifred wrote daily about living in an unknown land, dealing with this foreign concept of being a cattleman's wife.'

'It sounds like you've become quite attached to these.' He could see it.

***

'I respect her, Jake. Winifred Cullen is my hero, who had it tough. It was heartbreaking to read about her children dying, I had to admire her strength and determination to keep going. I have respect for how this place came to be, the struggles they went through and their triumphs. They couldn't ring up or email for things, and a lot they had to make themselves. It's so much easier now compared to back then.'

'Did you ever skip ahead?'

'No, that'd ruin the ending. Do you?'

'Always. As soon as it gets boring, I skip to the end. Same with magazines and articles—I skim them. I don't read the fine print. Not like you who reads a rule book on a competition.' He playfully nudged her with his elbow.

'We'll be giving them a run, that's for sure. Hey, it ruins the ending if you skip to the back. You'll miss the juicy bits, like ways to cook ox tongue, pig's feet, blood pudding—that was gross.'

'I'll skip that, thanks.' He reached for the last book and flipped through its pages. 'It's blank.'

'Winifred had a whole trunk full given to her as a wedding present. It's meant to be for the women, the cooks, who add their recipes and tips on station living. Rhonda told me she's written her own recipes in here, like her mango wine.'

'Rhonda made that last year. You should've seen Rhonda and Tom, they were rolling drunk at Christmas, it was funny to watch. It was almost as good as your jelly shots.' Jake chuckled as he grabbed the second-last book and flicked through the pages. 'This one's empty too.'

'I haven't gone that far.'

'I won't tell you the ending.'

'It'd be like ruining a good movie.'

'Hate that in movies, but reading, meh.' Jake grabbed the third-last book and flicked through the heavy volume.

'Here, there's blue ink.' He opened the covers wider and a white envelope fell to the floor.

Sienna picked up the envelope, turned it over and read the label. 'Jake, it's addressed to you. The return addressee on the envelope is Janice Cullen.'

'That's my mother.' His hands shook as the heavy journal fell to the floor.

'I'll get that.' She picked up the journal and flicked through its pages. 'This book's blank too.' She put it back on the shelf amongst the others that stood like silent soldiers full of stories. So where were Rhonda's recipes? 'Do you want me to give you a moment?'

Jake stared at the envelope, his hands trembling as he opened it. 'Here, take it. I'm tearing the letter.'

'I've got it.' She held his hands, gave them a squeeze. She opened the envelope and handed the crisp white sheets of paper to Jake.

'*To my darling son, Jake* …' He shut his eyes. 'Sienna, can you read this?' Thrusting the letter at her, he paced the floor, roughly scrubbing his hands over his face. 'The date on top … it's written the day before she died. I can't read it, you have to.'

With the letter in hand, she read:

*To my darling son, Jake,*

*Please don't be mad at Rhonda when you receive this letter. She's been a wonderful support during my illness and a true friend who's been there for me. She used to read these journals aloud in the muster room where we used to imagine how those women survived. We baked their many recipes in the wood stove you tried so hard to get for us, that kept me warm when nothing warmed my bones this last dry season.*

Jake stopped pacing to sit heavily at the end of her bed.

Sienna knew the wood stove represented some of his fondest childhood memories, and now this. She sat beside him, rubbing his back to offer him some comfort.

Head down, forearms rested on his denim thighs, his palms pressed together as if in prayer. 'Go on, Sienna.'

Sienna read the cursive handwriting:

*These journals are going to be or were (by the time you get this letter) hidden in Rhonda's room to save them from your father. He's burnt all the others and destroyed the false cupboard. Which was such a shame, when that cupboard helped so many in a terrible time in our Northern Territory history.*

*Kind of like our own family history, when you asked me what your father and I argued over on the night it all went wrong. How could Danbunnan's boss poison the land and herd? Why did your brother commit suicide, and why did I beg you to come home?*

*You had so many questions. And I had the answers, but I couldn't tell you why, only that the family was in trouble.*

*Because it was all my fault.*

'How?' Jake looked up at Sienna.

'Jake, I shouldn't be reading this.' She folded up the letter and held it out for him to take.

'Don't stop, babe, I have to hear this.' With his hand on her knee, he gave her a pleading look. 'Please read it.'

'Okay, then …' She took a deep breath and unfolded the pages:

*I used to write in the journals too. So did many of your female ancestors, beginning with Winifred Cullen who started the tradition.*

*Silly me, I'd forgotten what I'd written. Because it was inside the journals where Bob found out my deepest darkest secret.*

*It was about my affair.*

'What?' Jake's face twisted in disbelief.

'Do you want me to stop?' To hear his mother's faults would be hard for Jake, especially when he held her in such high regard. This was also the guy who would cringe on hearing his sister, the mother of the twins, wasn't a virgin. How was he going to cope with this?

'No, keep going.' Again, he wiped palms over his face as if to scrub away some internal imagery.

Sienna continued:

*I was so young, straight out of teaching college in Sydney, and at eighteen, I was the same age as Winifred Cullen when she started* these journals. I came here to start a new life. One of romance. Just like I'd dreamed about from the black-and-white movies I watched. So, I decided to head north, to Australia's final frontier.

I came to Darwin via cruise ship as soon as I'd graduated, with a promise of work. I ended up at Danbunnan as a governess, hired by the co-op to run a tiny outback school and to drive their old school bus.

They were long days—I began before sunrise collecting station kids; their mothers or the station cooks met me on the road—and I didn't get back until dark.

But one day my bus broke down and I met this road-train driver. He was such a larrikin, who made me laugh with his stories. He'd meet me at the school on weekends and helped me cope with the culture shock and isolation of running an outback school. He was a good friend, too, long before I met your father.

When I did meet your father everything changed. Soon after that Bob talked your grandfather into moving me into one of Danbunnan's cottages. I'd assumed it was part of the co-op's agreement where I'd been living in the school's office. But Bob wanted me at the cottage and used it as his excuse to check up on me, to make sure I was safe.

Bob was so handsome and this charming prince, the future cattle king of Danbunnan, that when he proposed I said yes.

The road-train driver was an older man, already married, and I was foolishly in love with both men.

But I chose your father because I loved him more.

As a wedding gift, Bob explained to me I'd inherited these journals that were part of the legacy of the women who married into the Cullen family who lived at Danbunnan.

In the beginning of our marriage, I wrote regularly in them, because I had no one else to confide in. I'd been separated from everyone and all I had were the journals and Duncan. Your father wouldn't let me befriend any of the staff, saying it was against the rules, because I was now the lady of the house. It was a job I took such pride in.

The journals contained my thoughts and a secret I'd kept for over thirty years, which was my affair with the road-train driver. I *never wrote his name in the journals, I'd just called him* the road-train driver. *Silly me, I wanted to protect him, when I should have never written about our affair in the first place.*

*Your father never knew until he found my journal entries. He's burnt all those I wrote in, so don't bother looking for them. Which is such a shame, because they also contained the stories of my growing children.*

*But I truly loved your father, always.*

*Sadly, when he became a mean drunk, I left him, a few times. But Bob always found me and charmed his way back into my good graces and I forgave him.*

*But this one night, I fled the house with Duncan in my arms, when he was barely five. The road-train driver picked us up, walking the track late at night. We had nothing on us. No food or water. But I couldn't stay at Danbunnan, not while your father was in such a mean rum rage.*

*The road-train driver took us to the deserted school. It was far enough away for your father to not drive after me while drunk.*

*The road-train driver had a wife and two children, and in that time, nothing happened. We were friends, and he was someone who'd helped me.*

*I stayed at that school for a week until your father found us. Of course, Bob apologised, begging for forgiveness and wouldn't leave until Duncan and I went back home with him. Which we did.*

*But, you see, I didn't know I was pregnant with you. And because of my absence during that time and finding out after I was pregnant, your father rejected you, refusing to believe you were his. It's because I'd slipped that I'd been helped by a road-train driver who'd brought us food and clothing during our time hiding at the school.*

Jake screwed his face up at Sienna. 'What the hell?'

But she just kept reading:

*Bob, the stupid fool, thought you were the road-train driver's child, but you weren't. No matter how much I swore to him you were a Cullen, Bob could never be sure. In the back of his mind, he always believed you weren't his son because you looked different to Duncan. Jess looked like me and he knew she was his daughter because I'd never left the station during that time.*

*But you are Robert Cullen's son.*

*It's Duncan who wasn't Bob's son, and Duncan's father is …'*

'Who?' demanded Jake.

*'Mick MacLennan.'*

'What the hell!' His face screwed up in horror. 'Tom's father.'

'Tom?' Sienna blinked at Jake a few times. 'Elliott's uncle, your 2IC, Tom?'

'All those years Dad gave me such a hard time—it makes sense. Aww, hell no … If Duncan discovered he wasn't Bob's son, on top of the poisoning and everything else—no wonder he killed himself.' Jake clutched the top of his head as if it was about to blow.

Sienna kept reading aloud, she had to finish it.

*I never wanted you or anyone else to know, but your father found my secret in the journals. I'd honestly forgotten what I'd written, because it was thirty years ago. It's what caused the biggest argument between your father and me and where for the first time in our marriage, I told Bob what an idiot he was for chasing his only son away. You.*

*When Duncan came to my rescue, I was sprawled across the kitchen floor after being slapped by your father. Desperately, I hid behind Duncan's legs, while he ordered Bob to get out. But Bob told Duncan that because he wasn't Bob's biological son, he couldn't kick out Bob and no longer had any right to Danbunnan.*

*My secret was out, and it was a relief to finally have it out in the open. But I had no idea how catastrophic the results would be.*

*Way back when you were a teenager covered in dirt, digging fencing holes, you said if given a choice, it wouldn't be the oldest son it'd be family who shared in managing Danbunnan. You said there was enough room to build houses for all the family to live and work there to share the load. You saw the burden Duncan was under, being forced to carry it alone, under pressure from Bob, without actually being the boss, waiting for Bob to retire.*

*I saw the same burden in your father, who never allowed me to share that with him. No one deserves to carry that burden on their* own, I just wished the fool man put his pride aside and shared with me. Bob said it was against the rules of the station for women to get involved with station business. Stubborn man.

But your father never believed that you were his son, and that was why he was always hard on you.

So when Bob realised he'd kicked out his only son and had raised another man's child, he got drunk and drove into that tree. We all know Bob walked away from that accident, poisoning the property, the herd, the station's reputation, and the long-term damage to everyone and everything on Danbunnan was catastrophic.

But I loved your father. Lord knows I was such a fool for that man, and no matter how mean your father got, I have always loved Robert Cullen.

But the thing was, I was pregnant with Duncan before we were married because I was sleeping with both men. Me, the governess who was young and foolish—I just never realised how much trouble it would cause.

Your father never knew the true name of the man I'd had an affair with. I only mentioned that it was a road-train driver, because Mick lived here, in a cottage, with his wife and children.

Yet, when I gave birth to Duncan, I knew he was Mick's son, and we both decided to never tell Bob. So when Mick passed away, I thought our secret went with him too.

Please believe me when I say, I never slept with Mick once I had agreed to marry your father. My marriage vows were sacred to me. No matter how many times I told Bob, the fool never believed me. I'm hoping Rhonda will get through to him to at least listen to me before I go.

Jake, I'm sorry to have put you through all of this and for how Bob treated you when you were younger.

But when your father kicked you out, you blossomed. I heard it in your voice. The stress of this place had left you and you seemed happier away from Danbunnan. When I heard all of your wonderful adventures, I'd hoped you'd find a place to call home and a lady to share it with. You deserved it.

But when Bob told Duncan he wasn't a Cullen, I saw the

*heartbreak in your brother's face. I begged you to come home because I believed you were the one to bring the family back together. You were the rightful heir, who cared deeply for family. It's why I made you swear to fight for her survival, because Danbunnan has always belonged to you, she's your home.*

*Forgive me, Jake, for what I've done. I honestly thought I was doing the right thing, keeping my secret. Hopefully, you'll read this after your father has passed away, so you don't take your anger out on him. You can see the guilt he's carrying now and he's very sorry with no way of undoing what he's done.*

*Anyway, I've given what is left of these journals with this hidden letter to Rhonda to keep them safe. They're part of your legacy to pass on to your wife, for your family that will be the next generation to call Danbunnan home. They helped me and I hope they'll help her.*

*I'm sorry I did this, too. Hiding the truth about Duncan's heritage and the legacy of this station that belonged to you.*

*I know you will repair this place from the damage your father caused and make it your own. Because Danbunnan is yours, Jake. And Danbunnan knows it.*

*Be good to Danbunnan and she'll be good to you, I believe it.*

*Forgive me, I love you and I'm so proud of you, always.*

*Love Mum.*

With tears streaming down her face, Sienna folded up the letter and slipped it back inside the envelope, passing it to Jake.

He stared at the envelope in his hand. 'All those years, that bastard treated me like scum, I could never understand what I'd done that was so wrong. I asked both of my parents why they argued that night, for Bob to drive away, and why Duncan got involved, and they never told me. I've been blaming myself for Duncan's death, for not being here.'

'I'm so sorry.' She hugged him, hoping to take away his pain.

Jake burrowed his face in her hair, to breathe heavily against her neck.

Then he stopped and glared at the letter before jumping to his feet and opening the door.

'Where are you going?'

'To find out if Bob was ever going to tell me the truth.'

# Seventeen

Jake was fuming as he stormed up to the house and ripped open the screen door to the kitchen. Inside, his sister was serving dinner at the kitchen bench while the twins were sprawled across the lounge room floor.

'Hey, want some pizza, Jake?' Jess asked.

'No, thanks.' He wiped his palms down his jeans as he tried to control his rage.

'It's movie night with the twins. Do you think I could interest you in watching the latest episode of *Barbie*?' Jess grinned at him, putting pizza on the twins' plates.

Just like Mum's movie nights, as a kid, camped in the lounge to watch black-and-white movies with homemade popcorn cooked in a pan. Now the twins shared microwave popcorn, pizza, and coloured cartoons on personal tablets. Some things changed, but a lot remained the same.

'Where's Dad?' That name was like acid off his tongue. *Bastard* was more fitting. *Bully* too. Flashbacks hit him from when he used to hide from his father when he was a kid.

He stared at the kitchen floor. Was that where his mother cowered from her husband? The mongrel who hit his wife. The arsehole who had disapproved of Jess leaving her cheating husband. When his own wife had ran away with a child in her arms down a dark, deserted dirt track with nothing.

Gritting his teeth, his knuckles whitened as his hands became tight fists. 'DAD.' The name echoed off the walls, making Jess wince.

Bob strolled in from the corridor. 'I was just putting away them sunglasses Sienna got me. She didn't have to … Son?'

'*Never call me that, again.* Outside. I want a word with you.' Jake trembled from the white-hot rage pumping through his veins. '*Get out, or I'll drag you out by the throat.*' He held open the screen door.

'Jake, what's going on?' Jess asked.

'Stay inside, Jess.' Jake slammed the wooden door behind him.

Bob stepped onto the garden path between the orchard and the house that overlooked the compound. 'What's wrong with you?'

'I know why you treated me like dirt and why DUNCAN KILLED HIMSELF. *Your secret's out, and now I want answers.* Did you or did you not poison this property on purpose?'

'No, it was an accident, and I was drunk. And angry.'

'You were always an angry drunk; you used to take it out on me.'

'What do you want to hear? That I'm sorry.'

'*Answer the bloody question.*' Jake spoke through gritted teeth, and it took all his inner strength to not grab the old man by the shirt front and shake him.

'It was an accident. I didn't see the tree when I went around that bend because I was drunk.' Bob heaved in hot air and bellowed, '*All right!* I didn't believe Duncan when he said the stuff was toxic, I didn't pay any attention to his words, because I'd just discovered he wasn't my son.'

'Duncan loved you like a father. He. Knew. No. Different.'

'I'm sorry. What else do you want me to say? Do you want me to leave? Kick me out?'

'I'll never be like you, a man who hits women and children. A man who scares his pregnant wife so much that she's forced to flee down a deserted track with a child in her arms, like Mum ran away from you.'

Bob's jaw dropped and the colour fled from his face. 'How did you find out?'

'The journals.'

'That's impossible. I burned them all.'

'Why?'

'How would you like reading about yourself as a —'

'A cruel drunken bastard?'

*'Who reads about my wife's affair with another man.* I found them in the trunk with her stuff, along with that cupboard she didn't think I knew nothing about, that was full of her secrets. So I dumped them all into the river.'

'Why?'

*'Because I never wanted you to know,'* shouted Bob. 'Your mother swore she'd never tell you while I was alive.'

'She didn't. She wrote me a letter that I wasn't meant to read until after you'd died. But guess what?' Jake stepped closer, towering over the old man. 'You're lucky I made a promise to Mum to take care of you, or I'd beat the crap out of you. But you have to live with what you've done, the only difference is now I know.'

'Jake, I fed you, clothed you, even sent you to boarding school. I didn't send Duncan to boarding school.'

*'Duncan never had a choice.* He was made to learn your way while you shipped me off to school because you didn't want me here, believing I wasn't your kid.'

'I tried.'

'Bull! You kicked me out *after* you treated me like a dog's slave to this place for as long as I could remember. But guess what?' Jake waved the letter in Bob's face. 'Here's Mum's letter, written the day before she'd died, swearing I'm your son, and I don't want to be.' And with pure hatred dripping from every word, Jake snarled out, *'Never call me son again.'*

# Eighteen

Inside her room, Sienna sat in her reading chair by the open window. She'd tried to work on her laptop, but Jake and Bob's angry voices echoed across the compound. Part of her wanted to run after Jake when he tore out of the compound in his ute, but she couldn't. This was family business, not hers.

She wished she'd never shown Jake those journals. He'd been getting along with Bob, finally, and now his family was again ripped apart.

Most of all, she wished she knew why Rhonda had lied.

Sienna had found none of Rhonda's recipes written in any of the journals. Why hadn't Rhonda stored them away with the rest of her gear? If Rhonda was so involved with the Cullen family, why did she go on a long holiday when they'd needed her most?

Sienna was destined to leave soon, which meant it was time to start making decisions. She grabbed her portfolio and pulled out a worn piece of paper hidden inside. It was her *to-live list* and unfolded her page of unfinished dreams.

'Sienna?'

'Tom?' She spun around in her seat to face the window to where the head stockmen stood in the shadows of her carport. 'Where did you come from?'

'Round the back.' Tom rested his elbow on the wooden rail that separated the carport and verandah. 'Did you hear those men before?'

'I'm just minding my own business.'

'Did Jake find the journals? I saw him help you unload your car.'

*Tom knows about the journals! Holy roasted coffee beans!*

Was history repeating itself, with Sienna and Jake having an affair like Jake's mum with Tom's dad? It was far too surreal to deal with right now. Instead, she blinked at the head stockman. 'The what?'

Tom said nothing but his silence spoke volumes as his grey eyes looked up to the house. 'Do me a favour?'

'Don't ask me to get involved, Tom.' She was far too involved already, with nowhere to run out of this corner she'd gotten herself into.

Tom balanced a six pack of beer on the wooden rail.

'Why do you have the boss's beer?'

'Jake needs a mate.'

'Do you want me to drive you?'

'Not me, you.'

'I'm not getting involved, that's family business and I'm only temporary, Tom.'

'You're also Jake's friend. And right now, Jake needs someone who won't see him as a boss, but as a friend.' Tom opened her car and placed the beer cans on the passenger seat. He then faced her with his normally stern expression darkening. 'Sienna, I don't want a repeat of what happened to Duncan because no one was there for the man when he needed it most.'

That thought alone had Sienna on her feet. 'Not on my watch!'

Like a lesson learned from her dash to Elsie Creek, she snatched her keys and laptop bag. 'Which way did he go?'

'I reckon the ponds, but I don't have a key.'

'I do.'

'I know. If you don't find him, come back and I'll organise a search party. If you're not back in twenty minutes, I'll assume you've found him.'

'I'll find him, Tom.'

Her toy-car's engine rumbled as she backed away from Tom standing in the shadows of the lean-to. Sienna didn't care how it looked — she only cared about finding Jake.

# Nineteen

Jake sat behind the wheel of his ute, parked beside the pump shed that overlooked the barra ponds. He'd turned off the engine, but couldn't let go of the damned steering wheel.

Behind him, the gate's heavy chain rattled. It was soon followed by a familiar engine rumble, and through the side mirror he watched the red car approach and park behind him. Sienna opened the passenger door and climbed inside the cab.

'Hi.' She slipped a six-pack of beer cans inside the car fridge and passed him one.

'Thanks, babe.' He opened it with achy hands, checking if he'd left a permanent indent on the steering wheel. He leaned back against the driver's seat and gulped at the ice-cold beer, hoping it would dampen his simmering anger. 'I don't know what to say,' he mumbled so low.

'You don't need to say anything.'

'Why are you here?'

'Tom thought you could do with a friend, and I agree.'

Without thought, he grabbed her, burying his face in her soft hair and breathed her in. The comfort of her arms, her small hands rubbing his back was his sanctuary. 'What do I do?'

'Don't give up.'

She pulled out a piece of paper from her pocket. 'And you never lose focus on your dreams.'

'What's that?'

'My *to-live list*.'

'I know you're all about checklists and notes, so what makes this list so different?' The off-white paper with browned edges was well creased and leathery soft from years of use.

Unlike his mother's letter. The letter of pain, that was a pristine white, lying in the fine layer of dust on the dash of his ute. Who knew paperwork could cause so much damage?

'I was like any other kid who made wishes on stars when growing up.'

'So it's your wish list?'

'It's my list *to live* beyond the world of bars, locked up not for doing anything wrong, but because I had no family. And no matter how messed up family might be, they're family.'

'I can't forget what he did.'

'Who says you have to? But you can tell Bob's a broken man. Its why Bob hasn't left the compound to see your work, Jake. He is sorry. You can see it.'

'If he was your dad, what would you do?'

'I don't remember my parents. Wish I did. So don't ask me for that sort of advice about family because I have none. But I do know what it's like to not have any and how lonely it is. Especially when there are days you want to give up and realise no one would even notice you're gone. You're invisible.' She stared at her hands in her lap, giving a slight shrug.

'I won't hurt myself.'

Her sigh of relief filled the cab. 'But I don't want you to give up either.'

'Right now, I want to keep driving.' Through the front window, beyond the bonnet of his ute, he gazed out to the sea of green trees. 'Escaping sounds good.'

'I did that. That's how I ended up here.' Her smile chipped away at the hatred inside his chest.

'How *did* you end up here?'

'Rhonda called in all her favours.'

'Before that?'

'I was drinking my way along the east coast.'

'Jess told me about your ex.'

'I was wondering if she did.'

'No secrets. Please? I can't deal with any more secrets.' His fingers brushed her hair, which spilled like fine spun silk in the sun.

'Okay …' She nodded, then held up the folded paper. 'This is my biggest and oldest secret. Even though I was a kid when I wrote this *to-live list*, every now and again I'll pull it out as a reminder of what I've been through. It helps me to keep moving forwards.'

'Can I read it?'

'Just don't laugh at it.' She cringed.

'I won't.'

'Um, okay.' She hesitated before she handed it over.

The paper was so flimsy and soft, yet leathery with permanent creases as he unfolded the single page. It was covered in different styles of writing yet similar, in many coloured inks and crayons, with a few of the items already crossed off. Jake read from the top:

'*Make and fly a kite.* I see you've already done that one.

*Have a midnight picnic to make up names of stars*—that's where you got that from?'

Her reply was a single shoulder shrug.

'*Have a country café.*

*Work in new fields.*

*Grow an edible garden and make something yummy from it.*

*Chase a tornado.*

*See a turtle in the wild.*

*Send a message in a bottle.* Another two crossed off. Well done!

*Take a road trip.*

*Surprise someone.*

*Play a new ball game.*

*Meet a prince?*' He cocked his eyebrow at her and smirked.

'I was a kid when I wrote that …' She blushed the colour of the dirt.

'*Go on a treasure hunt.*

*Go skinny-dipping, rock climbing, cliff jumping, and bushwalking.*

*Throw a dart at a map and travel to where it lands.*

*Be a mentor.*

*Create a business to walk away from.*

*Build something solid that would last a lifetime.*

*Ride a motorbike, a quad, an airboat, a helicopter and a horse.*'

'I wrote that before I fell off a horse when I was seven.' And her last effort at horse-riding ended up in a landslide.

He squeezed her thigh, then continued to read down her list.

'*Catch a fish and eat it the same day.*'

'You can cross that one off the list.' Her smile was so wide it matched the shine in her eyes.

'I will.' Jake was proud he'd taught her to fish that day. He snatched up his pen from the console and crossed it off her list, careful to not poke a hole through the worn paper.

'*Find snow and make a snow angel after falling off a snowboard.*' He chuckled.

'One day. That's why I travelled down the east coast, I was waiting for winter,' she said, with another shrug.

'*Swim in the sea and try to surf.*' He pointed to the line crossed off. 'It's very specific.'

'I was eighteen when I first saw the ocean where it was warm enough to swim.'

'Really?'

'I did adult swimming lessons. Mind you, I was the baby of the class.'

'I don't remember taking swimming lessons, I've always been able to swim.'

'Growing up here I'd believe that, like how easily you can ride a horse.'

'I'd be happy to teach you to ride.'

'No rush.'

But did they have time?

'When I finished my apprenticeship, I caught a bus and went to Queensland in search of warm weather. With one bag of clothes and that *to-live list* as my guide to forge ahead, it was all I had. The clothes and bags may have changed with every new season, but the *to-live list* is the same piece of paper. The items on it have changed, some were completed, and new ones were added as my goals changed. Like yours.' She waved her hand to the ponds that surrounded them.

'It's a cool list.' He was amazed at how simple some of her wishes were, with things he'd taken for granted as everyday normal items.

She grabbed his hands. Hers were so small, yet they gave him so much courage and comfort. 'Jake, I can hear your pride, your passion, and excitement every time you speak about this place. You're willing to sacrifice so much for this station, because there's more here that truly makes you happy too. Isn't there?'

He swallowed, digesting her words.

'You have a lot to be proud of, and you need to remember the positives that make you happy.'

Jake looked out to the ponds, where the late afternoon sun's reflection shimmered on the water. 'Yesterday, when I was showing Tom this place, I was bashing the golf ball around. This barra leapt out of the pond to try and catch it. Its scales and tail, flicking off the water, was full of rainbow colours from the sunset. It was beautiful.'

'I wish I'd seen that.'

They sat in silence for a while until Jake said, 'I feel like that letter has blown my world apart.'

'Hey, at least you found your answers.'

'They're not what I expected. I now understand why, but what happened to Duncan still hurts. It's why I'm doing everything I can to keep Danbunnan afloat for this family and our future generations.'

'Would you have liked to have grown up differently?'

'What do you mean? Dad would've never treated

Duncan the way he did, and I would have suffered as his number-one son.' He paused, narrowing his eyes. 'I got out.'

'You did. You had a whole life somewhere else, to live your way, that when you returned you used what you'd learned on your travels and made the station your own. If you'd been number-one son, would any of this be possible today?'

'No.' Cupping the side of her face, his thumb brushed over her cheek. 'You're very wise, and you bring me beer.' He sipped his beer can and patted his chest like a caveman.

Then he sighed, feeling the weight on his shoulders. 'What do I do about Dad?'

'Don't ask me.'

'I am, Sienna. What would you do?'

'Nothing.'

'Come on.'

'I learned a long time ago to let people carry their own burdens and I'll carry mine. It doesn't mean I won't help them, but you can't change them. I learned that harsh lesson the day my last blood relative walked away from me. He didn't like me and that's okay. Mind you, it took a while for that epiphany to sink in, but it did, and it makes sense. It might seem selfish, but it's all I have other than my *to-live list*.' She held up the folded piece of paper. 'My *to-live list* made me get up and keep moving forward. Believe me, there were days I couldn't, and then there were days I didn't need to fake it because I'd made it.'

'What else is on this list?' Jake snatched it from her hand. 'What's this blocked out in crayon?' He held up the leathery paper to the fading sunlight and read the letters hidden beneath the crayon that blocked it.

The letters spelled out: FAMILY.

He looked at her, as his heart fell for her. 'You blocked that out.'

'Some things never work out.' Sienna plucked it from his fingers and slipped it into her phone case, then into her pocket. Gone.

'What I'm trying to say was the *to-live list* was about surviving the crap. And with moments such as these, you survive first. Don't give up on Danbunnan, or yourself, not when you're this close to success.'

'Do you think I am?'

'I'm willing to bet on it. You asked what I get out of helping you, well ...' She smoothed out her dress, jutted out her chin, and said, 'I want a percentage as my fee.'

'Of what?'

'Sales profit.'

His eyebrows rose while his beer can froze halfway to his mouth. 'Huh?'

'Call it a finder's fee. With the sales proposal I've created, and after we've made any changes you might want, I'll release it to the buyers I find. But I'll want a set percentage rate. Meaning, I'll push for a higher price, and the higher the price ...'

'The higher your fee.'

She gave him a hint of a smile to those luscious lips but there was a definite shine to her wise eyes.

'You're not just a pretty face.'

'Never let the looks fool you when you're the man with the perfect poker face. Hey, I've got my laptop in the toy-car, we can finish working on the proposal. You can bash around some golf balls and I'll type.' She opened the door.

Jake grabbed her arm. 'Why do you avoid telling me what you do outside of Danbunnan?'

'Do I?'

'Every time I ask. Until last night I didn't even have your phone number. I don't even know where you live. Yet I know other things about you, but not the simple small-talk stuff about who you are when you're not here. I have no idea. If you want a percentage, answer those questions?'

'So I need to sell myself, is that what you're saying?'

'Babe, I said to you a while back you have a skill in selling things, and if given the proper resources, you'd do well. I already believe in you enough to let you do this for me, *with me*. It's because of you I'm doing this competition when I'd voted no with Dad. That's why I made him have that meeting, to let the crew show him none of us wanted to do it. But then you went and sold it. That's without credentials, just on your passion alone. And from the way you're powering through this other work, the business plans and proposals that are top class, it's obvious you know what you're doing. So why do you avoid questions about your past?'

Looking at her hands, she spoke in such a soft voice. 'Some days I like being known as just the relief cook.'

He reached out and gave her shoulder a tender squeeze. 'Why? When you should be proud of your business experience.'

'I used to be so proud of it.'

'Then what happened? The ex?'

'Everything. I'll show you something.'

'You're not changing the subject, are you?'

'No.' She headed for her car, soon returning with her leather compendium. 'Here's my card.' She handed him a business card from the group he'd spotted earlier, neatly slotted inside.

He read the print. 'Sienna Jacobs, Director of VA Enterprises. What the—'

'I own a virtual assistant company.' She showed him her tablet's screen. 'This is my website. It's not live because we have no access, but that's the business where I have over fifty staff and growing.'

'Why aren't you there?' This was nothing like he'd imagined.

'The way it's set up, I don't have to be there.'

'How is this possible?'

'As a virtual assistant, it's all done online. Most of my workers are mothers who work from home because I offer flexible working hours.'

'How, what? Where?'

'In Darwin. I have an office and a house that's rented out

while I've been on my road trip. I check in with Ricky weekly. He's earned his name as my BFF Mail-order Biatch by forwarding my mail to me whenever I stopped somewhere.'

'But I thought you were a chef?'

'I *was* a chef. I've never lied to you, Jake.'

'I believe you, but I'm trying to understand how you got from being a chef to this.' He pointed at her website.

'I wanted out of the kitchen, because I was sick of working nights and weekends.'

'Didn't you want to start a restaurant? Your *to-live list* said you wanted a country café.'

'I was so over the whole hospitality trade by then. But I wanted to do something else that still involved party planning. The education I received in the home was pathetic, so I started studying online to learn IT basics and bookkeeping. Yet to even get a business loan, I had to study to do business plans, so I got a job working for an accountant and then did night classes to get my business degree.'

'I remember you mentioned that when you taught me how to use my bookkeeping program.'

'At this accountant's I did books for lots of small businesses. Then before I'd finalised my qualifications, I'd set up a side business offering phone service, mail collection service and basic bookkeeping for sole traders. From there it grew so fast that I ended up supplying office space for these people to use too.' She showed him the site on her tablet. 'I have an entire floor fitted out into small offices that house over thirty different companies, right in the heart of the city, with access to a receptionist and three boardrooms. I enjoyed doing their product launches and we had some wicked office parties. But that's only part of it.'

He shook his head as he scrolled through the many images of a corporate world he'd never been privy to. 'I'd believe it, from one dish you make five.' Her entrepreneurial mind a wonder.

'I also help small businesses start, too.'

'Like you've been doing with me?'

'Except you're a much grander scale and I've never done livestock or primary industries before.' She waved at the scenery through the front window of his dusty ute. 'I'm talking small businesses, sole traders, when they first start out. It's my favourite part.'

'Why?'

'I remember how hard it was for me to start a business. Doing up business plans, websites, logos, business cards. Trying to get all this small stuff organised on the administrative side when all you wanted to do was the actual work of the job.'

'I hate the little details.'

'I know.' She grinned at him. 'I could also relate to these people because of my crappy education and having to go back to school to learn how to do business. So now I pass on what I've learned in layman's terms. Sole traders, especially tradesmen, want an honest sounding board for their business decisions and someone to keep an eye on bills, which is what my company does. For new businesses, I'll show my faith in their success by not charging them start-up costs but asking for a percentage of their profits instead. I know they'll do well and end up using my staff for bookkeeping too.'

'So that way you'll always know how they're businesses are going. To keep paying you?'

'Ah huh. My company offers heaps of other services to assist small businesses. From writing up grant applications to proofing annual reports and creating social media strategies. Darwin's so small a business community, everyone knows someone who needs help, so it's easy to network as well. Someone needs a plumber, I have ten on the books. You want a graphic designer for a logo, I have three on the books. I've even traded staff where I'd get a fee for connecting them or these services.'

'It sounds amazing.'

'Then it got pretty big, pretty quickly.' She sat back, rubbing at her temple as if fighting a migraine. 'I was working long days, seven days a week. I enjoyed the rush of going from one project to the next, and somehow it changed ... It became this chase to the next dinner party for the next deal, or for the next finder's fee. There were negotiations across boardroom tables, in cafes and bars. Taking conference calls in the gym or in airport lounges. I got so caught up living inside this bubble.'

'What happened to make you stop?'

Her shoulders slumped as she stared at her hands clasped in her lap. 'When I caught my ex in bed with this guy, it wasn't just that which upset me. Sure that hurt ...'

She looked so fragile. He gently rubbed at her tense neck. 'But?'

'The real issue was I'd been so caught in this little world, I never saw the obvious. If I hadn't been so wrapped up in my business, I would have realised my ex was gay. As much as he hurt me, I kinda feel like I let him down too.' She inhaled deeply, then faced him with such sad eyes he could see the scars of her life's past story. 'I got lost. And when I stopped and looked around me, I didn't like what I'd become, and I had no idea what to do or where to go. So I just went—no real plan, just travelling from place to place. Until I got the phone call from Rhonda to come here.'

'Are you still lost?'

'No.' She gazed out the window with a soft smile spreading across her lips. 'Danbunnan has helped me. I love this place and the people. Doing this project for you, and the many others I've done here, has been fun. It's so different to anything I've ever done before. Not only did this place take me out of my comfort zone, but it also brought me right back to the basics, like when I was a kid working in a kitchen. But different. Sure, the place triggered parts of my past, but I needed to face them and work through those issues. But there's no hidden agenda here. I wasn't working for profit margins. Sure I was streamlining and cutting costs, but it also made me remember how much I enjoyed helping people too.'

'What was your original plan for your company when

you started it?'

'It was on my *to-live list* to create a business that was self-sustaining. Where I could walk away from it while it kept making me money, and not get attached to it. I try not to get too attached to anything because I've been in a place where everything I had was taken from me.'

Did her lack of attachment include people? And him?

'I also hadn't realised the corporate world had swallowed me up. I never saw a sunset and never looked at the stars. I was so busy being busy, doing the same stuff in closed rooms, boardrooms, and airports, I forgot what it was like to breathe fresh air.' She inhaled deeply, as her eyes softened at the scenery through the front window. 'I would definitely have been too busy to sit in a ute and drink beer in front of a set of barra ponds as the water view of a golfing range.'

'Don't knock the driving range. It's been a great anger management tool for me. Do you want to see if you've improved any?' He cracked open his door.

'We should be working on your sales proposal.'

Jake took the tablet from her hands and closed the leather case. 'We've both been doing eighteen plus hour days, and we don't switch off unless we're goofing off together. How about we take a break and start fresh tomorrow? Let's live in this moment, babe.'

'Deal.' Her wide smile made his chest expand with pride as he helped her out of the passenger seat.

He kissed her lips, resting his forehead against hers to gaze into her wise eyes that showed her scars and the stars. 'Thank you, for being here.' She was the best thing in his world. It's a pity he couldn't keep her. But he could share the joy of today with her.

For tomorrow was another story …

# Twenty

The golden shimmering sunrise mirrored the land that spread further than the eye could see. Time stretched beyond a mere moment, where the dawn's hush had its own sound that increased as the sun crept higher over the expansive dusty horizon. Sienna watched the shadows disappear as the last of the men, in their convoy of vehicles, drove along the track that stretched like a long piece of red string. Leaving her at the homestead with one major mission for the day …

Determined, Sienna grabbed the large roll of plans, skipped past her thriving vegetable garden, crossing the horseshoe compound, aiming for the grand stone house that stood on the hill.

Even though her station was at the bottom of Danbunnan's employees list, she was about to overstep those boundaries. Today she was going to try and mend the rift that had ripped this family apart.

Through the outdated deserted kitchen, down the corridor of closed doors that once scared her, she stopped at Bob's bedroom and wiped her hands on her cook's apron. Smoothed over her hair, tightened the rolled plans in hand and took a deep breath before she tapped on the door.

Nothing.

With no time to waste she knocked again.

Still nothing.

But she knew he was hiding inside.

*Bugger him.*

'Bob. Bob. Bob. Bob. Bob. Bob,' shouted Sienna, knocking on his bedroom door.

'Go away.'

'Nope.' Her knuckles kept bashing on his door while holding that roll of paper in her other hand.

'Nick off.'

'Not today, I need your help. I'm coming in. Please don't make me come in there.'

The bedroom door whipped open and Bob glared at her with steely blue eyes, still in his pyjamas and bare feet. His grey eyebrows were so low they seemed like part of his eyes. 'What do you want, woman?'

'I want your help.'

'No, you don't. The place is working fine without me, find someone else to harass.'

'The men are busy, and I want to build a smokehouse.' She unrolled the plans and showed him. 'I want to make beef jerky and salamis.'

'Get a machine,' he growled and slammed the door in her face.

She burst in after him.

'This is my bedroom, woman.'

'Yeah, so what? Not the first time I've been in a man's room and don't go there, Bob, you're not my type. Get dressed, you're coming with me.' The room was big, dark, and musty and she didn't want to be in there any longer than necessary. But Sienna wasn't going to leave without the grumpy old man.

'Why?'

'Because it says I have to mix stuff for bricks and build stuff, from the stuff that Joe, our king of the junk pile, is sorting. I need your help because this is your great-grandfather's recipe.'

'Really?' He cocked a grey eyebrow at her.

'Yep.' She was hoping the ancestral connection would be enough to lure the ex-boss into leading this project. 'Everyone else is busy. But they've all told me you're the one who loves eating salamis. So that makes you the taste tester. Or should I call you the master of smoked goods?'

'What are you on about, woman?'

'Tom is the chilli king with his chillies and Anzac biscuits. Josh loves anything custard. Tyson ribs me if I overcook his choice meat cuts. The whole crew never holds back when it comes to their comments on cooked fish. Now it's your turn because you're the one with the refined palate for this product. So, I need you to get dressed and come with me. You've got five minutes, Bob.'

'Can I tell you to nick off?'

'You already did, that's twice now. So hurry up, or we won't have much time to perfect the recipe.' She closed the door and grabbed her phone from her apron's pocket and scanned over her list of much to do. The focus needed to complete a short-term project had the power to make her forget her own troubles. She was hoping this project would help Bob. 'I'm still here, Bob.' Tapping on his bedroom door.

'Nick off.'

'That's three. Come on, we've got loads to do and a deadline to beat.'

Bob opened the door, dressed. 'Why are you doing this? You know the boss hates me.'

'I'm not interfering with family business, Bob. I'm just the staff member in charge of kitchens for this competition. I've been told to use whatever resources are available that doesn't cost the company money. So, you're it.'

'What are we going to do?'

'We're going to build the best smokehouse ever, and I'll be your assistant today.' Hey, why not? So far in her time at Danbunnan, Sienna had shovelled chook poop, played in the gardens, done an office makeover, and had created a recycling centre. Originally hired to cook she'd fed feathered, furred, and scaled creatures, as well as humans, so this was just another new adventure. Who said station life was all about cows?

'Why isn't Elliott helping you?'

'Elliott is part of the painting party at the stockmen's quarters. Besides, Elliott doesn't know how to read a plan or do brickwork. I certainly don't. Do you?'

'Yeah.'

'See, all yours.' She forced the plans into Bob's hand then pulled him along by the shirt sleeve. 'Come on, I'll show you where I want it. You can tell me if it's a good spot or not.' She led Bob through the side door where he put on his boots and hat.

'You're not giving me a choice, are you?'

'No.' She couldn't let him hide in the house when he'd come so far. Hoping the father and the son could rebuild communications via food tasting sessions over salami.

'Does the boss know about this smokehouse?'

'Yes. It would cost over five hundred for a teeny tiny machine with consistent running costs for materials. I'd rather use that money on a commercial coffee machine. From what I've guesstimated, this homebuilt smokehouse will cost about twenty dollars to make, with zilch running costs.'

'A red-back? That's all?'

'Why are we talking about red-back spiders?'

'I'm not. Red-back is slang for the twenty-dollar bill.'

'Wow, another new word for the day.' Yes, the lingo of the land was an endless dictionary of discovery. 'There might be enough paint left over from the cattlemen's quarters for the smokehouse. If it needs painting? Hey, will paint melt from the heat?'

'I dunno about getting involved.' Shaking his head, Bob stopped on the edge of the verandah.

'Bob, you were instrumental with the muster room makeover and the office overhaul.' And he'd showed those places off with pride. 'This will be another signature building you've created, using a recipe from the Cullen line of men.'

'But—I ...' His shoulders slumped as he sighed heavily.

'I've made you an appointment this afternoon to talk to your mate over the phone, as an extra to your weekly appointment.'

'You did?'

'I don't think it'll hurt.' Sienna wasn't a counsellor and she'd only gotten to know Bob these past few months. If she'd met him as the old boss, she would've quit on day one.

But people changed. She believed that because it wasn't that long ago that she hadn't liked herself. 'So, let's keep moving forwards and enjoy this Goldilocks weather.' She hooked her arm around Bob's and led him towards the muster room, they had so much to do, with little time to do it.

# Twenty-one

It was late afternoon when Jake parked his ute in the worksched. The once cluttered benches were now cleared, and the concrete floor swept, but no one was around.

Voices echoed from the back, where he found everyone working by the flatbed truck. 'What's going on?'

'It's a junk party, Boss.' Joe gave a snort-laugh, wearing his toy crown over his oil-stained trucker's cap.

'You're literally playing king?' Jake chuckled, aware Sienna's cheap gifts she'd brought back from Elsie Creek were having a positive impact on his team's morale. It was needed after one of their own had hurt them.

'Boss.' Tom stepped in alongside. 'We're sortin' the junk for Lyn to take the first load to the recyclers.'

'Good. I don't think I've ever seen the back of these worksheds sorted out.'

'Me neither. But the truck's full of just aluminium beer cans.'

'Damn. I know we don't mind a cold beer on a hot day …'

'It's the Territory way, mate. Tomorrow we'll start on the other side. By the way, you've got a visitor.' Tom nodded towards the compound. 'Out back of the muster room.'

Around the corner, he found his best mate, without a shirt and in dirty jeans. 'Craig?'

Craig, the cocky cowboy, gave a wide smile. 'Well, it's about time you got back. This mob keep putting me to work.' Hands gripped, shoulders bumped, and backs were patted in a hearty greeting.

'What are you doing here?'

'I'm building a smokehouse, mate.'

The rectangular brick building resembled an outhouse without a roof.

'How did you get roped into this?'

'I hit up your relief cook for a cuppa and a feed. She said no worries, but only if I helped with the top layer of bricks on this thing.'

Sienna would've cleverly picked her mark. Craig liked to think he was a ladies' man, would've jumped at the chance to play hero.

'I've never built a smokehouse before. I did it with your dad, while that pretty cook ran off with your sister and the twins on a secret mission. Then I gave your crew a hand because I'm pretty sure I put a few of those cans out the back of those worksheds too.'

Jake glanced back at the cleared area that used to be piled with junk. They'd added to it over the years, even hiding there during school holidays to drink the beer they'd pinched from Bob. 'Are you chasing a cold one?'

'Mate, I've got an icy cold slab in the ute, with your name all over it. Hey, there's the slave driver now.' Craig's smile widened at Sienna coming around the corner.

Jake felt his own heart jump with the extra pump in the pulse at the sight of his lady, in her summer dress and half-laced town boots, with her sunglasses on, tablet in hand, her fair hair shining in the sun. What would she be like dressed up for her city job?

'It looks great, Craig. I'll put in a good word with the boss, he might let you stay for dinner,' said Sienna with Charlie beside her. 'What do you think, Jake?'

'Not much to look at, it's just a brick wall,' said Craig.

'That's why Charlie's here. He's our master of wood and water, who is going to provide the finishing touches.' Sienna handed the smokehouse plans to the bald stockman with the bushy Ned Kelly beard. 'Can I please have a door and high shelves? I'll hit up Joe for the hooks later.'

'No worries.' Charlie glanced over the plans, measuring tape in hand and pencil tucked behind his ear.

'Careful, the foundations are still settling,' said Craig.

'I want a smokehouse not a leaning tower for pizza goods,' said Sienna with a giggle. 'Jake, before I forget, when you get a chance can you check the invitations list, please? I need your final approval so I can send them out tomorrow?'

'Sure.' Jake winked at her. Damn, didn't her smile shine brighter than a sunrise. 'Come on, Craig, let's do a runner before she makes us do more work.'

Craig's head tilted towards Sienna as they walked past. 'Mate, I'd never leave the kitchen.'

'Don't go there, Craig. I don't need you breaking staff hearts when I need them focused on the job.' Jake frowned at Craig eyeing off his lady. If Craig knew, he wouldn't do it. Even though they were the best of mates with some codes that never got broken, this was one secret Jake couldn't share. 'Are you still playing golf?'

'Not for a while, why?'

'There's this driving range I visit this time of the day, it's a good place for a beer.'


'What the hell?' Craig stood with hands on hips, the same as Tom had done, when he'd first visited the barra ponds. 'You've got barra in that?'

'Yep, I'm farming fish.'

'But billabong barra? It's muddy this time of year.'

Jake was beginning to feel like a broken record as he gave Craig a rundown on the pond's history. 'Come on, I'll show you my driving range, while I do the pumps.' He climbed to the flat hilltop and frowned. 'What the—'

'Now that's cool.' Craig stopped beside him. 'This private driving range looks a bit flash, mate.'

'That's new for me, too.' Jake walked down the hill to where his simple net was no longer slung around the trunks of two spindly trees. It had been re-stretched tighter across two posts, with a sign on top that read *Danbunnan Driving Range*. In front of the net stood two painted targets, with holes in the centre, made from car bonnets. 'So new the paint's still wet.' He could smell it.

'I know.' Craig's laughter echoed over the ponds.

'How do you know?'

'Secret mission.'

'Give. Because last night this was littered with golf balls. We cleaned out every bucket and bag we had.' With Sienna for company, they'd used his ute's spotlights to illuminate the field, which attracted the bugs, making the barra jump for food, while they drank until late, smashing balls and watching fish jump.

'Don't look at me, mate, I just got here.'

'Where did all of the golf balls go?' Jake walked back to the pump shed where the pipes ran to the many ponds. 'No way.' Shiny tin buckets, filled with golf balls, sat beneath the old bench seat that used to sit outside the station kitchen. It used to be Sally's favourite place to sleep. But Sienna had bought her furry hero a new bed from her trip to Elsie Creek and had been proud for putting it together herself.

'Who's been decking out my private driving range?' Only one other person had a gate key to this area and liked her Goldilocks weather. 'Sneaky wench never let on.' Sienna was always surprising him.

'Come on, Craig, let's see if we can hit those new signs, while you tell me why the impromptu visit.'

Craig grabbed two beers from the fridge in the back of his dusty red ute and passed one to Jake. 'Your sister called me.'

'Why?'

'Jess said something happened last night. She's worried, mate. She said you might need to talk to someone. Even if you don't, it's a good excuse to drink beer.'

He'd thank his baby sister in the morning, knowing how sensitive Jess was. But where did he begin?

Jake pulled down the golf club from the corrugated roof and placed a ball on the tee that now sat in a strip of fake grass.

The cheeky wench must've had all this golf stuff stored in her toy-car while it was parked here last night. The lady was priceless.

He lined up the ball with a grin and *whack* …

The golf ball arced over the pond that reflected the sapphire skyline. It bounced off the newly strung net, onto the red dirt and rolled to a standstill. The place might seem peaceful now, but plenty of drama had erupted beneath its dusty surface only yesterday.

'Did Jess say what happened?' Jake asked.

'Only that you had some blue with your old man. Your dad's looking a bit bull-whipped there, mate.'

'I almost punched his bloody head in.' Jake scowled, then scrubbed it away with a rough palm across his face.

'What gives?'

Craig had witnessed Bob's treatment of Jake over the years. Mates from boarding school, then following the muster and rodeo circuit together, Craig had been there for it all. And here he was today, so Jake told all about the letter his mother wrote on her death bed.

'Bugger me.' Craig threw his empty can in the bin and got another round. 'So, what are you gonna do about your old man?'

'Nothing. I won't kick him out like he did with me.' If there was a spare cottage Jake would've moved in, but it didn't matter because he snuck into Sienna's room every night.

'I saw how good Bob is with Jess and the twins, playing granddad.'

'That was rough for a bit, too. It's because of the twins and my sister I haven't kicked the old man out to one of the outstations.'

'I was surprised to see Bob off the couch and working with Sienna. She was giving him cheek all day too. She single?'

'Don't go there, mate.'

'Ah huh?' Craig narrowed his eyes at Jake. 'How's your engagement going?'

'Angela and her dad visited the other day.'

'I wouldn't want Simon Simmons as my father-in-law. He'll take over, you know?'

'I'm biting my tongue until I've sold the cattle. I've got to make a sale, or I'm buggered.' And that meant being engaged to a woman he didn't love.

'What's happening with this then?' Craig nodded at the ponds.

'There's a few details to be completed before I can sell any.'

'Like what?'

'Licenses, transport, harvesting, and buyers. I've got someone putting out feelers now for those answers.' Sienna was his secret weapon.

Jake had deep bucketloads of respect for her, especially after last night, when Sienna had been there for him when he'd needed someone the most, never leaving his side until this morning.

'Did you get Barry out here to test these ponds?' Craig asked.

'Only the other day.'

'Our water boy's all grown up. Did he tell you he got engaged to Jenny?'

'He did and how we're playing groomsmen.'

'Just imagine the bridesmaids, mate.'

Why, when he had his own amazing lady—yet he couldn't tell anyone. 'Barry also told me he's having dancing lessons. Reckons he'll give you a run.' Would he ever get a chance to dance with Sienna one day?

'Never. Not when I've had years of experience,' said Craig, patting his puffed-out chest. 'Are you getting Ryan out here?'

'He's scheduled to visit in the next few days.'

'Does Ryan play with goldfish?' Craig grinned from behind his can.

'We'll find out soon enough. I've invited Ryan and Barry to the dinner. You're included. I could do with your help with the food tour.'

'I'm not sure on the boring table conversation. That's not me, mate, I don't do highbrow.'

'Me neither, but I'm learning. It's just a dinner party, no suit and tie, just a fancy feed to show off our produce.'

'I'd never say no to a decent feed, mate. So, count me in on the fancy dinner, the food tour, and definitely the shed party. I'll happily help anywhere, mate. I owe you stacks.'

'I appreciate it.'

'You know, it's all around the district about Bob accepting the competition nomination when Simon Simmons is saying you're producing pet meat. It's got people curious to see Danbunnan's first nomination.'

'Do you know who nominated Danbunnan?'

'Not a clue. But I do know you've got people talking about your organic techniques.'

'Good or bad?'

'It's a mixed reaction.' Craig shrugged, chugging back his beer. 'They want to see for themselves. And hey, Tom gave me a look at what you've got kickin' round the yard.'

'What do you think?' Because Jake truly respected Craig's opinion on cattle.

'You've got a prime herd, and I wouldn't spin the bull on that one. You've also got a great team who work well together and Tom's a good head stockman who knows his cattle.'

'Tom taught me.'

'I'm still willing to learn and Tom's got a great reputation. So if you're ever looking for stockmen, I'll toss my hat in the ring. Just don't put me in an office and make me do paperwork, I'm allergic to that claptrap.' Craig's blond curls shifted as he shuddered all over.

Jake chuckled. 'Fair enough.'

'Have you got anyone else lining up for work?'

'I've got loads of kids begging to be Danbunnan's next apprentice.' But Jake was wary after what happened with Annie.

'And that, my friend, is a good thing.' Craig patted Jake's shoulder, even raising his beer can in a salute.

'How?'

'If Simon Simmons and the co-op are saying your reputation's shot for cattle, it can't be. Not when you've got kids lining up to work here, and they'd know, their social media network is huge for sharing secrets.'

'That's because of Tom. He's the best at what he does.'

'But he's not Danbunnan's boss doing this.' Craig again tossed his thumb towards the ponds. 'Tom runs men and herd, on the instructions of his boss. He's happy doing what he is, you can see that. Did you know, he's had heaps of people offering him work elsewhere?'

'I'd guessed he might have, but I'm glad Tom never left.' Where would Danbunnan be without Tom forcing Jake to get up in the mornings, especially those times when Jake wanted to give in?

'Did you tell Tom about the letter? I just can't picture your mum and Tom's dad—' Craig cringed.

'I don't want to.' Jake shook his head. 'I haven't even told Jess yet. How the hell do I tell Tom?'

'I wouldn't wanna be in your boots for that conversation.'

'Look, if I have a vacancy, I might find your number.'

'In that case, I'll shout you another beer then.' Craig fetched a couple of coldies from the back of his ute. 'But I will never work for Simon Simmons.'

'That makes two of us.' Jake cracked open the beer can and drank deeply.

'You know Simon Simmons is ripping you off on purpose to get this place?'

'My future father-in-law is not hiding it, that's for sure.'

'But did you know, the co-op judges are getting a share

on what Simon Simmons will make in reselling your stock, if they keep blocking the sale of your beef?'

'No way!'

'It's true, mate. I had this hot date with one of the judge's wives who told all. She said her husband's planning a holiday to Bali on that payout.'

'That mongrel! I've been wondering how he was doing it.' Jake shook his head in anger.

'You're true competition now, with what you've got. Because I'm telling you, Danbunnan beef is not pet-meat standard. Any cattleman who knows his biz can see that.'

'Look, mate, I've kept the herd hidden and this fish farm quiet for a reason. I can't risk Simon finding out and dropping his offer, which is already lower than dirt prices. He's my last alternative. But he's snooping around, using his daughter as an excuse to visit.'

'I won't say nothing. So, have you got any other buyers? Coz I don't do sales.'

'Me neither. But it's a hurry-up-and-wait to find them.' And it was up to the winds of fate to decide on Danbunnan's future.

# Twenty-two

Fresh from the shower, Jake pulled on his shirt, heading into the kitchen. 'Morning, Jess. You're up early.' Or was he late?

'I wanted to catch you before you ran off with Craig.'

'Is Craig awake?'

'Dunno.' She turned on the new whisper-quiet kettle that had replaced the relic that cried like a choking curlew, waking everyone in the house.

'Craig told me you'd called him.'

'I was worried after you and Dad argued. What's going on Jake?'

'Here, read this.' He gave his baby sister their mum's letter and leaned against the counter to wait for her response.

'Oh, my word.' Jess's eyes widened as her fingers hovered over her open mouth.

'Yeah, that's how I reacted.' It's why he'd had Sienna read it to him. Since then, he'd re-read it dozens of times.

'Did Dad really destroy that chest? Because Dad throws nothing out.'

Jake scowled at the floor. 'Dumped it in the river.' *Stupid old fool.*

'So how many journals are left?'

'About a dozen, the original ones from our ancestors who'd started Danbunnan. They're with Sienna. She's using their recipes for the competition dinner. Some journal entries are even on the website and in our proposals.' Sienna had cleverly put these hidden things in plain sight.

'You should've seen Sienna yesterday. She banged on Dad's door and wouldn't leave him alone until he built that smokehouse. Are you going to ignore Dad? He's been good with me and the twins, you can tell he's trying to make up for the past.'

'Damage is done, I won't forget. But I've got other stuff to deal with.' Like saving the station from the circling vultures with his future father-in-law leading the charge.

Then Jake remembered Sienna had wanted him to go over the guest list for the dinner. He powered up his tablet, impressed he'd remembered to charge it after staggering inside last night.

'I know you bought that chair for Mum, but I'd love to chuck it, so Dad's not tempted to give up and sit on it again.'

The lounge room's open windows framed the sunrise that stretched beyond the roofs of the compound. It silhouetted the old reclining chair. A gift he'd proudly bought for his mother. Now ruined.

'Do it. And hey ...' He leaned over and gave his baby sister a peck on the cheek. 'Thank you for the golf sign and the targets at the ponds, they're brilliant. Was that your idea?'

'Sienna's. I needed to practise on something else before I did the front sign.'

'I'm impressed. We gave it a nudge last night, but never made it through the bullseye. Hey, is there anyone else you want to add to the guest list?'

'No, everyone I know is already coming. How long are your fiancée and her father staying? The cattlemen's quarters are booked out with the judges and your VIP guests, so I've saved the guest room for the Simmons. I don't think Dad or Mr Simmons will approve of Angela being in your room until you're married. Dad was like that with me.'

*Damn.* He hadn't thought of them and didn't want to. 'That's fine. I'm inviting Ryan, who'll bunk in with Craig. Barry and Jenny are coming and will need a room, they live together, so don't split them up.'

'They can have the twins' room, who can stay with me.'

He scrolled over to the guest list and there on top were the names Angela and Simon Simmons. *What the hell?* 'I've got to go.'

'Please don't hate Dad forever. He's trying and he's sorry. Anyone can see that.'

'I won't forget, Jess.' Was he ready to forgive? He was prepared to forgive his father for his nasty treatment as a child. But since he'd discovered the reason for that treatment, it was a struggle to forgive. Yet, with Bob disowning Duncan after they'd found out the truth...

And his mother, the woman he had on a pedestal, had a huge hand in damaging their family, too. She should have kept the secret to herself or said something sooner to not have everyone suffer like this. Then maybe, just maybe, Duncan would still be here today.

Slipping his hat on, he headed for the muster room.

And there she was, Sienna, the beautiful blissful break to his routine of days. Behind the counter, inside the muster room, giving her hint of a smile with eyes that glistened like diamonds in the sun.

This is how he liked his mornings—once out of her bed—with the scents of her fresh baked bread and cakes that mingled with the strong coffee aroma. He loved to sit with his elbows on the counter, watching the cook swivel in her skirts, while sipping the best coffee on the station, discussing plans for this upcoming event.

Jake nodded to Tom in his seat, his Akubra on its own reserved chair. The rest of the men spread out at the dining tables. While Craig leaned on the counter facing the kitchen, watching his lady. *Oi!* 'Morning.'

'Morning, Boss,' the crew mumbled.

'Morning.' Sienna slid his coffee across the counter.

'Ta.' Jake wanted to wink at her. He wanted to give her another one of those Hollywood kisses that made her eyes dreamy and her body pliant in his arms.

He'd missed her last night. But they'd gotten back late and didn't want to wake the one person who started earlier than the entire station.

'What service, mate.' Craig gave his cocky grin, leaning his hip against the counter. 'You get coffee with a smile, without even asking.'

'I'm a regular, not a ring-in like you,' said Jake.

'True that. Thank you for breakfast, Sienna, that's the best feed I've had in a long time.' Craig emptied his cup and grabbed a pen and paper from the bench. He scribbled on it, folded it in half, then held it out. 'This is for you, Sienna.'

'What's that?' Sienna asked. The oven timer rang its shrill bell, and her skirt swung as she moved to the oven.

'It's my phone number. I'll leave it here on the counter.' Craig placed the pen on top but never looked away from the relief cook. 'Next time you're in town, gimme a call.'

*Son of a bitch!*

With oven mitts, Sienna transferred a tray of hot bread onto the cooling racks. Not once did she look up at Craig or his number. 'Don't you work at a station that's out of range doin' a boundary run?'

'Usually. But I'm only an hour out of town. I'd love to buy you dinner sometime, let the cook have the night off. And if I hear of any cook's work going, I'll let you know?' The cocky cowboy gave his wide smile that won him many a lady.

'Oi, Boss here. Stop chatting up my staff.' *And my lady.*

The other men in the muster room scowled as if they were ready to help throw Craig out the door.

'Mate, once word gets out about this swanky dinner your relief cook is making, work is gonna come at her left, right, and centre. You wait, Sienna, it's coming.'

*Damn.* Craig was right.

'I'm not that popular.' Sienna laughed, stepping into her favourite hiding place, the coldroom.

'A decent station cook's hard to find, you know. I'll talk you into a date when I return for the party.' Craig then nodded to the men. 'Catch ya later, fellas. Thanks for a top afternoon yesterday. Tom ...' He held out his hand to

Danbunnan's 2IC.

'Craig. Thanks for the help.' Tom shook the younger man's hand.

'No worries. If you ever need an extra stockman, gimme a call.'

'I'll have to talk to the boss first.' Tom picked up his mug, expressionless as always.

Jake glared at the paper with Craig's number that lay on the counter. 'I'll walk you out.'

'All right, you mob, it's time to move out,' called out Tom, and the men shuffled for the door.

Craig collected his hat off the horseshoe rack, and they headed to the red ute adorned with aerials and spotlights. Its tailgate was covered in stickers of the many places they'd been. 'So, Boss, you should be proud of yourself, it's the best I've seen this place.'

'Thanks. And thanks for the session last night.' Jake shook Craig's hand.

'No worries. You've been there for me plenty of times, it's what mates do. I'll catch you at the competition, and don't be shy to call me anytime.' Craig opened his driver's door with its familiar creak.

'Will do. You stay outta trouble.'

With a fingertip salute against his hat's brim, Craig shared that cocky smile the ladies loved.

'I wish.' Jake watched the red ute until the dust settled. It was soon followed by the small convoy of work vehicles. '*Sienna*?'

'Here,' she replied, coming out of the coldroom with a handful of containers.

'I'll get the esky.' Elliott fled through the side screen door in the blink of an eye.

'Your mate's a major flirt,' she said, going back into the coldroom.

'What happened to Craig's number?'

'I don't know? It must have blown off.'

'Are you going call him?'

She kicked the coldroom door shut and dumped an assortment of vegetables on the bench. 'Are you serious?'

'He was flirting with you, I don't like it. You could've told him to stop.'

'It's just a game to Craig. I already told him no a few times yesterday. And how's your form? When I've never said anything about you and your fiancée playing happy families.'

*Happy families? Ha, there was no such thing.* 'Why is Angela and Simon on the dinner list? Only the judges and guests do dinner.'

'Your fiancée needs to be present at all events.'

'Why?'

'Because she's *your fiancée* who's there to support you. And her father, your future-father-in-law, is there to escort her. It's considered proper protocol. They'll be offended if you don't invite them, especially as they're part of the industry. It'll look odd if they're not there.'

She made a good point, but it meant making his fake engagement public.

'When do you think we can slot in a practice dinner?'

'Why do we have to have a practice dinner? Do I have to invite Angela then too?'

'You can invite whoever you want. But the practice dinner is because the kitchen needs to work out the menu kinks for service. The men want to perfect their new waiter skills, and your dad and sister aren't sure about their table manners. None of your team have done this before, and this will boost their confidence, which will only make you look good on the night.'

'Okay-okay. Do the practice dinner with no outsiders.' He didn't know what fork went with what either.

'Why did you make Craig build the smokehouse?' asked Jake.

'All the ladders were being used at the cattlemen's quarters and I didn't want your dad to stand on a crate, so Craig volunteered to do the taller parts.'

'Without his shirt on?' His anger was bristling in ways

he'd never experienced before. Especially over his best mate.

'Are you serious?' She matched his frown. 'Did you see me there? I showed up after you because I was busy elsewhere.'

'Doing what?'

'Here it is.' Elliott barrelled through the side door with the large esky.

'I'll take it with me, Elliott.' Jake wanted to say so much more. But couldn't. 'This is beginning to suck,' he grumbled as he walked towards Elliott, who was oblivious to the heated conversation.

'You're telling me,' she snapped back, going in the opposite direction.

'Grab a handle, Elliott.' Jake hated the sight of her walking away while mad at him.

But he was ticked, too.

They couldn't have a normal relationship. Plus, the pressure was building and time was running out over this competition. The mounting bills were biting his back like hellhounds bringing the heat, and there was so much to do, so much to say, yet he didn't know how to say it.

Instead, he walked away, because Danbunnan had to come first.

# Twenty-three

Sienna stewed on their argument all day. Even now, while standing at the sink washing the last of the dishes, she couldn't shake it free from her mind. She'd lost her focus, distracted by their heated conversation this morning.

She knew the pressure was building for Jake. Unlike Jake, working under pressure was one of her strengths.

As a chef she had to cope with the intensity of mealtimes. If she wasn't prepped enough, it was a nightmare. If her planning was perfect, it was like a dance across the kitchen tiles with a twirl of the tongs, giving her a huge adrenalin rush.

But this was different. She was putting everything into this—only for Jake to question her.

Didn't he trust her? She'd never given him any reason to be jealous.

But then she'd trusted her ex and look how freaking fantastic that turned out.

Fact: she had four weeks left on Danbunnan. Then she was out the gate and back to her own world.

But she didn't want to think that far ahead, when she needed to focus on the upcoming weeks, and she'd been enjoying the work—until today.

She was also tired from a lack of sleep because, like a fool, she'd waited for Jake to visit her.

But she got nothing. He never showed. And he never offered her any excuses.

Such was the plot of their one-sided love story.

She never found Jake, he found her. Always at the times that suited Jake, at secluded locations on the property. But only when he was ready.

Since when did she become the boss's biatch to be at his beck and call?

What the hell had she become? When she wanted flowers, dinners, romance, and conversation.

So okay, conversations with Jake were phenomenal. She liked how he taught her to catch a fish, and how to hit a golf ball while watching sunsets together. She'd enjoyed showing him how to use her camera, where his eye for photos was a brilliant and unrealised natural talent.

Yet she was unable to brag about her boyfriend's talents or achievements because he wasn't her boyfriend. She couldn't even hold his hand or tousle his hair in public.

Sadly, all forms of affection were restricted to the times he'd made himself available to her. That was mostly when he snuck around in the dark.

And like a fool, she'd always been there for him.

When was he there for her?

She pulled the plug from the sink and dried her hands. 'Night everyone.' She picked up Sally's bowl, leaving through the screen door. 'Sally?'

From her new bed the cattle dog rolled to her feet, her nails click-clacking across the floorboards. With lolling tongue ready for action, she sat and waited for dinner.

'Here you go, girl. *Bon appétit.*'

The bowl met with the snout first, and in a matter of moments the dish would be pushed across the deck until it was licked clean.

Sienna craned her neck back to face the night skies. The galaxies felt so close, it was as if she could balance them on the tip of her nose, where satellites spun their colours amongst the stars that held countless wishes. How many of her own wishes had come true?

'Making a wish?'

'Jake?' Her heart pounded from fright.

Leaning his shoulder against the outer wall, he was hidden in the shadows.

Once he'd been her full moon, driving away the shadows of her night. Except now she wanted to cry at the disappearing slither of a moon's glow that represented their untouchable unspoken love.

'Babe?' He reached out to grab her hand.

'Don't.' She stepped away from him, digging nails into her palms to stop herself from touching him. 'Don't call me that.'

'Don't you like it?'

She did, that was the problem. 'I don't want you to accidentally say it in front of the others.' She did it to protect Jake because it was all about Jake.

'Are you still angry at me about this morning?'

'You were angry first, remember.'

'I'm sorry I was jealous of my mate. Look, if Craig knew he'd treat you like a friend or a sister.'

'So, Craig doesn't know?'

'No one does.'

'And that's how it will remain.' A dirty shameful secret because he was sleeping with the staff while engaged to another woman.

'Have you spoken to Tom about the letter?'

'No. I did talk to Jess about it, this morning.'

'Good. I could see your sister was upset, but I didn't say anything.'

'You never do. But it upsets you about Angela, doesn't it?'

'When it shouldn't, because it's not my place.' She inhaled deeply, desperate to keep her strength as she said, 'I'm calling in our agreement.'

'No—'

'We agreed when we started this, that if we ever found it too hard …'

'Don't—'

'… we'd stop.'

'No, Sienna. Please don't do this.'

She pressed her hand to his chest. It had to be said now or never. 'You need to focus, Jake. I can count the weeks before I leave on one hand. We have so much to do and we can't let our emotions interfere with what we're hoping to achieve. Especially you. This is your business. Your livelihood. This is your future that everyone is counting on. You also need to call your fiancée and invite her to the dinner so she can get herself and her father organised.' There was more than one family involved in all this. And she wasn't a member of either of them.

'I don't want them here. I never wanted this engagement to be … real.'

'You need to remember why you're doing this, Jake. If I wasn't here, would you be so hesitant to invite Angela and her father and make your engagement public?'

His head dropped in defeat.

'I won't be the cause of any more distractions to your business.' He had too much at risk for everyone's sake.

'And what about you?'

Finally, he asks, but it was all too late. 'I'm doing this for me too. Believe me, I'm sorry.' She reached up and kissed his cheek as hot tears spilled.

'Sienna, please don't.'

'Night, Jake, get some rest. I'll still make your coffee in the morning, whether you drink it or not.'

She walked fast to her room, her vision blurred by her tears. Without looking back, and with shaky fingers she closed her door and slid to the floor.

Hugging her knees, she cried as her heart splintered into millions of shards that stabbed like ice into her chest, clawing at her raw throat as the unstoppable tears burned.

It was as if every past painful event in her life was piled up together, then doubled into this one crushing moment that hurt so much more.

But it had to be done today.

She had to finish this one-sided love story. Holding on to something she could never have was more exhausting than letting him go. She needed to return to that place before heartache had become a part of her everyday reality, which meant running from the only thing that felt like home to her—was him.

# Twenty-four

Jake sat in the office, frowning at the unopened golf kit, lying on the shelf. He just didn't have the heart to play with Sienna's gift.

She'd called in their agreement, the end of their affair. He thought he'd been prepared for this because he knew she was eventually leaving. Staff always did, where all that remained was the family and the dirt beneath his boots. But Sienna had meant more to him than any of the staff who had come and gone over the years.

He swung in his chair and eyed the photos on the wall. The black-and-white images of the original owners, his ancestors, Henry and Winifred Cullen. Droving their first herd from Queensland had taken over two years, costing the life of half the herd and their first-born child before they arrived on Danbunnan's soil.

They'd built this house by hand, carting river rocks to create a home. The evidence of their legacy covered the office wall, his family's history showcasing their achievements, their sacrifices, their lives—way back since 1885.

Now here he was playing with Danbunnan's future, trying to keep this station alive—no matter the personal costs to his soul.

'Bugger it.' Jake snatched up the phone. He'd been procrastinating over making this call. It was all about protocols and politics, for what? For the bloody neighbours' sake, or for the buyers he had yet to find.

Which meant keeping the one and only buyer he had

happy.

'Hello, Simon Simmons speaking,' came the gravelly baritone over the phone.

'Morning, Mr. Simmons, it's Jake Cullen.'

'Morning, lad. You're early.'

'I was hoping to catch Angela before she got a start to the day.'

'Sure, I'll call her.' Something muffled the phone, stifling Simon's shout, '*ANGELA, Jake's on the phone* ... So, how are your competition preparations going, lad?'

'Getting there. I'm hoping you'll be available to come with Angela for the competition stuff.' There he'd said it, and now he hoped for a no.

'I'm not a judge.'

No, Simon Simmons owned the judges. 'I'm not sure what the judges want with my beef, that's almost sold as yours. Of course, you'll understand I've got to try and find a better price, being my first muster as Danbunnan's boss.' Was his BS too thick in trying to con a conman?

'I've been trying to get you a higher price, lad, but no one's touching the Danbunnan brand. It's considered pet meat, you know. I'll have to re-brand them to sell them because reputation is everything in the cattle industry.'

Jake could hear a chair creak like it was about to break under the gloating toad. 'Being a man of your reputation, it'd be good to have you present for the judging?' Jake tried not to gag at his own suck-up to the head vulture ready to pick this place clean.

'Sure, I'll be there.'

*Damn.* 'The invitation will be emailed through shortly.' Shame he couldn't blame it on losing it in the snail mail anymore. 'It'll be a dinner on Friday night at the house, a tour the next day, with a shed dance on Saturday night.'

'Aren't you doing a rodeo?'

'We can't afford it. Besides, I don't keep rodeo horses. So, it's a basic feed and drive-by of the station.'

'Wouldn't bother, lad, the judges won't wanna see too

much. But then again, few people have been beyond Danbunnan's homestead, only the staff.'

'We've never been able to show the place off before, not with Dad being a judge. But you've been in plenty of these competitions.'

'I have.'

'Have you got any tips?' Should he throw up at his own words?

'Good feed, good cattle, and show the work crews a good time. That's it.'

'*Daddy*,' cried Angela's voice in the background.

'One more thing, before I go, young Jake?'

'Yes, *sir*.' Jake now understood why Sienna used *sir* like a swear word.

'I'll happily give you a loan. Of course, there's a bit of paperwork involved, but it's there any time you need it.'

'Thanks, I'll keep that in mind.' No doubt the interest rate would be so steep he'd foreclose in a month—just like Simon Simmons had done to the other neighbouring stations, increasing his empire by crushing the competition, with Danbunnan now in his sights.

They'd have to bury him in the family cemetery before he let Danbunnan go to another man's hands.

'*Daddy*, Jake phoned me, remember,' cried out Angela in the background.

'Now, look here young Jake, call me anytime you need advice from a man who made it himself. I'm not like your father, who had it all handed to him. And there's no shame in walking away, either. I'm quite able to write off all that stress with a cheque, today.'

No doubt at a quarter of what the land was worth. Could you put a price on a life's legacy of blood, sweat and tears?

'I appreciate the offer, sir.' Jake rolled his eyeballs. If there was anything he'd learnt from Simon, it was how to crush a man while they're down.

Angela's bubbly voice came over the phone. 'Heya, Jake.

You're early? What's up?'

'Can you come to Danbunnan's competition dinner? I've emailed you the invite.'

'Dinner?'

'Yeah.'

'Why?'

'I'd like my fiancée there, please?'

'Oh, right.' Angela giggled. 'Can I get a new dress?'

'Sure.' Hoping he didn't have to pay for it because Angela had an expensive taste.

'Goodie.' She clapped her hands in the background. 'Heya, I've been meaning to call and warn you that Daddy's got all the judges tucked away in his pockets.'

'Angela, where's your father?'

'Outside, I can see him talking to Pete. Did you know Daddy's had the judges here? Pete's livid over it and he told me some of the other neighbouring crews are too.'

'What for?'

'Daddy's stacking the market, calling your stuff pet meat. Daddy's also offering to share the profit from the resale of your stock to the judges in the co-op if they keep blocking you from selling. They know it's good stock and Daddy told them he's offering you below dirt price.'

'I know.'

'You do?'

'Craig told me.'

'I should've known, Cowboy Craig gossips worse than the girls. But it's wrong. Pete says Daddy's monopolising the co-op. If Daddy buys Danbunnan's beef cheap, what chance do the other stations have in getting a fair price for their future herds too?'

Jake hadn't thought of that. But he wasn't doing this for the neighbours when he was just trying to survive.

'Please tell me what I can do for you, Jake. I want to help you, I do.'

'You are, Angela. What you're doing means a lot. Look, Jess has you booked in for the guest room to share with your father. I'm sorry, you can't sleep in my room.'

'Aww, why not?' They both laughed.

'Not until we're married. Dad wouldn't let Jess do it.'

'Sometimes you've gotta love a tradition.'

'You're not offended?'

'Gotta have a thick skin living in this house. And heya, there's a murmur running through the mob about Danbunnan being in the competition. Heaps of people know who you are.'

'What? That I'm the stupid mug trying to save my family legacy?' How soon could he get out from under this gossipers' microscope?

'Everyone knows Danbunnan was ruined and that the long-lost son, the Black Prince, has returned to save the family station. It sounds kind of romantic, doesn't it?'

'Sienna would agree if she heard that.' Sienna loved all things romantic, none of which he could give her, of course. *Damn,* he was such a selfish prick. His heart suddenly felt like a chunk of cold coal, as his heavy head fell against his desk, defeated.

'Is that the relief cook? Heya, can't you keep her? Because I don't want Daddy to sack China to bring in a pretty face. China's been here for years.'

Jake winced as his heart squeezed like a dish rag oozing all liquid happiness from his soul. 'I can't. Rhonda returns from her holidays soon.' Too soon.

'Oh, heya, everyone thinks the fundraiser's a great idea, which includes me. So expect a big donation from Daddy's chequebook for that one. I miss your brother.'

'Me too.' Would his big brother, Duncan, approve of the changes and all the risks Jake was taking for this competition?

'So, who nominated you?'

'Wasn't it Simon?'

'No. Daddy doesn't know and asked a few of the judges. I know Daddy was shocked that Danbunnan got nominated in the first place, because it kind of ruins his plans of buying you out on the cheap.'

Well, that killed Jake's theory on this competition being a pre-liquidation sale. So who nominated Danbunnan?

'Look, I've got to catch my work crew. So, do I put you down as a yes?'

'Dinner, yes. New dress, definitely. I'm happy to help set up for the dance or anything you want, I'll be there.'

'Thanks, Angela, for everything.'

'I loved Duncan, too. See ya.'

Jake leaned back in his seat and checked it off the competition's to-do list. If he presented Danbunnan well enough, it should earn him a right to be part of the co-op and sell his cattle.

Even though he hated to admit it, Sienna was right. He had to keep his focus and maintain the façade of his fake engagement to Angela. If this whole thing didn't pan out, the backup plan was selling his soul to save this station.

# Twenty-five

Sienna kept herself scarce from Jake and everyone else, focusing on nothing more than the project. Something had to give and soon. If she didn't find any buyers, then all this sacrifice and hard work was for nothing.

Jake was counting on it. Everyone was.

She'd kept to her side of the kitchen counter and still made his coffee, timing it with her best morning view of Jake and his perfect fitting jeans. The view that once brought her joy now released lead weights that dragged razor-sharp hooks to shred what was left of her heart. The damage was irreparable. Worse than what she'd ever gone through with her ex-fiancé, who she now realised she'd never really loved, not like this.

Because she was soul-deep in love with Jake.

Sadly, it would take a thousand deaths to forget this one love. It was such a beautiful tragedy, with an ache that could only be soothed by the one she could never have. For she was nothing more than his dirty secret affair.

Now, she was all business focusing on this project to hide her heartache. It's all she had left. She couldn't run away from this. Danbunnan was home to these people, and she'd sworn to Rhonda she'd stay. And Sienna owed Rhonda.

A phone rang in the distance.

She cocked her head at the unfamiliar sound that used to be so common in her world. The land of phones, cars, smog, and the perfume clouds of many in crowded elevators, to the chorusing click-clack of shoes carrying across the concrete that made up her everyday life.

Now the dead weight of suffocating dread filled her at the thought of returning to that world.

The ringing stopped at the farmhouse, and it wasn't long before the twins tore across the compound.

'SIENNA,' shouted Aaron, beating his little sister to the doors. 'There's a phone call for you up at the office.'

'Uncle Jake said you've gotta come now, it's long distance.' Kate huffed and puffed, pulling on Sienna's hand.

'Elliott, in case I'm not here, this pack of morning tea, thermos and extra travel mug is for Jake.'

'Are we getting visitors?' Elliot asked, flinging the tea towel over his shoulder.

'Boss's business. Come on, twins, I'll race you.' She dashed across the compound, climbed the stone steps of the grand house. New plants were flourishing in the once-empty pots, and the verandah was free of cracked paint, swirling dust, and cobwebs.

She passed the front door she'd never seen open, through to the office to find Jake at his desk.

'Um, morning,' she squeaked out.

Jake looked far too good in his tight T-shirt showing off his strong muscular arms and toned chest. He had the figure of a working man. A real man. Her lungs squeezed the last of her air, and she fisted nails into her palms to stop the need to hug him.

Jake's chair rolled back as he stood. 'Morning, I'll give you some privacy.'

'Ah, yeah.' She stepped in, Jake stepped out, their chests barely millimetres apart, the closest they'd been in days.

She inhaled his soap and deodorant. But his normally shaven chin had a few days' worth of stubble, and his blue eyes were rimmed with red. The emotional pain etched on his face was also carried across his shoulders.

'Your coffee's ready.'

'Thanks.' With a nod, he looked at her, like really looked

at her. It made her heart cry out for him like a child raising their arms, demanding comfort.

But Jake was engaged to another woman; he ran a station the size of a European country, and had a family to care for. Sienna only had herself.

'Hello,' she said on the outdated phone that had a curling cord. How long had it been since she'd spoken on a landline?

'Sienna, it's Karl.' One of her former colleagues who she'd been in contact with trying to set up buyers.

'Karl, why are you calling me on this line?'

'You have no mobile reception.'

'I told you to email me.'

'Darling, do you want some good news or not?'

'I'd love some good news, my friend.' It was time to put on her game face to try and forget her pain.

***

'Twins, go finish your breakfast.' Shooing them back into the house, Jake hesitated for a moment by the office door. Sienna sounded happy talking on the phone, and her delicate floral fragrance lingered.

Sadly, she'd become a piece of priceless art in the museum, where you could look but never touch. Even though his hands itched to slide across her skin, he clenched them into fists.

Once she'd been his safety net, his friend and lover, now they were nothing but two passing bodies in a doorway. She would soon return to her world, and he'd be stuck here.

Why hadn't they met before he'd returned to Danbunnan?

Heading back into the house, Jake was curious to know who Sienna was talking to on the phone, and whether it related to the competition. It had sounded like a long-distance connection. But, then again, everywhere outside of Danbunnan was a long-winded hike.

'Who was that on the phone?' Jess asked, seated at the

kitchen table, where the twins had resumed slurping away at their cereal.

'Someone for Sienna.' Jake wanted to talk to Sienna too. But now it was like a heavy rubber band had strapped itself around his ribcage to squeeze his lungs whenever he tried to speak to her. Once he used to spill everything to her, but not anymore.

Jake grabbed his hat and headed for the muster room, even if the suspense was killing him. If Sienna had any news, she'd find him.

'Morning, Boss.' Elliott plonked his travel mug on the bench. 'Sienna said this thermos and morning-tea pack is for you.'

'Thanks.' Jake grabbed the cup, the aroma familiar and the flavour hers. But she wasn't here. So he turned to face the person who had been on Danbunnan since before Jake was born. 'Tom, the vet's coming in this morning to conduct some tests on the herd.'

'Is there something wrong?'

'I'm getting him to prepare a medical report.' Jake knew Ryan would be blunt about the results, which is just what Jake needed, support from a mate.

'To present to the judges?'

'And any buyers.' If Sienna found any. 'The vet will be checking out the barra, too. So, boys, it looks like you'll be going fishing today.'

'We never took the rods out of the ute, Boss,' said Tyson, nudging his best mate Josh.

The pair's camaraderie reminded Jake of working musters with Craig. Of boarding school meals with Craig and Barry and Ryan. 'Josh?'

The young jackaroo sat taller, giving an eager nod. 'Yes, Boss?'

'Can you see Joe about clearing an area for your snake cages?'

'Why?'

'Aren't you and Tyson going to bunk together for the

competition?'

'Yeah mate, I'm not sleeping with no snakes when I've got my own one-eyed python.' Tyson chuckled, safe to indulge in trash-talk because the lady was no longer in the room.

'My wife would appreciate not being near any snake cages when she's cleaning,' said Charlie, seated nearby, stroking his long beard like a cat's back.

'But, but …' Josh faced Jake with puppy-dog eyes like he was about to have his baby blankie taken from him.

'Don't stress, Josh, it's a recommendation from the ranger for your snake permit. Look, the vet's a mate of mine and he'll just have a chat with you.'

'Thanks, Boss.' Relief flooded Josh's face. 'So, I'll be hanging with the king of the junk pile for the day?'

Tyson asked, 'Can we take that crown off him?'

'I'm surprised the bloody thing's lasted this long,' said Charlie with a chuckle.

Jake leaned against the counter and grabbed a muffin, grinning at the men. It was still a café atmosphere, just no Sienna.

Then he spied Sienna coming out of the office. The spring in her step, that seductive swing of her skirt, the lush peek of those legs that led to heaven he'd tasted.

He swallowed down the desire that settled into a lump of heated concrete in the centre of his chest.

When she was halfway across the compound the phone rang again.

'*Sienna, phone call!*' Jess called from the office doorway.

Sienna turned and bounded up the steps again.

'That giggly girlie might be on the phone all day, Boss,' muttered Tom as Sienna disappeared into the office.

Was Sienna getting calls to work at other stations, being so close to the end of her contract?

# Twenty-six

Jake leaned against his ute with his tablet in hand, his coffee rested on the bonnet. Ahead in the morning haze, a small fixed-wing aeroplane landed on the dusty airstrip. It taxied back towards him and slowed to a stop. The door opened and out jumped the pilot, dressed in cargo pants, a polo shirt with the collar flicked up and boat shoes. His thick black hair was shoved straight up behind his aviators. With freckles on his nose and green eyes, Ryan stepped out like a millionaire landing at the yacht club. But he wasn't. 'Your airstrip has more holes in it than a moth-eaten quilt, mate.'

'Good to see ya too, brother.' Their palms slapped together in a strong grip followed by a hearty man-hug. 'Is the strip that bad?'

'It has a few potholes. I've landed on worse.'

'I'll put it on the list.' Jake grabbed his tablet and added it to the list. *Huh*, he'd been trained.

'Look at you, the Black Prince and his tablet of stone.'

'Smart arse.' Grinning at the cretin.

'Are you civilised out here, yet?' Ryan tapped on the edge of Jake's screen.

'Yes, but we've still got no reception. But they do come in handy.'

'I agree.' Ryan grabbed his large bags from under the plane's cargo hold. 'So, Barry filled me in on the ponds you've got, and I also believe I'm here to do beef and snakes too?'

'I've got a jackaroo the crew calls the snake whisperer

going for a permit with the rangers.'

'I'd heard you had a snake bite the other week.'

'Where do I begin?' It'd been a while since they'd spoken, but they were the type of mates you could pick up a conversation as if it was yesterday.

'You drive and talk, mate. And if you need it, I'll gladly volunteer for the dinner and food tour you've got happening. Craig told me what Simon Simmons is doing. Craig said he's inspected your stock and swears you don't have pet meat.'

'Craig said you only did goldfish.' Jake's grin was mirrored by Ryan's.

'And lots of pampered purse puppies.'

'I've heard Sienna say that to someone, once.'

'Sienna?' Ryan gave a sly smile. 'Is this your relief cook I've heard about?'

'What did Craig and Barry tell you?' His protective feelings for Sienna were strong, even if they weren't together anymore.

'That she's a great cook and that you're engaged to Angela.' Ryan rubbed at his hair that stuck up any way it wanted. 'I thought she was Duncan's girl.'

'Angela's been helping me out. And you don't need an invitation to visit, mate. Look, I'm sorry I haven't kept in contact, but I just didn't want to impose on you when I couldn't afford your services.'

Ryan's jaw dropped as he leaned over the ute's bonnet. 'Brudder, you've helped me out so much over the years I've been waiting for you to ask. And this goes way back to boarding school, when you stopped those kids who were bullying me. So, where do we start, Boss?'

'Cattle first, stock horses and cattle dogs while you're here, and we've got some buffalo too.'

Ryan climbed into the passenger seat. 'Sounds like my day is fully booked, so lead on, brudder. And, coz I'm a professional you can't afford, I'll be brutally honest as always on your stock.'

'That's what I'm hoping for.' Jake put the ute into gear

and the tour for the health check on his herd began.

Ryan swivelled on the muster room verandah, staring at the compound. 'The homestead has never looked like this before. What the hell happened here?'

'Sienna's what happened. She's been working on it.' Since the first week she'd arrived.

'It looks good, mate. So where is this relief cook?'

'She should be here.' Jake poked his head inside the kitchen. Her music was on, and her coffee and bakery aromas filled the air, but no Sienna. He looked towards the cook's quarters where her red car was parked. '*Sienna*?'

She walked around the back corner with Sally at her side. 'Hey, lunch is ready.' Skipping up the steps in her simple cotton dress, with her smile wide and gracious. As a whole she was stunning.

'Oi, mate?' Ryan nudged Jake in the ribs.

*Bugger.* Busted by Ryan for admiring the lady. This separation sucked because he wasn't sleeping well without her. 'Sienna, this is Ryan.'

'The flying vet?' She shook hands with Ryan.

'And part-time friend to Jake. Hey, isn't that Duncan's old dog?' Ryan pointed to the blue dog seated by Sienna's half-laced purple town boots.

'Sally's more like Sienna's shadow these days.' The dog defended Sienna as a faithful companion and was spoilt in return. Jake got used to being spoilt by the lady, and what did he do for her? Nothing. How selfish was he?

'Sally's not my dog. I don't know how to look after them,' replied Sienna.

'Luckily, I do.' Ryan squatted to pat Sally. 'Did Jake tell you about Sally?'

'He told me Sally wouldn't bite me when he taught me how to pat her, and that Sally's a good snake dog.'

It wasn't all that bad, Jake had taught her how to pat the dog, to fish, and hit a golf ball—which she was lousy at. He also wanted to show her everything this place had to offer, but they were running out of time.

'Sally is one of the finest breeds of cattle dogs around. Duncan used to show her,' said Ryan, inspecting the dog's fur, teeth and even her ears.

'Did Sally get all glammed up and parade amongst the other purse puppies at those dog shows?'

'Told you she used that term,' said Jake, chuckling to himself. 'Sally's not that kind of show dog.'

'Cattle dog competitions are shows of obedience and stance, as well as performing time trials for herding cattle,' said Ryan. 'Sally won a lot of gold in those time trials. Duncan made a small fortune on her puppies.'

'Since when?' Jake asked.

'I think you were working out west then. I've got one of Sally's grand-daughters at home.'

'So, is Sally okay?' Sienna asked Ryan.

'Sally is in excellent condition. She's old, so don't expect her to run hard, but she's healthy.' Ryan gave the dog a hearty pat. 'Don't feed her onions or chocolates.'

'I don't.' She opened the door. 'Gentlemen, lunch is ready. Handbasin is past the bench on the left by the screen door.'

'Same place as last time.' Ryan wiped his boots on the mat before stepping inside. 'Whoa, what happened to this place? I'm at the wrong cattle station.'

'Sienna did, that's what.' Jake was proud of her efforts, holding the door open to let her through first.

'Jake, I have an idea on diversification. Now the vet's here ...' Sienna scrunched up her shoulders.

'Go on.'

'I have questions to do with buffaloes, the smokehouse, and puppies.' She grinned wide.

'Hey, I deal with puppies,' said Ryan, heading to the small handbasin.

'It's just an idea because I don't know pets or cattle.'

No, she feared the Brahmans he bred. 'Why don't you

join us for lunch and explain your ideas.' He could count the times he'd dined with her on one hand.

'I can do that.'

At least he could enjoy these snippets of happiness in what little time he had left before Sienna left him for good.

# Twenty-seven

When Danbunnan's work crew entered the muster room one by one that late afternoon, there was no Sienna or Elliott, and no red car parked at the cook's quarters.

'Where's the kitchen crew?' Josh asked, lifting the lid on the biscuit tin that sat next to the urn.

'The banyan tree, I'd reckon.' Tyson reached for the wide screen's remote control. 'We usually don't come in this early.'

'There's no Sally around, I'd say that's where they've gone.' Tom picked up a mug and began to make himself a cuppa.

'I've put in an order with the cable contractor for wi-fi in the muster room, so they don't have to work out there.'

Jake searched for the familiarities he enjoyed in the muster room, but there was no coffee pot made. Only Sienna's super-stock simmered in the corner on the wood stove. There was no music and no lights. The kitchen wasn't going to be the same without her in the not-too-distant future.

'Don't ask me about wi-fi,' said Charlie.

'Do you even own a phone?' Josh asked.

'I do. My wife carries it because I've drowned too many of them.'

The familiar rumble of the red toy-car cruised past with the *doof doof doof* of thumping music, its occupants hidden behind tinted windows, parking under the lean-to at the cook's quarters.

'Have you found a buyer yet?' Tom asked Jake.

'Not yet, but I have faith, Tom.' Buyer or not, Jake was doing his checklist of what he needed to do to sell his produce. Even though the scope was widening on diversification ideas because, again, Sienna was making him see the possibilities.

He watched her approach in her swimming shorts, with a baggy singlet over the bikini top he'd once taken off with his teeth. Her sunglasses hid her wise eyes, while her sidekick Elliott yakked beside her, and the cattle dog led the charge as part of her entourage.

Sienna wasn't country. She didn't have the boots, the denim jeans, she didn't even own a hat. But he liked that about her.

They were almost at the back door when Jess called from the house. '*Sienna, phone call.*'

Sienna passed her laptop bag to her offsider and jogged for the house on the hill.

'Oh, hey, you're back early.' Elliott turned on the kitchen lights and then the gas oven.

'Where've you been?' Tyson asked.

'We went for a swim at the waterhole. Other than that, we've been doing the final research on the menu with the Queen of Busy in her office at the banyan tree. Of course, that's in between her serving lunch for flying vets, slamming on her keyboard, taking conference calls, checking my blog and my course assignments.' Elliott pulled out the large trays from the coldroom and put them on the centre bench, then lowered the oven's door.

'Must be a popular lady,' said Charlie, with Joe nodding beside him.

'Was Sienna talking to the park ranger? She's organising a Skype meeting for us to learn about the antivenene kit she got me,' asked Josh with hands full of biscuits.

'It was way over my head, conversations about export fees and quarantine certifications. But there's Sienna now.

Ask her yourself.' Elliott pointed to the window.

Sienna rushed down the stone steps and ran across the compound with a wide smile and a piece of paper in her hand. 'JAKE?'

'Here.' Jake caught Tom's arched eyebrow as he spun round to the compound, because she'd never called out to him, not like this.

He met her halfway in the compound far enough away so nobody could hear. Even if everyone was jostling for a view by the screen doors.

'What would you say if I found you not one, not two, but *three* buyers for your beef?'

'You didn't?'

'I did, *here*.' She gave an excited squeal passing him a piece of paper. 'All the buyers comply with international animal welfare standards. You've got one for local, another for interstate, and one for the export trade. That's the figures I've offered them, and one of them is also interested in the barra. So, that's three who've said a big *maybe* at being potential buyers once they see the stock. With four more nibbling at the bait in the background. That's what you say, right? For fishing?'

'*You bloody ripper.*' Jake hugged her, that heavy burden starting to lift from his shoulders.

With a shove from the heel of his palms, the muster room's screen doors flew open and Tom's boot heels stomped across the verandah towards the couple standing in the middle of the horseshoe compound. 'Good news, Boss?' Tom asked as the rest of the men followed.

'Sienna has found us a buyer.' Jake wrapped his arm around her back with the paper in hand.

'You'll have to negotiate prices, but one of them is definitely interested in your offer and they'll be here early next week,' said Sienna.

'When?' Jake asked.

'Monday. He's on a stopover from Sydney. So where can a private jet land? I heard this place has an airport?'

'Airstrip. Although Ryan said there were potholes in it.' Where Jake had just waved his mate off only an hour ago from the vet's whistlestop tour. Ryan had told Sienna she was cute, to her face, asking her to become his receptionist, to streamline his vet's surgery, when she finished at Danbunnan. Would she?

'Is this plane strip thingy big enough for a private jet?'

'Yes.' Jake's head tilted at her.

'Who do you know with a private jet, Sienna?' Josh asked.

'Buckle up boys, because Andrew Sulliance, a buyer from a very rich country in the Middle East is coming to Danbunnan. His company owns a purpose-built cattle ship with their own onboard vet, and he sells to the millionaires' marketplace. Top shelf, baby, I give you top shelf,' she said, patting Jake's chest.

'You did it!' Jake hugged her again, this time lifting her off the ground. Her laugh was music to his soul.

'I'll get them here. The rest will be up to you and the station.'

'Damn.' There was a lot of work to do before then. Would they be ready?

# Twenty-eight

Sienna awoke with her brain whirling into gear. Another day, and lots to do. At three in the morning, she'd bounded out of bed, showered, dressed, and was in the station's kitchen powering through her routine.

'Morning,' called out Elliott with a yawn. 'Did you sleep?' Pointing to the bench laden with food.

'Lunch and breakfast are done, and this is for you.' She tapped on a piece of paper lying on the bench.

'What's this?'

'You can finish the dinner prep.'

'Without you?' His chocolate-coloured eyes bulged wide.

'Elliott, if I didn't believe in you, I wouldn't leave.'

He flicked his fringe to the side as his cheesy grin widened. 'Well, if you insist.'

'Now, the coffee's brewing. Don't touch it except to drink it. Save the boss his one cup. Josh and Tyson have half cups only, leaving you plenty for four. Will you remember that?'

'Sure. But where are you going?'

'I need to make a few calls.'

'It's a bit early, don't you think? The sun's only coming up now.'

'Time zones. Sorry for doing the dump-and-run on you, but I have absolute confidence you'll do a magnificent job. If you need me, I'll be in my office.' She grabbed her well-stocked laptop bag, and with her torch shining along the path beside the vegetable garden, she headed towards the cook's quarters with her faithful furry friend shadowing her.

With the sun starting to rise, and with Sally in the passenger seat beside her, Sienna buckled up as her toy-car's engine rolled with its familiar rumble.

Peak hour was a little different in the outback. Instead of watching for pedestrians, bike riders, and other vehicles, here it was dodging wallabies, buffalo, possums, and dingoes who all seemed to love the dirt tracks at sunrise.

The toy-car rumbled low exiting the compound. Once on the hill, she flicked the lights to high beam, grinning at the deserted dirt road ahead.

'Hold on, Sally, we're gonna beat the change in the traffic lights.'

The dog gave her an air lick, as Sienna giggled, and gunned the toy-car into action. It roared like a jet over the runway and raced towards her office under a banyan tree amidst the landscape of an awakening Danbunnan Station.

This is why she loved her projects, and today she loved her job.

\*\*\*

Jake had been tempted to go to the muster room when he'd seen the lights on at four in the morning. He couldn't sleep, so he'd been up early this morning re-prioritising work plans for his men, working on a way to show off the place to strangers.

He wasn't a salesman. You could ask him about cattle and how to raise the product to its current standard, and he'd tell you. But selling, he'd never trained for that.

Grabbing his tablet, he went in search of a coffee and some answers.

'Ah, um, morning, Boss, h-h-here.' Elliott's hand shook as he plonked the travel cup on the counter inside the muster room. 'S-s-si-enna mixed it before she left.' And with a flick of his tea towel over his shoulder, Elliott rushed to the wood stove to stir the super stock.

Jake sniffed the coffee with suspicion. It smelt the same, tasted the same, but it wasn't the same. Because it wasn't served with a smile from the lady. 'Where is Sienna?'

'Where else, her office on the hill.'

'And she left you in charge?'

'Scary, huh?' Elliott gripped his tea towel in a knot, giving a nervous grin. 'Don't worry, Sienna left me a list.' He nodded towards the paper on the bench. Jake recognised the handwriting.

He trusted Sienna knew what she was doing, taking his coffee to then snatch a muffin from the cooling racks spread across the counter. The woman was still doing all the cooking he paid her for, not to mention all the other work she powered through. Did she ever stop?

With coffee in hand and tablet tucked under his elbow, Jake sat at the table next to Tom. 'Elliott seems to be coming into his own with his cooking?'

'Sienna's done good training the lad. He's only got a few assignments to complete for his certificate,' mumbled Tom, who then sipped on his black billy tea. 'So, what jobs do you want done today, Boss?'

Jake swiped his tablet to light up the screen. 'As a priority, the airstrip needs a fine mow and the potholes fixed. I'm also after a head count on the buffalo we've got.'

Tom looked over the schedules and gave a nod. 'Done.' The man had an elephant's memory; he only needed to be told once. 'Do you know when this buyer's arriving?'

'I'd say that's what Sienna's finding out now. I'm not sure when the negotiations will happen when he gets here. I'm guessing it'll depend on how shiny we make the cattle look, and how well Sienna feeds him with our beef.'

'That giggly girlie will do it, no sweat. They've got the smokehouse working big time.'

'Have they?'

'Yeah, your dad's into it.'

Jake still hadn't spoken to Bob since they'd had the blow-up over the letter. And he was in no rush to either. Not with everything else happening. 'Do you have any questions on the workload?'

'Aren't we having a practice dinner sometime?'

Jake shrugged. 'Soon, I guess. Do you want to sit in at the dinner?'

'No friggin' way.' Tom sat back with arms crossed over his chest. 'I volunteered to pour the grog at this fancy feast.'

Jake chuckled. 'I can't picture you doing that.'

'Me neither, but I don't trust this mob with all that fancy booze.'

'Fair enough.' Jake smirked as he stood, patting Tom on the shoulder. 'I'll go ask the relief cook when we'll be doing the practice dinner, because you do pour a bloody good beer.'

'I taught you.'

'And got me drunk.' Jake chuckled at the rarity of Tom's smile. Hoping that the winds of change were finally turning in his favour.

Ten minutes later, the banyan tree loomed high on the hill surrounded by an open field. It was a beacon of green amongst the gold and ochre landscape typical for the dry season.

Except for a tiny red car, and the woman sitting cross-legged on the roof working on her laptop. With the orange haze of the sunrise behind her and the expansive countryside surrounding her. She was a unique and beautiful addition to his world—the one he'd miss the most.

Jake parked his large ute up beside her tiny toy-car. A slight breeze carried the cool sweet scent of an awakening earth before the sun began to bite in a few hours.

'You know, I got you to do that makeover of my office, so you didn't suffer with sinusitis, and I don't mind sharing the workspace.' Jake leaned against his ute to sip his coffee and admire the vision she was.

'Don't you like my office? People pay a fortune for window views.' Sienna smiled from her perch, taking in the scenery as she inhaled deeply. Her new habit, she'd told him, because breathing fresh air was a rarity in her life in the closed-up corporate world.

'Good news, Andrew has officially accepted your preliminary offer. I've confirmed his visit on Monday for a face-to-face price negotiation.'

'I checked out the market prices this morning.'

'Excellent, so you'll know what to play in the number's game. What about the vet's certification?'

'It'll be ready. Ryan emailed me his preliminary reports, which are great.'

'I never doubted it.' Sienna showed him her laptop screen. 'I've used the same document we did for the competition and changed a few things to give to Andrew. I'll print it off for you to check. We also need to work out an itinerary for him, to email it to his assistant today.'

'So, it's really happening?'

'You bet. I hope you don't mind …' She hesitated, with a rise of her shoulders as she lowered her neck like a turtle. He always took that as a sign that she'd been pushing boundaries again.

'Out with it.'

'I sent the same offer to another potential buyer, at a much higher price that would include shipping fees.'

His coffee mug halted halfway to his mouth. 'Really?'

'You have your backup plan and that's one of my many.' Sienna closed her laptop and swallowed the last of her coffee. With sunglasses on her head, she started to climb down.

'Here …' His hands gripped around her delicate waist, effortlessly lowering her to the ground. 'I don't want you slipping off.' He wouldn't mind catching her in his arms again.

'Um, thanks.' And she went redder than the sun that rose behind her.

'Do you think this guy might pull out? Is that why you did the backup plan?' How many backup plans did Sienna have, when Jake only had one?

'Andrew is so keen he's rescheduled their entire itinerary to meet you.' Sienna put her laptop on the back seat, holding the door open for Sally to climb into her car.

If only he had a drop of her confidence. 'Tom has asked when we're doing the practice dinner.'

'Friday night. I'm looking for feedback on the menu.'

'What about the rest of the place?'

'The painting of the cattlemen's quarters is completed and looks amazing. Bob and I are trying to work out the kinks for the smokehouse. And Elliott and I are going to pressure clean Tom's cottage later today.'

'You're not going to draw flowers on his walls, are you?'

'I'm going to draw chillies for the chilli king.' She giggled.

Jake chuckled picturing Tom's face.

'And the rest of the women, including the children, are meeting Joe at the hay shed late this afternoon to create a work plan for the shed dance.'

'You never came up with a fancy title for the dance, huh?'

'No. But all the invitations are out. The judges and all of your neighbours have accepted.'

'Shocker.' Both laughing.

'So, um, with the guest list … Um, is Simon Simmons coming with…' Sienna turned to face the scenery, fiddling with her car keys.

This situation hurt her just as much, but he was trapped. 'They're coming. Angela also told me her father has offered to pay the judges a share of the profits on the resale of my cattle. That bastard even told me he'd re-brand them under his name too.'

'Can he do that?'

'If I sell the cattle to him, he can do whatever he wants with it.'

'So, are they coming … for all of it?' She winced at him.

'Yeah.'

'Good.'

'Is it? I don't want Simon here, but I can't see a way out of it.'

'That's your business, Jake. I'd better get back—'

'One thing.' He grabbed her arm before she escaped. 'I don't know sales.' He paced the dirt as he spoke. 'Dad doesn't know sales either because it was always done through the co-op. I've only worked at producing, so I'm clueless about negotiations and sales spin. I've already asked too much of you, but if you've got any tips, tricks, please …' He rubbed his forehead feeling the beginnings of the mother of all headaches building. He hated being this vulnerable to anyone.

She faced him squarely. 'You can do this. I'll help with the buyer, but I can't be there when you're meeting with the judges and cook at the same time. We have time to perfect your sales pitch. How about we use my notes from that day tour of the property? They're your words we'll polish up, so it'll come naturally to you, and we'll do the same for your speech for the fundraiser.'

He shook his head. 'I don't do speeches.'

'You can't talk your way out of it, buster. But my only tip on that one is to have a drink in your hand when you do.' She patted his chest like she'd started his heart all over again. 'You can do this.'

'With you at my side, I know I can.' It just came out, but he meant every word.

'Come on, I've got a tonne of work to do. I don't want the boss to catch me slacking off.' She jumped into her driver's seat. 'Do you want a coffee refill?'

'I dunno. That last one wasn't the same.' He shook his head, keeping a serious face as he scooped up his travel mug.

'What was wrong with it?'

He sniffed dubiously at the cup. 'I think Elliott might've changed the formula.'

'He'd better not! It took me years to get that right.'

'I think your reputation as the best coffee on the station's shot.'

'I'll fix that. The kitchen staff wants a coffee machine, you know.'

'I didn't.'

'We've been waiting for the right time to ask the boss.' She laughed over the familiar rumble of her small car's engine. 'I'll have a coffee waiting. Race you.'

'Not against that thing.'

She roared off with a wave, heading back to the homestead.

Yeah, they could be friends. Shame the benefits of the physical kind were untouchable, but the rest was still there, and right now he'd take whatever she offered, before she was gone from his life for good.

# Twenty-nine

'A delivery truck came today,' said Jess, seated at the dining table with the Cullen family. 'It was the party stuff.'

Jake ate and nodded while skimming the newsletter articles lying on the vacant chair beside him. Bob sat at the other end, the twins on either side of their mother.

'We got to play with bubble wrap, Uncle.' Kate giggled, as Aaron eagerly nodded with his cheeks full of food.

'Bubble wrap, that's fun.' Even if conversations were stiff between father and son, Jake kept up appearances for the sake of Jess and the twins.

Once it had been Bob who controlled the conversation, while Jess sat silently, fidgeting with her fingers. Now it was Jess doing all the talking.

Jake glanced at the vacant seat. One day he'd hoped Sienna could sit beside him, to share a meal, like he'd hoped to dance with her—just once. Yesterday, he'd had lunch with her and Ryan, but it'd never happen with the family. It was an impossible dream. 'So, what was in the boxes?'

'Plates and glasses,' said Kate.

'Boring stuff.' Aaron rolled his eyes.

Jake winked at his nephew. Yeah, he couldn't get excited over plates either.

'There was also new linen for the cattlemen's quarters, and cutlery,' explained Jess.

'Most of that stuff is hired, so don't get too attached because it goes back when we're done.' The sale of their recycled rubbish was paying for everything, painstakingly budgeted for while working alongside Sienna in the office. It's where she'd made him practise his speech, while playing with his new golf game. She was always coaching him, supporting him, when he had no way of repaying her. Sure, Sienna wanted a percentage of profits, but she deserved something special. But what?

'What are we doing with all that stuff, Uncle?' Aaron asked.

'It's for a fancy dinner party.'

'Are we allowed to be there too?'

'Good question. Jess?'

'We'll all be part of the rehearsal dinner tomorrow night, now we've got the gear to practise with.'

'And on the night?' Jake asked his sister.

'The twins will be in the muster room watching movies with headphones on. Sienna said when the pressure is on the language can get quite colourful in the kitchen.'

'Yes.' Aaron's fist punched the air the same as Sienna, whenever she had a win. 'Eating in the muster room is like eating in a restaurant.'

Footsteps were heard approaching the screen door.

'Knock, knock,' yelled out Sienna with her arms full of large plastic bags.

'Sienna?' Jake jumped to his feet and opened the door.

'Oh, you're still having dinner. Sorry for the intrusion.'

'It's okay, come in.' Jake guided her inside where she flung her large bags over one of the empty dining chairs, flushed with excitement that shone in her eyes. Damn it was pretty.

'I've got a surprise for you,' said Sienna.

'What is it?' Kate clapped her hands, her bangles jangling.

'Is it sweets?' Aaron asked, with a forkful of food hovering over his plate.

'No, just sweeter,' replied Sienna, messing up Aaron's hair before she squirmed uncomfortably. 'Now, Boss, I know

I should've gotten your approval first.'

'Go on.' Jake returned to his chair.

'Well, I just couldn't resist, and it was all last minute.' Sienna beamed with excitement like a child with a new toy. She unzipped a bag and pulled out a long-sleeved business shirt. The Danbunnan brand they stamped on their cattle was now an embroidered logo on a shirt. 'What do you think?'

The woman had surprised him, again. *Damn*. 'Is that our cattle brand?'

***

'Yes, it's the Danbunnan logo. I hope I've got the right sizes.' Sienna handed out the long-sleeved shirts to the family.

Jess and Bob disappeared down the corridor, while Sienna helped the twins with theirs. Jake stood up at the table and just tore his T-shirt off.

'Oh, no.' Desire washed through her so fast she collapsed into the nearest chair. She just couldn't stop peeking at Jake's naked torso. His strong arms pushed through the sleeves of the shirt, checking the fit on the shoulders. He could make a fortune as a stripper, wearing just his Akubra, jeans, and boots.

Jess soon returned wearing her new shirt. 'They're fantastic, Sienna.'

'Um, yeah,' Sienna's voice croaked. Jake looked better than fantastic, she had to turn away. 'So, err, Jess, are the twins' sizes okay?' She tried to focus on the children, and not climb across the table to run her nails over Jake's chest while nibbling at his jawline.

Jess checked her children's clothes. 'It's a good fit, Sienna.'

'What d'ya reckon?' Bob strolled through the doorway with shoulders back, full of pride.

'You guys really look the part.' She was pleased with her spur of the moment decision.

Jake's blue shirt brought out his blue eyes that sparkled in the kitchen light. 'Did you get one?'

'No.' Sienna put young Aaron on a chair and turned him around like a model. 'I thought we could get a different colour to distinguish between staff and management for the judges visit.'

'Great idea,' said Jake.

'They're smart-looking shirts. I feel all businesslike, huh?' said Jess, with a raised chin.

'You look great. All of you do,' said Sienna. 'So, we have enough money in the budget to order enough for everyone, Boss.'

'Do it.'

'Excellent. I'll make sure those shirts are available for the competition dinner. These are for the first buyer, so consider it a corporate uniform.'

'Good idea.'

'Well, I'll leave you to it. Sorry for disturbing your dinner.' It was time for this staff member to do the back-door exit.

'Sienna?' Jake followed to where Sienna stood in the shadows of the deep verandah. 'Thanks for this, it's a great surprise.'

'I hope it'll give you that extra bit of confidence when you do your sales pitch. Not that you'll need it. That colour really suits you.' Sienna brushed at some of the fine lint from his shoulders.

Without thought, her palm glided from his shoulder, stopping in the middle of his chest. But it was his enthralling eyes that trapped her. She swallowed at the intensity of his royal blues that exposed a rare moment of pure vibrant emotion. There was no boss face here, it was all Jake, and she was spellbound.

He stepped closer, trapping her hand to his chest, pulling her in, body, heart, and soul. His touch sent trembles of heat internally, while his warm breath brushing her cheek sent shivers externally, arousing her emotions to give flesh to her fantasies.

His lips feathered against her skin, whispering a secret

symphony. She sighed, closing her eyes as his lips grazed against hers and all thoughts of logic crumbled for the clarity of love. She drowned in his taste of hot syrup and summer where his lips recited a language that only her soaring soul could hear.

Her palms slid across his broad shoulders where she gripped him like she missed him. Lips against lips, she delved into his strength, scent, and flavour. Kissing him completely until the world disappeared.

The outside light flickered from a moth attracted to the light.

'Stop.' Sienna pushed him away as her fingers touched her heated lips, plump from his kiss. They were only a few metres away from his family, where the moth *tap tap tapped* on the yellow light above the kitchen door.

This affair was like a streetlight story that only came to life after dark, and she was the bug attracted to his heat and light, only to get burned.

'No more.' It was so easy to fall in love, but it was a battle to find her courage to walk away. But she had to. No matter how much she wanted Jake, she had to remember it was just a job.

# Thirty

Amidst the fragrant frangipani and heady jasmine that surrounded the house garden, the jacaranda tree towered above the flickering candles lighting the outdoor table.

Jake sat at the head of the U-shaped table, joined by Jess and the twins, Bob, Joe with his toy crown, and Charlie stroking his long beard. The rest of the vacant chairs were filled with an assortment of teddy bears.

'Do we really need to do this nonsense?' barked out Tom, standing nearby with his arms crossed over his barrel chest. Beside him, Tyson and Josh were doing the same.

'It's a teddy bear's dinner by candlelight.' At the end of the table, Sienna wiped away happy tears, with Pina, Lyn, and Elliott giggling nearby. 'I've always wanted to do a midnight picnic to name the stars.'

'I'm with Tom, I don't want to do this,' said Josh.

Sienna approached the staunch cattleman who'd volunteered to be the barman. 'Tom, you'll serve the wine in opened bottles. Red wine on a tray. White wine in an ice bucket, and all the glasses will be on the table. That's it.' She passed him a simple set of instructions.

'That's it?' His grey eyes squinted at the document.

She hesitated, biting her lip. She'd never given Tom a work plan. Ever. 'Um, yes?'

'Okay.' Giving her his usual nod.

'Josh and Tyson, your turn.' Sienna hooked her arms through their elbows and escorted them to the table. 'You'll serve the meals. The teddy bears each have a golf ball balanced on their heads. If you get too close you'll knock them off, and if any fall, we'll—'

'Throw eggs at you later,' said Elliott with a snigger.

Lyn laughed so hard she was in tears, while Pina hid her giggle behind her hands. That left everyone at the table shaking their heads, while the twins were proud to have their teddies as guests for dinner.

Tyson crossed his stocky arms over his chest. 'You're killin' our reputation.'

'Hey, I didn't know I'd be entertaining teddy bears who've got more hair than Charlie.' Jake plonked his elbow on the table, his palm shading his eyes as he laughed.

'The dinner will be set in this same U shape,' Sienna said, 'and this spare table in the centre is—'

'For me.' Elliott waved his arms as if to clear the air like a magician about to perform before his tortured audience.

'Now, when the guests arrive there'll be platters of nibblies. Josh, you serve.' She handed Josh the platter that had been arranged sparingly, hoping he didn't spill it. But this was their practice dinner to work out the kinks.

'Fine. Look at me, being all la-di-da.' Josh exaggerated his hip sway in his dust-stained jeans, parading in front of everyone. 'My mother would be so proud.'

Sienna held up her phone, recording him. 'I can send this to her, so she'll know you're thinking of her?'

'*Oi*. That never leaves the property.' Josh lowered the tray as if to hide behind it.

'What are you gonna pay us for it?' Elliott teased.

'Moving right along … The side verandah will be the bar area.' Sienna pointed to the mesh of eskies used for tonight's demonstration.

'I'm there,' said Charlie and Joe, both making a move from their chairs.

'Guarded by me.' Tom crossed his arms and barricaded their entrance.

'See, right man for the job,' called out Jake.

'Never had this in my bloody job description,' mumbled Tom.

'On the table is the homemade bread, pâté, and dips for you all to try.' Sienna grinned at their eagerness to eat.

'The first course will be the consommé.' With a soup terrine at the end of the table she dished out bowls for Josh and Tyson to serve to the teddy bears.

'I'm spilling the soup everywhere,' said Tyson, holding one bowl with two unsteady hands.

'Okay, this is good.' Sienna nodded with encouragement at the stockmen playing waiters.

'How?' Josh also spilled his soup, and he hadn't made it to the table yet.

'We're doing this practice run to work out the kinks. So, do we get Elliott to serve the soup from inside the U section?'

'Allow me.' Elliott picked up the large terrine and placed it in the centre table and served the soup with a steady hand, making his way around to everyone. 'You guys get to eat the teddy's dishes. They're already stuffed.'

Sienna stood behind Aaron and Kate. 'Start from the outside and work your way in ...' Everyone watched while Sienna showed the twins which spoon to use, answered their questions and the practice dinner was well under way. 'For the other courses, Joe and Charlie will be the runners bringing the dishes up from the muster room.'

'Muscle power.' Joe snort-laughed, giving a reverse bicep curl.

'Pina will be here in the house kitchen. I'll have a glass dishwasher for the occasion—sorry, Boss, about the bore and power.'

'All good, we'll make sure all tanks are topped up for the night.' Jake gave her a sly wink.

Her stomach swirled like a whirly-whirly of soft dust that heated her insides, all from that one look. *Ugh, why did he do that?* She tried desperately not to blush in front of everyone, doing her best to avoid him. 'So, basically the house kitchen will be the back of a bar for glasses, and coffee to go with the cheese platters that'll be served after desert.'

'Can we get a sheet with instructions like you gave Tom?' Tyson asked.

'Great idea.' Whipping out her mobile phone from her apron's pocket she made a note. 'We'll have heaps of time to practise in the muster room, so don't stress, guys. Now, it's a long meal of small portions.'

'Why?' Josh asked.

'I wanted to make sure we showed everything Danbunnan has to offer in the food. Elliott will explain each dish.'

'Go on, luv, tell us the dishes,' called out Lyn.

'Oh, that's my cue.' Elliott pulled out his cue cards and cleared his throat. 'The consommé, made with Danbunnan beef, was perfected by the original Cullens, a family recipe dating back to 1885. The hand-ground whole-wheat soda bread and consommé was a favourite for senators through to the stockmen who came to visit the station. During the Great Depression, Winifred and Henry Cullen sheltered many families at Danbunnan, where they fed countless with this soup and bread combination. Wow, the Cullens are a family of heroes.'

'That's cool,' said Josh, with Tyson nodding beside him.

'What else is written on those cards?' Jake asked.

Elliott inhaled so deep his skinny chest rose and posture straightened, as he read from the cards. 'Henry Cullen's salamis and cured meats were a recipe perfected by Danbunnan's first stockmen. And the chef's special pastrami and the bresaola—you so nailed that, Sienna.'

'Stick to the cue cards, Elliott.'

'So, what is the menu, exactly?' asked Tyson. 'In English, Elliott?'

'There's a reason these foods have been selected with the utmost—'

'I agree with Tyson,' said Tom, 'what's the short and sharp version.'

'Ditto, I might be king, but I've got no idea on this

schmancy food,' said Joe, tapping his toy crown sitting over the brim of his trucker's cap.

'Okay then ...' Sienna smoothed down her apron. 'The first dish is a clear soup made from the super stock that is always simmering on the wood stove. The wood stove is how they originally cooked all their meals, which is why I've made the first course to represent the ancestral dish of the first pioneers who created Danbunnan. This is followed up by newer dishes to represent the generations of the Cullen family, right up to the current owner.' Sienna pointed to Jake, the boss, and son of the ex-cattle king. As the man in charge, Jake needed to believe he was king. Not Bob.

'It's a Shakespearian drama representation interpreted in the food,' blurted out Elliott, holding a fork in the air like a silver torch to the gods.

'Oh, no.' Tom moaned, rubbing his eyes beneath the lowered brim of his Akubra. 'Who let the kid out of his sandbox?'

'The soup and soda bread recipes are older than Banjo Patterson's *Man from Snowy River* story. It was savoured long before they turned the lights on in Adelaide City, invented Vegemite, or kicked their first football at the Richmond Footy Club, *and* it survived the great depression.' Elliott waved his cards in the air like a fangirl chasing his idol for an autograph. 'They lived by gas lamps, telegrams, Coolgardie coolers and ice boxes, way back when the Territory wasn't the Northern Territory but under South Australia's regime and there's—'

'Breathe, Elliott.' Sienna squeezed his skinny arm, just loving his passion.

Jake shook his head, wiping at his crooked grin. 'Sienna, you might be better at explaining.'

'Well, everything, except for the dairy products, has been handpicked, caught, or grown within Danbunnan's borders. For the soda bread, it's hand-ground wild wheat I collected with the twins, Jess, and Elliott. The recipe is from the original Danbunnan ancestors, and it's been baked in the wood stove. From there the rest of the menu gets a teeny bit fancy.' She scrunched up her apron.

'How fancy?' Josh asked.

'Instagram-worthy,' said Elliott with chin held high.

'Will you be taking photos while serving?' Jake asked Elliott.

'No, Sienna banned my phone.'

Josh raised his hand in the air like a schoolboy in class. 'I'll take photos if you want, Boss?'

'Good lad, we'll put them on the website.' Jake nodded from his place at the head of the table.

'You can use my camera, Josh. But no photos of me in the kitchen or I'll post your video on Elliott's blog.' Sienna grinned at Josh.

'So, what's after the soup, luv?' asked Lyn.

'We'll be serving the barramundi terrine with a macadamia sauce. The wild-goose pâté, which is another one of the ancestor's recipes, along with buffalo chilli balls, using Tom's chillies married with a bush-tomato salsa.'

The men chuckled while Elliott served large platters.

'What's this?' Charlie asked, sniffing at the plate. 'Main course?'

'Entrée,' said Elliott. 'We're still getting to the mains and the dessert finale.'

'Gawd, what's for mains, then?' Joe asked with pieces of salami in his hand.

'My mother would be so proud. Look, Mum, pâté.' Josh scraped the tiniest slather of pâté onto the largest toast square he could find.

'I'm high-browin' it now with this top tucker.' Tyson shoved a canapé into his mouth with exaggerated pinkie in the air to scratch the tip of his nose.

'Bloody cowboys,' Elliott mumbled with arms crossed over his skinny chest.

'Elliott, you can explain the mains, and with flair. Come on, he needs the practice.' Sienna shrugged at the men's grumbles.

Brushing the hair out of his eyes, Elliott read from the card. 'Main course will be served in two parts. First will be the crispy-skinned barramundi baked in banana leaves, with my Uncle Tom's chilli and lime sauce. It will be served with a petite garden salad, delicately drizzled with a wild hibiscus tea dressing.'

'Now I'm hungry,' said Pina in her Spanish accent.

'Wait, there's more.' Elliott's index finger waved in the air like a conductor at an orchestra. 'Then it's the bush-pepper rubbed rib eye on the bone, with a wild mushroom sauce, served with baby vegetables and a roasted wild pandanus-pineapple puree. And for dessert we have the divine banana and native honey baked cheesecake, with a choice of bush lime, Kakadu plum, and mango sorbets, topped with a macadamia, rosella, and chilli crumb.'

'Yum,' said Jess, licking her lips.

Sienna, followed by Pina, carried large trays and placed them on the table. 'Here's a taste of the mains. Elliott will be in the centre and the guests will focus on him, so Josh and Tyson can serve on the outside.'

'How many people are we serving?' Josh leaned in to inspect the food on the platters that Pina and Sienna carried to the table.

'Eighteen people.' Sienna passed him a plate of food. 'Josh and Tyson, do we need Pina to help you guys?' Watching them serve the seated guests was like watching the awkwardness of a tomboy learning to walk in heels for her first school dance.

Josh and Tyson didn't hesitate to say, 'Yes please.'

'I said I'd help for lunch and anywhere else you need me.'

'Thank you, Pina. Elliott will also help from the centre once he's carved the meat.'

'But that could take ages,' said Tyson, their skilled butcher.

Elliott sighed, his slim shoulders sinking in defeat. 'I know, I'm only learning.'

'Most of the meals will already be plated by me. Elliott is there more to explain the dishes, and to offer any second serves of the meat, which is what Danbunnan is about. We want the food to speak for itself along with its history so they can get a true taste of what you guys produce. Hope you guys like it?' She took a teddy bear off the chair and they all sat at the table and dined together under the stars on the lawn.

Sienna put down her cutlery, satisfied with the standard of her dishes, but also enjoying the rare pleasure of sharing a meal with the crew. It was her first time.

It was even nicer when Pina and Lyn took away the dishes, which also made Elliott smile. 'Okay boys, your turn.'

Josh and Tyson dashed to the front of the house.

'What are them lads doing now?' Tom asked.

'I'm guessing we're about to have another one of Sienna's many surprises,' Jake said from behind his beer glass.

He knew her so well, which was scary. 'You'll see.' Hoping she hadn't gone too far with what they were about to propose.

Josh and Tyson soon returned with a plastic frame and a large box with electrical wires spilling out.

'That's not one of our flamin' sheets for the stockmen's quarters, is it?' called out Lyn.

'It's an old one, Lyn. You can blame Sienna,' said Josh, helping Tyson set up behind Elliott's table.

'No such thing as loyalty amongst thieves, right? I'll get the lights.' At the side door, she was ready to play with the light panel. 'Hit it, boys.'

There was a moment of blackness until their eyes adjusted to the dim candlelight and the stars. Then the stretched sheet displayed a photo of Danbunnan's homestead.

'You've made a film projector?' called out Charlie,

stroking his beard. 'How?'

'Sienna came up with the plan,' said Tyson. 'She just didn't know how to build it, because we all know she's not mechanical.'

'Don't I know it.' Joe, the station mechanic, gave another one of his signature snort-laughs while tapping his crown.

'What's this in aid of, Sienna?' Jake asked.

'I wanted to show everyone the website. And, at the dinner, we can use this as a backdrop.' Sienna nodded to Tyson who pushed a few keys on the laptop and a video of cattle grazing played in black and white on the bed sheet.

'It's almost like those movie night's we used to have with Mum,' said Jess, sitting straighter at the table.

Sienna knew it was a fond memory for Jake too. 'I wanted to create a unique atmosphere by using this as a backdrop for the dinner. I'd love to do the same for the shed dance.'

'You don't think it's too much for just a dinner?' Tom asked.

'Did you not hear me read out the menu, Uncle?' Elliott cried out. 'It's a gastronomical festival of food carefully choreographed to show the history of Danbunnan Station.'

And it was. Sienna had put a lot of thought into this menu. 'This screen will add an extra layer towards creating a unique atmosphere. You have the beautiful stone house, the exotic gardens that make up the oasis of the outback.' She pointed to the heavens. 'A ceiling of stars, surrounded by the fresh air and expansive countryside, that will only complement the food. So why not have this as an extra? Tyson and Josh are willing to do a slideshow for us too.' She was proud that the cowboys-of-cuteness were willing to get involved with the details. Jake should be proud.

'Slideshow of what?' Jake narrowed his eyes at them.

'Um ...' Tyson wiped his palms on his denim thighs. Josh hid his hands in his jeans back pockets, toeing at the lawn with his boot. Both looked at Sienna from beneath their hat brims.

'Go on, tell him. It was your idea, guys.'

Tyson cleared his throat. 'Um, well, Boss, we want to use those old photos you have in the office, to make a slideshow. Sienna said it'd be good to show off Danbunnan's history and we can put it to music to run on a loop, while you're eating dinner.'

'What music?' Tom asked. 'It'd better not be that rap crap Elliott plays.'

'As long as it's not your deaf-dog-whining country music, Uncle.' Elliott screwed up his nose.

'May I make a suggestion?' Sienna timidly raised her hand in the air. 'I think we should use music from the classic black-and-white movie era. Perhaps some Frank Sinatra?'

It might be a sore point, but she wanted to represent all of the members of the Cullen family who'd played their part in Danbunnan's history.

'You want to do it as a tribute to my mother?' Jake wore his poker face.

Had she gone too far?

Jess patted her brother's forearm that rested on the table. 'Jake, I think it's a great idea. I remember most of Mum's favourite songs and I can get the photos from the albums. I'd love to help.'

Jake looked at his sister, then at Sienna, wearing that unreadable boss face. 'Josh and Tyson, do you think you can put up pages of a journal on that slide show too?'

'We can put up anything you want, Boss,' said Tyson, with Josh eagerly nodding beside him.

'Jess will help you,' said Jake, and the best mates sighed with relief.

Bob gave a quiet cough before getting up from his seat to head inside. Everyone was aware Bob and Jake were arguing, but very few knew why.

But Bob was also a grieving husband who missed his wife.

However, the division between father and son was worsening, when they needed to show unity for this upcoming event. But it wasn't Sienna's business to get involved, because she was just the staff hired to do a job.

'And so, that's not all folks …' Sienna needed to lighten the mood as she stepped in behind the laptop. 'We've still got dessert to try, so find a seat everyone. Jake, do you want to talk about this?' Sienna pointed at the screen.

'What Sienna is showing is the website, which officially goes live on Monday. There is a little spiel about everyone, but if you don't want it, we'll take it off. But as Sienna said, your positions as team members and the work you do here makes you a part of Danbunnan's story. Sienna can explain the rest.'

'By the way, all of the brilliant photos we've used on the website were taken by the boss.' Sienna took them through the website, showing off Jake's natural talent as a photographer. He had a gift for showing off Danbunnan in the best possible way.

'Wow, we're on the website too?' asked Aaron. His sister, Kate sat with mouth wide open as they stared at themselves.

'Yes, honey. Sienna's done a good job,' replied Jess, gently stroking her son's hair.

'You're family, and Danbunnan is a family station. It's a great photo, Jake.' Sienna had to admire the photo of Aaron, Kate, Jess, and Bob where he'd used the lush tropical garden as the background.

For each scene on the website, it shared a small paragraph, introducing those employed at Danbunnan.

'Man, I look good.' Elliott's chin rose, his wide brown eyes staring at himself working in the pig truck. His lips moving as he silently read the paragraph about his position at the station.

In Tyson's photo, he stood next to his shiny, black beast of a ute. 'Wow, my baby looks good, Boss.'

The next image was of Josh holding a python as he explained his snake whispering venture. Joe stood proud with his toy crown catching the light as the king in his workshed. Charlie, the water specialist, got caught working on a bore where a water spout flew high into the air. Pina stood smiling wide among a fluttering field of white sheets like she was in a cotton wonderland. Lyn gave a thumbs-up from the driver's seat of a massive road-train. Rhonda, in her apron, gave a wide smile before the wood stove. Tom's photo showed him leaning on a rail with his steely grey eyes overlooking the herd.

The last photo was of Jake. The boss. With his Akubra shading his eyes, he faced the never-ending vista of Danbunnan at his feet from on top of the North Ridge plateau.

'Oi? Where did that photo come from?' called out Jake.

'Surprise,' said Sienna. He looked amazing in that shot, as the visionary, the protector, and the man—no, a king—in charge of this massive country they called home. It was her favourite.

'It's a great shot, Boss.' Tom even gave a nod of approval.

'How come there's none of Sienna, Mummy?' Kate asked.

'Because I'm only helping out while Rhonda is on holidays.' Did she want to be permanent? It was impossible. She had her own business and didn't want to cook and clean all her life.

She couldn't look at their sad faces when this was meant to be all about building a team's morale. And she didn't dare look at Jake, or she'd cry.

'Now for the finale and one last surprise for the boss.' She pressed play on Elliott's laptop.

'You didn't?' Jake's eyes widened as the screen flickered to a movie and the tinny speakers roared in mono.

'That's a top movie.' Tyson picked up a teddy bear and sat at the table, with Josh doing the same.

'I haven't seen this in decades.' Tom dragged over an esky and took a seat with a beer in hand beside Jake, as the men gathered at the table to watch the big screen.

'What is it, Mummy?' Aaron asked.

'This was your Uncle Jake's favourite movie when we were kids.' Jess shared a soft smile with her older brother. 'It's called *The Great Escape*.'

Little Kate climbed into her uncle's lap, where Jake hugged her while watching the screen.

They all sat under the stars in the garden and watched the show. It was what Sienna imaged it would be like to have a family.

Slipping silently into the shadows, she headed for her room. She was leaving soon, and it was time everyone got used to her not being a part of Danbunnan, including herself.

# Thirty-one

On Monday the station kitchen was a hive of activity, yet Sienna still stopped to savour her favourite time of the morning, no matter how much she tried to resist it. And there he was—Jake making his way across the compound with his long-legged stride in those perfectly fitted jeans.

But today there were no dust-stained clothes. He was in clean jeans and polished boots, wearing his bad-boy black hat. She'd never understood the romanticism over cowboys, until now—because her hero was smokin'!

'Morning.' Her tummy did the butterfly giddy-up like a schoolgirl in the playground hoping the handsome boy said hello. Or was she having a fangirl moment from a lack of sleep? *Get a grip.*

'Morning.' Jake nodded, then his eyes widened.

She couldn't move as if glued by his stare. Sure, she'd copped the whistles and catcalls from the others in jest, but this mattered.

'No dress and boots?' Jake tilted his head, wearing his poker face.

'I hope I don't break a heel, but they're boots.' With a click clack of her heels on the lacquered concrete, she stepped around the bench, in dress boots, fitted black slacks, collared business shirt, with her hair washed and blow dried. It had been fun getting all dressed up again, putting on make-up and jewellery. Totally overdressed in her office chic, to stand in an outback kitchen in the remote Northern Territory.

'Still no denim?' he asked as his royal blues slow crawled from her boots upwards.

'Nope. I didn't see a pair of jeans I liked in town.' *Holy roasted coffee beans!* He was totally checking her out, as if his eyes could eat her. And she wanted him to.

Which was so wrong.

She passed him a cup of coffee, then picked up her portfolio and a plate of muffins. They were strictly business now, trying to force some cool formality back into her heated body. 'Take a seat and have some breakfast. It's the bacon muffins with extra pepper, just how you like them.' Even if they weren't sleeping together, she still spoiled him.

Jake latched on to her hand as she put the plates on the table. 'You won't be leaving us alone with the buyer?'

'I'll be with you every step of the way. You have your bottom price, Andrew will go low, and you'll go high, just like we practised. You can do this, Jake, I believe in you.' Sienna gave Jake a slight squeeze on the shoulder. She believed in him, and in his product, that she barely had to polish. It was Jake who needed to believe in himself.

\*\*\*

The nerves were eating him alive. Jake sat next to Tom, and stared at his food, doubting anything could get past the knot of concrete sitting in his guts.

'Are you okay, Boss?' Tom asked.

Jake shrugged, trying to swallow his coffee.

'Same. You both did fine work on these documents.' Tom flicked through the glossy pages of the portfolio.

'Sienna made it look good.' Jake had enjoyed working alongside Sienna, going over the many details. But today wasn't just about cattle and cattlemen, this was a freaking rich buyer. His *first* buyer.

'You both make this place shine, Boss. And the relief cook looks good today. Don't tell her I said that. Don't want to get into trouble,' Tom mumbled from behind his mug of billy tea with his grey eyes facing the widescreen.

'She does, huh?' Sienna was mouth-wateringly gorgeous. Beyond gorgeous if his vocabulary stretched further.

'I reckon young Josh has got another case of puppy love all over again for the relief cook.' And in a rare moment, Tom chuckled behind his cup.

'Are the men ready for this?' He was depending on them today.

'Yep. Josh, Tyson, and Charlie have the cattle spit-polished and waiting in their areas. What are the kitchen crew doing?'

'Good question? Sienna?'

She approached them with her coffee in one hand and tablet in the other. She was the executive that men in offices talked about, gathering around the water cooler to watch her walk by.

And she had his attention. 'Are you sorted for today?'

Sienna sat on the bench seat opposite. 'I am, and I've got Elliott following us in the kitchen ute to the airport.'

'It's an airstrip not an airport.' Jake grinned at her as he inhaled her floral–vanilla fragrance.

'So, no lights? Or those cone thingies for wind direction?'

'Nope.' Jake chuckled, and Tom smirked ever so slightly behind his cuppa.

Sienna pointed at the head stockman. 'I almost got a smile out of you, Tom.'

'Never.'

'Why is Elliott leaving the compound? Isn't he doing lunch?' Jake asked.

'Elliott's picking up the pilot and staff from the jet. They'll wait here until it's time to fly back.'

'Didn't think of that,' said Tom.

Jake winked at the lady who had planning down to a fine art.

'Lunch is all prepped,' she said. 'Elliott's serving with Lyn and Pina, who are finishing the table set up. It'll be similar to that morning tea with the Simmons, but with more fabulous food.'

Jake didn't want to think about his neighbour, not today. 'How much coffee have you had today?' Because she was firing on twelve cylinders, all sleek and shapely in figure-hugging long pants and collared shirt that showed off her curves to perfection. *This separation was painful.*

'Not enough. So, morning tea's prepped for the plateau as part of the tour, then back here for lunch. Do you want to show him the ponds?'

'Can we gauge it?'

'Sure. I'm always flexible at these presentations. You can always ask him if he likes fishing and see what he says.'

'Oi, I don't hold conversations with billionaires every day, you know.'

'You'll be fine.' She patted Jake's hand. 'And I've gotta get busy. Elliott, let's finish those eskies.'

His eyes followed Sienna's seductive hip swing in those long slacks, with her glossy hair flowing down her back.

'Jake, it's time.' Sienna tapped at her watch that had a fine gold band around her slender wrist, when he noticed she was wearing a ring. Was it her past engagement ring?

Like the crack of a stockwhip, it latched around his heart and squeezed with bite. Was she wearing it on her ring finger?

'Boss?' Tom asked beside him.

'Huh? Yeah, let's go.' Jake had to focus on his first buyer, who would either make him or break him.

# Thirty-two

'So, this is the airstrip?' Sienna screwed up her nose at the wide-open field. 'It's a strip of dirt and dead grass.'

Jake chuckled, leaning against the twin-cab ute. 'What did you expect?'

'I don't know. Something more runway-ish.'

'It doesn't get a lot of use, but we make sure to keep it mowed in the wet season.'

'Why?'

'When the roads are flooded, it's our only way in or out.'

'You have a plane?'

'Used to. If we need one, we'll charter one.'

'Can you fly?'

'Most people can out here.' Jake pointed to the aircraft that had begun its descent. 'But no one I know has a private jet. How do you know this guy?'

'Through Karl, his EA.'

Jake stepped closer, his cologne wove around her like an invisible rope, craving for him like a much-needed vice. 'Sienna, I interpret our lingo of the land for you, so I'd appreciate the same. What is an EA?'

Why was she falling into this needy pull of her emotions? Maybe she was tired?

'Executive assistant. Karl and I worked together. He ran the EA training classes to teach his trade to mums. They'd come in for a day for the class and bring their babies. We were all about flexibility.'

'Did it work?'

'It was a huge success. We were going to run more, but Andrew made Karl an offer he couldn't refuse. We didn't run any classes after that. But Karl is a first-class EA, and he was my BFF Mail-order Biatch's bitch for a while.'

Jake's laugh echoed around them. 'Some days you come out with a whole new language in your wordplay. Maybe I'll see what you're like in the city.'

'Sure, when you're in town look me up.' And that killed the mood, because in just over two weeks she'd be gone.

The jet taxied to a stop, the door opened and out stepped a hostess followed by the passengers.

'Sienna, are we doing the right thing? I can't—'

Sienna squeezed Jake's hand. 'Relax. Isn't that what you told me when you tried to teach me how to ride a horse—you can do this,' she whispered into his ear and felt his tension ease a little. 'Come on, Jake. Andrew is a nice guy. You'll get on well with him. Trust me on this.'

Jake took a deep breath and shared his crooked smile. Combined with the intensity of his royal blue eyes it made her heart leap. She pulled her hand away, licking her lips, trying to refocus.

At least her words of encouragement were working, even though she had to shove her own feelings into a box in the back of her mind in order to focus on the job.

Four men climbed out of the jet.

'Sienna, darling,' said her old friend with arms wide open. He was dressed casually in jeans, a tailored cowboy shirt, hat, and boots that looked brand new, while the other men wore suits.

'Andrew.' She was engulfed in a bear hug.

'I couldn't believe it when Karl told me you rang—you who drops off the face of the earth and never calls.'

'Thank you for returning my call.'

'Karl insisted you have what I want, and we trust your perfectionist standards. So, who do we have here?'

'Andrew Sulliance, it's my honour to introduce you to

Jake Cullen, owner of Danbunnan Station.'

'Welcome,' said Jake, extending his hand.

Andrew shook his hand. 'Thank you for letting us visit at such short notice.' He introduced two of the men as his lawyers, and then introduced Karl.

'It's nice to meet you all.' Jake faced Sienna for the next cue.

The poor man was so nervous. 'Jake, could you make the introductions to your team, and help everyone to their seats. Karl?'

'Hello, darling.' Karl hugged Sienna with a round of air kisses. 'Oh, cowboy cute.' Karl's hazel eyes slow crawled all over Jake's physique.

'Shh, don't call them cowboys, Karl. These guys are cattlemen, and they carry guns.'

'Where?' Karl's eyes narrowed at Jake's crotch only to fan himself with a wicked grin.

'Hey, I didn't say loaded pistols. Discretion, please.' She giggled at Jake's expression at being checked out by a male. 'Careful, Karl, the boss has a fist that breaks doors if angry.' Was the cattleman of hotness flattered? He should be because Karl was very picky. 'Come on, we've got a schedule to keep.'

*\*\*\**

The decorated table stood in the cool shade of the flourishing house garden, where they were enjoying their lunch after the morning's tour.

Jake sat at the head of the table with Andrew and Sienna seated on the other side of him. It felt right having Sienna near him. Whenever he needed her prompting all it took was a simple glance in her direction.

Now over his nerves, he talked freely with Andrew while Sienna caught up with Karl, as Jess and the twins entertained the lawyers.

'Jake? Why don't you, me, and our assistants go for a walk,' suggested Andrew, at the end of lunch.

Jake looked to Sienna.

'Jake's got an amazing stallion called Sampson that you have to see.' Sienna stepped in beside Jake for the final part of the meeting.

'Yeah, right this way.' Jake grabbed her arm and whispered, 'Don't you dare leave me.'

'You've got this.'

Side by side they walked to the stables for the negotiations to begin.

Inside the round pen, Jake's proud black stallion pranced around putting on a show. Sampson's black coat gleamed in the sun, his mane trailed like black fire, as his muscles moved with a raw powerful magic. A perfect show of what Danbunnan had to offer, a horse Jake bred and trained himself.

Jake adjusted his hat and began. 'Andrew, my family has produced cattle on this station for over a hundred and thirty years. Yet, I'm considered new to this market. But I know what I'm doing when it comes to producing top-quality beef. You tasted the beef at lunch, so you know the product speaks for itself, and I can supply that high standard of stock every year for a five-year agreement. You're a busy man, I am too, and it's obvious from the way you look at the cattle you know your product. I won't put a sales spin on it, because I'm not a salesman, but I do know what my cattle is worth.'

'Let's talk numbers,' said Andrew.

For thirty minutes numbers were exchanged with laughter and banter, until Jake held out his hand. 'You've got yourself a deal, Andrew.'

'You're good. That's the most fun I've had in negotiations in a while.' Andrew chuckled, as he shook Jake's hand. 'I like you, Jake.'

Sienna and Karl then held out their tablets to Jake and Andrew.

'What's this?' Jake asked, grabbing her stylus pen.

'It's the agreement you've both just made. You need to read it and if it's fine, sign it, initial the bottom. Karl and I will be the witnesses.'

'Our lawyers will draft the contract and send it through to you. You should have it this afternoon. Are you aiming for front-door seal of approval?' Karl asked while witnessing for Andrew.

Sienna watched Jake and Andrew. 'Working on it.'

'Good, Darwin it is. How's Friday?'

'Perfect. Your lawyer's office?'

'Yes. We'll be heading straight to Hong Kong after that,' said Karl.

'Tough life,' said Sienna, passing Karl's portfolio back to him.

'I love my job, but I must say this country life really suits you.'

'I agree,' said Andrew. 'You look great, Sienna. You're both lucky. I could get used to this lifestyle.'

Sienna closed her folder and smiled. 'It's addictive.'

Jake watched on in awe. What the hell just happened? And what was happening on Friday?

# Thirty-three

Jake parked his vehicle beside the house lawns, with Sienna seated in the passenger seat busily going through her lists.

'So, Boss?' Tom approached, wearing a hopeful expression.

'It's done.' Jake rolled his tight shoulders as he got out of the ute, feeling the tension loosen. 'We're now in the live export trade.'

*'Oh. My. Word.'* Jess hugged her brother as everyone gathered at the table where they'd held their teddy bear dinner.

'Well done, Jake. You did it.' Tom heartily patted Jake's shoulder.

*Jake, huh? Where was the boss?*

He shook Tom's hand even if it still hadn't sunk in yet. 'We did it, Tom. It went better than expected. It was like Sienna and Karl had it all worked out between them, and Andrew and I were only there for the handshake. I mean …' He hesitated to exhale long and slow, hooking his thumbs into his jeans' pockets. 'There are contracts to sign, trucks to coordinate, and cattle to cart.' He couldn't get too ahead of himself.

'But will it be worth it?'

'Hell, yeah! I've been offered twenty times more than Simon was offering me. Andrew is paying by the head for first-class stock for five years. All we have to do is get them to the quarantine yards and he'll ship them out, end of story.' But he'd only get paid once his cattle boarded that ship, and that was one long plank to get them there. He couldn't and wouldn't let himself get too far ahead until that money was in the bank. He just couldn't.

'I don't know about ships and exporting. I only know what we do here.'

'I do, so does Cowboy Craig. It's his specialty. Craig ran the quarantine cattle yards out of Darwin as a stock inspector for a while.'

'Looks like your mate might get a job here after all?'

'Only if you want, Tom.'

'Craig's got a good reputation as a stockman. He got on well with the crew that day hauling rubbish with us, so he'd fit in alright. Still, I didn't approve of him sleazing onto Sienna like he did the other morning. But it won't matter, Rhonda will be back in a few weeks.'

'Yeah.' Jake frowned at the thought. 'Where is Sienna?' She'd been doing that a lot lately, stepping away from team sessions. On the movie night, when he wanted to thank her for the tribute to his mother. Now this—he wanted her to celebrate with him. 'Jess, where did Sienna go?'

'Into the office, mumbling something about emails and phone calls.' Jess smiled widely, carrying a champagne bottle and glasses to the table. He knew his sister had been worried about today and was glad she was celebrating.

'You'd better get that giggly girlie a drink, Boss,' said Tom, patting Jake's shoulder. 'I need another beer.'

'Not wrong.' Jake walked up to the office. The wooden door was closed. Inside he found Sienna leaning back in his office chair. Her boots rested on the desk, her thick hair fell down her arms, as she twisted the phone cord around her dainty fingers.

The door closed with a click and Jake sat in the guest chair next to her.

Today he'd seen a new side to Sienna. She'd kept her cool with the questions and was confident under pressure.

Qualities he admired. Now he was admiring her shirt that gaped to give him a hint of the delicate lace of her bra.

Jake couldn't help himself, he was restless without her, now running on adrenaline from the deal. He gently captured one of Sienna's long curls. It was like holding soft silk between his fingers, following it all the way down her arm. Her sharp breath led the tiny goosebumps that he traced with his fingertips, to entwine his fingers with hers.

Sienna kept talking on the phone. He wasn't listening because she fascinated him like the perfect puzzle.

His palm slid across the soft material of her slacks, up to her outer thighs, pulling her closer. He was either going to get slapped or he was about to take a trip to heaven.

\*\*\*

Sienna tried to concentrate on her conversation, but she was unable to resist or stop Jake. She wanted to push him away, she really meant to, but Jake trapped her hand and kissed each of her fingertips, sending electrified tingles throughout her body.

Shifting her legs from the desktop to across his lap, he rolled his chair closer, to skim the outline of her slacks and up to her hips.

That's when his lips caressed her neck.

She'd forgotten what she was doing. Who was she talking to? But the pendulum in her heart had begun to swing.

'Can you hold for a second longer, Sienna?' asked Anthony, the contracts lawyer, on the other line.

'Ah, yeah, sure.' *No*, she shouldn't wait, not when she had no resistance to the man in front of her. Not when his lips were on her skin. Not with his hand sliding under the edge of her shirt, to skim over her bare stomach to caress her curves.

Her breath erratic, quickening with each rise and fall of her chest, she could barely breathe. He was above her, and all she saw and felt was the curve in her universe and it was everything Jake.

Jake lifted her effortlessly from the chair and placed her on the desk. His hot mouth and lips trailed down her exposed throat, as his fingers unbuttoned her shirt, kissing her cleavage towards each of her breasts. She arched her back surrendering to the immense pleasure of his touch.

'Sienna, I'm back,' called out a small voice on the other end of the telephone line.

*Who?* What was she doing?

*'Sienna?'*

'Anthony?' The archaic handpiece fell onto the desk, she scrambled to pick it up. 'Sorry, Anthony, are you still there?'

'I've received the email and I'll look it over tonight. If there's anything I don't like, I'll let you know.'

'Thank you...' She tried to beat the foggy tide of overwhelming pleasure created by Jake's lips and hands touching, marking, and claiming her skin.

'I'll see you in Darwin on Friday.'

'Yeah, thanks. See you then. Thanks, thanks.' She dropped the phone; it bounced off the cradle. She didn't care, her body was in Jake's hands and there was no fighting it.

'Contract draft conditions are with the lawyer to do what they do.' While she let Jake do what he was doing as the butterflies in her belly burst into a galaxy of stars.

'Ah huh.' He held her face between his hands and kissed her deeply. This is what love tasted of, where loneliness and regret were forgotten.

'Hey, you two? Why aren't you outside celebrating,' yelled Jess from outside.

Sienna pushed Jake away and jumped to her feet. Her pulse pounded in her ears, blinking as if she'd been ripped awake into a frightening reality.

'Just. *Great.*' She straightened her shirt, annoyed with herself for not being in control, and how fast it all happened.

Again, they were in the same risky and frustrating position.

'Out in a second, Jess.' Jake gripped the door handle, his

forehead rested against the doorframe, where he took deep forceful breaths to gather himself. 'Are you okay?'

Sienna glared at him. *No.* Not while she was here with him. Not when they could never have an *us*.

Jake grinned, opened the door, and dragged her out of the office. 'Come on, let's have a night off. We deserve to celebrate this moment.'

'What moment? Where we almost got —'

'Come on you two.' Jess met them on the verandah and hooked her arm through Sienna's. 'Sienna, you must have some champagne with us and no sneaking off like you did the other night.'

'Yeah, like my sister said.' Jake gave her hand a slight squeeze then let her go.

Sienna hated him and adored him all at once.

But she couldn't say no when she wanted to celebrate their victory of the job — even if her private life was a mess. 'I'm up for a party.' Realising she still enjoyed the game that used to be her job.

She was ready to go home.

# Thirty-four

Rubbing the sleep from his eyes, Elliott walked into the kitchen and did a double take when he saw Sienna, to then give her a low wolf-whistle. 'Now how come you don't dress like that when you're working here?'

'Yeah, Sienna, how come?' Jake asked, leaning against the kitchen wall.

She hadn't heard Jake sneak in, but she saw him now in black jeans, his belt buckle shining in the light. A black jacket with collar up, cuffs folded back, and that black Akubra. He looked better than good. He was wickedly bad.

For the past few days, she'd powered through the competition preparations, confirming appointments, reading contracts. It felt like she'd only now stopped and blinked. But she'd also managed to avoid being alone with Jake, with her focus solely on the job.

But how was she going to avoid him now, when they were going to be alone for four days on their trip to Darwin?

*Just. Grrreat.*

Jake pointed to the small suitcase by the door. 'Is this your luggage?'

Sienna nodded, unable to find her voice. Was it too late to send Elliott?

'Funny, I thought you'd pack at least four suitcases, one for each day.'

'I packed light for the occasion because there's always time to shop on a business trip.'

'Finally, she speaks.' Jake chuckled as he picked up

Sienna's bag. 'Ready to go?'

*No*. 'Yes.' With laptop bag over her shoulder, she grabbed the travel mugs and headed for the door. 'Elliott, you have my number, and my email if you have any issues.'

'I'll be fine.' Elliott nodded. Then he shook his head with huge eyes. 'Won't I?'

'Pina, Lynn, and Jess will help if you need it. You did the pig truck, just think of the station kitchen as a spread-out workspace. You can do this, Elliott.'

'Okay, okay, okay.' Convincing neither of them.

'Keep an eye on the smokehouse and check the temp gauge. Bob will do the same. There are checklists on the pantry wall for the meal preps. And please don't forget about Sally.'

She squatted to pat the dog sulking on her bed. 'I'll get you a gift, Sally.' At least getting a half wag from the old dog's tail.

'She'll be fine,' called out Jake, securing the load in the trailer.

Honestly, she'd have to leave Sally eventually, which was going to break her heart when the time came.

Inside Jake's ute, Sienna put her laptop bag on her seat. 'I've forgotten something?'

Elliott pushed back his dark hair. 'What?'

'How do I know what I've forgotten when I've forgotten it?'

Jake's dropped his large hand on her shoulder. 'Relax and let them do their jobs. Now get in the ute so we can go.'

She gave her trusty offsider a hug goodbye and took her seat in the cab. As they drove off, she waved to Elliott standing alone in front of the muster room, it was the only light shining at the homestead at four in the morning.

Jake slipped his coffee into the cup holder and kept his eyes on the dirt track for the long five-hour drive ahead.

He was so big he filled the cab. She had to crack open the window for the cool air.

'What's wrong with you?'

'I'm so wired from rushing to get everything done, making sure everything's perfect.' She couldn't fail, for Jake's sake.

'I saw that. I remember you telling me you'd go full steam. So now, sit back and enjoy the ride.'

'I'm trying, but there's not much to see.' The dirt road was illuminated by his bank of spotlights that were as bright as a hundred camera flashes on freeze. Sunrise wasn't due for a few more hours and they were the only lights in the entire country. 'This,' she said, waving at the windscreen, 'makes me realise how big and far away this place is.'

'It's another world. So, I'll be your guest in the city.'

'Please let's not do the country boy in the city clichés.' Rolling her eyes as he winked at her. 'When did you last visit Darwin?'

'I can't remember. I've only gone as far as Katherine these past few years, trying to sell cattle.'

'Well, you've sold some of your herd, and we're on our way to selling more.'

'The cattle are only sold once they're on those ships and the money is in the bank, which will take how long?'

'I'm not sure. I wish I could offer you an exact time frame. I can get the contracts signed and organise meetings for introductions, but as for the rest ...' She shrugged. 'I don't know about cattle tariffs and carting cows like you do.' But she knew all Jake had to do was give Simon Simmons a phone call and he'd show up with his trucks and chequebook to buy out the entire place.

'I know, but your help has been amazing, Sienna. I appreciate everything you've done for me.'

'We're not done yet.' *Yes, we are.* She looked away. She had to remember that this was just a job, and she should have never mixed business with pleasure.

'So, what's the plan for this tour of Darwin?'

'We've got an appointment at the barra farm before we hit Darwin's industrial district. That's where we'll visit the quarantine yards, the market wholesalers, and the meat wholesalers.'

'Have you marked all of those places on the GPS?'

'Absolutely. I know how to play navigator.'

'Why did you stop racing rally cars?' Jake sipped his coffee. The rich caffeine aroma blended with his manly scent, filling the cab.

'I'm not so good at racing. But the navigating side is fun. It's so me, the planning ahead, then to react under high speeds, while having that driver trust me as we're hurtling around a blind corner. I loved it. Learning how to drive on dirt gave me more confidence on the road, and it was just fun.'

'Would you do more?'

'I like where I am now, I'll never race.'

'Why did you do it?'

'I used to have to schedule a time to get out and play. Yet, at Danbunnan it's a part of your daily lifestyle.' His world was unique, but not a permanent place for her.

She scrolled through her tablet's list. 'So, we've got the fish markets just outside the CBD. Then we can go to our hotel in the city, then the final appointment is the best one of the day.'

'What's that? Your tone has me wary.'

She grinned, not letting out the surprise. 'Dinner tonight is with my fabulous BFF Mail-order Biatch, Ricky, and his partner. You don't have to come, but you should. We'll be wine tasting for the competition's menu. Just so you know they're a gay couple. Is that going to be an issue for you?'

'I'm not a bigot.' He sniffed at her with annoyance.

'So, you'll join us for dinner, then?'

'I'll be there. I could do with a wine education.'

'Excellent, you won't regret it. We'll be trying to negotiate a decent discount. If you think I can negotiate, wait until you meet the queen of negotiations. But we can't get too drunk because we have a breakfast meeting with the water guy, then we're meeting your lawyer at Parliament House.'

'Why at Parliament House instead of their office?'

'Because we want the Minister for Agriculture to use his office to fast-track it through the normally long-winded departmental channels.'

'Is this that front-door stamp of approval you and Karl talked about?'

She nodded, hiding her grin behind her coffee.

'How did you score that?'

'I know people. You'll be making the minister look good when you let the guy witness the contract.'

'What's it gonna cost me?'

'It's a contra deal. The Minister will take a photo with you for PR. He'll then remember you at grants time giving you a heads-up on what would suit Danbunnan's future needs. You'll still have to apply of course …'

'Ah, I see. You're sneaky,' he said, with a relaxed grip on the steering wheel.

'Then we've got a meeting with the Minister of Mines, which will depend upon the university talks.'

'I can't believe I'm going to Parliament House and I'm going to meet with two ministers.'

'Have you ever been there?'

'Nope, but I've been thrown out of a few Darwin nightclubs.'

'There'll be none of that this trip, thank you. You have a reputation to keep up as the owner and director of Danbunnan Station.'

His grip tightened on the steering wheel as he peered down the dirt road.

'Are you okay?'

'I'm not used to being called that. Remember, I wasn't meant to have the title.'

'I know.' She patted his arm. 'Well, you are, Jake, so be proud of it.'

'Are we going to see that fancy office of yours?'

'No.'

'Why not? I'd like to see it.'

'We don't have time. This trip is all about you and Danbunnan. If I do visit, I'm …' She grimaced, hugging her tablet.

'Are you scared you'll get sucked back in again?'

'I know it's silly, but you're right … I created it, yet I'm okay not being a part of it anymore. It's working well without me. That project is done, and I'm enjoying this new project helping you.' She didn't get attached to anything in case it was taken away from her, which was the story of her life and how she'd survived.

'How can I repay you for this, Sienna?'

'You are paying me; it's in the contracts.' It was a job, even if she was going beyond the call of duty, but Jake needed this and she wanted him to succeed. 'So, back to the itinerary. We'll go through any questions we have for these meetings, and we'll have time to rehearse your speeches.'

'Great, all work while playing taxi.'

'You'll have playtime on Saturday, while I'm sleeping-in and squeezing in some shopping. You're booked to play golf with Barry and then dinner with Barry and Jenny at the casino. I'll catch up with you Sunday for the drive back to Danbunnan.'

'Aren't you coming with me on Saturday night? And the golf?'

'You need mate time with Barry playing golf and I still can't hit. I'll only slow you guys down.'

'You're getting better, and Barry wants to know what to expect when he comes out for the station tour. At least come to dinner and meet Jenny.'

'I don't think I should.'

'You're pulling away, aren't you?'

She couldn't lie to him. 'I leave soon.'

'But we're still friends. I'll still need your help.'

'I'll only be a phone call or an email away.'

'That's not the same, Sienna.' Jake frowned as he faced the dark road ahead.

No, it wouldn't be the same, but right now they had to finish the job first. Even if this was her first time back to the place she'd fled in her time of distress. This trip would tell her if she was truly ready to return.

# Thirty-five

Jake stood beside Sienna in the hallway of their hotel, waiting for the elevator. 'Did you know, I haven't left Danbunnan in three years, except for business? This is like a mini holiday for me.' Not that it had been much fun so far, going from meeting to meeting, with more lined up for tomorrow. It was the business side of the job he'd never expected. Thankfully, Sienna was there to help him every step of the way.

'I've been on a summer holiday for the past year,' said Sienna.

'Even at Danbunnan?'

'Yes, because it's not permanent.' Didn't that kill the mood.

'Where are we going now?'

'It's a surprise.'

'I should be used to your surprises by now.'

Into the lift, down to the foyer and out through the streets, Sienna hooked her arm around Jake's.

'Sienna, you're touching me in public.' And he liked it.

'No one knows us here and I don't want you getting lost.' She led him through the mixed crowd of office workers and backpackers. They entered a building through glass doors and into a cool blast of air-conditioning.

'Where are we?'

Black marble floors met walls made of mirrors. There was a chemical smell in the air, stronger than any cattle dip, reminding him of bleach. Elliott's style of music pumped in the background and the room was full of women wearing black capes with their hair being coloured, cut, curled, or straightened, while some wore tinfoil like aliens.

He'd definitely walked through the wrong door. 'I think I left the lights on in the ute ...'

'Don't you dare. It's just a haircut.' Sienna latched on to his arm.

'I only do barber shops.' And certainly not this room full of women watching him like an insect under a microscope. 'Look, you get your hair done, I'll be at the nearest pub.' Jake turned for the door. Even if Sienna still hung off his arm, he wanted out.

'Come on, it won't hurt, I promise.'

'What won't hurt? You said it's just a haircut, and I don't have that much hair.' He usually clipped his own hair that was kept under a hat, working on a station where no one saw him.

'*Sienna, angel*?' cried a high-pitched voice from a man who flounced towards them. '*You're home!*' He hugged and kissed Sienna on the cheeks like long-time friends. 'Oooh, who is this?' He squealed, moving as if ready to leap into a hug.

'Sienna?' Jake backed away for the safety of the door. He only liked being hugged by one person.

'Ricky, be nice, this is Jake's first time.' Sienna put a protective arm around Jake.

'Soooo, you're Jake...' Ricky tapped his fingers on his chin. 'The cowboy? A real live cowboy, in my emporium. Oh Cinderella, dreams do come true.' Ricky shook Jake's hand while ogling Jake's physique.

'I'm leaving now. Your mate just called me a cowboy.' Jake was ready to run.

'Ricky, no touch.' Sienna snatched Jake's hand back from Ricky, while tightening her grip on Jake.

'Okay, okay, I'm backing off.' Ricky lifted his open palms in the air as if under arrest. 'Sorry, mate, I was just having some fun with the protective little princess. I'll behave, or it'll be another year before I see her again. Now, please allow me to welcome you to my little corner of paradise.' Ricky clicked his fingers and two assistants appeared. 'Take Sienna through to the main salon. It'll be the full treatment for both. Jake, you go the other way into the back.'

'Where am I going?' When escaping through the front door looked a helluva lot better.

'Relax Jake, it's just a haircut and a little pampering,' said Sienna with a wave. 'You'll love it. I always do.'

'Good thing I trust you.' Yet Jake wasn't sure about this at all, following a woman with the weirdest green hair. Feeling like one of his cattle traveling down the chute before loaded onto a truck. What kind of ride was he in for now?

# Thirty-six

Jake had a head massage, a haircut, and the closest shave he'd ever had in his life, along with his first manicure. And they even gave him a beer for the effort.

Then Ricky skipped into the room of mirrors, sinks, and fancy barber chairs. 'Now, how did we do, hmm?' Ricky stood behind Jake, checking out his haircut.

'Okay?' Jake shrugged. No big deal.

'I see … Did you know Sienna's my bestest friend in the entire universe, and that she adores you?'

Jake slipped on his poker face.

Ricky flitted around Jake, inspecting the cut and shave. '*I said* Sienna adores you a thousand times more than she ever did that ex of hers. It's true love.'

'What?'

Ricky patted his heart with two hands. 'Oh, yes, it's the whole soul-consuming, love of soulmates, kind of love.'

'With who?'

'With you.' Ricky fussed with Jake's hair the same way Sienna perfected a plate of food for presentation. 'Which of course, she'll never say out loud. But I can see it. Do you need your eyes checked?'

'No. Do you?' He was over being touched by strangers and ducked his head away from Ricky.

The smell of hairspray carried along the corridor that echoed the noise of hairdryers as Ricky preened in front of the mirror. 'I've known Sienna forever, so I know how deep that girl feels for you.'

Ricky then leaned in closer, narrowing his green eyes at Jake. 'There had to be something special to keep Sienna in the middle of nowhere.'

'Sienna came out on a promise to Rhonda.' Because Jake doubted Sienna would have applied for the job under normal circumstances.

'Well, Sienna rarely makes a promise, and she does owe Rhonda, so okay, I'll give you that. But ...' Hand on hip, Ricky frowned at him through the mirror. 'Sienna adores that dirt land of yours. I've seen the photos she sends me with her real smile that makes her eyes all shiny. I used to get postcards from her that were these one-liner touristy words of droll, and from the word player, they had no pizzazz. But that place, that dirt land—or maybe it's you, or both—it's helped her.'

'How?'

'The girl's got her smile back.' Ricky twirled his finger on either side of his face as if drawing a large smile. 'She'll kill me for saying this, but I care, and you need to know this too.'

Jake's protectiveness over Sienna burned low in his gut. 'Know what?'

'That Sienna was a mess before she left here. Did you know her work used to be her happy place, where she was being so busy being busy? She was like one of those toys where you would pull the cord and it would go round and round in circles. That was Sienna. Sure, she got stacks of stuff done, chasing the adrenaline rush. But she never stopped to admire her achievements because she'd jump straight into the next project. When she left here she was a proper brain-fried mess.' He sighed heavily, only to then straighten up. 'But now she's found that playful spirit again. Taking the time to enjoy herself, learning new things like that golf range in dirt land. Fishing in those dirt ponds. Driving her toy-car instead of having to schedule a time to get it dirty. Growing her own edibles in dirt—that's on her *to-live list,* you know. Have you seen the *to-live list*?'

'Yes.' Was Ricky talking to Jake or Ricky's reflection?

'Wow, you're privileged, because she never shows anyone. Except me. But ...' Ricky sighed as he fussed with his own hair in the mirror. 'Did you know that *to-live list* is Sienna's reminder to have fun? How many things has she crossed off that list since she's been there in dirt land?'

'It's called Danbunnan.'

Ricky flippantly waved. 'I couldn't do it, but Sienna's happy in dirt land because of you, for you, with you. You. You. You.' Ricky pointed at Jake's reflection in the mirror. 'Now, don't be an idiot and let her go. And don't expect her to cook and clean for too much longer, because that phase is almost over with that fundraiser finale of yours.' Then with a wave of a soft dust brush, the black hairdressers' cape was whipped off as if Ricky was a Spanish bullfighter. 'You're free to go.'

'Where's Sienna?' And where was the quickest exit?

'As if I'd let you leave without Cinderella, she's rather protective over you. Follow me.' Ricky led him down the corridor. 'Soo, any thoughts, questions, gossip?'

'What do you want me to say, Ricky?' His mind was still reeling at the fast-babbling speech.

'Oooh.' Ricky smiled with his mouth open. 'You care about her too.'

'It's complicated.'

'The best love stories always are. But if they're worth the fight they work out to be the stories with the happiest happily ever after. You wait right there in that chair, and I'll go find our little Cinderella, who's going to bitch slap me for blabbing. I can't help it that I care about Sienna closer than a sister—if I had one. Just so you know, I'm scared if you reject her, I'll lose her forever. She's my family from a place of no family.'

'You and Sienna grew up in that home together?'

Ricky nodded. 'It was Sienna who helped me create all of this, she helped me find *my* happy place.' Ricky gave a dreamy smile at the salon. 'Now it's Sienna's turn, and I think she's found it in dirt land with you. So don't be some silly lonesome cowboy, because time is running out for the both of you.' Ricky flicked out a card like a magician holding an ace up his sleeve. 'If you get stuck with Sienna, call me. I'll do some intervention or rescue or whatever to help her. Just bear in mind, I don't do dirt.' Ricky then straightened his shirt and raised his chin. 'Now, if you'll excuse me, I'm off to get my bitch slap. Back soon.'

Jake collapsed into the chair, dumbfounded, to stare at Ricky's business card. *What the hell? Was it all true?*

A few moments later Sienna emerged with her fair hair, sleek and shiny like a halo, spilling softly past her shoulders.

'Babe, you are stunning.' Jake had to fight the urge to stroke her soft hair and watch it spill like water between his fingers.

'Thank you.' Her hair was glossy with a city chic to it, but her blush was the same colour as Danbunnan's red dust.

'Now, I'll see you both for dinner tonight.' Ricky gave Sienna a quick peck on the cheek and flitted off to gush over somebody else.

'Come on, I need another beer after this. My shout.' Jake held out his elbow, stoked when Sienna slipped her hand around his arm, and they walked down the street together.

He was keen to see where she came from and what made her happy. To see if this place was where she truly belonged.

# Thirty-seven

A jazz band filled the wine bar with their music, where Jake sat at the corner table with Sienna, Ricky and Ricky's partner, Mark. Over dinner, they'd gone over various wine choices for the competition events. Jake got on well with Mark and even Ricky—who was so different away from the salon. It'd been great to sit and share dinner beside Sienna and have a cattle-free conversation.

Through the wall of windows, there was a never-ending passing parade of people as part of the city's nightlife. He now understood what Sienna meant about people watching and was enjoying the beginning of his long working weekend.

Then the tempo of the band changed.

'I know this song.' His mum used to play it on her records in the schoolroom late at night like a lullaby that floated through the house when he was a small boy. He never knew the names of those songs, or the musicians that his mother favoured. But they told of her moods and kept her company under many a moon where she danced in the shadows on her own.

'May I?' He held out his hand to Sienna.

'Umm ...'

Her hesitation was normal, expected even, because of where they'd been. Yet no one from his world was here.

And for the first time he felt that taste of freedom, shaking off those shackles, unleashing the collar that had been strapped around his throat for so long.

He smiled at her, because he'd dined with her by candlelight, seen her dressed up for the city and she looked amazing, and he was proud to be beside her. Now he wanted this too. 'Just a dance, Sienna.' He'd always wanted to. 'At least once, please?'

***

Sienna's heart skipped a beat. It was the first time he'd asked her to dance. She'd seen Jake dance at the rodeo with Angela, with his sister, and even with his niece. Back then she'd pined for him to ask her, and of course he hadn't.

Whether it was the wine, the relaxed company of her friends, or the dimly lit atmosphere, Sienna nodded. Lost in his earnest royal blue eyes, there was no boss mask here. Just the man.

Jake guided her to the dance floor to join the other dancing couples. No one looked at them, dancing among a roomful of strangers where no one knew of their history. They were like any normal couple.

Jake caressed her lower back, drawing her closer to his chest as they slow danced to the sultry blues. She rested her head on his shoulder, immersing herself in his warmth, inhaling his divine musky-spiced cologne, as his strong arm wrapped around her. She tried to control her racing heart and tingling body, but the music drowned out any thoughts of resistance.

Jake's smooth lips pressed against her neck. His warm breath feathered against her ear, his strong heartbeat drummed against her chest, as his fingers entwined with hers. They shifted seamlessly from one song to the next, as other couples slow danced around them.

He squeezed her hand, then released his grip to let his fingertips glide up her arm to her shoulders where shivers squirrelled through to the rest of her body.

Sienna lifted her head and held her breath as his cheek brushed against hers, only then for his lips to brush her jawline. Until his fingertips held her chin, that was when Jake kissed her. Publicly.

Her lips were flush with his in a kiss that went so much deeper than the physical. She forgot where they were.

Until he stopped.

His body against hers, wrapped in the safety of his strong arms, she stared at him. Speechless.

His eyes searched past her flaws to make her feel beautiful, as if she was the only other person to share the room with him.

Again, his warm lips pressed against hers and she melted into the flavours of a midnight supper full of mystery and magic, a place of candlelight dinners, dancing, and romance. He was her forbidden fruit, his glorious taste of endless sultry summer breezes that was a part of the untamed outdoors that made up the man.

The song finished and Jake whispered, 'Let's get out of here.'

She looked at him. No longer afraid of losing what she could never truly have, for tonight she could pretend this wasn't the end.

At the elevator Sienna stepped inside, Jake stood with his back against the far wall. The doors closed and Sienna lunged at Jake and kissed him. The urgent desperation in their lips meshing, igniting the intensity that was both focused and wild, where her hunger for him could no longer be ignored.

*Ding.*

As the elevator doors opened, Jake carried her to her room, which was only a few steps from the lift. Not once did their lips part.

Sienna fumbled for her swipe card while Jake undid the ties on her dress, walking her into her hotel room backwards.

Jake kicked the door shut as he ripped off his shirt, hunger darkening his eyes.

Her dress opened, he slipped it off her shoulders, leaving her to stand in only her underwear. He clutched her lace covered breasts, Sienna groaned with a deep boundless pleasure. Bra cups lowered, breasts exposed, his hot mouth greedily worked from one to the other, his tongue trailing up her neck to find her mouth that he possessed with his.

Her lace panties disappeared in one quick tug, and he placed her onto the counter. His hungry hands were hotter than fire, taking her to the edge of ecstasy.

His jeans undone that they both hurriedly pushed down. She pulled him closer, and he entered her with such ferocity it shapeshifted their souls, latching onto each other where even a breath of air between them was too much distance.

Jake cupped her butt-cheeks, thrusting deeper with each motion. Moaning into her mouth, his groan travelled from his chest to hers.

Her hips met his, she clutched his shoulders as fingers dug into backs that bent together.

He lifted her and spun around. Two steps to the bed and he laid her on top, still inside, never stopping the momentum. With a rebel's grit of passion in the power of the slide and ride, he drove deeper, where all of their restraints were smashed. The pent-up denial of the past weeks was broken. The hard-fought emotional control they had maintained towards each other shattered into a raw possessiveness that made up the wild ride to the passionate finale.

Sienna arched her body and her climax hit new heights, as Jake roared with her.

This was their world.

Their union.

But she knew it was only for the now.

# Thirty-eight

Late Sunday afternoon Jake's ute pulled up at the front gate. The sign loomed overhead that read in fresh clear paint: *Danbunnan Station*.

Sienna jumped out of the passenger seat. In her sandals, she tiptoed over the steel cattle grid, then raised the hinge and pushed the large gate open. This time it didn't scream in protest.

Jake steered the ute through, and she shut the gate behind him. This time the sign didn't shudder or threaten to fall but hung strong and proud.

'Jake, what's wrong?'

He'd parked the ute in the shady avenue of symmetrically planted trees. They gave the impression of a formal garden setting, that was a stark contrast to the open outback scrub that surrounded them. Wearing a sombre expression, Jake stood under their shade facing the track that led to the homestead.

'Did you know that each of these trees signifies a member of my family. There's one for every Cullen who has ever lived here on the station? This tree …' He pointed to the largest tree that stood closest to the front entrance. Its treetop hidden in the branches that created an expansive canopy. 'This one is for my great-great-grandfather, Henry Cullen. He used to be in the navy, hated it, even if most of the terms in this place are naval.'

'Like the cook's quarters and I've heard Tom call the kitchen the galley?' Sienna asked and he nodded. 'I thought it was like some grand hotel name.'

'Naval terms, according to my grandfather. He said Henry Cullen planted this tree to represent himself, putting down roots to always remain a part of this land and not the sea. That one opposite is for my great-great-grandmother, Winifred Cullen.'

'She's my hero.' Especially from what she'd read in the journals.

'I know,' he said with a deep sorrow in his voice. 'Henry Cullen started the tree planting tradition to represent the Cullen family's arrival. This tree is for my great-grandfather who married my great-grandmother ...' Jake continued to walk past each tree, lining both sides of the track, saying the name of his ancestors. 'This is my father's tree, my mother's tree, my brother's...'

He pointed to the opposite side. 'That tree is for my sister, with the next three for her ex-husband, Brian, and the twins.' He paused as his posture stooped, as if carrying a heavy burden across his shoulders. 'That one is mine.' The last one on the left side of the track with nothing after it.

Jake walked to the tree planted in his honour. Its coarse trunk beneath his palm, craning his neck to peer through its thick green canopy.

He rested his forehead against the rough bark and his eyes closed as he said, 'I've always been proud of my family, of this property, and felt a connection to Danbunnan's history. Yet, at this moment, I hate it.'

'Why?'

\*\*\*

Jake rested his back against the large trunk, to face her natural beauty. He so wanted to give her the happy ending her eyes asked for. But he couldn't yet. Andrew was only taking a certain portion of beef, when he still had a large herd to sell with the competition and the co-op closing in.

Instead, he faced the homestead's direction. 'Because when we go down that driveway, I will no longer be able to hold your hand whenever I want. I won't be able to walk up to you, kiss you, or hold you anytime I want. These past few days with you have been amazing, babe. I don't want it to end.'

'Me neither.' Stepping closer, her delicate floral perfume with the scents of earthy bark mingled deep into his lungs. 'We both know it has to. I'm leaving soon, and you—'

'Hey, you and I, there might not be an *us*, but we don't end—not like this.' Jake pulled her to his chest where she belonged.

He kissed her, tasting a fear of fate, of failing, and the fear of living beyond this moment without her. Then he held her tight. 'I'm sorry for this whole situation with me, the family, the station, everything.'

'Don't be, Jake, it'll be okay. You have to believe that Danbunnan will have a future because of you.'

'I wish I'd met you before I came back here, when life was so much simpler.' Even if she'd found him in the wrong place at the right time, would they have ever managed to be together?

'Guess we all can't get what we wish for.'

'Yet I wish for you.' Jake held her tighter.

The leaves rustled with the breeze, as a pair of grey brolgas gracefully skimmed above the wild grasses that shifted like waves on a golden sea.

'We better go, or they'll come looking for us,' said Sienna.

He gently wiped the silk strands free from her beautiful face. His lips pressed against hers as if it was a goodbye and then he led her by the hand to his ute. Sienna climbed into the cab, and he closed her door, walked around to the driver's seat, and drove them further down the track.

He held her dainty hand until the last turn, then kissed the heel of her palm and each one of her delicate fingertips, then with a sigh he let her go. Gripped the steering wheel tight and entered the place he was supposed to call home, but in this moment, it felt like a prison …

# Thirty-nine

It was late in the afternoon when Jake drove his ute through the rear of the worksheds, to park his ute inside, with Tom riding shotgun. Joe, with his shiny crown over his trucker's cap, waited for them wearing a cheesy grin.

'What's with Joe?' Tom asked Jake.

'No idea. But I'm surprised that crown is still going.'

With five days to go, the place had gone through a major transformation. Inside the workshed, the benches had all been cleared. A fenced area had been set aside for Josh's snake cages, and all their tools and equipment were secured behind mesh doors. 'I've never seen the place locked up like this.'

'I have. Your grandfather would insist on it at times,' said Tom. 'But I've never seen it looking so clean.'

'Are we ready for our presentation for the judges? We still have time to fine-tune if we need to.'

'Besides giving some of the cattle a scrub for the stock inspection, we're good. It's a lot of work for one show. I don't think the other stations do this.'

'Other stations aren't under the kind of pressure we are. As much as I'd like to ignore them, I need those judges for the stock inspection, then they can leave.'

'You're not ignoring the judges, are you?'

'Oi, Boss,' called out Joe. 'Have you finished with your ute for today?'

'Hope so. Why?'

'Yours is the last of the fleet to be detailed,' said Joe.

'Fleet?'

Joe slapped a magnetic sign on the door that read *Danbunnan Station* with the brand they used for the cattle. 'You've got a fleet, Boss. See?' Joe pulled open the workshed doors to reveal the homestead's compound.

'No way.' Jake cocked an eyebrow at the row of work utes, gleaming in the sun, all wearing matching magnetic signs. 'Where did the signs come from?'

'Who d'ya reckon got 'em … they look good.'

'Did you clean them, Joe?' asked Tom.

'Me, no, the blokes who brought those beasts did all the detailing.'

'They're here, good. Tom, come check this out.' Jake strode out into the compound of cars.

'What the hell is that?' Tom pointed at the two new vehicles.

'Four-wheel drive tour buses.' Jake grinned at the buses, wearing Danbunnan logos. But it was Tom's jaw dropping reaction that made him chuckle the most.

'They're not practical for cattle.' Tom wrinkled his nose at the safari-style tourist buses.

Jake climbed inside. 'One bus is for the guests, the other is for the judges, to drive them around in air-conditioned style.'

Tom removed his hat and stepped inside. 'How much is this costing?'

'It worked out cheaper to hire these than it would've cost carting around eighteen people in a convoy. You'll be driving the guests in one of these puppies. It's just like a troop carrier, only better. I had a play in Darwin.'

'Flash lookin' troopie. But hey, if you insist, Boss.' Tom settled into the driver's seat, one arm rested across the back, as his grey eyes took in the details.

'Jake, you have to see this,' said Jess, rushing up to the doorway. 'Come on.' She tugged on his shirt like a little kid eager to show off her new toy. 'It's the shed.'

'Have they finished cleaning it?' Jake, along with Tom, followed Jess past the stables and calving sheds and out of the mouth of the horseshoe compound towards an old hay shed that stood furthest from the homestead.

'Uncle Jake, look at these,' Kate called out, seated beside her brother at a fold-up table under the shade of a nearby tree.

'What are you two doing?' Jake chuckled at their paint splattered clothes and faces. Their mother obviously wasn't bothered by the paint in their hair, because she was smiling at her children with pride.

'We're making signs. See? Dubai is that way. Sydney is that way, and Darwin is that way.' Kate pointed with a jangle of her bangles at the scrap wood painted with place names and kilometres.

'North Pole is that way. So where does the Easter Bunny hang out?' Aaron poked his tongue out the side of his mouth as he painted between the lines.

'No idea, mate. Rabbits live in burrows.' Jake then shrugged at his sister.

'The delivery trucks have been coming in and out all day. Sienna had me put up some signs, so they knew where they were going, and to stop stirring up the dust in the compound. She said it would also be good for the guests, so they don't get lost. I'd never thought of it,' said Jess.

'It's not the first party Sienna's organised.' But it was Jake's first. 'The signs look great, Twins.' But he was curious to see what they'd done to the old shed.

As they continued on to the hay shed, Jake glanced back at the track that led to the working yards and the rest of Danbunnan's open country.

But the view was blocked by massive rolls of hay that stood on the back of the road-train trailers that lined the track. *Damn, it looked good.*

'Why are the stockfeed rolls lined up like that?' Tom asked Jake.

'To hide the herd and to create an impact when we start

the tour. Sienna's suggestion—all about the wow factor.' It had his attention.

Jake tapped the brim of his Akubra at Lyn, who waved from the semi-trailer cab she drove with amazing skill. It was polished, with a magnetic Danbunnan sign on the door. She parked it beside the station's utes and trucks gleaming in the sunshine before the worksheds. 'Huh, I have a fleet.' He raised his tablet and took a photo of them.

'It's like a wedding,' said Jess. 'All vehicles polished—'

'No, it's not, this is a …' *What did Sienna call it?* But Jake soon forgot what he was saying when he spotted what was inside the enormous hay shed.

The rusty old shed, which was barely more than two half walls and a roof, was now cleared of hay and cobwebs.

Smaller rectangular hay bales had been stacked in a curved arc to create an impressive backdrop. Hanging in front was a massive projector's screen, with an area cleared for a dance floor, surrounded by large round tables and chairs.

Along the far-right side Charlie was constructing a bar made from scrap timber and pallets. Josh was hanging chandeliers from the corrugated roof, with Tyson running the power leads. To the left, Elliott worked by the nest of tables with Pina to create a serving area for meals, leaving a group of six plastic-covered red couches to one side.

'What's with the couches?' Tom asked.

'It's the lounge area,' said Sienna, holding out a plastic container. 'Here take this, I can't stop eating it.'

'What's this?' Jake wanted to hug her, to kiss her, or put his arm around her, but couldn't. That was for after dark and sneaky moments away from everyone.

'It's a new batch of salami.'

Jake took a few slices, then handed the container to Tom. 'You're spoiling us.'

'Tom, there's a new chilli-style salami we've made. I'd appreciate your honest opinion,' Sienna said.

'If you insist,' said Tom with container in hand. 'Rhonda

would love this, she loves a good party.'

'Has anyone heard from Rhonda?' Jake adored the station cook, and missed her. But he didn't want Rhonda to return because he wanted Sienna to stay. Not forgetting he was engaged to another woman, and Sienna wasn't going to cook and clean forever especially when they couldn't have an *us*.

*Damn*.

It was the only subject Sienna and Jake didn't talk about, remaining focused on this event ever since they'd returned from Darwin. But he made sure he snuck into her room every night and took advantage of any small snatches of time to be alone with her.

'What is that mob doing?' Popping a salami slice in his mouth Tom headed towards Elliott with Jess beside him eager to explain.

'What were you taking photos of?' Sienna's dress hem flowed with the slight breeze, as a fine sheen of red dust settled on her half-laced town boots. With no make-up or jewellery, and hair tied back, she was more beautiful now than when she was all dressed up in the city.

'I have a fleet.' Jake grinned back at the group of parked vehicles all clean and shiny with their matching signs.

'I'll get the camera.' She'd walked to the side where her laptop was stationed, where Sally the cattle dog was asleep under the table. 'Here, you have the natural eye for this.'

Jake took the digital camera and aimed it towards the fleet. He'd never thought he'd get into photography, but he enjoyed it. He got a kick out of seeing it on the website, and Sienna had suggested he should put photos on Instagram, like Elliott. Yeah, *not*.

He took more photos of the work in progress, starting with the twins painting the signs. Then the ex-mining couple, Joe and Lyn, holding hands as they strolled towards them from the worksheds. The renovated buildings of the compound where smoke trailed in a whisper from the smokehouse as its latest addition.

He took another bite of salami. The flavour of smoky meat made his taste buds dance. 'Hey, this salami is good.'

'It is?'

'I wouldn't lie to you.' He never would, swearing to keep no secrets from her, even if their relationship was one big secret.

'We changed the wood,' Sienna said. 'Mahogany works well.'

'And I've got plenty of that weed lying around the place.'

'You told me that, which is why I'm trialling it.'

'I like how you listen, and your initiative, your smile and that tight piece of—' Stopping at her arched eyebrow.

He peered around the shed where everyone was busily setting up for one night. 'Yeah, I'll behave.' Even if he didn't want to. 'So, are the magnetic signs for the fleet the only surprise I'll find today? Like your explanation on the red couches, please?'

'Well, the front entrance will be under spotlights, making sure the first thing guests see is the sponsors' banners. The banners will create a wall here, and the sofas will create a wall on the right. Guests entering will be requested to at least offer a gold coin donation for the Black Dog appeal.' She pointed to the areas inside the shed and explained, 'The left side is where food will be served, with tables set for dining. The dance floor and stage are in the centre. The right side of the shed is for drinking and mingling at the bar. Leaving the right corner for the couches so people can lounge a little further away from the noise. So I've created rooms. Eating, dining, dancing, drinking, and lounging.'

'Where did the chandeliers come from?'

'Your dad bought them decades ago.'

'Dad bought a lot of junk.' Jake still wasn't talking to his dad. He'd been okay with the lifetime of being bullied, but he still struggled over Bob's treatment of Duncan being told he wasn't Bob's son, including how he'd treated his mother, and the damage he'd done to Danbunnan itself. How could he forgive when he couldn't forget?

'Okay, I'll admit the chandeliers make a nice touch, it gives the place some class.'

Her eyes lit up. 'I love these chandeliers. Tyson's wiring them up for solar. I can't wait to do a test run tonight. We may need to add more fairy lights. And we're testing the projector, too.'

He was impressed at how everyone was here chipping in—except one. 'Where is Dad?'

'Your father is avoiding this place, Jake,' she said with a sombre tone. 'Bob keeps saying he's busy with the smokehouse and won't leave the compound. But this shed is just down the road, path, track—whatever you call it.'

'Track will do. That's Dad's deal if he wants to sulk. Not my issue, and I don't want you to worry about it either. And this is where you show me something new.'

'Well, I could use your opinion, because I'm not sure how you're going to react? This way.' With shoulders hunched, she nibbled on her lower lip, pointing to some large rectangular posters spread across the round table. 'They're for the walls.'

'No way...' They were black-and-white images of his ancestors, the outstation, and other historical photographs of the past hundred-and-thirty years. Photos that had once lived inside albums that collected dust in the old office, were now life-size portraits. 'What are you going to do with these?'

'Charlie's making frames so we can hang them on the corrugated walls, and we'll put spotlights on them like artwork in a museum to add to the atmosphere.'

'Babe, you've taken this to a whole new level. It's not a shed party, is it?'

'No, it's more of a product launch for you, as the new cattle king of Danbunnan.' She looked at him squarely, as if to see right through to his soul, deeper than anyone had ever looked before. 'You know, I'd never fully grasped the concept of what you did as boss until we went over the sales portfolios and Danbunnan's business plans. What you do is huge. I've worked with lots of people in many different industries, and I will say one thing ...' She poked his chest lightly and said, 'You're not a simple bloke in the country with that hat and crooked grin. You, sir, are a brilliant man.' And then she walked away from him. 'Elliott, can we please go higher with those lights to deepen the loop? It needs to be even with what Josh has done on his side or it'll look odd.'

Jake stood with the camera in one hand, salami in the other, and watched her walk away.

Whenever he felt like he couldn't do something, Sienna would say let's work out a way and they were off. He said a tree was a pest, so she found a way to make smoked smallgoods out of it. They could do anything together — except go public about their relationship.

'I like the posters,' he called after her, and was rewarded with a smile over her shoulder. She knew him so well, yet it'd take a lifetime to know all about her, which would be a challenge he'd enjoy — if he could.

But first he had to survive this weekend, and then maybe — just maybe — he could plan for a different kind of future that didn't feel like it was draining his soul.

# Forty

Inside the cook's quarters, the slight *tick tick tick* came from the rotation of the ceiling fans that stirred the cool air. The red numbers on the alarm clock were the only light that highlighted the bed made of the finest soft linens where Jake and Sienna slept.

They jolted awake at the knock on the door.

'*Boss*.' It was Tom.

'Damn.' Jake slipped on his jeans and rushed to the door.

'We are so busted,' mumbled Sienna, hiding beneath the covers.

Jake stepped outside, not sure what to say, when he spotted the stockman's face. 'What's wrong, Tom?'

'There's dingoes up at the north valley makin' a helluva racket.'

'Meet me at my ute. Grab the shotguns.'

'On my way, Boss.' Tom nodded, and with a steady stride he marched for the worksheds.

Inside, Jake turned on the bedside lamp, bathing the room in a soft glow. 'Sienna?' He sat on the bed, put his boots on and slipped his arms through the sleeves of his shirt. 'Babe?'

'We are so busted.' Her muffled voice coming from under the covers.

He pulled the covers down, her fair hair was spread out everywhere. 'I have to go.'

'What's wrong?'

'I'm going to check on the cattle. Back soon.'

'Be safe, please?'

His heart melted at her genuine care, even half asleep. 'I will. Go back to sleep.' He kissed her forehead, slipped on his hat, and rushed out of the room, buttoning his shirt. Right now, he didn't want dingoes near his cattle. It could end up being very costly if they did.

Jake drove his ute along the dirt track as spotlights sliced through the blackness. In the passenger seat, Tom cradled his rifle and swept the area with a handheld spotlight. Two shotguns and boxes of ammunition rested between them. With solemn expressions, there was a sense of urgency in the air as they made their way to the valley near the North Ridge.

The spotlight found a bleating wild-eyed heifer trying to get up, covered in blood with her hind torn apart by the wild dogs.

'Aw, hell …' Jake hated this.

The echoing shotgun was soon lost in the night as he put the poor beast out of its misery.

'She's calved Tom, that's why they're after her. Search for a calf. I hope they didn't get it.'

'I can't see it.' Tom used the handheld spotlight to scour the area.

Jake climbed onto the back of his ute, unclipped a large spotlight from the roof's railing and swivelled its wide beam a whole three-hundred-and-sixty degrees. '*Dog, two o'clock, Tom.*'

A dingo stood blinded by the light with blood dripping from its jaws. Guilty.

*Boom*. The shotgun echoed its justice, and the wild dog was done.

'We won't find any more tonight, coz that pack would've hauled arse outta here.' Tom approached the dog to ensure it was gone.

They resumed their search for the newborn, Jake on the back, as Tom drove the ute around the restless cattle. But there were no more dingoes.

'*There, I see it.*' Jake tapped on the roof of his cab. '*Nine o'clock.*' He aimed the spotlight at the group of spindly trees where a small calf stood on shaky legs. Before the ute had stopped Jake leapt off the back and carefully approached the newborn.

'Hey, little fella.' It was trembling, spooked from a rough first night. He scooped it up in his arms. 'Hey, it's all right, mate, you're okay now.' Trying to soothe the struggling young animal, he held it tight to his chest.

'Have you got him, Boss?'

'Yeah. There should be an old rag behind the seat. We'll wrap him up and take him to the calving sheds.' The calf bleated, its big brown eyes were wide with fear, pressing its wet nose against Jake's shoulder. It didn't fight but shivered as Jake held it to his chest. 'How old would you say the dog was?'

'Less than a year.'

'New litter. Damn.' Cradling the newborn in his arms, Jake climbed into the passenger seat and Tom drove them home. 'I want an electric fence set up in this area. Be sure to whack up the juice for a bit. Get Tyson and Josh onto it, they can clean up the mess, too. I also want to run a random rotation of boundary riders as a dingo deterrent.'

'They'll get the message soon enough. They're not dumb animals.'

The calf rested calmly in Jake's lap as he stroked its big ears and glanced out the window passing the main herd that needed protection. 'See if the crew will take turns playing night watchmen over the herd.'

'Joe and Lyn are always keen for camping.'

'Good. I don't want to lose any more. It won't be long, and we'll start shipping them out. Tomorrow we'll scour the herd for any ladies that are due. I missed this one. I don't want to miss any more.' The smell of birth attracted dingoes, just like blood called to sharks in the water.

'Yes, Boss.'

'Any suggestions?'

'Nope.' No, Tom never did put suggestions forward. He'd say if something was right or wrong, and nothing more. But it was always for the good of Danbunnan.

Inside the calving shed, Jake had just finished bottle-feeding the newborn in the small stall, watching it snuggle up to the other babies. 'Tom?'

'Yes, Boss.'

'Where else did you look for me before you came to Sienna's room?'

'Nowhere. I went there first,' replied Tom, his gaze direct.

*Damn.* Jake lowered his head and shut his eyes. 'Is it that obvious?'

'I don't think anyone else has noticed. I won't say nothing, coz it wouldn't look good, not with you being engaged to someone else.'

Jake hated his fake engagement. 'Tom, you know you're a part of this place and have the right to say how you feel. I respect your opinion.'

'Still …' Tom cleared his throat. 'It's not my place to say, Boss.'

Jake hadn't spoken to Tom about his mum's letter. How could he strike up that kind of conversation? And what would Tom do if he knew Duncan was the half-brother they'd shared?

Flat out with the competition preparations, Jake hadn't thought about it. As Sienna would say, business came first, and Tom and Jake were all about putting Danbunnan first.

Without Tom, who knows where Danbunnan would be today.

Jake leaned his forearms against the pen's railing and watched the future of his herd sleep. 'Tom, how come you never left this place, when you've had plenty of job offers?'

'Didn't want to be anywhere else.'

Jake glanced at Tom. 'Sienna said you knew about the journals being in Rhonda's room. Is that true?'

'Yeah.' Tom removed his hat and rubbed his clipped black hair with flecks of grey highlighting his temples. 'It's obvious you've found them, using them for this competition.'

*Damn, Tom knew all this time.* 'Look, um, do you know about my mother … and your …' Jake winced.

'My old man?' Tom gave a sharp nod.

'Why didn't you say something?'

'Coz I wasn't sure if Duncan was my half-brother, or you were, but either way I had a brother. That's why I stayed, and I've always loved working here. Your family has always been good to me. Your grandparents helped my dad and me after my mother left with my sister. Your family put me through school, gave me a job, and helped me with my dad's funeral. You helped me get Elliott here and helped me look after him. So yeah, your family have done a lot for me over the years. Besides, I'm a simple bloke. I don't want nothing, don't need nothing, when I've got all I want right here.'

'Why did your mother leave?'

'Mum didn't like this place, she liked the city. We've both seen enough people who come out here to know that they'll either love it or hate it. Mum hated it.'

'So how did you find out about my mum and your dad?' That still made Jake cringe.

'My old man went on a huge bender and told me how much he loved your mother but couldn't offer her anything, except to watch over her. Dad reckoned he'd failed her a few times with how Bob used to treat your mother when he was on a rum bender.'

Jake frowned at the childhood memory of Bob bullying his mum.

'That night my old man spilled about your mother and said I had a brother. He never said which of you boys was his. But the way your father treated you, I figured Bob knew about the affair. Your mum swore she never told Bob who it was because we were working here.'

'Bloody hell ...' Jake rubbed his palms over his face and blurted out the words on a conversation filled with awkwardness. 'Tom. I found a letter from my mother, stuck inside one of the journals when Sienna showed me how she'd learned more about Danbunnan's history than Dad did. I know Sienna promised Rhonda to not tell, but ...'

'You gave her no choice?'

'Sienna told me Rhonda wanted her to look after them, which Sienna has, Tom. Sienna calls Winifred Cullen her hero and can relate to what's written in those journals. I've learned a lot myself from those journals about their old farming techniques too.' He'd loved the times he'd shared with Sienna reading them aloud while he held her against his chest feeling her voice against his skin.

'Those journals were meant to be kept in the cook's quarters until Bob passed away or when Rhonda and I thought it was a good time to give them back to you. They've always been yours. We just promised your mum to protect them, so your dad didn't try to burn them again. It was the safest place because Bob never goes to the cook's quarters. He's crashed on my couch plenty of times when he's been on the rum.'

'That's why they're still with Sienna.' The anger in his voice only a drop compared to what he felt for his father who had done so much damage. 'Jess is ticked Dad destroyed the original chest. It had Mum's movies and records.'

'I know.'

'Where was I when this happened?' Jake would've done anything to save that stuff for his mother.

'Working out east in Queensland. It was right before your parents had that huge argument with Duncan. I spotted Bob dragging that chest full of journals across the compound with your mum begging him to stop. But he wouldn't listen. Rhonda and I wanted to do something, but we couldn't. It wasn't our place.'

'So, how did those journals end up in the cook's quarters?'

'Your mum begged me to follow Bob, who'd dumped that trunk into the dinghy and was heading for the river in his ute. She was worried Bob would fall in the river being drunk, and you've seen how big those crocs are.'

'Yeah, I have.' He'd seen those sneaky crocodiles take down a full-grown water buffalo in seconds.

'By the time I got there, Bob had poured fuel over the trunk, set it alight, dumped it overboard, then took off. I tried to save what I could from the bottom of the trunk and the rest sank or got burnt. It broke your mother's heart … And that was the start of everything becoming a bloody mess after that.' Tom shoved his hands in his pockets and exhaled heavily.

'But the place is coming back. Nah, it's better than back, coz it's beyond anything I'd ever imagined.' Tom adjusted his hat, then squarely faced Jake. 'Back at the meeting, that giggly girlie asked me what my favourite place was on this station. Well, it's all of it. To see Danbunnan alive when that sun rises every single morning does it for me, and it's looking prettier than ever.'

'We did this, Tom.'

'No, you did this. I only helped you, just like that girlie up in the cook's quarters, she supported you too. Sienna sees what you are.'

'I don't want her to go, Tom, but I don't know how to keep her here either.' There, he'd voiced it. It was out. 'I'm not looking past this weekend.'

'I know, but I'm bloody glad I nominated you for this competition.'

Jake gave Tom a questioning frown. 'You nominated Danbunnan? Can you do that? I thought only the bosses had the power to nominate?'

'And head stockmen.'

'Why? Truth, Tom, not as a boss, but as me, Jake. Please, no more secrets.' He'd had enough of secrets and the damage they'd caused.

'Fair enough, B—Jake.' Tom sighed, rubbing the back of

his neck. 'I saw the crappy stock Simon Simmons had on show at the rodeo. And then I watched them judges grill you about being Danbunnan's new boss. It ticked me off when Bob spouted off a load of bulldust, calling your management techniques some hobby—my arse—when he's never left the compound to see what you've achieved. We worked damned hard, you most of all, and I wanted to show off the work you'd done, coz I'm proud to be part of Danbunnan and her changes. The highs and the lows.'

'I'm sorry you were involved with the lows.'

'That's life,' Tom said with a shrug. 'But don't ignore those judges either. Be proud of what you've done here. The team's worked hard. And I dunno what Sienna is—coz she's no simple cook with what she's been doing—but you can see that giggly girl's putting her whole heart into this. Mate, she's making this place and you shine. You're a Cullen, and even if we don't win that competition, I'll follow you as a boss coz you're a natural leader. Danbunnan is alive because of you.'

Jake blurted out in one breath, 'Duncan was your brother, not me, but we shared the same brother. Tom, you've always been there for me, and I'd be proud to call you brother.'

Tom did what Tom always did and gave his signature nod. 'Thanks, Jake, that means a lot.'

They both blinked, cleared their throats, sniffed at the air while staring at the sleeping calves as if to regroup after that heavy conversation.

'Hey, who else knows that you nominated Danbunnan for the competition?' Jake asked.

'The committee treasurer and secretary, and there's others,' Tom mumbled, staring at his boots shifting across the dirt floor.

'Who? Because Simon Simmons and the other judges don't know.'

'Most of the competition committee is made up of senior staff members elected by other permanent staff or station owners. The judges are the bosses for the beef and overall station performance. The rest is done by the peers, like the cooks judge the cooking, the stockmen do the same. Then, it all gets tallied together. They hold meetings that are more gossip sessions, kind of like country women's groups where some have Tupperware parties while we're having a beer and barbecue.'

'Do you go?' Jake couldn't picture Tom swapping Tupperware lids while discussing the latest in must-have plastics.

'When I can.'

'I only knew Dad's deal as a judge, I wasn't interested in the competition.' Now here he was spending everything he had on one weekend.

'Nah, you were too busy holding up the bar.'

'That's true.' Jake chuckled. 'So, who else is on the committee?'

'Rhonda's secretary.'

'That explains all the Tupperware in the storeroom.' Jake shook his head. 'Rhonda's on leave. Does she know about Danbunnan's nomination in this competition?'

'Yeah.'

'But if you're both working on the same station, you would've needed someone else to second your nomination. Who did you get?'

'China.'

'You used Simon Simmons's station cook?'

Tom nodded. 'China doesn't want to lose her job to Sienna.'

'Bloody hell.' Jake rubbed his forehead at this unfolding twist of a night. 'Who else nominated Danbunnan?'

'Nearly every head stockman from every other neighbouring station and beyond backed me.'

'Do you have that much pull?'

'No. It's because of you, Boss. I told them what you were doing out here. We're all aware Simon Simmons is stacking the market, calling our beef pet meat, which is a load of bollocks. The other head stockmen in the region, they've seen what Simmons is doing. These competitions used to be for a reason, but now they're trapped with Simmons taking control of the co-op. So don't let them buzzards beat you, but don't short-change yourself by ignoring that mob either.'

'We're going beyond the competition stuff, Tom.' Too tired to explain.

'You and Sienna are resetting the boundaries on this competition, and it needs it. Remember, the contractors from this last muster? They want to set the record straight because they want to come back for the next muster. As a lad, I saw those men who'd line up to stay here because the cattlemen's quarters were the first of its kind in the Territory. Now you've got kids lining up to be your apprentice, who aren't bothered by the rumours the co-op is spreading. That's a whole new generation choosing to learn from you.'

'If they were all like Josh, it'd be great. Annie was a lesson learned.'

'How's that kid doin'?' Tom's hard eyes softened with concern.

'Annie's mum emailed me. Annie is getting help and back at home with her family.' It still bothered him how that had turned out, but they were paid to show apprentices a trade, not to babysit them.

They both watched over the small baby calf, babysitting of a different kind, now fast asleep.

A *tap tap tap* came from a beetle tapping on the lamp hanging off the gate. There was no breeze, but the scent of hay and rich earth still reached them where the corrugated iron sheltered them from the dew that kissed the earth goodnight.

'I'll take the next feed. Go rest up, Boss, you've got a big day tomorrow. Will you let the twins know there's a newborn to look after?'

'I'll tell them in the morning. Thanks, Tom.' Jake patted Tom on the shoulder.

He headed to the house, showered, and went into his bedroom. It was the same room he'd had all his life, a place to sleep and change his clothes. But why sleep here when he had sleeping beauty waiting for him, with what little time they had left.

Jake messed up his bed to keep up appearances. Grabbed a clean shirt and jeans from his dresser and spotted the photos he'd stuck in the mirror's frame as he got dressed. They'd been there so long he never noticed them anymore.

They were still images of his graduation with his mum, sister, and Duncan. His rodeo win with Craig. At university partying with Ryan and Barry. Then there was the image of the golf crew, Jake and his three best mates with golf clubs in their hands as men, beside the photo of them as boys in uniforms outside their boarding school.

Then there was Tom standing beside Jake when he broke in his first horse. Tom had always been there for him, teaching him about cattle and the land, as well as how to fish, ride motorbikes, and drink beer.

Jake took the photo of Duncan and put it beside Tom. Now he knew what he was looking for, it was easy to spot the similarities.

He was so glad that the 2IC had stayed and been a big part of his life. They'd shared a brother, which made Tom family and Danbunnan was Tom's home too.

This house, this room, was part of a home, but not where Jake wanted to be right now, so he headed back to Sienna's room.

Inside the cook's quarters, he took off his boots and slid between the silken covers on her bed. He'd never bothered about fancy sheets before, but had to admit it was nice sleeping in luxury. Even better sleeping next to his lady.

'You're back.' Sienna stirred in her sleep, reaching for him. 'Is everything okay?'

'Shh...' Jake cradled her against his chest. 'Nothing that can't wait until morning.' He listened to Sienna's deep breathing as she snuggled up to him in her sleep.

Tom was right about the competition—he couldn't afford to ignore the crooked judges. But what was the best way to deal with them?

If Sienna was awake, she'd help brainstorm this one. They could discuss it before anyone else made it to the muster room like any normal couple sharing breakfast. Except Sienna cooked for everyone, and he got to sit at the kitchen bench sipping her coffee with the best view of the relief cook swivelling in her skirts.

Again, Tom was right. The support he got from Sienna made him feel capable of achieving almost anything. He held Sienna tighter, because she was his dream and this little piece of luxury was his heaven at home. He just had to work out how to keep all of them—his home, his lady and the family—together, before it was too late.

# Forty-one

Sally barked as Jake's ute pulled up before the house on the hill. From the muster room Sienna watched him bound up the steps, and that was her cue.

She dashed across the compound to Jake's ute, placing an esky and a large envelope on the passenger seat.

She swallowed down the lump in her throat while staring up at the house with dread. 'Please don't hate me. Please don't hate me.' She repeated the mantra as she walked up the steps to the verandah and around the corner to the side door.

'You're here,' said Jess, opening the screen door.

Sienna didn't want to be, but there seemed to be no other way to do this. 'Where are the twins?'

'In the schoolroom. Come on.' Jess dragged Sienna into the house kitchen.

'Sienna?' Jake stood at the open fridge holding a juice bottle he'd been guzzling.

'Jake, don't move,' said Jess, disappearing down the corridor.

'Why? Where are you going? You called me in here. You said it was important.'

'I'll be right back.'

'Please don't hate me.' Sienna scrunched her shoulders to her ears. She stood by the door ready for a quick exit because she was about to cross that line today by getting in the middle of family business.

Jake approached her in those dust-stained jeans made perfectly for the man, with his earnest eyes that saw straight through her, pinning her to the spot.

'I'd never hate you. What's wrong?' Jake's aroma of outdoorsy male was intoxicating.

'I, ah ...' *Hurry, Jess.* She peeked over his broad shoulders to the empty doorway.

Jake blocked her view and placed his palm on the wall beside the doorframe, trapping her. 'Babe, tell me?'

The man was clever and could see straight through her. 'You know your issue with the judges and bus arrangements?'

'I hope you've found a solution because I haven't. We need someone to answer the judges' questions, because I'll be busy concentrating on our special guests, and you'll be busy cooking and doing everything else behind the scenes. Can't we give those judges a map and say, *there you go, send me a postcard, and tell me how you get on?*'

She giggled. 'I may have a solution. Although you might not like the idea? Um, so you've done your cowboy in the herd thingy for the day?'

'I'm not a cowboy. Don't play your word games on me.' He kissed the tip of her nose, which made her smile. 'I rode Sampson today and we sorted through the herd, it was good. It gave me time to think, until Jess called me in for something. But hey ...' His fingertips brushed her hair around her face. 'If you've got time we could nick off for an hour or two?'

'Tempting.' *Hell, yeah.*

'Come on, Dad.' Jess's voice carried down the corridor.

'Please don't hate me, Jake.' Sienna ducked away from him just before Bob and Jess entered the kitchen.

Jake spun around, wary. 'What's going on, Jess? You said you needed me.'

'I do. Well, no, you need Dad.'

Jake stood tall and frowned so hard it could've cracked the foundations of the building. 'No, I don't.'

'See, the boss doesn't need me.' Bob turned away, but Jess refused to let him go.

'I'm leaving.' Jake turned for the door.

'No.' Sienna stood in front of Jake. 'Please listen.'

'You two men, STOP!' The normally timid Jess was so loud they stared at her.

Sienna had to bite her tongue to not cheer at the mini mouse that roared.

'*You men need to sort this out, right now.*' Jess's hands shook as she clenched them into white-knuckled fists, her face reddening as she glared at the men in her family. 'Sienna, this was your idea.'

'Great, dob me in.'

'Sienna, what's going on?' Jake faced her with a questioning frown.

'All right.' Sienna raised her hands in appeasement. 'I'm going to be brutally blunt here, and you may hate me for this, so here it is ... The judges are coming because you, Bob, accepted the nomination, which means you're involved, whether you want to be or not. And right now, Jake needs you.'

'No, I don't.' Jake crossed his arms over his chest.

'Yes, you do. Bob, you've been a judge for decades. You know what they're looking for and can answer their questions. So, Bob, you'll be the judges' host, while Jake looks after the guests and everyone else.'

'Hmmm.' Jake tilted his head at Sienna then looked at Bob.

Great. She was halfway there. Now she had to convince Bob.

'Why me?' queried Bob.

'Who better than you? This is meant to be a family function and right now Jake is carrying everything. Bob, I know you're helping, but you don't understand what's out there and it's time you did.'

Bob shook his head with arms crossed. 'Nope, I will not get in the way.'

'You won't be in the way, that's the thing. We know stuff went down, and that you're sorry and want to fix it. This will help, because Jake needs someone to babysit the judges and who better than an ex-judge himself.'

'Dad has never bothered listening to me before.'

'You have to make him listen, Jake.' Sienna turned back to face the ex-boss. 'You ran things your way, Bob. Now you have the chance to see what the next generation is doing, to see Jake's way of doing things, and the amazing things he's achieved. So please be open-minded to these changes. Remember, you created change in your time when you did the cattlemen's quarters, and now you've got the smokehouse—and you should know why we're doing that too.'

'We're just smokin' meat. So what?' The crevices deepened on Bob's weatherworn face.

'Think bigger picture, Dad.' Jake's stance was solid with arms crossed over his steely chest. 'You could've told him, Sienna.'

'No, that's for you to *show* him as you explain why.' Stuck between both men, Sienna said, 'You both have lots to sort out and you're not expected to fix it overnight. But right now, we need unity—even if you have to fake it. Come on, we're putting on a show for these people, promoting Danbunnan's history as a family-run environment, *and I bloody well want to see it.*'

'What do I have to do?' Bob asked.

'Follow me.' Sienna grabbed Jake's hand. Jess did the same with Bob and they followed Sienna out the door.

Jake was furious, with that tell-tale vein ticking on the side of his forehead.

'Hate me later, fine, but I'm doing this for you.' She opened Jake's ute, hoping he saw sense once he got past his anger. 'Sorry to both of you, but if I'd asked you first, you would've said no.'

'Dad won't do it.'

'I think he will. Please try. You know I'm making sense.'

'Unbelievable.' Jake rolled his eyes as he jumped into the driver's seat.

'Dad, come on, you need to do this for Jake, for Danbunnan, and for me. Please.' Jess tugged on Bob's hand as if pulling a stubborn mule.

'Come on Bob, get in the car. You have your glasses now, so you have no excuse not to see what amazing things Jake has done.'

'Nick off, woman,' grumbled Bob as he climbed into the passenger seat.

'*Oi, don't you dare talk to Sienna that way,*' said Jake with a low frown over his darkening eyes.

*Wow,* even mad at her, Jake cared.

'Sorry, Sienna.' Bob clipped on his seatbelt, and Jess passed him his hat and sunglasses.

'It's okay, Jake, I said I'd be brutal when I started this conversation. You can both hate me now, but I leave in less than a week, so there's no ulterior motive coming from me except I want this to work. At least try to sort this out for Danbunnan's future, which means showing the judges family unity so there's no excuse for gossip.'

Jake gripped the steering wheel, the engine running. 'What am I meant to be doing?'

Sienna patted Jake's strong arm. 'Do the food tour. This will be the perfect practice run, so treat Bob like a judge. Bob, please listen and learn from Jake, because you'll be giving the same speech in the bus carrying the judges. There's a brochure in that envelope on top of the esky, which I've filled with food and drinks. Now if you'll excuse me, I've got a meal to prepare. You can fire me when you get back.' She tapped Jake's door and headed back to her side of the compound.

'Women,' Jake muttered, shaking his head at Sienna, and for the first time in years he drove his father out of the compound to take a tour of their own backyard.

\*\*\*

It was late that night when Jake walked into the muster room looking for Sienna. Only to find her asleep at Tom's table with needle and thread in hand, attached to the hem on a pair of men's jeans.

'What the hell?' Whose jeans were those and why was his lady asleep at the table? He glared at Elliott, Josh, and Tyson seated at the other tables, then looked to Tom for answers.

'Sorry, Boss, we didn't have the heart to wake her,' whimpered Elliott, like a timid child.

Jake leaned over and whispered, 'Babe?'

But there was no response, she was out of it.

He removed the sewing needle and thread from her hands. Placed her arm around his neck and scooped her up against his chest.

Tom opened the screen doors. 'Sorry, Boss. I don't think she's stopped all day. She must have dropped like a light. I didn't even notice.'

It annoyed Jake that they'd let her fall asleep in the kitchen. If he'd known, he would've forced Sienna to take a break. But he'd been with his dad sorting out their issues.

Had she been waiting for him to find out what happened today?

Jake couldn't stay mad at her when her heart was in the right place. And she'd been right. He was relieved Bob was on board to babysit the judges. Maybe, just maybe, they could share a proper father–son relationship—but at least a conversation had begun.

He placed Sienna on her bed, removed her boots, loosened her clothing, and covered her with the soft doona. He checked her alarm clock was set, stripped off, and climbed into bed beside her.

With a fingertip he stroked the outline of his sleeping beauty's face, admiring everything about her. 'I love you, Sienna.'

He wanted to tell her when she was awake, to see her reaction. But he didn't dare tell her the truth.

He brushed his lips against hers then switched off the bedside lamp and listened to her deep breathing. Holding the only woman he'd ever truly loved, and dared to dream of an indescribable destiny shared.

Did dreams come true?

He wished they did, like he'd wished for her.

# Forty-two

Sienna awoke with a start, switching off the alarm before it erupted and eased out of bed.

'No, you don't.' Jake pulled her back and cuddled up to her. 'Ten more minutes.'

'We've got lots to do today.'

'Five more minutes,' he mumbled, nuzzling into her ear.

She melted against his warm skin, enjoying his arms around her, as his lashes feathered against her cheek. 'How did I get to bed last night?'

'After visiting Joe and Lyn last night, who were playing nightwatchmen, I found you asleep at Tom's table and carried you to bed.' He rolled on top of her and lightly kissed her. He kissed her top lip, then her bottom lip, slowly dragging it between his teeth as if savouring his favourite dessert. 'Good morning, beautiful.'

She truly felt beautiful, as if she was his entire world just with that one look.

So, was she forgiven for yesterday?

'And a good morning to you, kind sir.' Her fingertips skated along his strong jawline, then down his chiselled chest. Her palms glided over the heat of his muscular arms, and it was like she was awakening inside a dream.

'Are you sure we can't have ten more minutes?' His eyes darkened with a hunger.

Did she give in or get out?

'I won't be able to see you tonight.' His lips feathered

against her throat.

She sighed under his touch, as he stole her soul with lips that traced her jawline.

Why did she bother pretending to resist? When surrendering to Jake's enthusiastic sexual pleasures was the most spectacular way to start the day.

Showered and dressed, Sienna was greeted by Sally's tail thumping on the porch. 'Morning, Sally.'

She patted the dog, who responded with old dog groans. Soon followed by a full-body shake of her coarse fur, then the *click clack* of nails across the deck before the cattle dog jumped to the compound's soil.

Above was a wondrous galaxy of stars, so thick and endless it was like staring at the gateway to heaven.

'Coffee, Boss?' Sienna slipped on her apron as a signal for her mind to whirl into gear.

Jake closed her cabin door behind them. 'Absolutely. I'll go check my emails and collect my tablet.'

They were like most modern couples, synchronising their schedules for the day ahead over coffee. In that short time they shared together, before the rest of the crew joined them, they achieved a lot.

'Hey, we got an extra phone. The telco contractor did it late yesterday. I put the paperwork on your desk. Sorry, I forgot to tell you.'

'You were asleep.'

'Good thing I don't talk in my sleep then.' She kissed his prickly chin.

'Do you remember anything about last night?'

'Not when I asked you how I got to bed.'

'Well, there was this knight in shining armour—better yet, I can show you how he carried you to bed, if you want?' He gripped her hips, walking her back to her door.

Her palm pressed against his strong chest. Her laugh came so easily, as did her smile, bubbling up from the warmth inside her, all from Jake. 'As tempted as I am, we both have a huge day ahead.' *Just huge!*

Jake leaned his forehead against hers, to tenderly press his lips against her. She forgot everything else, except this man and his kiss.

'Don't work too hard, babe.'

'You, too …' *Wake up, princess. Today is D-day.* 'Gotta go or the boss might get shirty because he has a thing for his coffee being on time.' With torch in hand and the dog escorting her, she blew him a kiss, and headed for the muster room as Jake went to the house on the hill.

Today was the day.

ETA for the judges and guests was five that afternoon, and there was an awful lot to do before then. The moment of truth was here. Everything had to go off without a hitch for the next thirty-six hours. And it had to be perfect for Jake.

*Hello, stress, my old friend.*


The muster room's kitchen was at full steam, with Sienna finalising her menu preparations. Her team sat in the dining room sharing breakfast together.

Sienna emptied a sack of potatoes into the deep industrial sink. 'Tom, I need you and your men back in the compound showered, shaved and in your new shirts by four-thirty.'

'Why so early?' Tyson asked. 'Dinner isn't until six.'

'Jake needs you guys to help sort out the guests' luggage.' She sorted out the pastries sitting on cooling racks.

'We're baggage handlers now?' Josh asked, screwing up his face.

'For the night. You'll be driving Bob's bus tonight and tomorrow, and if Jake takes you to the airport—'

'Air*strip*,' the crew chorused.

Rolling her eyes, she placed a plate of pastries on the table. 'Extra custard, Josh, tell me what you think of the danishes? The guests will have them for breakfast tomorrow if I do this recipe right. Savoury one for you too, Tyson.' She mirrored Josh and Tyson's grins as they snatched a pastry each.

'Jake's printing off the time schedules so you'll know what we're all doing these next few days. And a big thank you up front for your amazing teamwork, guys.' It had to run perfectly.

Sienna peered through the window just in time for her perfect morning view of Jake in his dust-stained jeans and that confident long-legged swagger. The tight waist, straight strong shoulders, muscular arms, and the Akubra that topped off perfection. The man was a heartbreaker—hers. Because Jake could never promise her anything when he had a legacy that already owned him.

Jake stepped inside with the black leather compendium she'd left as a gift on his desk.

Unzipping it, he removed some documents. 'Is this the only surprise I'm getting today?'

'You like?'

'I think it makes me look good.'

'You don't need help with that.' *Oops!* She glanced at the others who were oblivious to what she'd said. She then slid over his coffee. 'Is that the time schedule copies for the team?'

He winked at her as he took a sip. 'Yes, I'll hand them out while you take this phone call.'

'Phone call?' The new cordless phone sat on the wall beside the large radio. 'Did anyone hear the phone ring?'

Elliott carted another sack of potatoes to the sink. 'I didn't. So, when do we get wi-fi?'

'The modem is in the snail mail.' Jake plucked the phone from the wall, pressed the call button. 'Are you there, Rhonda?' He paused to listen to the phone. 'Good, didn't lose you. Okay, here she is. For you, Sienna.' He held out the new phone.

'Wow, it's the first phone call to the muster room,' cried out Elliott. 'We're so new-world! Like a man landing on the moon.'

Sienna took the cordless handset. 'Hello?' Phones were such a novelty these days when they used to be a daily necessity. Was this a moment to be recorded in the journals as part of Danbunnan's history?

'Hello, honey.'

Sienna instantly recognised the nasally twang. 'Aw, hey Rhonda. How's the holiday?'

'Honey, I'm having such a wonderful time and I'm about to be a grandmother again.'

'Congratulations.'

At his table on the other side of the kitchen bench, Tom's frown faltered, his hardened eyes softening as if pining for something—or someone. But then he turned away.

'It's due any day now, and I'm hoping you'd be willing to stay for another four weeks?'

'What? Stay for another month?'

All eyes in the room were on her.

'Err, I'm kind of swamped at the moment.' Sienna scooped up her coffee and headed out the side door, it was time to test the range on this new gadget.

'Jake told me you've got the competition dinner on tonight. He's excited, and it sounds good. Wish I was there to help.'

'Why aren't you, Rhonda?'

'I'm on holiday…'

Sienna walked down the path between the kitchen and the thriving vegetable garden. This morning she'd come by torchlight under the stars, now the sky was the palest of blues. At the back corner where a stack of plastic milk crates was kept, she flipped one over and took a seat.

The cook's quarters were to the left, with the worksheds to the right, where the pig truck and smokehouse were stationed. But before her was an unhindered view of the sunrise that stretched beyond the morning mists, to mix with the rising dust stirred by the herd. This was her spot, hidden from the compound, with her own special view.

It was a holidayer's view.

Yet like all holidays, they had to end sooner or later.

'Rhonda. Why did you go on holiday?'

'Sorry, honey?'

'From what I've learned about Danbunnan's recent history, I can't understand why you left. Jake told me that you're the secretary of this competition's committee and you knew that Tom nominated this station. I also know why the journals are hidden in the cook's quarters and how you cared for Jake's mother before she passed away. And I know you are the type of person who would have never left Danbunnan without a good reason, especially when they needed you most. You love these people as much as they love you. So, Rhonda, I don't want any more half-truths, please. I deserve to know the whole truth.'

Rhonda's heavy sigh carried over the phone.

Sienna could picture Rhonda smoothing out her apron as if dusting off some invisible flour. Perhaps a pat to her soft grey curls, trying to work out another way to *not* answer the question.

'Rhonda, I need to know why, if you're asking me to extend my stay.' Sienna sipped her coffee and waited as Sally walked up and lay at her feet with a groan and a grizzle. Sienna patted the cattle dog as if she'd been doing it all her life.

'Jake needed help,' replied Rhonda. 'When China told me Jake was engaged to Angela, who's always been Duncan's girl, I knew it was wrong. I knew that boy didn't love Angela but was selling his soul for the station. You should've seen him, honey. Working sixteen hours a day trying to save the station. Jake was so exhausted, collapsing onto his bed fully clothed, he would've forgotten to eat if I didn't make him.'

Sienna's heart squeezed in pain to hear this about Jake. 'He had Tom, he had you.'

'He did. But when I found out you were still wandering around after what your ex had done, I knew you needed something to get you back on your feet, too.'

'Nooo, you didn't plan this, did you?' She sat taller, caught between horror and disbelief.

'Tom helped me.'

Sienna jumped to her feet and paced in the dirt. *'Are you kidding me?* You played me? *Both of you?'*

'Don't get mad, honey. Listen, when I learned you were still wandering around, I knew you were searching for something. You just didn't know it.'

'I was waiting for winter to make my first snow angel.' It was on her *to-live list*, still safely tucked inside her phone case.

'Jake needed someone like you.'

'I'm not that special.'

'Oh yes, you are, honey. You have skills that man needed. Jake needed help for the business side of things, and you're all about business, honey. I figured the only way I would get you to Danbunnan was to get you cooking again. I knew you'd have the job down pat in a week and would start searching for your first project.'

Sienna glanced at the cleaned wooden rail on her verandah where her ex–porch perchers created her first project of fixing the chook pen. From there it snowballed to the orchard, the vegetable patch, the cook's quarters, and the rest of the compound. *Holy roasted coffee beans!*

'Honey, you needed something to focus on. Tell me it's helped.'

'I'm only here as your relief cook.'

'You're beyond station cooking. But you've helped that place, haven't you, honey?'

'It's up to them now.' Sienna couldn't do any more. 'Was this holiday real, or …' She didn't want to call her friend a liar.

'It was real. Tom and I worked out you'd need a few months to kick into high gear, with at least a month to settle in and for Jake to spot your full potential. He's good that way.'

'Was Jake in on this too?' *He'd better not be.*

'No. It's up to you if you tell him. Tom won't say nothing.'

Tom was the sneakiest dark horse in the pack. She'd been played!

'Tom never smiles for me,' said Sienna, 'but he adores you. You know that, right?'

Rhonda gave a curious giggle. 'I care about Tom, too. So don't be hard on Tom for not telling you. Tom witnessed all of Danbunnan's drama. It was Tom who refused to let Jake give up, saying he had a debt to pay to the Cullens for all the good they'd done for him. He wanted to help Jake, who'd been through hell already and had no one else to help him. Tom also did it for Duncan. They grew close in those last few years, it hit Tom hard when Duncan left us like that.'

'Poor Tom.'

'Anyway, honey, don't you worry about that man, he's proud of Danbunnan's changes.' Then Rhonda sighed. 'You know, I was hoping that by bragging about having an internet lover he'd do something.'

'And have Tom confess his undying love for you and beg you to stay? Sorry, I can't picture Tom doing that. Why did I even say that?' Because that stuff was for fairy tales and happy endings, and this Cinderella still had a full day ahead of her of playing with firewood and stoves.

'Tom only rings me to talk about Danbunnan's stuff. He's all about the station, same as Jake. But from what they've both told me, you've done more than expected.'

'You could've asked me.' Irritation prickled across her scalp, while the hurt smouldered like a deep burn inside her chest—they'd manipulated her and that hurt.

'What would you have said?'

Seated on her milk crate, she leaned against the corrugated wall, admiring the amazing view. 'I would've said I was busy.' It was her excuse for everything, so busy being busy she never stopped to stare at her surroundings.

Yet right now, she inhaled the crisp sweet morning air.

Before she'd arrived at Danbunnan she never saw the

stars, barely spotting the sky at all as she moved from one air-conditioned room to the next. She'd never sipped her coffee watching spectacular sunrises because she was too pre-occupied staring at a small screen.

She'd never heard the haunting sound of a dingo serenading the moon until Danbunnan. Never witnessed the daily waddling parade of hens at sunrise, or known how rich free-range eggs could be.

She'd never heard of such a thing as the bubbling water dance of the billabong barramundi where ponds reflected rainbows on sunset. Nor had she been still enough to watch tiny red finches feed off the ends of bending golden grasses that surrounded the grazing herd of water buffalo.

Here, time stretched while the world of chaos spun outside of Danbunnan's borders. It was a place filled with a magical wonder if you only stopped and dared to look around you.

'I'm sorry I lied to you, honey,' said Rhonda. 'I truly believed that you needed a project to focus on, and Jake needed someone to give him the right type of support. Yours. You do it for strangers.'

'I used to.'

'I'd guessed your heart wasn't in it anymore or you would've gone back to your office ages ago.'

She hated to admit it, but Rhonda was right.

'Is it true about the new grandchild?'

Sienna could hear Rhonda's smile. 'Yeah, honey, my youngest was keeping it as a surprise for me. She's due in a week and it's her first child. They've asked me to stay for an extra few weeks to help them settle in, if that's okay with you?'

Sienna's mobile phone beeped in her apron pocket, and she pulled it out to look at the screen. Her phone wasn't used to call anyone these days, but it held her notes, her music, and it was her cooking timer. And here she was on the phone for the first time in ages. How surreal.

*Focus—the mobile phone beeped for a reason!* 'I've got bread and pastry cases in the oven.'

Sienna dashed for the kitchen with the phone cradled between her ear and shoulder as Rhonda spoke of her holiday. She removed a tray of tiger bread, turned the pastry cases, and checked the coals through the grate. She was a pro now with the wood stove, having won the bake-off battle. *And how country did that sound!*

'Rhonda, can I get over this weekend first?' She reset the timer on her mobile phone, while talking on another phone, as she scanned her schedules on her laptop, that rested on the kitchen bench.

Deja vu hit her squarely across her shoulders, as if she'd been hit with a blast of icy air, she blinked at the laptop's screen.

This is exactly what she used to do all day, every day, in an office. Not in a kitchen on a remote cattle station in the Northern Territory. But was it the same?

She was employed to complete a project for a client chasing a profitable future.

Oh no, it was!

'Hey, good luck tonight,' called out Rhonda.

'Thanks. I'll call you later when I get a chance and we'll talk more. See ya.' She hung the phone back in the cradle while everyone stared at her.

Unfortunately for her, the muster room's first phone call just sucked.

Sienna blatantly glared at Tom. 'Rhonda says *hi*.'

'Blimey.' Tom lowered his head, to stare at his tea mug.

Jake looked at Tom then over to the relief cook. 'Sienna?'

'Rhonda's about to be a grandmother again. She wants to stay for the birth and extend her holiday for another month.' And the way Jake looked at her, he knew.

Did he know everything that Rhonda and Tom had planned? Manipulating her to do a job!

'So, are you staying?' Jake wore his poker face, sitting very still.

What sort of a fool was she to not have seen this sooner?

*Arseholes.*

She slipped on her oven mitts, turning her back on them all, to shift the piping-hot tiger bread to the cooling racks. 'People, our first show is on in nine hours, and we have a schedule to keep. Elliott, I want twenty spotless plates for each course ready on the bench, please. Pina and Lyn, can we please take the linen to the house for the table setting. The cutlery needs to be in boiling water and vinegar then polished.' She slipped easily into her job, after all that's why she was here. Even though she was fuming underneath at Rhonda and Tom for using her, she would turn her anger towards finishing this project.

And then she'd walk away.

Job done.

# Forty-three

Jake leaned against the safari-style tour bus, watching the small plane land at Danbunnan's dusty airstrip. As it taxied forwards, he directed the flying vet's aeroplane to the side of the field.

The plane stopped, the door opened, and Craig's boots landed with a thud in the dust as his sun-bleached curls bounced. *'We made it. Thank you, God.'* Craig waved his Akubra to the air then bowed down to the dirt.

'You're no flamin' pope, are you?' Barry said, stepping out in board shorts and thongs with his fiancée, Jenny, passing the cowboy kissing the red dirt.

Ryan, with his hair that fell any way it wanted, stood at the open doorway of his plane. 'Oi, tell me you gave me off-street parking for a reason. Or you're just jealous I've got a plane?'

'I've got guests arriving by charter plane in a few hours. But we fixed the potholes just for you.' Jake heartily man-hugged his mates, glad to see them. It'd been a while since they'd been together. 'Hey, Jenny.' He gave the lady who'd won the water boy's heart a peck on the cheek. 'Welcome to Danbunnan.'

'We've brought our testing kits, in case you need it,' said Barry, following Ryan to the cargo hold.

'We only brought the cowboy to carry the luggage,' teased Ryan, opening the plane's hatch.

'Also for my good looks, and because someone has to

dance with Jenny.' Craig grabbed his bag and threw his swag over his shoulder.

'Listen, mate, I've been having dancing lessons, so I'll be dancing with my own lady,' said Barry.

'I'll dance with Sienna then. Where is that cute cook?' Craig asked, passing the gear to Jake.

'Busy.' Jake remained expressionless as he grabbed their luggage and loaded up the bus. 'For the dance, you'll all be staying at the house. Craig and Ryan are in the twins' room. Barry and Jenny, you've got the spare room.'

'Who got the guest room?' Ryan closed his plane, passing his medical case to Jake. 'I'd assumed we'd all camp in there like we've always done.'

Jake loaded the last of the luggage onto the bus. 'My neighbour, Simon Simmons and Angela have that room.'

'So the engagement is going public?' Craig pushed up the brim of his Akubra.

'But I like Sienna, she's fun,' said Jenny.

Barry put his arm around her. 'Honey, remember we can't talk about that here.'

'I knew it!' Ryan pointed at Jake. 'Are you sleeping with the cook? If you're not, I'll ask for her number because I need an office manager to streamline my surgery.'

'I already gave Sienna my number,' said Craig.

'Your number is written on the wall in the women's toilets in the Elsie Creek pub,' said Jenny.

'True?' Craig and the other three men stopped beside the bus and looked at her.

'It says *For a one-time good time call Cowboy Craig*,' Jenny said with a giggle.

'Well, at least I don't have to lie on the one-time thing.' Craig grinned, his thumbs hooked into the belt loops as the sun caught his champion rodeo belt buckle.

'Come on you lot, I've got a schedule to keep.' Jake climbed into the driver's seat.

'So, what's the plan, my man?' Ryan asked, heading for the back seat.

'Dinner first at the Oasis of the Outback. You'll then be bussed to the camp site where you'll sleep in these fancy tents up at the North Ridge. Tomorrow you'll start with a camp breakfast then the food tour begins, where the competition presentations are done.' That part he wasn't looking forward to. 'Jenny, can you ride a horse?'

'I've only had a few lessons. But I want to do the trail ride.' Jenny took a seat in the centre of the bus.

'I'll set you up with the horse Sienna rode.'

'Take the lady on a romantic horse ride, did we?' Ryan tugged at his sunglasses caught in his floppy hair.

'Nothing romantic about it. Sienna helped me babysit the twins and ended up in a landslide.' The woman had been through hell and still stuck it out helping him.

From the driver's seat, Jake looked back at his best mates since boarding school, with Jenny now part of the package. 'Look, I want to say thanks for coming and doing this, guys. I appreciate the effort it takes to come here and what you've all been doing for me.'

'Hey, I'm only here for the feed and to perve on the pretty relief cook. It's my mission this weekend to get her to say *yes* to going out with me,' said Craig, settling into the front passenger seat.

'*OI*.' Jake loved Craig as a brother, but Sienna was *his lady*.

Barry closed the bus door and took his seat next to Jenny. 'Watch out, Craig, the Black Prince is giving you his signature black look.'

'Remember, our Black Prince has got those magical make-up fists that fight first and asks questions later in the colour you'll wear for a week,' called out Ryan, manspreading his place in the back seat.

'Can't you see Jake adores Sienna,' said Jenny.

'Jake is engaged to Angela.' Craig aimed his wide, white-toothed smile at Jake.

'Okay, okay. I'm with Sienna but it's complicated.' Jake locked eyes with Craig, to make his point crystal clear.

'Sienna is mine, so back off.'

'*Finally*, the truth is revealed.' Ryan waved his hand in the air like he'd won bingo. 'I picked it when Jake forgot I was standing next to him, going all watery at the mouth for the lady.'

'Was not,' snapped out Jake.

'I saw it too, *before* they came to Darwin,' said Barry from the centre of the bus.

'They were the cutest couple in Darwin, it was nice to double date,' said Jenny.

'Meh, I knew Jake was a goner for the girl ages ago,' said Craig, shrugging.

'Bull—you only see cattle, cowboy,' called out Ryan.

Craig swivelled to face the back, thumbing up the brim of his hat. 'Listen, puppy panderer, I spotted the Black Prince and his lady way back at the Simmons's rodeo. When you', he said, poking at Jake's chest, 'couldn't keep your eyes off her. Of course, we'll tease Sienna to keep up appearances because, mate, we understand you're whoring yourself for this place.'

'We're all the Black Prince's whores this weekend.' Ryan then tapped lightly on Jenny's shoulder. 'Jenny's excluded.'

'Thanks, mate, didn't feel like bashing you to defend my future wife's honour.' Barry gave his fiancée a kiss on the cheek.

'We get no phone calls. No emails. No love for months. Until the last few weeks and bang—it's on with all these requests for our wonderful presence and expertise. And all our top-class service is costing the Boss a feed and a bed. That's whoring,' said Ryan.

'What am I?' Craig waved at himself. 'I'm not needed for the presentations.'

'You're just the permanent manwhore.' Jake laughed, patting Craig's shoulder. 'But I'm glad you're here, mate. I'm grateful to all of you guys for your support. Hey, no one knows about Sienna, so, please don't spill.'

'We won't say nothing. We're happy to help the Black

Prince,' said Barry, with Jenny nodding beside him.

'That's a ditto from the crowd that matters at the back of this bus. Secret's safe with us, mate, we've got your back about the lady.' Ryan slipped on his aviators. 'Isn't that right, bubble butt up the front?'

Craig replied, 'I'm not a bubble butt, you flying puppy panderer with hair worse than an unclipped poodle.'

Jake chuckled, grateful for this reprieve from the stress ahead. 'Buckle up, peoples, it's tourist time at the station.'

# Forty-four

The lush tropical garden was the backdrop for the house on the hill, its manicured lawns spread like a soft green carpet beneath the flourishing jacaranda tree. The late afternoon sun making the hanging crystals sparkle like falling diamonds.

Fine china, polished silverware and assorted glasses stood on crisp white linen. Vibrant wildflowers were the centrepieces on the U-shaped table that faced the expansive view that was all Danbunnan Station.

Outside the compound, the hay shed stood alone on the distant rise, dark and deserted. At the station's entrance, by the track's edge, stood a tall wooden post with painted signs pointing in various directions: Darwin, Singapore, Sydney, Dubai, Melbourne, and the North Pole. On top the sign read: *Danbunnan Station Homestead* that pointed towards the horseshoe compound.

On the right stood the stables, calving sheds, and worksheds, all closed. Lined up before the corrugated structures stood the polished fleet.

Beyond that was the renovated muster room, alive with voices and music, with its enticing aromas and a thriving kitchen garden nearby. The freshly painted laundry shed, and the cattlemen's quarters created the bottom apex of the compound. To the left, was the lush orchard where the hens waddled along in their afternoon parade towards their pen. And back to the grand house on the hill, with its wide verandah where the colours from its rich rock walls were highlighted from the late afternoon sun.

There was a hush to the area. An air of expectation amidst the calm, where Jake stood in the centre of the dusty compound and looked around the place with pride.

Danbunnan had never looked better, all because of one woman. The one and only lady he couldn't call his own.

But he was determined to find her and headed into the muster room.

Inside the staff had gathered, and his sister was sorting out the twins in front of the wide screen.

'Look, Boss, it's official.' Elliott stepped out from behind the kitchen counter wearing a white chef's uniform.

For once the lad spoke first and wasn't doing a runner. 'Aren't you meant to be wearing the station uniform?' The rest of the crew were in their white shirts displaying the Danbunnan brand. He'd never thought he'd see his stockmen looking like waiters.

Elliott adjusted his white chef's hat. 'Sienna said I should look the part for service. I am the entertainment, you know.'

*God help them.* 'Where is the head chef?'

'Out back, indulging in some do-not-disturb chill time.'

'Look, um …' Jake cleared his throat and faced the dining room where the staff had gathered. 'I want to say something now in case I get caught up later … Thank you everyone for your help with tonight. I appreciate all you've done to get us here.' He was lucky to have such a great team of individuals behind him.

Jess, all prettied up for dinner, smiled at him with the same pride he felt.

But there was one more person he wanted to see before the evening commitments began.

Out the side door, there was no Sally on the dog bed, and the red car was parked in the cook's quarter's lean-to.

Past the veggie patch and out the back of the kitchen he found Sally lying in the dirt beside Sienna's fully laced town boots.

Seated on a milk crate with coffee cup in hand, Sienna wasn't wearing her usual dress, scarf, or apron. Instead, she wore long black slacks and a white singlet, with her fair hair plaited and looped into a tight bun.

'That's the first time I've seen those town boots of yours fully laced.' He grabbed a crate from the stack and flipped it over onto its lid and sat beside her, giving him a great view of his herd.

'Hey, Sal.' He gave the old cattle dog a hearty pat. He then put his arm around Sienna's upper back, kissing her soft fair skin on her upper arm, the side of her slender neck, her jawline, up to her cheek as she giggled and squirmed.

'Are you feeling nervous?' Sienna asked.

'No.' He knew most of those who were coming. 'We've planned for everything, now it's just doing. Are you nervous?'

'Nope.' She sipped her coffee and leaned into him. Resting her head against his shoulder as they listened to the sounds of the station. 'Are your friends here?'

'They're getting ready for dinner. I told them about you. Us.' He winced because there was no *us*.

She sat forward and his arm fell away as she tossed the last of her coffee into the dirt. 'Did you tell them that you're having a dirty affair with the relief cook?'

'Oi! It's not a dirty affair. Don't say that.' His fingers massaged the back of her neck, feeling the tension in her shoulders she hid so well.

Resting her elbows on her knees, she stared at the empty cup cradled in her hands. 'Rhonda and Tom set me up. All of it.'

'What do you mean?' Tucking a stray strand of silk behind her dainty ear, she faced him with hurt and anger in her eyes. His chest ignited with that fierce protectiveness he had for her. 'Babe, what's wrong?'

'Rhonda took a holiday with the hopes of forcing me to come here to help you.'

For just a moment he gazed at his herd grazing on his

grain. 'Rhonda would've known all about your skills and your company?'

'Of course, she did. Whenever Rhonda came to Darwin she stayed with me, and the only place she'd find me was at work, because I was always working, never at the house.'

*House*, he noted. She never called her Darwin house a *home*.

'You told me you were here because you were travelling around lost.'

'That's true. Rhonda knew it too. She begged me to come here, saying she needed a break from cooking. But she didn't. Rhonda and Tom got me out here under false pretences. They tricked me.' Her frown shadowed the shine in her eyes that showed her scars of the past. She had every reason to be angry.

'If Rhonda had asked you to work on this as a project manager, would you have agreed?'

'I would've said no.'

'That's understandable because you didn't know me back then. But now ...'

'I'll still give you one hundred percent effort to finish this project.'

'Don't you dare think I used you. I had no idea any of this was happening. Look, no matter what happens, I have you to thank for all of this and I'm trying to work out a way for you to stay.' He held her close to his side, wishing he could take away all the hurt she carried inside. 'But what do you want?'

'I get my percentage, it's my normal fee.' She stood and stretched, twisting her spine.

*Damn, that was cold.*

He wasn't just a job to her, was he? 'That's it? Just a percentage? Don't you want more?'

Before she could answer Sally barked and bolted towards the front at the sound of a vehicle entering the compound.

'*They're here.*' The twins' voices carried across the

compound.

'That'll be the judges.' Jake turned Sienna around to face him.

Sienna never said what she wanted. She never asked for anything unless it was to do with the job. His job. *Dammit.*

Sienna brushed his shoulders and checked his collar. 'Good luck, cowboy. You have every reason to be proud of who you are as the Boss of Danbunnan Station.'

'I'm no bloody cowboy. I'm a cattleman.' And he wasn't just a damned job to her either.

He pulled her close and his lips meshed with hers in a Hollywood-style kiss with all the love he felt for her, a kiss he wanted to last forever. But couldn't.

'I'll see you soon, babe.' He left her reeling as he headed off to greet his guests.

Jake wanted to tell her he loved her, but the impact of their kiss had to be enough for now. Expecting her to push him away to finish this project.

They weren't just a project, they were so much more than that.

But right now, it was up to fate to decide the future for everyone on Danbunnan Station.

It was showtime.

# Forty-five

*ead chef is in da' house!* With dinner well under way, a
constant stream of delectable dishes were created,
that time just flew. Sienna twirled her tongs as she
swivelled on her boots and danced across the tiles, giving the
last inspection of every plate that left her kitchen. And
tonight, as head chef, she loved it.

Her best work had been presented in a menu that told a
story using the finest ingredients found on the station. It
wasn't just the meat, it was the hand-selected wild
mushrooms she'd foraged alongside Elliott, Jess, and the
twins. There were wildflowers from the meadow that
decorated the tables. Fruit from the orchard. Eggs from her
ex–porch perchers, and vegetables from the kitchen garden.
Everything carefully harvested to create the ultimate feast of
flavours for twenty people that was of a world class
standard—it's what Danbunnan deserved.

Now, all she could do was hope it was enough to
impress Jake, the judges, and his guests.

'Well done, everyone. The kitchen is closed.' Sienna
removed her apron and threw it into the laundry basket,
checking her phone for the time. *Right on schedule.*

'So, what happens now, luv?' Lyn asked, flicking soap
suds from her hands at the deep kitchen sinks. She'd been
tonight's kitchen hand, singing along to their extensive
playlist.

In the dining room, Joe and Charlie ate at the table, in

between playing runners and babysitters. While the twins wore headphones, staring wide-eyed at the big screen.

'They'll have the coffee and cheese platters for half an hour, then onto the buses.'

'What time did you start this morning, Sienna?' Joe asked.

'Four. I'll have a break when they leave.'

'And tomorrow?'

'I'll start at three. I need to bake stuff for the camp breakfast. I can nap on the road. Don't worry, I'll sleep when it's over.'

The front screen doors opened and in walked Jake. 'That's the best meal I've ever had.'

'Hear, hear.' Joe nodded as he scooped the last of the sorbet from his bowl. Beside him, Charlie waved the slab of meat he'd been attacking.

But Jake's crooked smile was real. The worry lines around his eyes had lessened and his shoulders were strong and so was his stride. He looked way too good dressed as a bad-man in black.

'Um, how did it go?' *Why was it suddenly so hot?*

'Why don't you ask them when you meet them? Cute uniform.'

She rolled her eyes at her unflattering chef's jacket. 'I'll stay here, thanks. I don't do after-dinner natterings.' She backed away, eyeing the coldroom. Even if it was the worst hiding place ever, she could hold onto the shelves. 'I'm not dressed to be presented.'

'Could've fooled me, luv, you look good in that uniform,' said Lyn.

'As the boss, I insist.' Jake grabbed Sienna's hand and led her from the kitchen.

'Great, pull the boss card on me.' The touch of his hand sent a tickling warmth through her veins, leaving her with no choice but to follow. It'd be easier if she didn't connect with him on all levels.

When reality hit her, she snatched her hand away. 'You

can't walk in there with me. Your fiancée and future father-in-law and the judges and—'

'Sienna, it was a magnificent meal. Elliott did a wonderful job in presenting. In fact, the entire team did well serving dinner, and the place looks amazing because of you. You made me proud tonight—not just for tonight, but for everything you've ever achieved in this place.'

'Right now, you should be with your guests, it's not over.'

'You're right. This, you and me,' he said, with his finger pointing between their chests, 'it's not over, babe. Remember that.' Then his lips met hers, kissing her into silence.

It was her punishment to suffer the magical bliss of his warm lips against hers only to know they'd part ways, again. But this bubble of denial was perfectly divine for one fleeting moment.

'Come on, I want you to meet the guests.' He led her by the hand towards the house. Kissed her fingertips before giving her hand a final squeeze. Then he let her go as they entered the light.

Music greeted them, where Danbunnan's stockmen had gathered by the open front door of the house.

'Told you the boss would get the queen of the kitchen here, instead of me fetching her,' said Elliott, waiting by the stone steps.

'I didn't have a choice,' mumbled Sienna. 'Hey, I've never seen that door open.' The front door with the corridor that had once triggered her past, no longer affected her. 'Is everything okay?'

'The guests want to see you. They loved it. I loved it.' Elliott fanned his face as if showering himself with the accolades of his own stage performance.

'I'll admit it was fun.' Josh was beaming.

Tyson dusted off his stocky shoulders. 'Just another skill to add to my many talents.'

'Elliott, take Sienna out and introduce her. If she doesn't go, Tom, drag her out with a rope.' Jake laughed over his shoulder, heading for the corner towards the garden.

'Yes, Boss,' replied Tom.

'I don't think so.' Sienna glared at Jake and then faced the 2IC. 'I'll want a word with you later, Tom.'

Tom never smiled, just nodded.

She then realised where Jake had learned to keep a poker face, his boss face—it was from Tom.

'I'm guessing I'll need a beer for that kind of conversation. Elliott, go do another yakking intro and tell that mob who the relief cook is. Kid's an MC in his own bloody circus.' Tom shook his head.

'Uncle, I may have found my true calling—the arts.' Elliott palmed his skinny chest and held his head high, eyeing off his shadow on the wall.

'Man, I can't breathe. He's stealing our oxygen.' Josh shook his head.

'I'll go introduce myself.' Sienna tried to control her laugh as she walked around the corner with the rest following.

The glistening stars blended with the soft fairy lights that wound around the trunk of the jacaranda tree, as the candles cast a warm glow over the tables. The sheet screen showed a continuous loop of black-and-white images of Danbunnan's history and the Cullen's ancestors, while the smooth sounds of Sinatra, as the tribute to Jake's mother, serenaded them like a seductive whisper. It was perfect. Romantic even. Was this something that Winifred Cullen would have been proud to see?

'There's our little relief cook now.' From his seat in the corner, Bob sloshed his beer glass in her direction.

Sienna raised an eyebrow at Bob's flushed features. 'I hope you enjoyed your meal?'

'Your best yet, woman. Hey, fellas, this is our relief cook I was telling you about.' Bob waved his glass at her like she was some heifer cow in the stockyards.

*Awkward much?* She turned to leave. She should have never left the kitchen.

'Don't go, Sienna. I'll do the introductions.' Jake stood, raising his wine glass as if in a toast. 'Everyone, it's my privilege and honour to introduce you to Sienna Jacobs, who isn't just a relief cook but a lady of many talents. She's our head chef and projects coordinator for this weekend's events.'

Wow, what an intro from the boss.

Jake introduced her to the six judges seated on the left side of the U-shaped table. She shook their hands as they returned polite nods, until she faced the last of the bosses, Mr Simmons, the neighbour, and shook his massive hand.

Simon Simmons licked his thin lips and stared at her breasts, as usual. 'Good to see you again, Sienna. Brilliant meal.'

*Eyes up, buddy.* Sienna was tempted to duck and say boo, yet grateful for the double-breasted thick chef's jacket that hid all. 'Thank you, Simon. Angela, nice to see you again.' Sienna gave a nervous smile to Angela and her amazing blonde curls. While guilt scratched up her spine for deceiving Jake's fiancée.

'Heya.' Angela waved a flash of jewels that covered each finger, sharing a friendly smile.

Then it was on to Jake's closest friends, seated at the centre of the U-shaped table. 'I'll skip this crew.'

Craig's rodeo champion belt buckle sparkled under the candlelight as he reached out and caught her by the shoulder. 'Not nice, when I gave you my number.'

'I think the wind carried that away.' She shook his strong working hand, grinning at his wink. Then on to the next. 'So, did the flying vet bring that plane?'

'Want to come for a joy ride later? I'll show you where you'll be working as my new office manager?' Ryan grinned with his thick hair flopping everywhere.

'Not tonight.' She didn't mind Ryan, who was loud and fun. 'Jenny, wow, your hair is amazing.'

'Thank you. Your BFF Mail-order Biatch was brilliant and sends his love,' said Jenny, patting her sleek new style.

'I'm so glad Ricky came through. Barry, thanks for being

here and for everything.' She shook his hand and leaned over and kissed the cheek of the water expert who'd been instrumental for this event.

'My pleasure, it's what mates do,' said Barry.

'Oi, where's my kiss?' Craig tapped his cheek.

'I wouldn't kiss that cheek, you've got no idea where it's been,' mumbled Jake, giving his mate's shoulder a friendly tap. 'Sienna, these are our guests.' He gave her a hopeful expression.

With a deep breath, Sienna turned and smiled—*it was game time.*

She'd been to many of these types of dinners in her past life and she'd done her homework. These three men were part of a big pond she wanted to tap for the ultimate ripple effect. Shaking the hands of the guests that mattered: Patrick and Jasmine Lambell, Warren and Karen Payne, and the big one—Lance Snadden and his wife, Dianne.

Lance stood to shake her hand. 'Please join us for a drink, Sienna.'

'Tyson, Sienna will have the red wine,' called out Jake, not giving her a choice. 'Josh, a chair for the lady, please. She's been on her feet all day.'

'Well, if the boss insists.' Sienna sat at the end of the table near Lance and his wife, Dianne, and spoke with the guests she needed to impress.

Twenty minutes later, Sienna's phone beeped in her pocket, and she turned off the alarm. 'Jake, you have a bus to catch.' As a woman who wore many faces, she slipped back into her EA role. Then nodded at Josh and Tyson who were tonight's designated bus drivers.

'Dad, can you sort out the judges? Jess will help you.' But then Jake had to help the intoxicated Bob stand, with Jess coming to his aid. 'Sienna?'

Poor guy, his dad was a mess.

Not good when they needed to impress their guests.

'I'll look after the guests. Please take this wine and your glasses for the drive. Consider it a nightcap.' Sienna passed a bottle each to Patrick, Lance, and Warren as their partners scooped up the glasses with a smile.

'What happens now?' asked Karen Payne.

'You're going glamping in these amazing tents. You'll love it. I hope you will because I haven't been camping yet to compare.' Would she have time before she left Danbunnan?

'Elliott, the gift bags please?' Sienna escorted the guests to the waiting buses at the bottom of the stairs.

While Jake and Tom wrangled Bob into the other bus with the judges, Elliott approached with a large box.

'Thank you, Elliott.' From the box, Sienna handed out a small backpack to each guest as they boarded the bus. 'These day packs are a gift from Jake to make your stay more comfortable. There's water bottles, hats, sunscreen, and all sorts of goodies, especially for those going on the trail ride tomorrow.' All branded with the Danbunnan logo. 'And if there's anything extra you might need, please don't hesitate to ask.' This wasn't her first rodeo, especially when Sienna was aiming for high-end corporate country class to leave a long-lasting impression.

Jake closed the door, trapping everyone inside the guests' bus. 'Thank you, ba—'

She frowned, opening his passenger door. It was definitely the wrong time to call her *babe* in front of everyone. 'Please make sure your guests are shown to their tents *first*.'

Jake hesitated before he climbed inside. 'Am I forgetting something?'

Yes—her! 'No. I put your notes and tablet on the front dash. I've set your alarm for the morning. Please don't drink all night with your mates.' Because they were all watching from the back of the bus like fish in a goldfish bowl.

'I won't. I'll see you in the morning. Get some rest.' Jake gave her a sly wink and that crooked grin that made her heart glow as he closed his door.

With Jess and Elliott by her side, they waved the buses out of the compound.

'Thank the stars that's over.' Sienna undid her top

button, ripped off the black neckerchief and headed to the garden. She plonked into her seat, exhausted. Everything ached, but this was only part one.

'Thank you everyone for doing a magnificent job. Please help yourself to a knock-off drink because I am.' Sienna raised her glass and soaked up the atmosphere. 'Were there any issues tonight?'

'I didn't see any,' replied Elliott, stripping off the table linen. 'No one left a skerrick of food on their plates, and all the men asked for seconds on the beef.'

'And the fish?'

'The crispy-skin barra was a huge hit.'

'Simon Simmons couldn't stop raving about it,' said Jess, taking a seat alongside Sienna. 'Jake never mentioned the barra farm, he just told them that all the food was either Danbunnan produced, caught, or grown. My favourite was the wild-goose pâté. And the bush bee honey sorbet. Did I mention I liked the dessert?'

'There's plenty in the coldroom for a midnight snack. Tom, did you see any issues tonight?' Because the ever-watchful 2IC had side row seats, manning the bar all night.

Tom plonked his beer on the table and took a seat. 'Nope.'

'Did the judges mingle with any of the guests?'

'Nope. That mob kept to themselves with Simon Simmons in charge.'

'Jake talked to everyone, right?' They'd discussed Jake's duties as a host, even consulting the journals for correct entertaining etiquettes. Afterall, in Danbunnan's long history they'd entertained senators, even a Duke, a few Lords, and lots of other dignitaries this past century, with each visit recorded within the journals. *Thank you, Winifred Cullen.*

'My brother was so confident, like a real boss, and kept the conversation going. The food was amazing, and the wine was delicious. It was the best dinner party I've ever been to, and the dessert was my favourite.' Jess giggled behind her usually fidgety fingers.

'I can now see where Aaron gets his sweet tooth from.'

'Why did you separate the guests from the judges?' Tom asked as he sipped his beer.

Sienna eyed the head stockman. She didn't have the energy to yell at him now for his part in Rhonda's plan. 'Jake and I guessed the judges would want to keep to themselves.'

'How did you figure that, when you've never met them and it's your first competition?'

'My *only* cattle station competition. I'm not doing this again.' Not when there was too much emotional involvement. 'I'd learned from the Simmons's rodeo that those judges were a herd amongst themselves, with Simon playing top dog.' Hold on, did she just sound like a local including herd in her speech? 'We'd assumed the judges wouldn't bother with the guests if they appeared to be part of Jake's group of friends.'

'Aren't they all Jake's mates?' Jess looked at Tom and Sienna for answers.

That sounded promising. 'No. Some of them are VIPs.'

'So why were you separating the guests from the judges?' Tom asked.

Jess frowned with confusion. 'What do you mean? They faced each other over dinner.'

Tom narrowed his grey eyes at Sienna, pointing his beer glass at her. 'You used Elliott in the centre as a distraction.'

'I did.' Sienna suppressed her grin behind her wineglass, watching Elliott lead the charge in cleaning the tables, just like he did daily in the muster room. 'Let's hope we can keep them separated until tomorrow lunchtime, at least.'

'What do you mean by that?' Jess asked.

'Because at morning tea we'll be dropping the bomb.'

# Forty-six

The food tour was under way as the safari buses followed the dirt track. In the lead vehicle, Tom drove while Jake explained his organic concepts, and the use of green energy, including an inspection of his prize cattle.

'I'm really feeling like a tour guide now,' said Jake in the front passenger seat.

'And I'm a tour bus driver,' mumbled Tom. 'I noticed how Sienna had separated the guests and judges last night. You're not ignoring the judges, are you? You're sidelining them.'

'Dad's giving them what they want. As per the rules they get to inspect the cattle and crops.' Jake was pleased how Sienna had used the judges to explain to their guests what it was they were looking for in the cattle, keeping it all transparent as part of the competition. His cattle were polished to perfection, led around a small arena on leads by Jess and the twins putting on their own show. It had made their guests, and even some of the tough judges, soften. Except for Simon Simons, whose frown only deepened to discover how pristine Jake's herd of cattle was. It wasn't pet meat. It was top shelf beef that was impossible even for the judges to deny.

Jake checked out the guests and his mates all chatting like one group of friends in the back of the bus. It'd been such a casual atmosphere with this group, hoping it stayed like this for the rest of the day.

'Good, the horses are ready.' Saddled horses were lined up against the horse truck where Tyson and Charlie waited beside Lyn.

'And there's the toy-car.' Shining in the sun, the piece of modern machinery stood out in the valley. The other bus, containing the judges, pulled up beside him.

Jake opened the bus for his guests. 'We've got some morning smoko before we go for our trail ride.'

He led them to a table laden with food beneath the shade of the tree, where Sienna waited, dressed the same as she had for Andrew's visit.

'Nice change.' His eyes walked over her long legs in those black slacks and that tight business shirt. But her shirt showed no Danbunnan brand like the rest of the crew wore with pride. Wasn't Sienna part of the team, too?

'Sienna, where's that cute chef's uniform gone?' called out Ryan, shoving up his sunglasses to get lost into his mop of hair.

'In the wash.' Sienna held out a platter to their guests. 'Tea, coffee, cakes, and you must try the salamis.'

'You're feeding us too well, Sienna,' said Craig, helping himself to the food.

'All part of the plan.' Sienna passed the platter to Jess and smiled at Jake. 'Any time you're ready, Boss.'

'Ah, yeah.' Jake headed for the far side of the table, feeling her close, supporting him right when he needed it the most.

'It's just like we rehearsed,' she whispered. 'I'll back you up anytime you need it … I've got the flick chart ready.' Sienna pointed to the chart on a stand as if for a boardroom presentation, except the backdrop was a wide-open valley floor with water buffalo grazing in the distance.

Every stop on the food tour had been carefully choreographed for maximum effect to sell his product. But this was the moment of truth. He was so nervous he was tempted to jump on his horse and escape the pack.

Instead, Jake inhaled deeply and turned to face the

group. From here the surprises would keep on coming.

It was time to nail it home.

'Everyone, there'll be a small presentation as the final part of the competition requirements. Then we'll split up, because some of you have elected to not join us on the trail ride.'

With arms crossed over his massive chest, Simon Simmons stood a head taller than the other judges. 'We spend enough time riding our own horses on our own properties, thank you.'

Which is what Jake had been counting on.

'For those unaware of my background, I grew up here and did my degree in agricultural studies. But my apprenticeship didn't end there. For the next six years I continued learning, not only from my family, but also from Tom, my head stockman, and from many other brilliant cattlemen I've had the honour of working with right around Australia. I've worked as a contractor following cattle musters, and I've even done the rodeo circuit with my mate, Craig.'

'That's me.' Craig tipped his hat for the crowd.

'Don't let the larrikinism and looks fool you, as Craig was chief stock inspector in charge of the export yards in Darwin.'

'Yeah, mate, but you don't see me taking meetings with Middle Eastern buyers.'

'What's this?' Simon's frown deepened as his face got redder.

'Sorry, son, I forgot to tell them.' Bob gave a sly wink and sipped his tea.

'You haven't seen the main herd yet, Simon, but you will.' As much as Jake would've loved to see the judges' faces when they did, his dad would have that privilege. 'In the next few weeks, some of the herd is being shipped out as part of a live export agreement to the Middle East.' *Damn, that sounded good.*

Lance Snadden removed his sunglasses and said, 'That's

a billionaire's market known for accepting only exclusive top-quality products.'

'And that's where my organic cattle's going.'

'All of them?' asked one of the judges.

How much were the judges expecting to receive as their pay-off from Simon for blocking Danbunnan's beef sales?

'No. I've diversified my organic products to expand into regional niche markets.'

The judges raised their eyebrows.

'As of this month I'm registered as a certified organic producer in livestock and stockfeed. This whole valley is organic.' He waved at the scenery behind him. 'Those hay bales we drove past last night on the way to our tents are organic. There are no chemicals kept on this property for a reason.'

'Everyone knows about the poisoning,' said Simon.

'What poisoning?' Karen asked, standing beside her husband Warren.

'Sienna, please.' There were some things he just couldn't say.

Sienna flipped over the charts' cover page to reveal a map of Danbunnan Station and pointed to the area. 'About three years ago, there was an accidental toxic chemical spill within this region, which spread into the water channel. It poisoned all the cattle meant for market.'

'Oh no,' said Karen. The other ladies gasped as their husbands murmured surprise.

'My brother killed himself over it,' said Jake quietly to Karen. 'That's why I banned chemicals and went organic, and why we've chosen to have a fundraiser for mental health at tonight's party.' That was the true story in one simple sentence.

'What happened to that area?' asked their guest, Patrick.

'It was re-channelled and quarantined,' replied Sienna.

'Can we see it,' asked a judge.

'No.' Jake frowned, crossing his arms over his chest. That area wasn't a tourist destination to be judged, it was sacred.

Sienna said, 'Jake's leased it to the Department of Mines and Environment for rehabilitation.'

'Why?' asked another judge.

'Because the toxic spill is similar to a mining accident,' replied Sienna. 'They'll be trialling techniques to fast-track decontamination methods. Eventually that contaminated area will become a natural wildlife corridor in honour of Jake's brother, Duncan. Just so you know, the soil and water on Danbunnan has been extensively tested and found to be clear, including that area.'

'How can you prove the water's clean?' asked one of the judges.

'Barry can.' Sienna pointed to Barry.

'And you are?' Simon wheeled around like an albino gorilla about to squash a field mouse.

Barry grinned at Jake at the secret shared. 'I'm the Federal Government's leading water analyst in charge of the Top End's extensive artesian water basins. As per national environmental protection standards, I regularly test for chemicals, bacteria, nitrates, trace elements and other contaminants within this region via chemical and biological samples. I've been randomly testing this region every six weeks since the contamination occurred three years ago. It was on my recommendation, backed by my test results, that showed this area was prime for rehabilitation. Sienna and Jake have the reports if you need them.'

'So, how is the water?' Lance asked Jake.

'Crystal. You've all been drinking it ever since you arrived.'

'Don't let the dusty outback fool you, as Danbunnan has a bountiful water supply and many natural springs, where the quality is proven to be higher than anything else in today's marketplace.' Sienna turned the page on her chart to show a diagram. 'The quality is so pure it will be bottled for distribution, scheduled to commence next month where one of Danbunnan's mineral rich springs will be tapped, filtered, then micro-filtered into 15-litre water coolers with future expansion into stylised bottles for restaurants. I can't wait.'

'Since when are you selling water?' Simon said.

'I signed off on it last week,' replied Jake. It had been one of the many meetings they'd had in their whirlwind tour of Darwin.

'But wait, there's more …' Sienna's excitement was heard, as she turned over the page on the flick chart. 'Danbunnan's organic certification involved soil testing, just like this valley we're standing in, which received the tick of approval in excellence for soil quality. Same again for the assorted natural grains and grasses, that's in those hay bales you saw by the homestead.'

'What's the feed ratio?' asked Warren.

'I was so hoping you'd ask that question.' Sienna pulled out a large envelope from her leather portfolio. 'For you, Warren. Inside, you'll find the testing stats on the ratios of fibre, mineral, and nutrient content within the stockfeed varieties that Jake has available. Feel free to speak to Jake after this presentation should you have any further queries and he'd be happy to discuss this or any of his products at length.'

Sienna returned to her place by the chart and continued to address everyone. 'Last night you ate the wild rice from this field. The wild mushrooms, wheat, and other grains I carefully harvested by hand for the bread and pastries you've been eating since you've arrived. The menu was specially created to use everything that Danbunnan produces, because this station isn't just about beef. It's diversified as part of Jake's plan for this station's long-term future.'

'If you've gotten into Dubai, you've got my attention,' said Lance. 'Have you sold all your cattle, Jake?'

'No. I'm looking for a regional buyer because I believe in promoting local industries. I plan to use the local meatworks, who have agreed to take Danbunnan produce first thing on a Monday to avoid contaminating it with any other lesser quality meats they process.'

Simon cleared his throat as the rest of the judges mumbled, shifting their boots in the dirt.

'Sienna, please?' Jake's jaw tightened, getting sick of Simon's attitude.

Sienna flicked to a new page on their chart. 'Which brings me to Danbunnan buffalo. Eye fillet and rump from our buffalo herd has been sold to the five-star restaurant trade, starting with Darwin. The rest will be for mincing.'

The judges now wore permanent frowns, mumbling their disgust.

'Danbunnan buffalo mince is being used for specialised sausage production through a boutique butcher who supplies exclusively to Darwin's best restaurants. It's what you ate this morning for breakfast. The buff mince is so popular for boutique sausage meat we've been inundated with orders for the upcoming tourist season. But this week ...' She hesitated and looked to Jake. 'Do you want to share the news?'

'No. You do it.'

Sienna's smile ripped wide. 'The NT's Minister of Tourism and Trade has offered to take Danbunnan produce to the tourism trade show in Sydney.' Surprised murmurs grew. 'And just this morning we received an invitation to be part of the NT delegation for the tourism tradeshow in Singapore, where Jake will have the opportunity to display not just the buffalo but all of Danbunnan's products to the world.' She clapped her hands, which led the rest to do the same.

*Damn.* Jake dropped his head to hide beneath his hat's brim. Again, she'd surprised him.

'Be proud, Jake.' She squeezed his upper arm.

Jake now understood what *front-door stamp of approval* meant, and the enormity of Sienna's contacts. The lady was gold.

He could see they'd shocked his family, his friends, and the judges. Most all it was Simon, who blinked as if his eyeballs were full of grit.

Now for the finale that'd either make or break his

reputation within this region. 'Wait, we haven't finished on the buffalo yet, Sienna ...'

'The rest of the buffalo meat that's not suitable for human consumption will be minced to create these buff rolls.' She held up a clear plastic bag. 'These are hand-rolled and smoked using traditional methods from Jake's family by the master smokehouse chef, Bob. Again, this product meets the highest quality for organic standards, but it's for canines. We've had an independent pet store in the city take our first batch, which sold out in a day.'

Simon scoffed, 'You're making pet meat?'

'Your idea, wasn't it, Simon?' Jake retorted.

'May I have a look?' Patrick asked.

'I was hoping you'd ask, Patrick. Here's a sample we've prepared just for you. On the platters Jess is serving we have Bob's re-creation of his ancestors' family recipe for salami and beef jerky, created for the first stockmen of Danbunnan. They're all for human consumption.' Sienna passed the plastic bag and an envelope to Patrick. 'This sealed pack and information is for the pet-feed market, including our research results. But don't ask me about the quality—ask our flying vet.'

'That's me.' Ryan put his hand in the air with sunglasses pushing up his floppy black hair. 'I've read through all their clinical results.'

'What did you make of them?' asked Patrick.

'It shows the nutrients needed for canines is off the charts from this organic buffalo Jake's got getting fat in that valley.' Ryan thumbed towards the grazing buffalo behind them. 'Sienna and Jake gave me a box of those buff rolls and I've been testing it in my surgery. I've also given samples to the local air force base for their security dogs—who all loved it—and they want more.'

'And that concludes the presentation for the station competition.' Sienna approached Lance, holding out a large envelope. 'This is for you, Lance. Don't worry, Jake's got something special for you later.'

'Thank you. I was feeling a little left out.' Lance took the package under his arm.

'If you have any further questions, please ask Jake on the ride. For the other gentlemen, Bob has your portfolio presentations, as per the competition rules, waiting on the bus. Jake?'

'For those of you riding we'll be going down this valley where you'll see the crops, cattle, buffalo, and a few of our natural springs up close. Then we'll be having lunch at one of the waterfalls.' Jake spoke to the guests that mattered, glad to be rid of the judges who were wandering back to the bus scratching their heads.

Now the fun could begin.

'For those unsure on riding, don't worry you're in good hands. Craig and Tom have taught hundreds of people over the years. These horses aren't racehorses, they're Danbunnan bred, and we've selected those most suited for gentle trail riding.'

'Can you ride, Sienna?' Craig asked.

'She's learning,' said Jake with a grin. 'If you can get her out of the kitchen.'

'I won't be there forever, but I've got to head back now. There's a dinner to perfect.'

Jake stopped his frown at her blasé comment on her time here at Danbunnan. He cleared his throat and looked to the horses and his team. Yes, his team he could keep—but Sienna?

'Those riding, if you'll follow Tom and Craig, they'll get you saddled up. The rest with Dad and Jess.' Jake grabbed Sienna's arm and led her away from the others to the far side of her car.

'I think it went well, Jake.'

'It was brilliant.'

'So, what's wrong?'

'I don't want to show the judges the barra ponds.'

'Are you sure?'

'Yes. We've done what's needed for the competition, and

you can see the judges have had enough.'

'You're right, you don't want them ruining the mood when your guests are excited.'

'So, what do you suggest? You said you're always flexible with these things.'

'What about detouring to the ponds on the horses? You could let your guests catch their lunch and have the crew cook them at the waterfall.'

'We can do that. What about the rest we've got planned?'

'Let the guests chill longer at the waterfall, it'll be relaxing for them. I'll serve lunch in the muster room for the judges. Pina can help me. I'll meet you at the barra ponds. Can I bring Josh with me to the ponds? He loves fishing and he can help me pick up any golf balls lying around.'

'Do it, babe. Ask Josh if we could borrow his fishing gear. He knows where the rest of our fishing gear is in the workshed.'

'Good idea, because I still don't know what's in those sheds, and my tools interpreter is busy.'

All his team were busy, with Sienna the busiest behind the scenes coordinating it all. 'Anything else?' Did he dare ask what she wanted that wasn't work related?

'No, leave it with me. Ride safe and enjoy it, please? The hard part is over.'

'Thank you. You know I'd …' He wanted to hug her and kiss her and show his gratitude.

She gave him a wink as if she'd read his mind. 'Go, cowboy, your guests are waiting.'

'I'm not a cowboy, I'm a cattleman.'

# Forty-seven

In the rich red clay lay six dams, the size of massive swimming pools, with large silver fish lurking below the watery surface. The pump shed stood silent on the small rise, and the golf driving range signs sat in wait. Sienna, with hands on hips, looked over the ponds with a picky presenter's eye. 'There's no way to pretty this up, right?'

'Why?' Josh pushed up his hat's brim. 'It looks good. You can see the changes from when I first saw it.'

'Do we have everything?'

'Fishing rods with barbless lures, check. Water for horses, check.'

'Did you discuss your snake whispering project with the judges?'

'Nope, they talked cattle and gossip. Correction, Simon did the talking, the rest just sat there.'

'How did they react when they saw the main herd?'

'That was cool. Bob made me slow right down, I felt like a proper tour driver cruising past the herd.'

'It's impressive seeing that many cattle together. I know I was stunned to see it the first time.'

'That mob of judges didn't say a word all the way back to the cattlemen's quarters. They still didn't say nothing when Pina was there ready to show them to their rooms like it was a proper tourist resort. Do you think we'll win?'

'Don't care.'

'Because you won't be here when they announce the

winner? I wish you were.'

'Aww, I'll miss you too, Josh.' She tapped the tip of his hat. 'Hey, whose extra club is that one?' Sienna pointed to the iron clubs poking through the grooves of the corrugated roof struts.

'Charlie's.'

'Does Charlie play golf?'

'Nah, he uses it for cane toads.' Josh pulled it from the roof. 'That way when we're manning the pumps, we both get a hit.'

'Good idea.' They both put a ball on the tee and *whack*. Josh's ball slammed into the net and Sienna's golf ball flew sideways and *plonked* into the pond on the far right.

'I thought you were getting better, Sienna?' called out Jake, riding up on Sampson.

Her heart literally stopped at the view, only to jackhammer hard at his crooked grin and the intensity of his royal blue eyes shaded beneath his Akubra. 'I was warming up.' With her body temperature going through the roof.

Jake looked amazing, in control of his stunning black stallion, with everyone trailing behind him like a camp ride. 'How was the ride?'

Jake dismounted with ease. 'Good. What have you done to my ponds?'

'Nothing. I've just set up a small table for the guests. Josh said the horses would need water and shouldn't drink from the ponds.'

'Knew there was a reason for you to bring Josh. Well done.' Jake patted the jackaroo's shoulders. 'Okay, Josh, help Tyson and Charlie with the guests. We're not here for long, so don't unsaddle the horses.' Jake passed the reins to Josh, who led Sampson away.

Craig headed straight for the table of food waiting under the shed's shade. 'More food! I'll be rolling home.'

'My plane won't have the power to carry you, Craig, if you keep eating the way you are,' said Ryan, also helping himself to the table.

'Okay everyone, this is the last of the show and tell,' announced Jake.

The guests, who wore matching Danbunnan caps, rubbed their butts, and wore wide smiles from their riding adventure.

Sienna again stepped in as hostess, passing out bottles of water to everyone, as they gathered inside the pump shed.

'What is this place?' Jasmine asked.

'Ponds,' said Jake, 'filled with billabong barramundi.'

Lance removed his sunglasses to polish them on his shirt to take in the view. 'Is this your surprise for me, Sienna?'

'Surprise.'

Jake cleared his throat and began his explanation. 'So, this wild barramundi is channelled into these ponds, hand fed, and spring fed with the aid of these pumps. I'll admit this is a new venture for me, but it's part of my diversification plans for Danbunnan Station. We've just got our licenses and sold a batch to the local fish markets, and they're keen to buy more.'

Lance asked, 'Is this venture certified organic too?'

'Close. Sienna?' Jake looked to Sienna.

'The paperwork is with the certification committee as we speak, waiting for approval. They don't sit for another six weeks but we're confident of passing as we've surpassed all their requirements.'

Jake continued. 'We've delivered some fish to selected Darwin restaurants, where, again, it's been well received. I'm not the only barra farmer in the territory. Most of the others do large-scale production. I'm doing—Sienna?'

'Plate-size, spring-fed, free-range billabong barramundi, perfect for the signature size for restaurants.'

'The crispy-skinned barra we had last night, that's this?' Jasmine pointed to the ponds.

'Yes,' said Sienna. 'I know it doesn't look pretty.'

'I've seen worse. But none of them have a driving range. Now that's clever.' Lance pointed to the painted targets and net.

'*We know*,' chorused Craig, Ryan, and Barry, wearing boyish grins that made Jake chuckle.

'How long have you had these ponds, Jake?' Lance stepped closer to the ponds.

'A few years. The ponds are currently stocked at their peak levels. The university has agreed to show us how to breed them, because I want to release a proportion back into the river to keep up their natural breeding processes, so they return to Danbunnan's waterways.'

'So, what's your vision then for your products? Because I'd assumed you were all about cattle and buffalo, not barramundi too.' Patrick shook his head, laughing, his amusement spreading easily amongst the other guests.

Jake inhaled deeply, sliding his hands into the pockets of his jeans. 'I've almost reached the cattle and buffalo numbers I want. Now it's all about improving their quality. You see, there's a delicate balancing act I have with this place. If I go much bigger the scales will tip and I'll be raping from the land instead of reaping her rewards. I don't want to be *big*—I want to be *select*, using what I have to diversify and not destroy.'

Jake pointed to the river beyond the fence line. 'Sienna and I've researched this thoroughly. I'm responsible not only for the land but also the water systems within Danbunnan. That includes three rivers that runs all the way to the sea.'

'How big is Danbunnan Station?' Lance asked.

'Danbunnan is bigger than Greenland. In the wet season, this place is as green as Ireland and full of wildlife, it's paradise. And I'm responsible for her, so I won't let her be destroyed by over production.'

Jake looked beyond the ponds to the sea of green tree tops, mirrored by an enormous blue sky. 'I won't lie, Danbunnan was heading that way, and I've seen other farms go that way. Look, gentlemen, I only want select buyers, which is why you three have been invited as guests to this property.'

'Wasn't it for the competition, too?' Warren asked.

'This weekend is more about showing those judges what I've done and to kill a lot of local rumours. Look, I'm just a bloke trying to make a living for my family. My techniques aren't new. I even went back to what my ancestors did and learned from their documented mistakes and wins. I've also used what I've learned from my own travels to produce a quality product.'

He paused, facing the horizon as if speaking to the land itself. 'In the end, it was Danbunnan who taught me the most. She's been in my family for a long time, and I want her to be here for many generations to come. She deserves to be treated with respect because there's nowhere else like it. Danbunnan's shown me how pure she is, and as my reward for looking after her she looks after me and my family.'

'So, what do you want to do with the fish?' Lance asked Jake.

'Sell it to a select market. You've seen it, tasted it, and it's produce is up for sale. I just need to find the right buyers.'

'Well ...' Lance glanced back at the ponds, then grinned sideways at Jake. 'Are you going to show me how to catch one?'

'Right this way.' Jake gave a nod of his Akubra, escorting his guests to the water's edge. 'Tom, give us a hand.'

'Yes, Boss.' Tom then spoke softly to Sienna beside him. 'Are you alright, girlie?'

'Ah huh.' Sienna sniffed as she wiped away the tears and slipped on her sunglasses to put on her game face. She had to remember this was just a job, even if the guy running the show was pretty close to perfect.

Jake had his future set. He knew exactly what he was doing because he'd found his vision. It was a rare and powerful thing to witness.

But it was more than that. Jake truly believed in himself, and Danbunnan had finally found her true king.

But would there ever be room for her as his queen?

# Forty-eight

Back in her chef's uniform, Sienna entered the hay shed. 'Hello, girl.' Sally greeted her, wagging her tail with a wide yawn, happy to receive a big pat as Sienna untied her.

'Why'd you tie the dog up in here? Isn't she your mate?' Gone was the crown and footy shorts, Joe, the station mechanic, was dressed to play bartender alongside the bearded Charlie.

'Sally has plenty of food and water. Besides the booze is here,' explained Sienna, walking past the bar to the far side of the shed.

'Good idea, no one would dare come inside with Sally playing guard dog,' said Charlie.

'Hey, guys! The stage is over there,' she shouted to the band as they walked in from the afternoon sunshine of glorious Goldilocks weather.

'You don't just play country, do you?' Elliott asked the guitarist.

'Elliott, the utensils go by the bain-marie so we're not searching for them later.' She started removing the plastic covers from the red couches.

'How do you want to do this, luv?' called out Lyn, helping Pina drag a trolley of stacked milk crates filled with wildflowers.

'It's three jam jars with candles in the centre of each table then wrap the wildflower wreaths around them. They don't need to be perfect as it's a party, not a wedding.'

'It's a brilliant touch, something so simple as a girl doing daisy chains.' Pina held up a wreath of delicate yellow, blue, and white wildflowers, mixed with native eucalyptus leaves.

'Kate loves her flowers, like all girls do. Like I do.' The handwoven rustic wreaths on the tables looked amazing. The whole place did, she couldn't wait to see the guests' reactions.

'Excuse me, no smoking in here, okay?' Sienna said to the band's guitarist, who had an unlit cigarette dangling from his mouth as he stood before a carefully curated wall of hay. 'I'll have Elliott fetch you an ashtray for outside, how's that?'

'Sorry, bad habit.' He gave her a shrug.

Sienna put out reserved signs on three tables at the front of the dance floor for their VIP guests. In her past life she used to sit at the VIP table, now she was working behind the scenes again. Where would she find that balance of both?

'Who are the reserved tables for?'

Sienna spun around at that question.

'Angela. Hi.' *Oh no, Jake's fiancée.* 'What are you doing here?'

'I thought I'd give you guys a hand.' Angela held on to her hat gawking at the shed's interior, as her many rings caught the light.

Sienna carried a crate to the bar and spread out the candles in their jars. 'The reserved tables are for family and guests, like you, Angela.' Who wasn't meant to be hanging around with the staff.

'But this is amazing. So are the chandeliers and the red couches.' Angela stood in the centre of the corrugated shed. 'It's not a country shed anymore. It's a rustic ballroom when you step inside. This is not what I expected, it's brilliant.'

*Yesss!* Sienna refrained from the air punch. 'Thank you. That's the effect we were after. Okay, are you guys all good?' When she got the nod from the crew, she headed out. 'I'll be in the kitchen if you need me.'

'Anything I can do?' asked Angela, still shadowing

Sienna.

'We're good. But thank you for offering.' Where were the family hiding when they should be attending to their guests? 'Excuse me, I've got a meal to prepare. Elliott?'

'Coming.' Elliott snatched a large bottle of coke and two six packs of beer, passing one to Sienna.

'Why did you give me this?'

'They're for us to celebrate in the kitchen when the meals are done.'

'Good idea.'

'How hot was that guitarist?'

'I saw him checking you out.' She bumped him playfully with her shoulder. 'Which reminds me, could you go to the recycling centre and fetch a batch of empty coffee cans for ashtrays, please? And for safety's sake, grab a couple of fire extinguishers for behind the bar.'

'Done, done, and done.' Elliott palmed off the rest of the beer and headed off on his mission. Leaving her with arms full of drinks she headed for the muster room with Sally trotting alongside.

'Here, let me help you carry that.' Angela took a six pack from Sienna's arms.

'Thanks, but you don't have to do that. You're a guest.' Not just any guest, but Jake's fiancée. *Great*. Again, that guilt factor scratched along her spine.

'I'm bored. I knew I should have gone horse riding.'

'Why didn't you?'

'Daddy will only ride our horses.'

'Where is Mr. Simmons?' Sienna hadn't seen anyone since she'd returned from the barra ponds.

'Daddy's yakking with the rest of the judges at the cattlemen's quarters. He's still griping after that morning tea presentation.' She pulled a face. 'He likes your boobs.'

'Hmmm. Well, I won't be taking China's job, okay?'

'China will be pleased. She'll be here tonight and said she was gonna hunt you down, so I'll head her off.'

'Thanks for that.' *Um, awkward.* But Sienna kept walking

towards the muster room.

'You've done a good thing here, Sienna. The place has got spirit. Duncan would've loved this, and Sally is in excellent condition. Must be that food you're giving her.'

'She's not my dog, just my mate.' It was going to be heartbreaking saying goodbye to her furry companion, trotting ahead with her tail wagging.

'Duncan used to say a dog picked their owner, and Sally picked him. After he died, Sally stayed on the muster room's verandah and never moved, waiting for him to come home. It was so sad. And now look at her.'

'You were Duncan's girlfriend, weren't you?'

'Yes. He was a good man, gentle like Jess. They're both like their mother. Jake's a little like his dad—but not.'

'I've noticed.' But Sienna also noticed there was no Bob or any other family member in sight.

'Jess told me who Duncan's father was. It made sense, you know. Duncan said that Tom was like a brother to him. I can understand why Duncan was so upset when he'd given everything to this place only to find out he wasn't Bob's son.'

'The whole thing is sad, and I'm sorry for your loss, too.' Sienna could see Angela was hurting.

'I'm doing okay, though there are days I still miss the guy. I loved Duncan, but with him Danbunnan came first. Guess that's why I love Pete so much. He's willing to run away with me, as we're both just hanging here for Jake's sake.'

'Um, what?' Sienna stumbled a little, checking to see if anyone else was nearby.

'Jake told me you know about our fake engagement. He loves you, you know.'

Sienna shook her head and kept on walking. 'I'm just staff.'

'You're more than that. Any fool can see that.'

'No, it can't be that obvious.' *Was it?*

'What, that you're more than a relief cook?'

'When did Jake tell you?'

'Last night up at the North Ridge, we had to hang out together or our fathers' would've been suspicious.'

Sienna was not going to get jealous of Jake spending time alone in the dark with a woman he was engaged to. *Nope. Nuh uh.*

'We haven't told the guests I'm Jake's fiancée. But I am secretly engaged to Pete. Here, this is Pete's ring.'

'Um? Congratulations? Nice ring.' It was a stunning set of shiny diamonds, even though this entire conversation was incredibly awkward.

'We told the guests I was Angela, the girl from next door.' Angela sighed, swinging her beer bottles like a little girl dragging her teddy bear.

Poor thing looked lonely. 'You don't fit the profile of the stereotypical girl next door. Not when it takes two hours to get to your place, instead of looking over a fence.' Sienna opened the muster room's doors and followed Angela inside.

Angela gave a dazzling smile before peering around the empty dining room, to lean over and whisper, 'You know, Duncan and I had planned to use the horses not good enough for Daddy's stock for training, specifically for little kids to ride. It's always been my dream to run a place to teach little kids to ride horses, especially those with disabilities.'

'That's amazing. I can't ride—but teaching disabled children, that's incredible. Why can't you still do that?' Sienna fetched the large farmhouse bread loaves rising on the counters, and slid them into the wood oven, stirred the coals, and set the timer on her phone.

'Daddy thinks it's stupid because there's no money in it. But it's always been my dream. Duncan said he'd help me once Bob retired, and we were going to get engaged, then married.' Angela sighed again, watching her finger draw invisible lines on the bench. 'But for Duncan, it was always next muster, then the next muster, and then he left us.'

'I'm so sorry.'

'It's okay now.' Angela looked around the muster room with a widening smile. 'Just look at this place.'

'Why did you get engaged to Jake?' Her curiosity speaking before her manners could catch up.

'I'm not ready to see this place get swallowed up by Daddy. Not after Duncan tried so hard, and Jake too. China says cattlemen treat their country like sailors who love the sea as a mythical goddess. My Daddy, Bob, Tom, Duncan, even Jake, are all like that—they're in love with this land first and, if they marry, their wives come second.'

'Isn't this your home too?'

'I'm only staying to help out Jake, otherwise, I would've eloped with Pete a year ago.'

'Does Jake know this?'

'Of course, he does. But this whole fake engagement was my idea.'

'Why?' It was none of her business, but she had to know.

'When I learned Daddy was paying the co-op to block anyone from buying Danbunnan beef, I had to help Jake. I couldn't do anything to save Duncan. I tried to take Sally with me to take care of her, but she wouldn't leave. Bob was a mumbling mess, Duncan's mother got sick and died, and then Duncan's little brother, Jake was killing himself with work. All while Daddy sat back waiting for Jake to quit.'

'Jake's not a quitter.' Sienna admired that strength of his.

'I know. Do you know why they call Jake *the Black Prince*?'

'No, but I've heard his mates call him that.'

'He's the black sheep of the family, but so much more. You see, Bob was the cattle king who had two sons. Duncan was promised the land as number one son, the Crown Prince. Jake was the second son that wasn't needed, and Jake was *baaad*,' Angela said with wide eyes.

'How bad?'

'Jake got banned from all the pubs in the neighbouring towns for brawling. Duncan had to bail Jake out of the lock-up a few times.'

'Men make mistakes.' How angry was Jake to fight like that?

'But Jake was underage, drunk in the pub, brawling with these bigger men while on school holidays.'

'That naughty man.' She tried everything to not laugh. She wasn't exactly Miss Goody-two-shoes in school either.

'Jake had quite the reputation, surprising everyone when he passed school to go to university.'

'Jake's a smart man. Many people underestimate him.'

'I agree. I was shocked, too. But Duncan knew. He talked Jake into going to university. He wanted Jake to be his partner after graduation, so they could manage Danbunnan together. And Jake did ...' Through the windows, Angela scowled at the house on the hill. 'You know, Bob had Jake cleaning troughs, doing the boundary run, or fencing when he returned after his graduation. Until Jake wanted a day off to go to the rodeo with Cowboy Craig. Bob said if Jake left, he couldn't come back because there was no room for a freeloader.'

'Is that why Jake got evicted?'

'Duncan told me Jake had worked for a month straight, working harder than the contractors, for nothing. Yet Bob said Jake was the worst worker they had, barely earning his room and board.'

'That's so unfair.'

'But Duncan gave Jake's wages to his mother to pass on to Jake. The problem was Bob caught her with it and they argued, and he was going to hit her. But Jake jumped in and punched Bob. I think he broke Bob's ribs and that's when Bob kicked Jake out. I know Jake offered to take his mother with him, but she said this was her home and she stayed. So, Jake left with only his swag and one bag, jumped into Craig's ute and didn't return for six years. Jake was then forever known as the Black Prince, an heir to nothing but heartache.'

'That is so sad. Why are you telling me this?'

'Because I loved Duncan, who loved Danbunnan like Jake does. And I hate that my Daddy not only controls me but he's happy to use me as his princess pawn to increase his empire. He knows I don't love Jake that way, because Jake has always been Duncan's little brother to me. Jake was meant to be my brother-in-law, but it never happened.' Angela then frowned as her posture straightened. 'I'm disgusted by what Daddy's done to the co-op and to Danbunnan, and Pete's the same. It's why Pete's been so supportive and patient, waiting for me because I won't let my Daddy win. He's won everything else by cheating, but I won't let him win this time. From listening to what you and Jake have organised for Danbunnan, I don't think he will.'

'But you're willing to sacrifice your own happiness for others, aren't you?'

'Isn't that what you're doing, too?'

'Me? I'm only hired as a relief cook.'

'You know Jake is happy with you. And he is so in love with you. You can see it. At the speech today, it's Sienna this, Sienna that. I can tell he's in love with you.'

'Who's in love with Sienna?' Jess asked, coming in through the front doors in a dressy shirt, ready to party.

'You look nice. How was the swim?' Sienna asked, steering the conversation in a new direction.

'Amazing. The twins are exhausted.'

'Shame I missed it,' said Angela.

'Ladies, coffee and cake for afternoon tea is there, help yourself. Excuse me, I have a beast to baste. Nice talking to you, Angela.' Sienna dashed out the screen door away from sisters, neighbours, guests, and her guilt for misjudging Angela.

Angela was right, the men here did have a strong connection to the land. She'd seen it today in Jake when he spoke of Danbunnan as if it was a woman, like a captain's love for his ship.

Fully aware she was just a visitor, who wasn't going to take second place to dirt. She deserved better than that. She just had to get through tonight and her job was done.

# Forty-nine

'That's it, this kitchen is *closed*.' In the muster room, Sienna noted the time on her phone, pleased to be ahead of schedule. She then carried the final dish to the kitchen ute parked in front where Josh, Tyson and Elliott waited to deliver them. 'Is everyone enjoying themselves?'

'You should come and see for yourself,' said Josh, putting the tray in the back seat.

'I'm not going anywhere looking like this!' Not when she'd spent the day sweating in front of the wood stove, an industrial oven, two large gas spits, and wood coals from the smokehouse.

'Here.' Tyson shoved a Danbunnan cap on her head. 'We'll sneak you in the side.'

Elliott tugged on her sleeve. 'Come on, you're the only one who hasn't seen the place.'

'I've got a kitchen to clean.' But she struggled to find the energy.

'Five minutes.' Elliott pushed her towards the car.

She climbed in, still wearing a dirty black apron and with a tea towel over her shoulder. Elliott, in his pristine chef's uniform, sat beside her as they were driven to the hay shed.

'How many cars are here?' When she'd been here last it was daylight with an empty field. Now the paddock was filled with assorted utes, vans, four-wheel drives, and tents.

'Boss says over a hundred people are here. For my next

party I'm calling you to organise it, Sienna,' said Josh, grabbing a tray from the car. 'How's my twenty-first sound, in two years? We could have it here.'

'I won't be here, remember? I'm only the relief cook.' Avoiding their sad expressions, she helped them unload. 'Come on, let's get this food inside so I can clean up the kitchen.'

'You look like a kitchen hand instead of the head chef Elliott's been posing as all night,' teased Tyson.

With tray in hand, she peeked inside the wide-open doorway then ducked her head to hide under the cap's brim, away from the attention of visitors. 'I don't think I should go inside.'

Elliott tugged on her sleeve. 'Yes, you can. This way.'

Inside, the chandeliers were like sparkling centrepieces in the sky, as fairy lights looped like spun web from the shed's corners. On the tables, thick candles flickered in clear jars amongst the wildflower wreaths. Spotlights highlighted life-sized black-and-white historical images framed by corrugated walls. The projector's screen displayed black-and-white moving images behind the band, while couples danced before the tables. It was so much better than expected.

'Sienna?' Josh gave her a gentle nudge with his elbow. 'We don't want the relief cook getting ticked-off for letting her food get cold.'

'Oops, sorry. I was gawking like a tourist.' With head down, she followed Josh to the bain-marie. 'We'd better put lids on the trays, so the food doesn't dry out, then turn the temperature down, and that'll do it for the night.'

'Have you finished playing kitchen wench yet?' asked Cowboy Craig, all spiffed up for the occasion.

'Why aren't you dancing?'

'Soon-ish. Dinner was divine as always.'

'Good.' Finally, her first comment from someone who wasn't staff. 'Where are you sitting?'

'With Jake. Are you coming to join us?'

'You're kidding, right?' Staff sitting at the VIP table,

when she looked like the help. *Not gonna happen.*

Through the crowd she spotted Jake, like her eyes were drawn to him, seated with Angela, Jess, and the twins, like a family with their friends. Jake's eyes captured the candlelight and his smile was true. He was proud of himself, and he should be. Today, as boss, he'd proved he was the newly crowned cattle king of Danbunnan Station, who'd earned his place amongst his peers.

Jake looked up and she held her breath waiting for him to notice her, to give her one of his crooked smiles that'd tell her she'd done a good job.

Instead, his gaze skimmed past her to focus on another face in a room full of people she didn't know.

Once again, she was invisible to the world, lost in a sea of people.

'I've got stuff to do. Later.'

Craig grabbed her chef's sleeve. 'Are you coming back?'

'Not dressed like this, I'm not.' She pointed to her splattered apron, then walked away and didn't look back.

Outside in the cool air, she tried to soak in some energy from the scented dew kissing the dust goodnight. But tonight, the band music echoed, people talked, while car exhaust fumes and fuels tainted the air in the once vacant field. It all seemed so loud.

With a heavy tread of her boots in the red dust, Sienna slipped off the cap displaying the Danbunnan logo and left it on the kitchen ute's dashboard. It didn't belong to her because she wasn't permanent staff. It was over.

Angry men's voices caught her attention and she peered into the shadows. Jake didn't need this sort of drama, not when tonight had to be perfect.

Over to the side of the dirt track, on the edge of the shadows, stood four men, three with wide-brimmed hats and one with a white shirt.

'Elliott?' Her offsider was being shoved around by the three men and she instantly saw red. '*Hey*, what's going on here?'

'Nothing to do with you, rack off and leave us with the gay boy,' said a young man wearing a white cowboy hat.

Sienna stood in front of Elliott to shield him. 'Not when you didn't say *please*. Not when I've worked my arse off for two days that I'm so wired, I don't need some little bugger, like you, telling me what to do. So *you* rack off!' They were in their teens, but it didn't matter their age, because they were ganging up on Elliott.

'Little gay boy has to have a woman to protect him.'

'He's more of a man than you'll ever be. Come on, Elliott.' Sienna grabbed his arm.

'We're not done, cow.' The guy in the white Akubra grabbed her arm.

'Don't you touch me. LET GO. She struggled to pull free and kicked him in the shins.

'*Ow.*' He jumped around and his white hat landed in the red dust. 'You'll pay for that.'

'*Run, Elliott.*' But they were blocked off by the other two. She shielded Elliott behind her, hands clenched into fists, and searched for an escape.

'OI! WHAT'S HAPPENING HERE?'

'Tom?' She turned to see the 2IC, Tyson, Josh, and Craig with him. 'We could do with a hero about now.'

'Sienna, what's going on?' Craig asked.

'She kicked me in the shins, and mucked up my good hat, stupid bitch.' The guy dusted his white hat against his jeans.

'You called me stupid!' She gasped, as a fire exploded inside. 'I told you to let me go, when you *had no right to touch me or my mate. So what if he's gay, he had more integrity than you'll ever have you mindless sun-fried little freak. You're nothing but a bunch of bullies. Real tough guys with your class act of three onto one. And don't tell me to rack off either, especially today, tonight, or whatever freaking day it is.*' She shouted at him mere inches from his face as her fists shook with fury.

'Sienna.' Tom's large hand landed heavily on her shoulder. 'We'll deal with this. You go back to the kitchen and cool off. Elliott, take her with you.'

She shrugged off Tom's hand and pointed up at the bully. 'I'm not done. I'll get my frying pan and I'll give you what for, you little maggot. And you're lucky the dog is on the chain too.'

'*Sienna, get,*' shouted Tom.

'Come on, Sienna.' Elliott hooked his arm around Sienna's and dragged her towards the compound.

'Arseholes.' She stormed down the hill with hands in fists, still hearing them talking behind her.

\*\*\*

'Who would've thought she'd go off like that.' Craig chuckled, and then he sobered up, narrowing his eyes at the three boys. 'Do you know who you've just upset?'

The guy dusting his white hat said, 'Cranky kitchen hand?'

'That, boys, was the relief cook.'

The young man put on his dusted white hat and adjusted it, then shrugged. 'So?'

'Here's the thing,' said Craig as he crossed his arms over his chest. 'You do realise you're standing on Danbunnan Station's soil, right?'

'Yeah,' the three young men replied.

'Like all stations it's got a boss. Now when Danbunnan's boss hears you've upset that little relief cook on *his* land, you're dead. Simple. You'll probably cop a hiding before being thrown into one of Danbunnan's rivers to feed the crocs, and we'll be powerless to stop him.'

'Bull. Not over a smart-mouthed camp cook.'

'Haven't you heard the stories of Danbunnan?' Tyson asked, hooking his thumbs into his jean's belt loops. 'The last guy who gave the relief cook grief got smacked in the face with her frying pan. She smashed him so hard that he flew backwards through the muster room's doors. He then rolled into the compound while she kept using his head like a cricket ball. She made a mess of that stockman, and that's *before* her dog got him on his back.'

'I heard her dog shredded his jeans and then the boss punched a hole through the door when he found out. Was that true?' Craig asked. 'I know Jake's got some anger issues, where he'll punch first, talk later. If you make it.'

'Oh, yeah,' said Josh with a nod. 'The boss's fist went straight through the whole wood panel and the door fell off the hinges onto the deck, busted. From one punch.' Josh's hand mimicked the falling door. 'And that was *after* the boss punched that stockman's nose to a pulp for upsetting the relief cook.'

'We'd never seen the boss that angry before,' said Tyson, shaking his head. 'He was so mad that when we tried to hold him back, the boss shrugged us off as if we were nothing. And the thing was, there were over a dozen men in that room trying to hold him back. Now there's only us.'

'You see, boys, the way it is on this station is that if the relief cook's happy, Danbunnan's boss is happy. And right now, she's not happy.' Craig pointed towards the muster room's direction.

'I suggest you three leave before the boss does find out,' said Tom. 'And just so you know, *that's my bloody nephew you were bullying.* NOW GET.'

The three men skidded in their boots dashing across the car park.

'Josh, Tyson, make sure they leave,' ordered Tom.

'We'll take my baby and blind them with her lights. They'll think a road-train's up their arse, it'll give 'em a hurry-up,' Tyson said to Josh. Their laughter followed them as they disappeared into the shadows.

'I'll go rescue my drink.' Craig chuckled to himself. 'I like Sienna's spirit, she's tougher than she looks.'

Tom nodded. 'I'd better go find her before she decides to get in her toy-car and chase after them with the flamin' dog and frying pan.'

# Fifty

'I'm sorry, Elliott. I'm so, so sorry.' Sienna sat opposite Elliott on the coldroom floor as the warmth from their breaths puffed like mythical dragons. 'I didn't mean to out you like that, but I got so mad.' This was not how she wanted to end the night.

'They would've bashed me if you hadn't shown up.'

'How did they get you on your own all the way out there? I thought you were serving inside.'

'I'd been talking to the smoking guitarist, who wanted a light. We'd been flirting with each other all night, ever since you'd sent me up to light the candles. And this other guy yelled out could I give him a light, and I did. Next thing I know, I'm dragged further into the dark and they started shoving me around until you showed up.'

'I'm so glad the crew showed up, right?' Things could've gotten complicated, and poor Elliott didn't have the backbone for a street brawl. Ah yes, the days of the home had toughened her up making her protective over the few she called friend.

With knees up to his chest, Elliott hid his face in his palms. 'What am I going to do? They all know now.'

'I'm sure it'll work out. At least you don't have to hide the wonderful person you are. Come on, the crew must know, if those three guys did and they're strangers. I wonder what station they're from?'

'Oh nooo.' His whole face screwed up. 'You mean the whole time they knew?'

Poor guy, she couldn't begin to imagine what he was going through, having to hide his true self in fear of others. The only thing she hid was her past as the kid no one wanted.

She'd tried to fake it by making out she was all refined like royalty of some kind. But here she was all over again, as an adult, sitting on a coldroom floor covered in kitchen gunk. Still that same homeless little girl who worked in the kitchens and kept herself busy to hide her loneliness.

Her past is what made her who she is today—and she was okay about it. She had nothing to be ashamed of, and sat taller, proud of everything she'd achieved.

Sienna placed her hands on Elliott's, grateful she'd found another true friend to add to her family. And she did have a family, which included Ricky, Rhonda, and Elliott. They were the few who'd fully accepted her, and she adored them more for just being different too. 'Hey, is this why you're scared of Jake?'

'I've been so worried he'd kick me out, even Uncle Tom.'

'Oh, honey, I'm sure the boss will be fine. Jake met Ricky and Mark and he got along with them just fine. Oh no, I hope no one tells the boss about my dummy spit, he's got guests.' Her perfectionism had failed.

'We need something to drink.' Using the shelves laden with fruit and vegetables, she pulled herself up, and from the top shelf she grabbed a beer each. 'Here, this beer was escorted by none other than the boss's fiancée.'

'Beer?' Elliott screwed his nose up at the bottle.

'It's the best I can do at such short notice. Hey, I needed to cool down, even if this is the worst hiding spot ever.' She'd been so pumped she would've punched the wall and kicked the oven.

'You were pretty angry.'

'I'll admit I overreacted. I'm tired and overemotional from the stress of these past two days. But now it's all over, let's have our own little party in here. No one will know to bother us.' Because only the staff came near the kitchen tonight and she wouldn't be missed, and she was okay with that.

She passed Elliott an open beer bottle and raised her own for a toast. 'Thank you for your help, Elliott. You are a great cook and a wonderful person. Please don't hide your magnificence.'

'Aw, thank you.' They clinked their beer bottles together in a salute to each other and drank. 'Yuck.'

'*Ugh*.' Her face screwed up at the bitterness of the meaty full-strength stout. 'I'd batter fish with this, but to drink … There's got to be something better than this or we're on to cooking wine.'

'This is terrible, who brought this?'

'You stole it from the esky, not me.' She searched the shelves for something else. 'Hold on, here's the boss's beer, we'll steal one.' And cracked open two cans. 'I think the trick is to drink the first part of the beer really fast and then carry on.'

'Okay, ready?'

'Ready.' They clinked their beers and said with wide grins, '*Go*.' They sculled back a few mouthfuls then burped and giggled like cheeky children.

'Let's party in here, shall we?' She'd outed the poor guy and wasn't going to leave him alone in his fragile state. This way she didn't have to face the true party either.

# Fifty-one

The band played and people danced as Craig wove his way through the tables and took his seat opposite Jake and scooped up his waiting rum.

Jenny leaned across her partner, Barry, and called out, 'Hey Craig, where've you been? Who was the lucky lady?'

'I just saw a woman with so much passion it reminded me of a little Chihuahua going off.'

'Why are you talking dogs? I talk dogs, not you,' said Ryan, seated on Craig's other side. 'She can't be that passionate or you wouldn't be here.'

Craig's nose screwed up. 'Sienna's not a dog.'

'Who's calling Sienna a dog?' asked Barry.

*'They'd better not.'* Jake's eyes narrowed and teeth gritted as he glared at Craig. 'What did you say about Sienna's passion and being a dog?'

'Whoa, Jake, no one said that.' Craig raised hands in surrender.

'Great! Who started the drama?' asked Barry, rolling his eyes.

'Bubble butt, who else.' Ryan tossed his thumb towards Craig.

'It was the puppy panderer who carried on about canines—'

'STOP.' Jake's leaned over the table towards Craig. 'What happened?'

'Don't worry, it's all been taken care of. It was just a

coupla young blokes getting a little argie-bargie with the muster cook for being gay. Tom told the kitchen crew to cool off.'

'Sienna's not crying again, is she?' Jenny asked.

'When was Sienna crying?' Jake looked to his friends for answers.

'When you gave that speech at the barra ponds about Danbunnan's future and what the place meant to you. Mate, it hit home.' Ryan patted over his heart.

'It was a top speech, mate,' said Craig. 'No wonder Sienna cried.'

'Yeah, even I saw that, and I see nothing.' Barry shrugged as he sipped his beer.

Expressionless, Jake stared at the candle's flame that flickered before him. Why hadn't Tom said anything? 'Has Sienna been in here tonight?'

Craig pointed over his shoulder to the food tables. 'Couldn't miss her, sneaking in with the boys to deliver the last load of food.'

'She looked cute in that chef's uniform,' said Ryan.

Jake looked around the room. There were people everywhere, dancing, eating, drinking, at the bar, and lounging on the couches. Sienna did this.

'Why didn't she stay?' Jenny asked Barry, who shrugged.

'Sienna was on her way back to change but ended up in some street brawl in the car park,' Craig said with his rum can halfway to his lips.

'*What the hell?*' Jake threw down his napkin, his chair scraped across the concrete as he rose to his feet.

'Well done, bubble butt,' snapped out Ryan.

Barry pointed his beer glass at Jake. 'And that's the face the guests didn't need to see.'

'Hey, Jake asked.' Craig shrugged at Jake leaning his fists on the table, waiting for an answer. 'Tom sent the kitchen crew back to the muster room after Sienna gave those boys an earful for hassling Elliott. And I wasn't lying when I told those boys to run, or they were dead for upsetting the relief cook, just by the black look the boss is wearing alone.'

'The Black Prince is in da room,' said Ryan.

Jake ignored them and made a move for the door.

Bob, at the nearby judges table, reached out and hooked Jake's arm. 'Son, you're not gonna make a scene, are you?'

'I'm going to check on Sienna.' They'd both been busy, especially Sienna in the kitchen, who would've chased him away if he went near her during service. But he sure as hell was going to find her now.

Bob followed, again grabbing Jake's arm. 'You have guests to attend to, don't bother yourself over staff.'

He hated that term, glaring at his father because Sienna was more than staff. He pulled his arm free. 'Excuse me.'

Bob followed, only this time he stood in front, blocking Jake as he said in a lowered voice, 'Tell me you did not fall in love with her.'

'Get out of my way.'

'Are you forgetting you're engaged to Angela?'

'Angela and I were faking it for Danbunnan. It's always been about saving Danbunnan.'

The shock of surprise was written all over Bob's face, then came the scowl. A look that once put the fear into Jake as a kid. 'How dare you. Am I some joke? Don't I —'

'I've got other things to deal with than your feelings, right now.' He'd kill those little bastards if they'd hurt her.

'No. You need to be clear on who to spend your time with. You've got Simon and the judges here that you've ignored all night.'

'You go babysit the judges. They're your mates, not mine. But our VIP guests are fast becoming my mates.' The guests never judged the golf driving range or complained about riding stock horses. They all had a great time, because the station sold itself just like Sienna said it would.

'You shouldn't ignore the judges. You need the co-op to sell your beef.'

'I don't give a damn about the co-op, who locked me

out.' They could rot for what they'd done to him. 'I have other options now. Do you know who my VIP guests are, Dad?'

Bob shrugged. 'Mates, or something. They're not the judges, who can get you into the co-op to sell the rest of the herd.'

'The Paynes own a stockfeed franchise. And he's bought all the stockfeed that's ready to ship out on the trailers.'

'I thought you did that to clear the shed?'

'We did that for a dual purpose, not just to hide the herd, but for Warren Payne to hear what the judges were looking for in stockfeed, where they'll now have to buy from Warren.' Jake chuckled, realising he was going to sell stockfeed to his neighbours with no mate's rates either— *sweet*!

'I thought Warren was just one of your mates. How did you find him?'

'Sienna did. When she was in Elsie Creek, I asked Sienna if she could check the feed store's current prices, because I had ample crop to sell. So, she did. Asking the owners who their suppliers were, and she followed the chain of command right up to Warren's head office in Adelaide. All from Sienna walking into the feed store not having a clue what those places do and asking questions. It's her skill. Elsie Creek's feed store is where she got the idea for the buff rolls, which Warren wants, too. But I doubt I'll have enough.'

'Why not?'

'Because the Lambells, my other guests you never bothered to talk to, own a pet-shop franchise that's Australia wide. Patrick has agreed to buy my buff mince and rolls for their stores and any seconds I have in beef and barra. Again, through Sienna, with the help from my old school mate— who you never liked—Ryan, who recommended Patrick.'

'And Lance?'

'He's the middleman. Lance was the one Sienna begged me to invite.'

'Why is this Lance so special then?'

'Lance is a select food supplier. He wants the best of our barra, beef and buffalo, where his top-shelf is gold plated. He's even offered to buy our bottled water for the exclusive Sydney and Melbourne markets, as well as Tom's chillies.'

'They're Tom's chillies—'

'That Sienna's been selling to Lance's Darwin store, out of the back of the muster room for months. That's what paid for Sienna's coffee we all drink, and it paid for Elliott's online cooking course we've all been benefiting from. Look ...' Scrubbing a palm over his face, Jake exhaled heavily to calm himself down.

It was obvious his father wasn't going to let him pass until he shared the answers. So why not tell the old man everything?

'Our Darwin market was stitched up when I was in town because Sienna had every minute scheduled with all of these meetings. We didn't just go shopping and sign those export contracts, we were flat out. Even on the drive to Darwin and back, Sienna made me practice sales pitches while we worked on all those portfolios and work plans for this weekend. It's here, done. And it worked.'

'No ...' Bob's jaw moved, but nothing more came out.

'Look, I was only thinking local places for buyers, because of the shipping costs. But Sienna went bigger and asked who has their own transport, so we didn't have to bother with that. Sulliance Industries has their own ships. All we do is get the cattle to Darwin's export yards. That we can do. Easy as.'

'And what about the fish?'

'Sienna found the solution. Lance's chilled delivery trucks come out here fortnightly on rural runs that normally leave empty. Except, now we'll be filling them up with my barra to deliver to the Darwin fish markets just down the road from Lance's warehouse. And that's just for the local trade.'

'How do you know about Lance's operations?'

'I didn't. Sienna did. Where do we tell every truck or

road-train driver to stop first when they come to Danbunnan?'

Bob's eyes widened as he said, 'The muster room.'

'Where Sienna is willing to have a conversation with anyone while offering a cuppa and a feed. Those drivers, who do the fortnightly deliveries, told Sienna about Lance and his gold-plated top-shelf trade along the east coast.'

'And this Lance agreed to buy from you?'

'More than that, Lance is stoked to use his chilled trucks more efficiently, which was all part of Sienna's contra deals and what she meant by her pond ripple effect.'

'When did you negotiate this?'

'It's in all those tailored packages Sienna handed out at morning tea. They showed our asking price, and any question you'd ever think of we've answered. It's what Sienna and I've been working on for months, and I shook hands with all my buyers over the barramundi ponds this afternoon. You know what the best part was?'

'What?'

'We used the judges and this competition to sell our products, and they didn't even know it. It was beautiful.' Jake chuckled at playing the bastards who'd been blocking his sale of beef. *Justice was sweet.*

'I, ah ...' Bob rubbed the back of his neck. 'You've found your buyer?'

'*Buyers*, Dad, with more interested from what Sienna's done. Don't you get it? I don't need to prove myself to anyone anymore, and I certainly don't need the co-op or those judges. I worked out today who I was and why I do what I do, with only the few true friends who've supported me.' Jake went to sidestep his dad.

'Stop. I need you to listen to me first—'

'Why? When you never bothered to listen to me before.'

'And that's my fault. My mistake and my own selfish pride too.' Bob sighed, shaking his head. 'I need to tell you, what I wished my father had told me, before you make one hell of a mistake that may cost you everything. Especially when it involves Danbunnan and family. Son, I don't want you living a life of regret, like I do. Just give me five minutes, then you decide what's worth it.'

# Fifty-two

Still seated on the coldroom floor, Elliott screwed up his face, hugging his knees. 'Ugh, how can anyone drink beer?'

Sienna took another sip. 'It has its benefits.'

*Knock, knock* on the door.

*'Go away, no one's home.* Quick, Elliott, let's hide in the freezer.'

The door opened wide to Jake, Tom, Craig, and Ryan looking down at the seated pair.

'I told you she hides in here,' said Jake.

'Worst hiding place ever,' she mumbled.

Craig chuckled. 'When Tom told you to go cool down, you literally did that.'

'And you're drinking my beer?'

Elliott hid his can behind his back as Sienna said to Jake, 'Sorry. And I'm sorry for making a scene at your party, Boss.' The only one, when this weekend required perfection. She could've handled it better.

'Aww, can I keep her?' asked Ryan. 'How can you stay mad at that face?'

Great, Jake was mad at her too?

'Sienna, out, please.' Jake held his hand out.

She couldn't resist, reaching for his large palm, that was strong yet gentle, sending heated tingles along her arm. 'But—what about Elliott?'

'Both of you, out.' Jake pulled Sienna to her feet and out

into the warm kitchen air that hit her like a sauna.

'Um …' What did they do now? 'I'll finish cleaning.'

'No, you've done enough, Sienna,' Jake said.

Yep, she'd done more than enough damage. What sort of professional was she to yell and scream like that in a car park?

'Elliott, you have half an hour to shower and change and be back in the shed. Tom, make sure he shows up.'

'Yes, Boss. Come on, Elliott.' Tom put a hand on Elliott's skinny shoulder and marched the lad out the door.

Sienna started to follow because Elliott could use the moral support, and that way she could avoid Jake.

'Not you. You're coming with me.' Jake led her through the side door, down the path beside the kitchen garden and towards the cook's quarters.

'Do you know what happened?'

He unlocked her cabin and flicked on the lights. 'Craig said you were in some street brawl in the car park.'

'Was not,' she barked out defensively as she stepped inside. Then she shrugged, fidgeting with the end of her chef's jacket. 'Well, nearly. Until the guys showed up. I'm sorry for being unprofessional.'

'I understand why you did it; you're very protective over those you care about.'

'But I outed Elliott. When I shouldn't have. It's not my place to do that, and he's scared what'll happen to him. That's why he's scared of you. I should go see him.' She made a move to the door.

'Nope.' He slammed it shut, blocking her exit. 'Do you think we're stupid?'

'No, never. You're a highly intelligent man in a very well made-up package.'

'Sienna?' He grabbed her chin, forcing her to look at him. 'When Elliott's mother got arrested, she told Tom that his nephew was gay *before* he came to Danbunnan. It makes no difference to us. Elliott is who he is, and he's been a great help around here.'

'You knew all along?'

'Sure.' Jake shrugged. 'But Tom's been terrified about the conversation they're about to have, so he never said anything.'

'Tom, really? It'd be like a father–son talk, right? Wow, Tom doesn't hold conversations and Elliott loves to ramble.'

'Look, we've always watched out for Elliott. He is Tom's nephew, and I consider Tom family, and Elliott too.'

She couldn't face him and rummaged through her small freezer to pour herself an icy glass of Grey Goose. She tossed back the shot where the cold liquor curled like a fire in her chest. 'That's good news for Elliott. It'll boost his confidence, and he has the skills. He'll be fine managing the muster room until Rhonda returns.' Decision made.

'You're not taking the extra time to stay?'

She hated this, but it had to be done. 'I wasn't going to say anything until tomorrow, but the job that Rhonda and Tom got me here for is finished. I quit cooking for a reason, and tonight I remembered why.'

'Why?'

'Because I always showed up to the party late, and I was invisible. People were having a great time, and you looked amazing. You have every right to be proud.' But everyone he needed was seated at his table tonight, there was no room for her. He could never promise an *us,* and there's no way she'd play second place to dirt. No, she'd find her own home, now she no longer wanted to hide herself.

'You got me there, Sienna. It was you who did this.'

'Now, that's where you're wrong. All I did was brush your shoulders and give you that pat on the back. I only showed you where to find things you were looking for and ask the questions you weren't sure to ask. It wasn't any magical formula. I'm just an EA and a relief cook, and you don't need to pay the wages for two cooks. Elliott's been here longer and deserves a shot. Hey, the last one on is usually the first to go.'

'If you think Elliott can cope without you and Rhonda

for the next few weeks, he can have the job.'

He was so cold, but she needed to be, too. 'Thank you. I'll pack my gear tomorrow.' She undid the top buttons on her chef's jacket and removed her sweat-stained neckerchief.

'Will you get changed and come to the party?'

'No. I'm going to take a long shower and catch up on some sleep. And you have a speech to give.' She peeked at the alarm clock sitting on the bedside table. 'Although you're well ahead of schedule.'

'Were you going to wear this tonight?' Jake pointed to her party dress hanging on the front of the cupboard door.

'I'd thought about it. But you don't need me there.' She plonked into her reading chair and unlaced her boots, grateful he was taking this so well. What she was doing now would hit her hard later, but it had to be done.

'That's not true.'

'Angela's there with her dad and your dad and ...' She didn't want to see the loving couple together, even if it was fake.

'You know, Angela said something to me earlier, and I saw it myself.'

Jake crossed his arms over his chest, wearing that unreadable expression. 'What was that?'

'Angela said cattlemen were like sailors in love with the sea. She said your father, Tom, Duncan, and you, were like that too, in love with the land and with this place. I saw how you spoke about Danbunnan, and it was beautiful.'

'Is that why you cried today at the barra ponds?'

*Who told?*

'I'm tired, and I'm a little delicate at the moment, or I wouldn't have cried today or reacted so strongly with those guys tonight. But it was a beautiful speech, Jake. You found your vision of what you want, and you have that self-belief to truly achieve all those goals, too. Trust me, that's a rare thing and I was proud to witness it. Danbunnan is lucky to have you as her king. But I'm just a visitor.'

His royal blue eyes narrowed at her. 'Is that what you

think?'

'Angela also told me about the plans she'd made with Duncan that were always delayed for the next muster. She said Danbunnan always came first with the Cullen men. It's why you were so willing to sell your soul and marry someone you didn't love. Not that I begrudge you. I'm actually jealous of Danbunnan; she's a worthy opponent that a woman can't bitch slap and say *hey, leave my man alone*.' She forced a grin. But he remained expressionless.

Great, that attempt at humour sucked.

It's a good thing she knew how fast she could pack her car, if needed.

'Are you finished?'

*Wow, that was cold.* His poker face was daunting, as he stood before her with his arms crossed.

'Um, yes.' Should she prepare for her marching orders?

'Do you hate Danbunnan?' Jake asked her.

'What?'

'Do you hate Danbunnan, because of the drama and all the tests you've endured to see if you're tough enough to live here?'

'No, never. It overwhelmed me at first, but it's a great place. I've always said you were lucky.'

Jake sighed, his stance softening. 'Remember, I wasn't meant to be here according to Dad's plan. I only put up with my dad and this place because it was for family and the promise I made to my mother.'

'I wouldn't know about family, not the normal sort of family.' She emptied her pockets, dropping her keys and phone onto her desk.

'Look, Craig told me what happened.' He picked up her mobile, glanced at it, and then put it back on her desk.

'Craig's such a gossiper. I bet none of the crew said anything?'

'They didn't. Dad said the staff had it covered, and they always do. I spoke with Dad before I came here. He gave me a speech warning me that I was about to make a terrible mistake and it was to do with you.'

'Me?'

'I told Dad I wasn't in love with Angela and why we'd gotten engaged. Dad said this place has been in our family for so long it's in our blood and he didn't want me making the same mistakes he had.' He wiped a hand over his mouth and then said, 'The thing is … I'm trying to say I'm sorry.'

*Great, here it comes.* She leaned back against the chair, gripping the armrests, swallowing the scratchy lump in her throat.

'I do love this place. But before you came here …' He crouched in front of her and held her hands. 'I hated it, worried I was turning into my father.'

'How? Your nothing alike—'

'My heated violence towards Chris. Threatening to sack contractors when in a bad mood. Being jealous over my best mate Craig for talking to you. But this...' He tapped his chest. 'It's this constant burden, this battle that Danbunnan had to always come first. I was just like my father... This place, this legacy, it was this invisible collar choking me, like I was a chained dog going in circles, never crossing the border.'

'Today you explained how much you understood the place. You could see you love it.'

'I do, but only because you showed me how.'

'Me?'

'Through your questions and the way you looked at things, you saw it differently. Before that, I was working with this possum biting my back, the same way I was six years ago. In fact, all my life here at Danbunnan I was the mutt who never got paid. But you showed me another way from that day I showed you the property, the falls, the ponds, the driving range. That was the day you helped me fall in love with this place, because that was the day I fell in love with you, Sienna. Your vision is what I see, and I can't do this without you.'

'But—your dad … the station's rules … Angela?' She was grabbing at straws, afraid to hope for something she had always believed she couldn't have.

'Dad told me one of the biggest mistakes he'd made in his life was choosing Danbunnan over my mother, for choosing *the way it is*.'

'I hate that term.'

'We both do. And we both challenge that term, the traditions, and the rules, making them into our own. You're right about Dad, he admitted to me that he's stubbornly stuck in his generation. He struggled because he chose to carry the burden alone, excluding my mother, and, while not an excuse for his drunken bullying, it was his reason for turning to alcohol that made him violent. The damage it did to Duncan too, the pressure took its toll on him mentally, even before my brother discovered he was not Danbunnan's rightful heir. Dad also told me not to make the same mistakes he'd made, which were many, but it all boiled down to one thing.'

'What was that?'

'Dad put Danbunnan before his family, where the land always came first. Henry and Winfred Cullen had the right idea of a partnership when they first arrived at Danbunnan, but in Dad and in my grandfather's time, they seemed to have lost that idea, shutting out those who were willing to share that burden with them, like their wives, family, and friends.' He gently grabbed her hands and said, 'I don't, and I won't do that, not with you. So, I called off the engagement to Angela tonight and she's telling Simon Simmons about her and Pete as we speak. If he doesn't like it, Angela is going to elope with Pete, tonight.'

'Wow.' She slapped the top of her head, blinking fast as if grit filled her eyes.

Again, he grabbed her hands, with those intense royal blue eyes focused on her. 'This—you and me—it doesn't end this way. If I have my way, it will never end. We're only just beginning, especially when I want you to be my partner.'

'But … I have my percentage.' And a duty to protect her heart, which had been burned far too many times, still feeling the sting in those scars.

'Look, you said when I left Danbunnan it gave me the extra knowledge to be a better boss. I agree. Don't you realise that with all of your skills you've helped Danbunnan too? She needs you. I need you. And I believe you're meant to be here, too. Call it fate that brought you here to help her, and in return she'll give you a home with me. Our goals are aligning like the stars, and I'm sure you'll have better words for it too.'

'I did this for you.'

'*For us. A*nd that's why you won't be getting that percentage you negotiated, because I'm bumping you up from a silent partner to my full fifty-fifty business partner. You will no longer be behind me, but beside me to help me run our projects together and live here with me.'

'*Here?* This is Rhonda's room.' *No way—this wasn't real.*

'At the house. We'll take the guest room, which is twice this size with a bigger bathroom that'll be perfect for us in the interim. We'll share the office like we've done these past few months, or I'll get you a desk that sits right next to mine. I'll also want you to bring the journals back to where they belong, with you and me as a family. I'll build a cottage for Dad and Jess, so we can make the house ours, because I want you there with me.'

'What about Simon's deal?'

'I don't need him. I told him, and I enjoyed telling him too.'

'I bet you did. So, the guests came through?'

'Babe, when you told me to bring them in, I was sceptical. All that stock feed you'd carefully displayed is sold. Lance and Patrick both want in on all our products, and I need your help to manage that with me. The guests know who you are because I introduced you as Danbunnan's project coordinator at our dinner. We all know you love projects and what we've created here at Danbunnan is a never-ending project.'

'Can you afford me?'

He gave her that crooked grin that made her heart bloom. 'No. You're priceless, babe, and not some percentage.

I want you as my partner, my lover, and my best friend because I want you to be my wife, too.'

'Nooo.' She slapped her hand over her mouth. 'What did you say?' she mumbled through her fingers.

He reached into his pocket to produce a small velvet jeweller's box. 'This is for you.'

*Holy roasted coffee beans!*

Jake pulled her hand away from her mouth and made her hold the box. 'It's a surprise. I owe you hundreds and I have a lot to make up for.'

Her fingers shook as she opened the lid to expose a gold ring with emeralds and rubies. 'It's exquisite.'

Jake took the ring from the box. 'This is Winifred Cullen's promise ring.'

'My hero …' She looked over to the journals sitting on the shelf. 'Not the ring her husband gave her, that she gave to her son to make his intentions—'

'His promise to marry someone. Yes. My mother gave me that ring, making me promise to take care of Danbunnan. And to give it to someone special.'

Completely stunned, tears blurred her vision of Jake and the ring. Winifred's ring.

'Like you, I rarely make promises and the ones we make we keep, so …' He got on one knee, taking her hand, and held the ring to the tip of her finger. 'Sienna, I promise to follow and support you wherever you go, because I love you and I only want to see you happy.'

'You do?'

'Of course, I do. I love you. I've been in love with you for a long time.'

'But—'

'Sienna, we don't end here, we're just beginning. I have so much to show you, right here on Danbunnan.' He jumped up and put the ring back into the box.

Sienna's head was spinning as she watched it disappear.

Grabbing her phone from the dresser Jake popped open the case and unfolded her *to-live list*. His grin widened as he pointed to the writing on the page. 'In case you hadn't realised, most of this *to-live list* is here.'

'No way?' She hadn't looked at in a while.

'I'll take you on a midnight picnic and we'll camp on the North Ridge where we'll lie under the stars and make up their names. I want to show you this place in the wet season, when it's our holiday time, and do some real fishing.'

Jake read off the next item on the list. '*Have a country café.*' He pointed to the words on the page. 'It's here, it's the muster room.'

'Seriously?'

'It's where I sit at that kitchen counter, sipping your coffee, while you swivel in front of the wood stove, serving everyone who comes and goes throughout the day, just like a café… You've also worked in new fields and grown an edible garden.' He reached for a pen on her desk and crossed those three items off her list.

'*Chase a tornado*: We call them willy-willies. Do you remember that time down the track delivering lunches with Elliott, the day you two got lost, you called them mini dust tornadoes and I know Elliott posted that photo on his Instagram feed.'

'The dancing dust storms that were everywhere. Okay, you can have that one too.'

He grinned at her as he crossed it off the list and read out the next item. '*Take a road trip*: Which is what brought you here. *Surprise someone*: From the moment I met you, when you surprised me by not being in Rhonda's age group and rocking up in that toy-car, and every day since. *Play a new ballgame*: I'd call golfing at the barra ponds a fair swipe.'

Her heart thumped heavily in her tight throat as he crossed off three more items on her *to-live list*.

'*Meet a Prince*: Me, even if I'm only known as the Black Prince to my mates. Tick.'

'*Go on a treasure hunt*: Hmm, I'll have to think about that one.

'*Go skinny-dipping, bushwalking, rock climbing, and cliff*

*jumping*: We've been skinny-dipping at the falls, many times.' They grinned at each other. 'As for the others, you did all of those in one swoop when you survived that landslide at the waterfalls.' And with a stroke of the pen, he crossed it off her list.

'*Throw a dart at a map and travel to where it lands*: We can do that tomorrow. We'll use the map of Danbunnan for you to chuck a dart at.'

'I'd probably miss.'

'I could blindfold you and you could play pin the tail on the donkey?'

'Ooh, that's possible.'

'We'll go wherever your dart lands on the map. Not once, but at any time—we could make it a monthly date for us.' Again, he consulted her list.

'*Be a mentor*: That's what you've done for Elliott. *Build something solid that would last a lifetime*: there's the smokehouse you and Dad built.' He put another swipe across the crinkled page.

'*Ride a motorbike, a quad, an airboat, a helicopter, and a horse*: You've done the horse ride, and I'll give you more lessons, I won't let you quit on that. I can also teach you to ride the bikes and drive a boat anytime, and on the next muster when the choppers return you can have a ride then.'

'For. Real!'

His hand cupped her jaw, as his thumb brushed over her cheek. 'I know you like to play on words, babe, and this *to-live list* is how we interpret it. So that leaves *Find snow and make a snow angel after falling off a snowboard*: We'll go see the snow and make snow angels together as part of our honeymoon, if you want?'

'Honeymoon?'

'I can tell you've carried this around with you for a very long time. You also said your *to-live list* changes and grows as you do, so ...' Using his other hand as a shield, he wrote on the top of her list, folded it over and passed it to her.

She opened the page and read out Jake's handwriting.

'*Live with Jake as a family and share Danbunnan as our home.*'
Tears blurred her vision as shaky fingertips covered her trembling lips.

'Babe, I get you. I understand what it's like to be alone, kicked out from my family and homeless. You were locked in a home with no family—I was locked in here because of my family. I've risked so much of my own happiness, but no more. I'll never risk the one thing that matters most, which is the love of a woman, the right woman. You.'

Again, he pulled out the ring and knelt before her. 'We'll make our own family and reinvent the meaning of family. We'll make a home our way, we'll have our *us* and all you have to say is *yes.*'

Tears streamed down her face. Her hair was everywhere, smelling of kitchen grease and wood smoke. She was a blubbering mess. Yet this moment was the purest and scariest ride of her life. Holding her breath, she whispered, 'Yes.'

He smiled, pushing the ring onto her finger. 'Say that again.'

'I said yes. *Yes.* YES.' She threw her arms around him and kissed him.

'Hey, you haven't told me, yet.'

'What do you want to hear?' Because she was still reeling.

'Sienna, you've done so much for me because you love me. I know you love me as much as I love you, so please say it.'

She inhaled, trembled even, and whispered, 'I … Love … You.'

'And I'll never stop loving you.' He leaned in to press his lips against hers and kissed her deeply and truly. Both on their knees, on the floor in the cook's quarters with arms around each other. The rest of the world didn't matter—they only had themselves. They finally had their *us*.

***

*Bang. Bang. Bang.*

'OI,' shouted Ryan on the other side of the door to the cook's quarters. 'Bubble butt says Jess needs the boss for some speech.'

'Damn.' Jake opened the door to Ryan, with Craig standing by the front rail.

'Tell me you kissed and made up. Or am I getting a new receptionist?' Ryan asked, disentangling his glasses from his hair.

Jake turned back to lift Sienna off her knees. 'Sienna, it's time to put on that party dress, because we have a reason to celebrate.' Hell yeah, he wanted to shout it out to the world.

Using the sleeve of her sweaty chef's jacket Sienna wiped at her tears. She was an emotional mess.

His thumb stroked at her tear-stained cheeks. 'They'd better be happy tears.'

'They are.' She buried her face in Jake's chest, and he held her. He never wanted to let her go again.

'Aw, just look at the Black Prince and his queen of the kitchen,' said Ryan, peeking his head inside. 'Cool bed. Hey, is that Egyptian cotton?'

'Excuse me, babe. You get ready while I take this moron out the back.' He kissed her forehead, spun her around and tapped her backside. He was relieved to see her smile as she peeked over her shoulder before she disappeared into the bathroom. He then turned to deal with the intruders. 'Out, you.'

Ryan walked backwards to the small porch with palms up in surrender. 'Oi, mate, I'm an animal lover, not a bust-in-the-dust kinda guy, like knucklehead over there.' He pointed at Craig.

'Only coz you fight like a blind fish with that mop you call hair.' Craig leaned against the rail with a beer can in one hand and a massive roasted leg bone in the other.

Jake chuckled at the cowboy. 'You look like a caveman.'

'Mate, I've never eaten so much and so well in my life.' Craig's white teeth tore at the meat on the bone.

'Me neither,' said Ryan. 'What's Sienna cooking for breakfast?'

'Sienna's not cooking anymore, except for me, and only if she wants to.' Jake heard the shower running. 'Bugger 'em, the guests can wait a little longer.' He'd waited too long and wasted too much time to miss out anymore.

'What do we tell Jess?' Ryan asked.

'I'm busy keeping the cook happy, who makes me happy, and my lady always comes first. I think she needs a hand scrubbing her back.' He headed back inside, booting the door shut behind him.

# Fifty-three

'I can't walk in there with you.' Sienna stopped on the edge of the light at the front of the shed where the band's music and the laughter of many reached them.

'I'm not letting go, so stop trying to shake me off.' Jake gave her hand a slight squeeze.

'Everyone will look at me.' What would the crew say? His family?

'Dressed like that, hell yeah they will.' Jake shared his crooked grin as his shining eyes grazed over her curves. 'I'm tempted to take you back to your room, right now.'

'You need to be here. You're the boss and you have a speech to make.'

'And we have a reason to celebrate.'

'But … in front of everyone?' If he let go, she'd run for the hills.

Jake squeezed her hand as if he read her mind. 'We're not hiding anymore. I'm proud to be with you.'

*Aww, how perfect.* 'Wow, so Elliott's not the only one who came out tonight.'

Jake winked at her, she had to smile. She couldn't help it, she was in love. She lifted her hand, checking out Winifred Cullen's ring, which fit perfectly on her finger.

'It's about time you showed up,' said Jess, rushing towards them. 'Where have you been?'

Jake put his arm around Sienna's shoulders. 'I was with my lady.'

Sienna braced herself for the sisterly rebuttal.

'Finally.' Jess clapped her hands together, sharing a huge smile.

Did Jess know, like Tom did?

She grimaced, feeling every eye on her. Could she really brag about Jake as her boyfriend? Wait—her fiancé? *Holy roasted coffee beans!*

'Let's go. You'll be sitting with me, babe. No more staff entrance for you. I've wanted you to sit with me for a while.'

'You have?' She was still unsure about going inside, but to no longer be staff and seated at Jake's table—did she hear right? She had to pinch herself to check that this was real.

***

'Before this whole competition ordeal started, I was having dinner with the family and remembered thinking about how much you'd love to dine with us. There's this empty chair next to me that used to hold my work manuals. It'll be your seat now.' And it felt right, having her alongside.

'Family dinners?' Her eyes widened and she looked like she was going to cry again.

'I told you, we're family. It's a done deal. You'll always be beside me, babe. Now, let's have a drink.'

Jess tapped her brother's elbow. 'Jake, I'll cue the band, shall I?'

'Why?' Jake pulled the chair out for Sienna, looking damn fine in her party dress that was turning heads. He had a reason to celebrate and poured her a wine and a fresh beer from the jug on the table.

'Speech, remember?' Jess tapped her bare wrist.

'I'd better get this over with. Back soon. We'll share some champagne then.' He emptied his glass, and whispered to Sienna, 'You stay right here. I don't want you running off and getting into any more trouble tonight.' He kissed her cheek and left her seated at the table, blushing. It'd been a while since he'd seen her blush.

The band finished their song and Jake stepped onto the

small stage as the singer adjusted the microphone stand. The dancing couples moved to their seats, while those outside gathered by the doors or filled the empty spaces and chairs.

All eyes were on Jake.

He hated giving speeches—how the hell did he get talked into this?

Jake then looked at his table and there she was, his pocketful of courage, Sienna, giving him all the confidence he needed.

He gave her a nod, gripped the microphone, and addressed the many guests before him. 'For those who don't know me, I'm Jake Cullen, owner of Danbunnan Station. This is the first time Danbunnan's been nominated for this competition…'

Jess worked the projector's slideshow, which began with the station's logo displayed on the large screen behind Jake.

'Tonight's dinner is the final festivity of the Northern Cattle Stations Competition, and in honour of my brother we chose tonight to be a fundraiser for suicide prevention. Did you know one in five Australians suffer from mental illness? It's higher in men living in remote areas, and in the Northern Territory we're higher in suicide numbers than the rest of Australia.' Jake slid a hand into his pocket and looked at the crowd. 'As blokes, we're Territory tough, and the *she'll be right* attitude works sometimes. But for mental health, there's no shame talking to your mates or family. If not …'

Jake looked back at the photo on the big screen and his stomach knotted at the sight.

'That's my brother, Duncan …' Damn, he missed his big brother. 'I wish I'd known the signs for what my brother was suffering, because I would've done anything to save him. So hopefully, the information you'll learn tonight will help someone or show them how to find help. Look, we have different stress factors to that mob in the city. We deal with extreme weather conditions, natural disasters, and isolation. We can't switch off from our jobs when we live it. We can't shut the office door at five when dingoes are attacking the herd or there's a bushfire jumping the firebreak. So, I urge you all to take a brochure to read later on, because there should be no judgement when it comes to mental health, especially if it can save a life.'

Jake sniffed, then cleared his throat before readdressing the crowd. 'So, today was all about being transparent and dispelling rumours surrounding Danbunnan. Here's a secret: when we were nominated for this competition, I said no.'

The crowd murmured their surprise.

'But, as you can tell, I got talked into doing this.' He waved his hand at the crowded shed. 'We even hung chandeliers from a rusty shed roof—who does that?'

The crowd chuckled, as some of the women cheered their approval.

'My dad told me that these competitions were originally about neighbours. He told me that when he was a boy, it took my grandfather five days travelling over corrugated roads, in trucks without decent suspension and no air-conditioning, to show up for dinner, only to turn around and head back home the next day.

'My great-grandmother wrote in her journals about her excitement attending these events, because back then it was mainly just to visit the neighbours. We all live and work in such a remote environment that few can relate to, and we can't explain it. So, having your neighbour show up with his crew to share stories, have a beer and even share trade secrets, that's the way it used to be. And to be honest, I don't care if I win or lose this thing, I'm just glad you mob showed up and I'm proud you made it.'

The crowd cheered with glasses held in the air.

'I was also told that this competition wasn't just about the owners; it was about the crew who worked here, too. On a station this big, you can't do this job on your own, so I'd like to acknowledge my crew. Please stand up as I introduce you. My father, Robert Cullen, the retired cattle king.'

Bob stood at the judges table and nodded with a wave to the crowd.

'My little sister, Jess.'

Jess waved with a wide smile from behind the projector.

'My niece and nephew, the twins, Aaron and Kate.'

The twins stood on their chairs at their table next to Pina. Kate waved with a jangle of bracelets and Aaron tipped his hat like the mini-cowboy he was.

Jake continued with a smile. 'That's my family. Now I'd like to introduce you to the amazing team, I'm lucky to have working with me. Please make your way up to the front. First up, Josh.'

As Josh stepped through the crowd towards Jake, the photos used on Danbunnan's website appeared on the big screen with Josh holding one of his rescued pythons.

'Josh is our sweet-toothed jackaroo, a promising all-rounder, and our resident snake whisperer.' Jake patted the lad's shoulder.

'Next is Tyson.'

As Tyson stepped forward the enlarged photo of Tyson's polished black ute brought murmurs of approval from many of the men at the bar.

'Tyson is trouble,' said Jake over the microphone, as he shook the lad's hand. 'With a ute that's won so many ute musters I've lost count. He's our solar specialist, our relief cook's favourite butcher, and a great stockman too.

'Next, Charlie and Pina.'

Charlie grabbed his wife's hand and walked to the stage to stand next to Josh and Tyson. The photo displayed Charlie staring up at the waterspout that shot over twenty feet into the air as the background while Jake shook Charlie's hand.

'Charlie is our master of wood and water, and one of the quietest stockmen I've met. His wife, Pina, is our cleaner, assistant camp cook, babysitter, waitress, fish grader and a lady of many other talents. Danbunnan is privileged to have her as part of the team.' Jake kissed her cheek, as Pina's smiling face shone among the white sheets on the big screen behind them.

'Next up, Joe and Lyn.' Jake beckoned to the couple who

stepped forwards. 'Joe's our station mechanic and a very patient parts-interpreter, who'll tell you he's our king of the junkyard.' Joe's wide smile and his grease-stained trucker's cap with the shiny toy crown flashed across the screen, followed by the image of Lyn driving the road-train. 'Lyn is another lady of many talents, and one of the best road-train drivers I've ever seen, currently training Josh for his truck license.' He shook Joe's hand and gave Lyn a kiss on the cheek, and they stood with the rest of Danbunnan's crew.

'Next, Elliott,' called out Jake and looked around the room. *Did the kid survive?*

'Oh, that's me.' With a big wave, Elliott skipped to the stage where his photo showed him working on the pig truck.

Jake held out his hand to Elliott who shook it with a limp hand giving a timid grin.

'Elliott is our muster cook, gaining his cooking qualifications while working as an all-rounder at the homestead. Elliott assists Rhonda, our long-time station cook, who is currently on holidays, and about to be a grandmother again.' Rhonda's smiling face came on screen.

'And that brings me to Tom.' Jake nodded to the big man himself.

A low murmur of approval echoed amongst the crowd. On screen, Tom appeared ten feet tall and Territory tough, leaning against a fence, wearing his sweat-stained Akubra, and with steely grey eyes, he watched over the herd before him.

'Tom is head stockman and like a brother to me. It was Tom who first called me Boss, and without Tom who knows where Danbunnan would be today. So, thank you, Tom.' Jake shook Tom's hand and gave him a man hug.

With his signature nod, Tom took his place amongst the team that lined up before Jake.

'Everyone, this is my team, who live and work here at Danbunnan. And they deserve a round of applause for the outstanding job they've done to get us here tonight.'

The crowd applauded as the Danbunnan crew waved or

tipped their hats at the crowd.

Jake held up his hand and the crowd quietened. 'Lastly, there's one more person I want to introduce. She's pretty damned special to me and my crew since she arrived as the relief cook.'

'No, he's not?' Sienna sank into her seat and hid her face in her hands.

'Elliott, go get her before she bolts for the door,' said Jake.

'Yes, Boss.'

'I'll get her.' Tom approached Sienna. 'Come on, girlie, time to get your giggle on.' He held out his hand and smiled.

'Tom, you smiled!'

'It's a rare thing, but the moment deserves it. I might have to call Rhonda and tell her about tonight,' he murmured.

'You know her internet date fizzled out, and she only did that to get your attention?'

'Really?'

'It's time to make a move or lose her forever, Tom.'

'You'll talk to the boss about the rules?'

'It's not my place to tell you, but just between us, those rules you mention are all in the past.'

'Well, I'm not surprised, since he's been breaking all the rules for you.' Tom grinned as he escorted her to the stage.

'You didn't have to do this, Jake.' Sienna looked up at him, blushing brightly.

'Yeah, I did. Come here, I want you beside me.' Jake's arm snaked around her waist and lifted her onto the stage as Jess walked up with a large bunch of flowers. 'Thanks, Jess.' Jake passed them to Sienna. 'For you, babe.'

'Flowers for me?' Sienna blinked back tears at the large bouquet. 'Thank you.'

*Damn*, her eyes shone and her smile was brighter than any sunrise. 'I've got a lot to make up for, babe, especially all the surprises you've given me.'

With an arm around her shoulders, holding her to his

side, he faced the crowd. 'Everyone, this is Sienna. She's the one who fed you all tonight and project-managed the entire weekend's events. She's the one to blame for the chandeliers and couches in the corner...'

A few women murmured their approval, while those lounging on the couches raised their glasses to give a cheer.

'Sienna's not just a relief cook. She's renovated the muster room into a country café, where we're spoiled with her cooking. But it's her uniqueness that is an inspiration to us as a lady of many surprises. Sienna arrived in what she calls her toy-car, where her off-road rally-racing skills broke the Danbunnan record, racing from here to town, getting a staff member to hospital after a snake bite.'

The crowd murmured, with a few surprised expressions.

'Sienna showed enormous courage saving my niece's life during a freak landslide. Suffered blisters and burns in the course of her job, enduring bake-off battles with a wood stove in her pursuit of food excellence. And for those who know Sienna are aware she isn't all about work either.'

The crew chuckled at the private joke.

'At Danbunnan, Sienna is famous for her jelly shots and zombie hunting expeditions on a full moon. She's stolen sheets from the stockmen's quarters to make a wide screen theatre to watch movies under the stars. Or she hangs out in her office, sitting on the roof of her toy-car under the banyan tree in an open floodplain.'

He nodded to Jess, standing behind the projector at the back of the room, and the screen changed to the photo that showed the North Ridge plateau. 'That's my favourite photo of my two favourite ladies, Danbunnan at the feet of the one person I have to thank the most, Sienna.' With palm to her back, he smiled at her and said over the microphone, 'Sienna is not only my business partner, but tonight, she's agreed to *marry me.*'

The crowd roared. Jess clapped with happy tears, the twins screamed for joy on their chairs. The staff cheered, with Lyn wolf-whistling loudest, while Jake's boarding school mates cheered just as hard.

'This is the last of the show, so let's shock 'em babe.' Jake pulled Sienna into his arms, removed his black hat, and put it on her head. It was big, but it was for a reason. 'That's me sending a message to all those other cowboys out there that you belong to me. You're mine.' And pressed his lips against hers to give her a proper Hollywood-style kiss in front of the entire room.

He gazed into her dreamy wise eyes, giving her exactly what she wanted and whispered, 'There is no end to us, because we're only just beginning.'

Sienna nodded, all her spirit and mischief returning, and said, 'And you aint no cowboy!'

OASIS OF THE OUTBACK DUOLOGY

## I HAVE A GIFT FOR YOU!

### Learn more about

## The Station's Story

- It's history
- The family tree
- Plus so much more

*Free & Exclusive!*
Simply go to:
https://melarowe.com/stationstory4u/

## What happened in Elsie Creek
when Sienna and Elliott raced to town?

You'll find that & more in the book:
**Doctoring Dust.**

As for Cowboy Craig, you'll find him in:
**Xmas Dust**
**& Muster in the Dust**

Find them at your favourite online bookstore.

# ACKNOWLEDGEMENTS

Thank you for hopping on this wild word ride that's been a few hundred thousand words long, filled with twists, turns, and the occasional misplaced semicolon!

Thank you to all those who have helped me on this amazing journey to get here, I wish I could name you all.

Thank you to the amazing Handbrake, who'll be sighing with relief this is finally over—until my next book! Thank you to my online writer friends and to the editing Deb team at DP Plus.

Lastly, to you, dear reader. Yes, I'm talking to you. Thank you so much for taking the time to read this epic story. It means the world to me, and I look forward to sharing more with you in that romantic *'Escape to Happily Ever After'*.


Until next time,

A. ROWE

# ABOUT THE AUTHOR

Australian bestselling author, Mel A ROWE, creates romantic escapes for today's busy women to enjoy from the comfort of their home.

Delivering stories with a dash of drama, witty humour and quirky family units, Mel is known for reinventing romantic versions of home, taking her common characters on uncommon journeys that lead from boardrooms to billabongs as they try to find their own HAPPILY EVER AFTER.

Living in Australia's Northern Territory, Mel enjoys random outback road trips, fumbling with her camera, annoying her family with her bad singing, and making new friends in the middle of nowhere—except for water buffalos. She's been chased by a few.

Find Mel at

## MelAROWE.com

Receive exclusive insights, book gifts, news
of upcoming releases by joining:
https://melarowe.com/newsletter/

# Also by MEL A ROWE

**ELSIE CREEK SERIES:**

The ART of DUST

DIAMOND in the DUST

CAKED in DUST

XMAS DUST

MUSTER in the DUST

ROLLED in DUST

WRITTEN in DUST

DOCTORING DUST


**OASIS OF THE OUTBACK DUOLOGY:**

The Station, Volume One

The Station, Volume Two


**STANDALONE STORIES:**

Avoiding the Pity Party

Unplanned Party

The Football Whisperer

Winter's Walk

Run Beautiful Run

The Sister Trip


**For story exclusives & more visit MelAROWE.com**